Rock Star

ROCK STAR

HEROES OF HENDERSON: BOOK 8

Liz Kelly

To Molly One more romance before your name is "Mommy"

This is one of my best. Enjoy.

Liz Kelly

Published by Kelly Girl Productions
©Copyright 2020 Liz Kelly
Cover design by Tammy Kearly

ISBN: 978-1-7338604-2-0

This book is a work of fiction. The characters, events, and places portrayed
in this book are products of the author's imagination and are either
fictitious or are used fictitiously. Any similarity to real persons, living or
dead, is purely coincidental and not intended by the author.

For more information on the author and her works, please see
www.LizKellyBooks.com

With gratitude to the band

Old Dominion

For their joy-producing concerts
where the feel-good high continues on for at least three days.

And to the daughters of my heart

Jody Cumberpatch
Liz Cumberpatch Hodgson
Caroline Dickson
Kate Dickson
Mary Southgate Dickson
Stacey Collins Ditlevson
Natalie Fleury
Heather Hodge
Hayden Williams

Who's Who in Henderson

Should you like a review, here is a reference to the primary characters in Rock Star you've already met in previous books.

McKenna Blakely
Journalist for the Henderson Daily newspaper, she dated Xavier Wright back in high school where the entire Wright family fell in love with her including Xavier's twin, Xander, with whom she's now involved in a complicated relationship. Mr. and Mrs. Wright consider McKenna the daughter they never had and eagerly anticipate an engagement between McKenna and their son Xander.

Laidey Bartholomew, a.k.a. Tweets
Originally from Dallas, Texas, she works for C.C. Henderson and is recently engaged to her very bossy, yet very sweet, fiancé Xavier Wright. She and McKenna Blakely are best buds.

Scarlett Langford, a.k.a. Red
A Henderson native and recent graduate of Ole Miss, Scarlett dates Davis "Pinks" Williams and is presently working on opening a wine shop on Henderson's Main Street and producing a record starring Major League Baseball's phenom, Cal Johnson.

Xander Wright
Twin brother of Xavier, he works in Charlotte, NC, and comes home rarely. Lately, he's been dating McKenna Blakely, Xavier's ex and the "daughter his parents never had."

Xavier Wright
Bossiest and oldest of the five Wright brothers. After a long stint in Arizona, he moved back in with his parents to help care for his sick mother. He quickly fell in love with his Tweets and took no time putting a ring on it.

Anna Beth Wright
Mother of five large, boisterous, trouble-making (in their youth) sons. She's recovering from an autoimmune disease that nearly killed her and has brought much of her family back to Henderson.

Jaxon Wright

Youngest of the five Wright brothers and the most recent to move back to Henderson. He works as a consultant for NASCAR race teams fine-tuning their engines for race day. He's mad for newcomer Jinx Davenport.

Jinx Davenport

Secret, long-lost daughter of Hale Evans. Jinx found her way to Henderson after applying for a library position. She and Jaxon Wright fell for each other at first sight.

Davis Williams, a.k.a. Pinks or the Ninja

Originally from Baltimore and a childhood friend of Missy McReady's, Pinks is now heavily involved in Henderson's economic recovery plan and Evans & Evans Investments. He's also heavily involved with Red, a.k.a. Scarlett Langford.

Hale Evans

Successful equity investor and Henderson's local multimillionaire. Twenty years ago, his first wife left him devastated. Now he's married to Lolly DuVal's mother, Genevra (pronounced Jen-ev-ra.) They now have a son named Beau. Hale owns Evan & Evans Investments with his thirty-year-old son Vance and is patriarch of Team Henderson. His mother, Emelina Flores, a.k.a. the Big Em is originally from Spain and lives with them.

Vance Evans (Bad Cop)

Part owner of Evans & Evans Investments and the Henderson High Bulldogs' baseball coach. He was the mayoral campaign manager for his best friend, Brooks Bennett. He's married to Piper Beaumont the girl who fell in love with him in fourth grade. Their son, Vance, Jr, is the same age as Vance's half brother Beau.

Cal Johnson

Orioles' rookie pitching phenom, whom Coach Cooper saved from drowning after Boston Red Sox fans tossed him into Baltimore's harbor. He showed up in Henderson to give a pitching demonstration for the Opening Day Spectacular and became a YouTube sensation by singing with the band at the after party. He's currently dating

Scarlett Langford's college roommate, Natalie Houser, daughter of MLB Hall of Famer, Nate the Great.

Harry the Bartender

Mysterious young bartender at Henderson Country Club with an uncanny knack for knowing your drink and reading your mind. His tequila shots have a way of bringing couples together.

Brooks Bennett (Good Cop)

Henderson's Golden Boy. He's determined to bring economic prosperity back to town and stop the mass exodus of the younger generation. He's recently been elected mayor and is madly in love with Lolly DuVal, a local girl turned couture dress designer who has recently set up shop in Henderson.

Missy McReady

Imported from Baltimore by Davis Williams to be Henderson High's girls' lacrosse coach as well as the town's Marketing and Event-Planning guru. She is now considered the CEO of Team Henderson and is heavily involved with Thurgood Watson.

Thurgood Lewis Watson III, a.k.a. Thor

Former Army Ranger and owner of a large plantation passed to him upon his father's untimely death. He's got a lot of plans for his land, and one of them involves marrying Missy McReady in the gazebo he's building.

See a complete list of characters at www.LizKellyBooks.com

CHAPTER ONE

Jagger Yates knew Scarlett Langford had a serious boyfriend. Still, he liked coming into her wine shop and admiring her pretty face. She was all North Carolina charm with intelligent green eyes over a pert, little nose and a blazing smile that liked to make you grin. Her fancy style matched her dark-red hair with long, manicured nails, party-girl dresses that showed off long, shapely legs, and always a flashy set of heels. He appreciated her Southern drawl and the easy-on-the-ears tenor of her voice, but he loved that she turned into spit and vinegar when it came to business.

Fortunately, Jagger enjoyed wine. Really good wine. And because he wasn't opposed to dropping some dime on the stuff, Scarlett didn't seem to mind him lurking in her shop, studying her inventory, eavesdropping on random conversations—*looking at her face.* And since he lurked repetitively, she also didn't seem to mind putting him to work stocking her shelves.

Reds had been unofficially open for one week, and Jagger had seen the inside of the store on a daily basis. The place smelled of wood and wine and a hint of perfume. All of it expensive. Each time he entered, more of the redwood shelving was filled with unusual varietals from small producers in California. He figured little Miss Scarlett must have a sugar daddy backing her place with the kind of bills she'd thrown around. Jagger was betting on her father, who stuck his head in the door around noon every day and asked how things were going.

Tucking himself deep into a row, back where the ports were shelved, Jagger had a new melody brewing inside his head while covertly admiring Scarlett's profile. The words to his new song "Her Pretty Face" practically writing themselves with this kind of inspiration. The hook was that she had a guy. A good guy. One she was seriously into. And in real life, Jagger was happy for her. But the song he was writing was from a different angle. The angsty angle of seeing something so striking, so perfect, so beyond your comprehension that your feet get cemented to the ground and you're powerless to move. Only your heart isn't grounded. Your heart blows up, and you're stuck with that.

Yeah.

Stuck.

Distraction entered through the front door in the form of a tiny, little darling who was all dark curls and old-school Keds under a fit-for-fall gray cardigan sweater and playful orange frock. Now there was a song just dying to be written. "Baby Girl, Whatcha Got On Under That Dress?" Jagger and his curiosity remained silent at the end of the aisle as he watched the newcomer approach Scarlett and ask for the specifics about Reds' Grand Opening event. Her voice was charmingly reserved—quietly shy—yet she enunciated beautifully, so he was able to pick up every word, his mind capturing the details of the grand opening as the two women spoke.

This Saturday evening.

Wine tasting with a food pairing.

Featured wines on sale.

Discounts on full cases.

Yadda, yadda, yadda.

After he wrapped his head around the petite brunette's unusual name—*Laidey*—Jagger went back to writing songs in his head while studying the labels on wine. He continually found himself snickering at the names. Like the ridiculous—*Flirt*. And outrageous—*Sweet Bitch*. Apparently Miss Scarlett liked her bottles to have a sense of humor.

When the door to Reds opened again, Jagger didn't bother looking up. He was engrossed in the *Sweet Bitch* label, thinking it would make a great title for a song. Not that he and his band could get away with something like that on country radio, but on an album? He was pulling out his phone to make a note when a feminine voice so authoritatively bossy yet, at the same time, so pleasing to the ear drew his attention away from his idea and made him fully focus on what was going down just yards away.

"You know I like red, and my mother likes red, and we are just too tickled that you've named this place Reds for all the various reasons you did. But you must help me select a white wine for Thanksgiving. I mean, white wine with turkey, right? I'm going to need a case, because this is my contribution to Thanksgiving dinner at the Wrights. I want it to be *good* wine, the *right* wine, and, since you are now the resident expert—thank God for that, by the way— I'm going to leave the entire thing in your capable hands. And, as you are well aware, I'm on a budget. So, I need you to cut me a deal in exchange for as much free publicity as I can give you in the Henderson Daily before my boss realizes what I'm doing and shuts me down."

Jagger grinned. Because all of that was said with two breaths in a rhythmic cadence, and she never missed a beat. With his interest sparked, he quietly maneuvered himself to a space where he could observe the three women who'd converged at the checkout counter. He assessed them as men did women because ... single.

The petite one with the bouncy black curls was way tiny.

The attractive redhead with the long nails was already taken.

But the new one? The taller one? The one in the well-fitted slacks and matching jacket who was all business until you got to her hair? That one, *that one* was just right. And ... *Holy shit.*

Jagger's heart rate sped up as all that layered, French-roast-colored hair swung around to reveal her startling profile. Because he'd seen this woman before. Not here in Henderson but three different times down in the pit. A year ago in Raleigh. Recently in Charlotte. And the first time in that honky-tonk bar in Somewheresville, Virginia. He may not recall the exact place, but he remembered her. Oh, he *definitely* remembered her.

In fact, he'd written songs about *her.*

He'd written seventeen fucking songs—and counting—all about *her.*

The one that got away.

And now, there she was.

Right there.

In Reds.

Jagger scratched his beard, incredulous. Standing mere feet from him was the dark-haired beauty who'd first bewitched him with her big, wide smile. Then those brilliant ice-blue eyes. And, if he remembered correctly—which he was damn sure he did—a pair of tight-fitting jeans and absolutely spectacular breasts. God, her breasts alone were worthy of so many songs. All that before he'd had a chance to let her bewitch him with her sass.

And *that* had been the game changer.

He stood and stared, his mouth going dry. His pulse pounding like a son of a bitch. His mind replaying the same recording from the first time he'd laid eyes on her.

Awe-inspiring beauty, the kind that stood out in a crowd. The kind most guys simply stood and gaped at while attempting to get their bearings. Because instinctively they knew—no way could they handle a woman like that.

He gulped.

Then he glanced down to where his boots were cemented to the hardwood floor.

Yeah. Definitely that kind of beauty.

Yet, after a brief moment's hesitation, he pushed up his sleeves, straightened his shoulders, and allowed a slow-growing grin to spread his lips. Because he remembered.

He wasn't most guys.

And this was going to be fun.

Stepping out from the cavern formed by the tall racks of wine, he made sure to appear all his badass, six foot two height.

"Ladies," he said, addressing the group before his gaze landed heavily on the one he wanted.

Like a deer caught in the headlights, she stared at him, transfixed. Finally, she stage-whispered to Scarlett, "He was supposed to have left town."

The little one, Laidey, stepped closer to his prey. In his peripheral vision, he saw Scarlett shrug her shoulders. "Apparently he decided to stay."

He took a step forward, squinting. "McKenna, right?"

"How—" She stumbled backward at his approach, bumping into a round table loaded with a display of stacked crates and wine bottles. One of which toppled to the floor, shattering in a magnificent splash.

Jagger didn't pull his stare from McKenna's eyes as he told Scarlett, "Put it on my tab."

McKenna blinked. Then her eyes bounced between him and the mess she'd created before she stooped down, picking up two large pieces of glass with a huff. "I can pay for my own clumsiness."

Scarlett came over with a dustpan and paper towels. "That was a fifty dollar bottle of wine."

McKenna flinched before briefly glancing up at him. "Fine. Put it on his tab."

He grinned as he squatted down on his haunches right in front of her, helping her pick up glass. "You remember me?"

Those blizzard-blue eyes flashed at him and then rolled. She shook her head back and forth as they both continued to clean up the mess. "I can't believe you remember my name," she spouted, standing and dumping the broken glass into the trash bag Laidey held out. Jagger did the same.

He took a paper towel from Scarlett, then dusted his hands together. "I not only remember your name but the totally bogus phone number you gave me. Want to hear it?"

After a quick glance toward Laidey, McKenna shook her head.

He recited it anyway.

"Pretty close," Scarlett said, drawing a harsh eye flash from McKenna.

"You left me with blue balls and a phony number." Her eyes locked on him even though she said nothing. He took a step closer. "Have dinner with me."

She backed away again, this time bopping into the end of a wine rack. "Watch it," Scarlett snapped.

"Sorry," McKenna said, gathering herself by picking up her beat-to-hell canvas messenger bag and putting it back on the shoulder of her navy pinstripe jacket. He noticed her white button-down was too buttoned up for his liking but definitely dug the hip-hugging trousers it was tucked into. She planted both her hands in the front pockets of her jacket.

"Have dinner with me," he pressed, working hard to stay where he was so she wouldn't back into anything else.

With eyes frantically looking between him and the two girls behind him, she said, "Ah ... I can't. I have a boyfriend."

Jagger folded his arms over his chest while allowing his gaze to drift down her body, giving her a very leisurely, very suggestive once-over. He licked his lips. "I bet a woman like you could use two."

Behind him, Scarlett burst out laughing. "Only Jagger Yates would say that."

"Right?" he said, twisting and grinning at Scarlett. "My band may be taking a sabbatical. Doesn't mean I'm not still me." He turned his attention back to McKenna. "So what about it? Dinner?"

"I told you. I have a boyfriend."

Jagger shook his head. "Not a deterrent. Dinner?" When McKenna just stared at him open mouthed, he asked, "Do you live here?" When she didn't answer, he twisted around to Scarlett and Laidey. "Does she live here?"

"Yes, she lives here."

"Scarlett," McKenna scolded.

"Well, you do," she told McKenna before she turned to Jagger and enlightened him further. "She's a reporter for the Henderson Daily. Interviewed every other band who cut a record with Cal Johnson. I thought it was curious when she was a no-show for the Cavaliers. I'm assuming you two have prior history?"

Without losing the staring contest he was presently engaged in with literally *the girl of his dreams*, he responded, "You could say that."

McKenna pulled her hands out of her pockets and let them drop in exasperation. "We had a conversation after one of his concerts."

"We had a conversation after the third concert where I noticed you in the crowd," he clarified. "After the third time you were in the pit, right up front, and had your eyes locked on me."

"I beg your pardon."

"Locked. On. Me."

"They were not."

"They so were."

She cocked her head and gave him a contrite smile. "I was trying to look past you. I have a crush on the drummer."

"*Bull*-shit."

She sputtered a short laugh and gave him a grin. A real one. Hell if he couldn't help grinning back. This wasn't the first moment they'd shared, but it was probably the best.

So far.

McKenna tried to hide her amused smile from him by looking down at her shoes. Black with pointy toes peeking out of the hem of her slacks. "I've got to get back to work," she said softly.

"Yeah? To the paper? You know, if you want to do an interview, I'm available. Like right now. Or over dinner. Tomorrow," he offered while she simply turned and headed for the exit.

Annnd … she'd already reduced him to begging.

She tossed a hand over her head. "Bye y'all," she said as she sauntered out the door.

Man, it was a good saunter. Jagger watched the door slam shut, watched her walk away from him through the large picture window in the front of Scarlett's shop. Then he kept watching a whole lot of nothing while his mind tried to catch up with life's latest plot twist. Finally, he turned and took in the two women who were staring at him.

"I need her last name, her home address, and her cell number," he told them, taking out his phone and handing it to Scarlett. Instinctively, he knew better than to try to wheedle this kind of information out of little Laidey.

Scarlett took his phone but gave him a weary look. "She's not lying. She has a boyfriend. Word on the street is that they're practically engaged."

"*Practically* being the key word there." Jagger motioned to his phone. "Put her in as a new contact. Give me everything you've got." When Scarlett hesitated, he added, "I'll buy two cases of the priciest wine you've got in stock right now."

"Done." Scarlett started poking at Jagger's phone.

"Scarlett," Laidey quietly chastised. "I'm not sure—"

"Shh," Scarlett scoffed. "I saw the way she looked at him, and if you ask me, Xander Wright could stand a little competition."

"Darn right," Jagger said as he took his phone and looked over the information. "Huh. McKenna *Blakely*. And the number she originally gave me was ... just one number off." He dropped his hand to his side, staring at the girls dumbfounded. "All this time, I've only been one digit away. Damn."

Laidey leaned forward on her Keds, giving him a curious look. "You honestly like her." She seemed surprised.

"Like her? Hell. I'm gonna marry her."

CHAPTER TWO

McKenna wanted to squeal.

Jagger Yates was *still* in Henderson.

Seriously. She could hardly breathe and would have totally done a happy dance if she'd been surrounded by her girl posse. Well, not Laidey, because ... Xavier. So, yeah. Not Laidey.

Instead, she made a beeline for Jinx Davenport. Jinx, the very young, very brilliant new head of Henderson's public library, was pretty much the *only* person she could talk to about what had just happened.

And yeah.

What. The. Hell. Just. Happened?

How was it *Jagger Yates*, hot—*so hot*—lead singer for the Cavaliers, her one-and-only celebrity crush, her one-and-only *obsession*—was lingering in Henderson? The band was supposed to come in last week, lay down a track with All-Star MLB pitcher and singing phenom Cal Johnson, and then hit the road. And as much as McKenna had wanted to be there when it happened—really, really wanted to be there to interview the band and to watch the whole thing go down—she'd ultimately decided to play it safe. Just in case Jagger Yates did somehow remember her from the hundreds of women he'd no doubt propositioned.

With the frame of mind she'd been in lately, if Jagger Yates hit on her again, she'd probably have put out and done it fast.

She sooo didn't trust herself around Jagger Yates.

Because she wasn't lying when she said she had a boyfriend.

But Jagger had never spoken truer words when he said she could probably use two.

Because said boyfriend? Xander Wright? Lived three hours away in Charlotte and came home to Henderson infrequently at best.

And, oh yeah. He was *dating another girl*.

As McKenna yanked open the library door, she spied Jinx off to the right, sporting her signature side-braid ponytail and issuing orders in that calm, balanced way she had. McKenna could tell they were orders because although Jinx was speaking quietly, she was focused on the older woman like a kindergarten teacher would be on an errant child. One who required repetitive instructions.

Compared to McKenna's own thirty years, Jinx was young. At the tender age of twenty-one, she'd recently been hired to oversee the library's renovation and the technical overhaul needed to accommodate an academic library. Jinx was a certified genius who held not only a master's in library science, but some other random master's degree as well. All to say she was up for the challenge. As an interesting aside, she also happened to be the long-lost daughter of Henderson's most prominent businessman, Hale Evans.

This little-known fact had been a secret McKenna had unearthed and kept quiet. And to assure Jinx she could be trusted with such heavy information (back before it all came out), McKenna had given Jinx a secret of her own. That secret being that McKenna was *part of a love triangle* when it came to her relationship with Xander. Which was such a big deal, on so many levels.

"Got a minute?" she asked when Jinx was free.

"Not unless it's urgent."

"What if it's crazy juicy?"

Jinx's brows shot halfway up her forehead. "Juicy I can make time for."

They headed to the library's meeting room where Jinx closed them in tight before turning to McKenna and wiggling her brows. "What's up?"

McKenna plopped into a chair, tossing her satchel on the table. "So, remember when you thought it was weird that I didn't jump at the chance to meet the Cavaliers when they were in town last week?"

"Right." Jinx slid into the chair facing McKenna. "Way weird, because you insist on listening to them whenever we are in the car together and also on Sunday mornings when we're cooking at the Wrights'."

"Yeah. They're my band of choice. They are. I mean, I've told my boss if ever he can't find me, check their tour schedule. I've likely run off with the band."

Jinx leaned in. "Right. Right. So why the heck didn't you want to meet them up close and personal? Afraid you would burst into tears like I did when I met Oprah?"

"You met Oprah!"

"A song for another time. Were you afraid you'd cry or something?"

"No. No. In fact, the last time I saw them in concert, I actually did meet Jagger Yates, their lead singer."

"The guy who's on your phone's wallpaper?"

"Oh shit." McKenna plucked her phone from her satchel and stared at Jagger's image. "Probably should change that."

"Why? What's going on?"

"He's here. In town." McKenna controlled her renewed urge to jump up and do a happy dance, but had no luck stifling the energy that compelled her feet to rapidly tap the floor under the table. "Jagger Yates is still *here in Henderson*. I just *ran into him* at Reds."

"Oh. Wow. Did you burst into tears?"

"What is with you and bursting into tears? No. No. It was just crazy surreal. Like I knew who he was, but he's standing in Reds, so my brain is like, *that can't really be him*, but my eyes are like, *oh, sweetheart, that is so him.*"

"What's he look like?"

McKenna pointed at her screen saver with a *duh* look on her face.

"No. In per-son," Jinx exaggerated. "Not on stage. What does Jagger Yates look like when he's standing in a wine shop?"

McKenna took a deep breath and then sighed loud and long as she fell back into her chair. "Oh, Jinx. He's …"

"Breathtaking?"

"Mmm. Yeah. And …"

"Gorgeous?"

"Oh, so very gorgeous. I mean, I was never a fan of the hipster beard thing until I saw him perform. Now I'm all about the beard. And up close, his beard is trimmed and neat and, God, I just wanted to reach out and feel the texture. I've never felt a beard. Have you? And, oh, he's taller than I remember. I mean, it felt like he was looming over me, because he's built—but not like he wrestles for a living. He's just fi-ne. All dark hair—shorter on the sides with longer curls on top—with chocolate, puppy-dog eyes and a loud, happy smile. The guy *really* knows how to smile."

"Well, he clearly knows how to make you smile."

Feeling that her face had indeed contorted into a goofy grin, McKenna immediately retracted it. She sat up, waving all that away, bringing forth her most weighty expression—except that she was bug-eyed. "He asked me to have dinner with him."

"Whoa." This time, it was Jinx who fell back into her chair.

"I know." McKenna's eyes grew even wider.

Jinx leaned in. "You mean your heartthrob, Jagger Yates, lead singer of the Cavaliers, your favorite band, asked you out on a date?"

"He did. In front of Scarlett and *Laidey*."

"Oh, crap. Laidey. Well, what did you say?"

"What could I say? I mean, for a moment I was stunned speechless. I couldn't even believe he was standing there, much less asking me to dinner. But then, of course, I told him I had a boyfriend."

"Because of Laidey."

"What? No. Well, probably no. I mean, it was probably good Laidey was standing there. Reminding me of the fact that I am, indeed, dating her future brother-in-law."

"So, what did Jagger say?"

"He didn't care that I had a boyfriend. No. No. What he actually said was—and get this—*that I could probably use two.*" Her hand rose up, then came down and sharply smacked the table.

"Get out!" Jinx's hand mimicked the move, also landing with a smack on the table.

They both cracked up.

"Can you believe this?" McKenna shrieked through her laughter.

"Well, if anyone can give Xander Wright a run for his money, I'd wager Jagger Yates can."

"I know, right?"

"What are you going to do?"

"I don't know. I mean, why is Jagger still here? In Henderson?"

"Henderson's great."

"Oh, my God. You've already drunk the Kool-Aid. Henderson is not great, and it's most definitely not Nashville, where the man actually lives and works."

"Then why don't you ask him? You could do an interview for the paper, find out everything you ever wanted to know about Jagger Yates. This is your big chance."

"Way too much temptation. I have a boyfriend."

"Who is dating *another girl*."

McKenna dropped a bland stare on Jinx.

"Come on. If Xander has two girlfriends, you can have two boyfriends."

"Really? You think Xander would be okay with me dating someone else? With me dating *Jagger Yates*?"

"I think he'd hate it. Doesn't mean you can't do it. Clearly, the two of you aren't exclusive. And, at the very least, this is definitely a conversation the two of you *need* to have. I've been saying this for months."

"I know. I know. I've been burying my head in the sand for too long. It is a conversation we need to have, but there is just so much riding on it."

"You mean because of his parents?"

"Yes. Of course, because of his parents. They love me."

"As I understand it, they've loved you for years. Their affection has nothing to do with you dating Xander."

"But now that we are … dating, they expect us to get engaged and make all their dreams come true."

"Only because they've been kept in the dark about Becca."

Becca.

The woman whom Xander was already dating when a chance encounter had McKenna hooking up with the love of her life before he could mention that he wasn't all that single.

He'd been as upfront about it as he could, under the circumstances. Circumstances being that McKenna didn't exactly give him the chance to mention his Facebook status before she jumped his bones. He swore that he and Becca had never had the talk declaring them exclusive, and that's how Xander ended up with two women. One in Charlotte whom McKenna assumed he saw on the regular, and one pining away in his hometown, waiting for him to throw her a bone.

"I've let this go on too long," she admitted. "I was so happy to have Xander back in my life I didn't want to pressure him to make a choice. But with his twin engaged to Laidey and you and Jaxon getting serious, the Wrights have convinced themselves that Xander and I are getting ready to tie the knot too."

"Because they can't imagine a more perfect girl for one of their five sons. For them, this is a dream come true."

"I know. And I thought it was for me too. But now"—she huffed—"Xander doesn't come home enough, he doesn't text enough, he certainly doesn't call enough, and I know I've got to deal with this. I mean, obviously the writing is on the wall."

"What writing?"

"He's choosing Becca."

"You don't know that."

She gave Jinx another *duh* look. "I kinda do, don't I? I just don't want to admit it."

Jinx shrugged.

"What's that mean?" McKenna asked.

"It means I should probably be on Xander's side, seeing as I'm dating his brother. But I can't help but think that if things go south with Xander, Jagger Yates would be a perfect rebound to help mend your broken heart."

McKenna grinned and actually licked her lips, unable to disagree.

"There's not going to be a better time to broach the subject with Xander," Jinx encouraged as she got up out of her chair. "I've got to get back to it, but do yourself a favor and think about it."

Somewhere on the sidewalk between the newspaper office and her daily stop into city hall, McKenna decided to simply text Xander.

Since we're not exclusive, I assume you're okay with me going on a date with someone else, right?

She stopped. Reread what she'd typed and then … Hit. Send.

It was done.

She'd put it out there.

She took a few steps and started to stuff her phone back into her satchel when it rang.

Xander.

Well, that was fast.

"Hey," she said, curious. Usually the guy liked to text, not talk.

"Who asked you out?"

Her brows shot up. "So … you got my text."

"Yeah. Who asked you out?"

She stopped walking and found a lamppost to lean against. "Does it matter?"

There was silence.

"Xander?"

"Yeah. Yeah. I'm here. I'm just struggling to find words that will not make me come off like a total douche."

She smiled at that. Bowing her head, she quietly suggested, "Why don't you just calmly tell me your thoughts."

"My thoughts aren't calm, McKenna. My thoughts are flipping out. Clearly, I don't want you going out with anyone else. But I can't tell you that, can I? Because then …"

"Yeah. Because then." Then she could tell him she didn't like being second string to Becca. She cleared her throat. "Can I say that I'm glad my text at least triggered a visceral response?"

More silence.

"Xander?"

"Look, McKenna. You know how I feel about you."

Her brows furrowed. *Did she?* "What I know is that you find it hard to keep your hands off me when you're in town."

"It's more than that. You know this. I'm crazy about you. I'm crazy about the way you take care of my mother and how you fit into my family. And I really like how *I* fit into my family when you're with me."

"Yes, and you like how Becca fits into your life in Charlotte."

"We've talked about this. It's complicated."

"Yeah, it is. So I'm simply looking for clarification. We aren't exclusive, right? We are *both* free to date other people."

There was a soft curse followed by, "Yeah, but I hate the idea of you being with anybody else." He'd used his low, sexy voice, which made McKenna smile.

"I'm glad to hear it."

"And I get that you feel the same way, and you've been more than patient."

"I do feel the same way, and yes, I have been more than patient."

"But see, you're a choice I never imagined I *could* make. In fact, you're the reason I stayed away from Henderson and made my life in Charlotte. Now? Hell. It's like the world has tipped on its axis, shaking things up to the point I don't know which way is up or down. My parents have never been happier, now that we're together. Who would have imagined that? And hell, I've never been happier coming back to Henderson these past few months knowing I have you by my side. You make me *want* to be a regular part of the family. You do. With Xavier back home and you in my life, I get it. This should be a no-brainer.

"But I have this other life, McKenna. One I've worked hard for, and it is not inconsequential. I know I have to choose. I do. And I'm sorry this hasn't been simple or easy on either of us. I just need a little more time to wrap my head around what's ahead of me."

McKenna was actually empathetic to all that. Choosing her meant he'd move back to Henderson. That he'd need to find a new job. Live in close proximity to his parents again. All of which she'd originally assumed he'd want to do. But apparently, he had mixed emotions.

"Look, until you make up your mind, I'm sort of stuck, you know? It's not like I can go on a date when the whole town believes we are moments away from becoming engaged. Word would get back to your parents, and then what? I'd not only appear to be the bad guy because they have no idea you're dating Becca, but I'm also the one who is going to be taking the heat when they find out, because I see them way more than you do."

"You're the daughter they never had. They'll forgive you."

"Eventually. But they are invested in us, Xander. Heavily invested."

"You think I don't know that? I know that. Since I'm dating you, I am now the favorite son."

"You've always been their favorite."

"Because I'm the only one who didn't act like a jackass. Up until now."

"It's becoming harder and harder to explain why you aren't coming home regularly," she said softly.

"I know," he said just as softly. "I'm sorry."

"Xander, is Becca seeing other people?"

"She's free to. She knows that. I've been upfront with both of you."

"But is she?"

"I don't know, but I doubt it."

McKenna found it physically hard to swallow. "Look, it's time you figure things out. Chips are gonna fall. There's no help for it."

"I know. So, who asked you out?"

She paused, not sure what to say exactly. "Just a guy."

"A guy, huh? You know I'm going to find out."

"You might." She thought of Laidey, who was engaged to Xander's twin. Laidey who was also her best friend. Her best friend who *didn't know* Xander had a second girlfriend. "Things are getting complicated," she said, mostly to herself. "You may be being honest with Becca and me, but I feel like I'm lying to everyone else."

"That's my fault."

"No. It's mine. But I can't go on like this. So maybe the answer is, we come clean to your parents. We explain that even though we are involved, we are definitely not exclusive."

"My dad will hit the roof."

"I'll smooth it over."

"So are you saying you really want to go out with this guy?"

"I'm saying that I've just started to realize the expanse of the lie I've been perpetrating."

"It's not a lie, McKenna. You and I ... we're definitely involved."

"Except no one knows there's a Becca."

"I hear you. Loud and clear."

"Do you?"

"Yeah, McKenna. I do. I'll figure my shit out, or we'll come clean to my parents—and shit, everyone else, I guess—that we are not, as you say, exclusive."

"I'm sorry this is so hard," she said in sympathy.

"Well, even though it sounds like a cliché, it's not you. It's me."

"In this case, I have to agree, it is you."

He laughed. "I miss you. You're good for me."

"I am. We're good together."

"Can't argue that. Talk later?"

"Yeah. Get back to work."

"You too."

"Bye."

"Bye."

And there it was. A conversation that gave her clarity about absolutely nothing when it came to Xander, but highlighted how deeply she'd buried herself in a misrepresentation.

CHAPTER THREE

"Gonna need a little help," her mother yelled from the front door. McKenna lowered the heat of the burner where her pasta sauce was bubbling and wiped her hands on a dishcloth. As she approached the front door, her mother said, "Someone left a huge box on our doorstep. There's a note, addressed to you."

Yep, at the ripe, old age of thirty, McKenna still lived with her mom. Since her mother was hardly ever home, she saw no reason not to.

She took a look at the box. "It's wine," she said as her mother handed her the note. "Scarlett must have found something that will work for Thanksgiving. This is probably the bill." She handed the note back to her mother, then hefted the case of wine inside. She tucked it to the side of the door, behind the cushy chair she liked to curl up in and watch her shows at night. "I'll take it over to the Wrights' tomorrow. They've got the room to store it."

"Thanksgiving isn't for weeks."

"I know. But I stopped into Reds today and told Scarlett I needed something good but affordable. This year, I want to contribute more than just your pecan pie and my ability to mash the potatoes."

"Whatever. My pecan pie is delicious." Her mom waved her hand over her head as she toddled into the kitchen and set down her large, worn-around-the-edges purse and monstrous tote bag. Cassandra "Sandy" Blakely was the physical antithesis of her daughter. At five foot three, her height, her body type, even her shorter hairstyle resembled a young Kathy Bates. And she was all business, all the time, working two jobs ever since McKenna could remember. Her nine-to-fiver was an office manager position for a moderate-sized insurance company over in Oxford. Only she worked it from eight in the morning until seven at night. Most Saturdays and Sundays, she was Henderson's lone female choice when it came to real estate agents. She made a decent living, enough to take care of herself and her daughter, and she continued to pay for all the household expenses, even though McKenna was now in a position where she could contribute.

"You *are* planning to show up, right?" McKenna dogged after her mother. "I know you like to go to the Hollis's, but I'd really like you to come with me to the Wrights' this year."

"Yes, I know. So the *in-laws* can get to know each other." Sandy sat down on a kitchen chair and bent over to untie her shoes.

"It's not like y'all don't know each other," McKenna protested. "My goodness, I've been spending time over there since I was in high school. It's just that …"

"I know, darlin'." Her mother softened. "Things are serious with Xander, and the holidays are a nice time to get both families together. I'm happy to be included. I can stop by the Hollis's after we've finished up at the Wright's. Have a second piece of pie with them. Whatcha cookin'? Smells good."

"Meat sauce. Pasta's almost done. Bought some shaved Parmesan on sale to top it off. Want a salad?" McKenna stuck her head in the refrigerator. "We've got bib lettuce and cherry tomatoes."

"Sounds fine. Mind if I take a minute to change?" Sandy took hold of the envelope she'd set on the table. "How much did you spend on the wine?" She slid her finger under the flap and pulled out the card inside. "Ah … this isn't a bill."

"No?" McKenna asked as she tore lettuce and tossed it into a bowl.

"Definitely no."

When there was no further information, McKenna looked over her shoulder to find her mother reading the note. "Well?"

Her mother shook her head and rolled her lips together before she spoke. "Um, it starts out, *Babe, Feeling a little guilty so I thought plying you and your mother with really good red wine might—*"

"Oh my gosh, the wine's from Xander?" McKenna headed toward her mother to check out the note. "We had a … a conversation today."

"Not from Xander." Her mother handed McKenna the note and got up from her chair. "You can fill me in over dinner."

"What?" McKenna read the note as her mother left the room.

Babe,

Feeling a little guilty so I thought plying you and your mother with really good red wine might loosen you up just enough that you'll say yes the next time I ask you to dinner. Which will be at ten o'clock tonight. So, drink up. And answer your phone when I call. As you can see, I know where you live.

~ Jagger (The one who stands in front of the drummer.)

After about thirty seconds of her brain swirling around with a whole lot of *Holy crap, it's from Jagger Yates*, she took a deep breath and read the note again. "Okay, I'll admit the 'stands in front of the drummer' part is cute. But addressing me as *Babe*?" She slapped his note on the table and went back to the front door to take a closer look at that wine. She pulled out a bottle of a cabernet she didn't recognize. Not that she knew much about wine except that she enjoyed drinking it.

At the Wrights' house.

With Xander's parents and his brothers.

A bottle in hand, she swung around and headed back into the kitchen. Tugging open the junk drawer, she rooted around for a corkscrew and a seal cutter. Both items were rarely used by the Blakely girls since they consumed boxed or screw-top wine at home. She reached for their best two wine glasses—the ones without silly sayings painted on them—and, after struggling a bit—she never was the one who uncorked wine—she poured two hefty glasses.

The aroma caught her attention, filling her senses as she poured the rich burgundy-colored liquid from bottle to glass. She stuck her nose into the rim to sniff and thought about juicy figs and decadent raspberry jam. She swirled the fragrant extravagance, mostly because it seemed like the right thing to do, taking a moment to admire the deep cherry color. Then, without taking a sip, she took both glasses to the table and set them down. McKenna stood back and stared at the wine before turning to pull out cloth placemats and napkins, setting the table more formally than she and her mother usually bothered to do.

"Jagger Yates," she whispered as she gazed at the table. "Sending me wine." Annnd because no one was watching, she raised her hands high in the air and did that happy dance she'd put on hold.

The wine was delicious, but the true gift Jagger had inadvertently given McKenna was the gift of time with her mother. Because of the wine, they dallied over dinner. Because of his note, her mother wanted to hear her story. So she pulled up her favorite Cavaliers playlist for background music and let her fangirl rage, waxing poetic about Jagger, his voice, his stage presence, and his *looks,* using more superlatives than she'd ever allow herself to use in newspaper copy.

Her mother snickered, then laughed, then spit her wine. "How is it you didn't jump at the chance to go to dinner with him? Or even sleep with him the first time you met?"

"Mom."

"Seriously. I've never seen you so animated. So enthralled. Not to mention, *he sent us wine.*"

"I know." McKenna laughed. "Why is he even still here in Henderson?"

Her mother shrugged and poured herself more of what Jagger had sent. "What about Xander?"

"Yeah. Well. About Xander." McKenna confessed it all. Their backstory in high school. How she ran into him this summer when on assignment in Charlotte. How happy they were to see each other and then how one thing led to another and boom—she's in a very nonexclusive relationship the whole town thinks is a done deal.

"Oh, my." Her mother sagged back in her chair, taking her wine with her. "Anna Beth and Maxwell have no idea?"

"No. When Xander came home for the Fourth of July, we were … a couple. Happy and head over heels for each other. So much so, I assumed he'd broken things off with Becca. But when he didn't come home as regularly as I hoped, I realized he hadn't. I didn't say anything to Anna Beth because she was so over the moon about Xander and I being together that I didn't want to disappoint her. And I didn't say anything to Xander because each time he'd come home, things were so good I didn't want to rock the boat. But now, as time's gone on, the whole thing has become exceedingly complicated. Laidey is my best friend, and she has no idea that Xander and I aren't … as tight as everyone thinks we are."

"Darlin', you have one of the strongest backbones of anyone I know. And you've never been shy about tellin' people what's what. Why in the world have you let that boy get away with this?"

"I don't know," she lied. Because she did know. She knew exactly why, and it wasn't something she planned on sharing with her mother.

"Figure it out," her mother insisted. "And have that singer boy come over here and sign all these bottles for us. I bet we can make a fortune selling some of them on eBay."

"We aren't selling Jagger's wine on eBay," she insisted. Though she didn't think it was a bad idea to have him sign at least one for her personal collection. Her mind immediately went to Pinterest and creative ideas for repurposing empty wine bottles.

It was a few minutes after ten when her cellphone rang. Her screen flashed UNKNOWN and a number she assumed was Jagger's. She bit her bottom lip at how surreal this was.

"Hello?"

His familiar voice sang low in her ear, stirring goosebumps along her shoulders that tingled up the length of her neck. "Did you receive the wine?"

She bit her bottom lip harder and squeezed her eyes shut just so she wouldn't let out the squeal she was holding on to while her legs kicked underneath her bedcovers. She dug down deep—into the part of her that was more about self-preservation than being a crazed fan—in order to pull off a cheeky, "I'm sorry, is this the guy who is constantly blocking my view of the Cavaliers' drummer?"

He laughed. And oh, God, his *laugh*. It was hearty, it was genuine, it was melodically beautiful. It literally brought her joy.

His voice slid low, wrapping her up in its seductive nature. "I'm only blocking your view because you can't take your eyes off me."

He wasn't lying. It was just sooo awkward to have him call her on it. And thank goodness this wasn't a video chat, since she couldn't stop grinning from ear to ear. "Since you happen to be the *lead singer*, I'm pretty sure most of the audience has their eyes on you."

"Maybe. But those few times I caught you in the audience, I only had eyes for you."

Swooon. Just kill her now. Those words—cheesy though they may be—combined with the way he said them, smooth and low and just dripping with honey …

She liked honey.

Really, *really* liked honey.

It took a moment for her brain to come back online and catch up with his story. "I noticed you the first time in that honky-tonk bar in Nowheresville, VA. It was crowded, but you were up front, locked in, enjoying the show. And you sang every freaking word, even the tracks that never singled on the radio."

McKenna's embarrassment was cast aside as she became caught up in the rush of memories from that night. It was the first time she'd seen Jagger Yates on stage. She hadn't known his name then. She just knew she was crazy about the three singles the Cavaliers had released. Liked those songs enough to download their album. Then hit up the band's website and check out their tour schedule. Then not even two weeks later, less than an hour away, she ended up going by herself and having the time of her life.

And because she was a fan—a true fan—she couldn't let this moment go by without gushing. She wanted him to know her most vivid memories attached to that first concert. "That night, you and your buddies on stage … y'all couldn't stop smiling and laughing over how packed the place was or how the crowd sang along to your songs."

"Oh, trust me. We were as giddy as grown men can get." His voice had the eagerness of a kid on Christmas Eve. "We'd been singing in dive bars for next-to-nobody for *years*. So a packed house?

And they'd actually come to see us?" He gave a low whistle. "That felt big time. None of us will ever forget that night. Sort of when it all came together after years and years and then boom. Proof we had a following."

"And now you're playing to sold-out arenas."

"Which is why the first thing I do when I get on stage is go over and look down into the pit. That is our base, and they continue to show up."

"You do do that. I remember you doing that in Raleigh."

"And I remember seeing you in the pit in Raleigh."

"How? I mean out of all those crazy fans …"

"I don't know. I mean, besides the obvious. You're a beautiful girl. But maybe because you were lit up. Having as much fun as I was. I don't know. I don't know," he mumbled. Which made him seem suddenly shy. "I had the thought to have someone pull you backstage then. But I didn't do it. And McKenna, I regretted that. Hard. So when I saw you in Charlotte—I mean, I was pretty sure it was you—I jumped at the chance to have a word."

She blushed to the point she was again grateful they weren't Face Timing. "I'm flattered. I don't want you to think I'm not. I'm a fan. A huge fan, as you can probably tell by the money I've dropped on VIP tickets."

"Well, you've got my number now, so that's the last time you need to do that. Just call, and a backstage pass will be waiting for you. Any city, anywhere."

"Oh. Wow." She grinned into the phone while she tightened herself into a ball, bringing her knees up to her chest so she wouldn't burst. She tucked her forehead to her knees, squeezing her eyes together in sheer glee. She couldn't believe this was happening.

"McKenna? You there?"

She exhaled on a laugh. "Yeah. Yeah, I'm here. That would be great. No, that would be amazing. I really enjoy your concerts. And the wine you sent—"

"Shared. The wine I shared with you because I had to buy two cases in trade for your contact information. I thought it only fair I share."

"You had to buy wine to get my number?"

"Yeah. Scarlett and her cute little sidekick weren't going to throw you to the proverbial wolf easily. I had to promise to take two cases of her most expensive wine off Scarlett's hands."

"Oh, Jagger." She laughed—she couldn't help it. "You're in *Henderson*. All you needed was my full name, and anyone on the street would have pointed you in the right direction."

"Turns out that's a damn good thing. Clearly you can't be trusted to remember your own phone number correctly."

"I'm sorry about fudging my number. But seriously. I didn't think you were going to call, and if you did, well, you're you, so ..."

"I'm me?"

"Yes, and as you, you have easy access to all sorts of ... numbers."

"And?"

"And ... I suppose I didn't want to be another notch on your bedpost."

"I'm a grown man. My bedpost notching days are long behind me. And gross. Is that what you think of me?"

"Well?" She thought about that, lying back on her bed and squinting at the ceiling. "I just assumed. I mean, you know, the whole rock-star thing and all that. Lord, you were so not my type. But after seeing you play guitar and sing a few songs, I totally fell for the whole beard-and-ripped-jeans thing, and seriously ... that smile ... killer."

There was an extended silence that allowed her to digest her own words. *Oh, shit.*

Then came his quiet, "So ... remind me why you turned down my invitation to dinner?" His smile was so blatant she could *hear* it over the phone. "I mean, you know, I could wear some ripped jeans, bring my smile ..."

"Stop," she groaned, more embarrassed than ever. Then she started laughing. At herself. At the situation. She shook her head as if to bring herself back into reality. "Frankly, I can't believe we are actually speaking on the phone."

"Neither can I, since you gave me the wrong number."

"I got nervous," she defended.

"Nervous?"

"Yes. I didn't expect to meet you one-on-one. I certainly didn't expect you to ask for my number."

"I wanted to get to know you."

"Oh." That was … nice. He wanted to get to know her. "Can I ask what you're doing in Henderson?"

"Sure."

After another silence, "Okay. So, what are you doing in Henderson?"

"Writing songs."

"Because Nashville isn't conducive to that?" She grinned.

This time, he laughed. "Nashville is conducive to a lot of things. Song writing being one of them. But Henderson is a small town. Not as small as some maybe, but a lot smaller than Nashville. There's also some hustle going on here. I just thought it might inspire a few lyrics is all."

"Hustle? There is hustle in Henderson?"

"That Scarlett is hustling, for damn sure. I still haven't quite figured out her gig. I mean, she's producing a record, opening a wine shop, and has her hand in creating a restaurant? And she's all of what? Twenty-two?"

"Yeah. Twenty-two, I think. She is hustling. God love her, because she's keeping me in business by giving me something to write about."

"She's giving me things to write about too."

"Really?"

"Well, the girl's got a pretty face. And then there's all this spit and vinegar underneath that catches the attention. The imagination."

"You're writing a song about her?" McKenna felt profoundly jealous.

"I am. Don't tell her. She won't let me creep around her shop if she knows."

"I doubt that."

"Nah. She's not interested in inspiring songs. Or, maybe she is. But if she knows I'm writing it, she'll want to produce it, and that ain't happening."

McKenna snickered. "She'd *totally* want to produce it."

"Right?"

"So what song did you sing with Cal Johnson?"

There was a slight pause. "Babe in a Bar."

"Was that his favorite Cavaliers song?"

"Nope. But it's one of mine."

"Mine too," she told him.

"Hmm."

"Hmm?"

"Nothin'. Just glad you like it."

"There isn't a Cavaliers song I don't like."

"I would very much like to hear about your favorites. And I think that's a great topic of conversation we should get in to over dinner."

Annnd that's when she remembered the position he was putting her in with Xander and the Wrights. "Listen, I would love to have dinner with you. Honestly, I would. But—"

"But—" he said at the same time.

"I have … obligations."

"To your boyfriend."

"It's complicated. In a way only a small town can make it."

"If you're seen with me, people will talk."

"Oh, people would definitely talk."

"Fine."

"Fine?"

"Fine. I'm not going anywhere."

"What's that mean?"

"It means, Mc-Ken-na." The way he exaggerated her name made her heart pound. "I'm not going anywhere. I'm not leaving … Henderson. I'm going to be here in town for the duration."

"The duration of what?"

"The duration of complicated. See if maybe I can help un-complicate things for you."

"But this isn't about you."

"I'm going to try to make it about me."

"But … it's not."

"Okay, so it's not. Still. I'm going to see if I can make it about me. And you."

Her burst of laughter was part shock and part hysteria. "You can't do that."

"I think I can."

"No. What I mean is, you *shouldn't* do that."

"Shouldn't, schmouldn't. I'm doing it. Watch me."

"Jagger. Stop."

"Watch. Me."

They were at an impasse. The silence proved that. McKenna's sudden dislike for her favorite singer was an uncomfortable curl in the depths of her belly.

"Listen, I want to thank you for the wine. I really do. My mom suggested I ask you to sign the bottles. And as a fan, I'd love for you to do that. As a fan, I think it's cool you're in my hometown, hiding out from whatever you're hiding out from."

"Who says I'm—"

"But as a fan, I don't want to be your friend. I don't want to know the *real* Jagger Yates. I'm afraid that would only ruin the magic."

And then across the airwaves came …

Nothing.

Just complete and utter … silence.

And, in that still, miserable void of sound, McKenna's heart wrung itself dry. Intuitively understanding that she had hurt the real Jagger Yates. In her desperate fit of self-preservation, she had stomped on his feelings—as if he had none or, due to his celebrity status, he was above them. When the silence drew out longer than she could physically bear, she whispered his name as an apology into the abyss. "Jagger."

His response was quiet and bordered on deadly. "McKenna."

That tone resonated within a place deep inside her soul, the space right between loneliness and self-loathing. The ensuing shame so great, she fell mute. Completely unable to respond.

She finally heard Jagger clear his throat. "Here's something I want you to keep in mind as you try to fall asleep tonight."

Yep—she was … still mute. Her mind so stuck that she didn't just hear every word that came next, she literally felt them.

"I'm. Not. Going. Anywhere."

With that, he ended the call.

Abruptly.

CHAPTER FOUR

McKenna didn't sleep much that night, or the next night, or the night after that.

During the two days in between she'd received two hey-what's-up texts from Xander and heard nothing at all from Jagger. The lead singer of the Cavaliers might not be going anywhere, but he wasn't interested in engaging with her either. She could hardly blame him.

So while she tossed and turned well into night three, she had a come-to-Jesus moment and got her facts straight.

Fact: She had been dedicated to Anna Beth Wright (Xander's mother) since her sophomore year of high school. (Ever since the woman helped her find a dress, fixed her hair, and did her makeup for her prom date with Xavier—Xander's twin. Yeah, there was a lot of history between her and the Wrights.) She didn't want to do anything that would hurt Anna Beth or the Wright family in general.

Fact: Xander was still dating Becca. For all intents and purposes, he was stringing McKenna along.

Fact: If she accepted Jagger's dinner invitation and allowed the two of them to be seen together in public, it would definitely stir the pot. And might get Xander off the damn fence.

Fact: If she went to dinner with Jagger and he smiled at her with that charismatic smile of his, there was a sixty percent chance she'd end up sleeping with him. (Not good odds if she didn't want to be another notch on his bedpost.)

Fact: No matter what Jagger said, he was just passing through town. Eventually he'd head back to Nashville. (Refer back to said notch.)

Fact: Marrying Xander and becoming a member of the Wright family in fact rather than just in theory was a dream she wasn't ready to give up on.

Fact: On her deathbed, she'd regret not having gone to dinner with Jagger Yates.

"Oh. You're here."

Jagger didn't know what to make of the young, dark-haired dude who stopped dead in front of him. It was midweek, and he was strolling down Main Street, sticking his nose into places it didn't belong on his way to hit up Reds per usual. But his path was thwarted by a guy with sparkling golden eyes.

"I'm Harry," the dude said, holding out his hand. "And you're …?"

After a moment, Jagger clasped the outstretched hand. "Jagger Yates."

"Jagger Yates," Harry said, as if listening to the sound of his name or maybe the way it felt as it rolled off his tongue. "Ahhh." The way the *ahhh* came out, it was as if Harry had arrived at an understanding.

"Ahhh?"

And then Jagger watched the guy's smile twist up just a bit while a definitive twinkle glistened from his right eye. "You've met our McKenna."

Jagger felt his eyes widen at the unexpected statement. "McKenna?"

"McKenna Blakely." Harry nodded absently as if he'd answered his own question.

"I have, indeed, met *your infamous* McKenna on several occasions."

"And that's why you're here."

"Ah—not exactly." *Was this the boyfriend? Was Jagger about to get a beat down?*

"Oh—ah, right then. So, here's the thing." Harry clapped his hands together and looked somewhere over Jagger's left shoulder before his gaze came back, hooking Jagger in with the unworldly glisten of his eyes. "I'm a bartender over at the country club." He jerked a thumb over his shoulder as if Jagger would know in what direction the country club stood. "I've got a knack for knowing people's drinks. By the way, you may think yours is a run-of-the-mill beer—but in actuality, you have a palate for appreciating the subtle differences of fine wines." Harry gave Jagger a firm nod. "I've also got a knack for knowing when to pull out the tequila shots that will get you where you want to go. Un-fortunate-ly," Harry dragged out, "I'm probably not going to be much help to you because … yeah, that dark-haired vixen has stolen one of the club member's heart."

"The boyfriend."

"As it stands."

"So you're warning me off?"

"No. Nah. Never. Just, ya know." He pointed to himself. "Out of my jurisdiction."

"How about advice? Is that out of your jurisdiction? The reason I'm asking is I made a bold move the other night, and it's gotten me exactly nowhere."

Harry held up his hands, palms out. "Anything worth having is worth working for."

"I hear that." Jagger wasn't going anywhere. He'd proclaimed that loud and clear. Not that the female in question gave a rat's ass, apparently. "So …" Jagger squinted, trying to understand what was happening, "you just saw me on the street and …?"

Harry shrugged. "I'm a bartender. I'm good at reading people. And sometimes … it's like the writing is in large letters, spray-painted on the wall."

"What writing?"

Harry just gave him a nod and shot him a wink before moving on past.

Jagger turned and shouted after him. "What wall?"

"All will be well," floated over Harry's shoulder as Jagger watched him walk down the road and disappear into the building that was undergoing construction.

"Glad you think so," Jagger muttered.

Jagger didn't realize just how much *hustle* Scarlett Langford could throw down. But on Saturday, as he sat at a rickety card table outside the door of Reds during the Grand Opening, he did realize just how badly he'd been hustled. Because he wasn't signing the actual CD that starred Cal Johnson and his favorite bands. No, he was signing copies of the cover art that fans—who pre-ordered tonight—could slip into the actual CD cases when they were received.

Scarlett, or Red as he'd begun to refer to her, was a master at publicity and sales. Combining pre-sales of Cal's upcoming collaborative album, the actual release of the Hunks of Henderson Calendar, and the opening of her wine shop seemed like a no-brainer to her. When she asked him to do the signing, he figured he couldn't say no. He also figured a little exposure wouldn't be a bad thing.

Because even though his intention was to lie low while in Henderson, lying low over the last several days hadn't gotten him any closer to where he ultimately wanted to go.

So he sat on the sidewalk of Henderson's picturesque Main Street with a modest but continually replenishing line of fans and curious citizens, signing autographs and allowing people to share their favorite Cavalier songs or moments. He was essentially an extrovert, born to be on stage, chat up fans, and sign autographs. So for the first time in three days he finally felt like himself. Chatty. Gregarious. High on life.

And then that high ratcheted up a hot ten degrees when McKenna and a woman who was probably her mother stepped to the end of line, ten people away.

He tried to take his time with the guy in front of him. With the kid who played guitar in his high school band. With the darling trio of coeds who lamented to his face how sad they were that he was waaay too old for them.

He was, *but damn.* Quite the bruise to the ol' ego.

He stood for selfies. Signed hats and T-shirts, which was kind of a thrill. Evidence that even here in Henderson, the Cavaliers had developed a following. He probably appeared as if he had his head together. He could fake it pretty good when he had to. Which came in handy, because in truth, he was so focused on the brunette at the end of the line—who was giving him a helluva run for his money—that he was just half paying attention to everything else.

What was she going to say after that sudden end to their telephone conversation?

What was he going to say to her?

How was this next mashup going to go?

He figured he'd find out as he said, "Thanks for stopping by," to the giggling teens that had been keeping her waiting.

"McKenna," he said, staring her straight in the eye. "To what do I owe the pleasure?" He didn't smile. He was hoping that through eye contact and body language he was actually conveying, *"Last we spoke, you got scared and I was an asshole. Now we're in public, so how should we play this?"*

"Jagger," she said, pointedly meeting his eyes. She reached beside her and wrapped an arm around a slightly built but well-dressed woman, bringing her forward. "This is my very good friend, Anna Beth Wright. Anna Beth, this is Jagger Yates, the lead singer of the Cavaliers."

The woman seemed frail as she stuck out her hand, but her smile radiated warmth and her eyes twinkled with excitement. Jagger was compelled to stand.

"It's a pleasure to meet you, Mr. Yates. McKenna introduced me to your music, and I mean to tell you, I am a fan."

Jagger's eyes shot between the two women for a moment before landing decidedly on the elder. He let his smile go broad and pulled his shoulders back as he took Anna Beth's hand gently in his own. "Please, call me Jagger. And the pleasure is all mine."

"I forced Anna Beth to listen to your latest album the day it came out," McKenna informed him. "She was bedridden at the time, so she was a captive audience."

"I was," Anna Beth said, leaning in. "And bless you, your music soothed me. It helped me heal. I believe that. There's a quality there, in your voice, in the melody, and in the clever turn of phrase within your lyrics. McKenna tells me you write most of the songs."

"Yes and no. Most of the songs on that album were a collaboration."

"My favorite song is 'Babe in a Bar.'"

Jagger tilted his head and grinned slyly. How could he not? "Is it now?" He nodded vigorously, glancing at McKenna before returning his gaze back to Anna Beth. "You know the part where he finally gets the phone number, then tries to call the woman who has captivated him and finds out he's been duped?" She nodded. "Actually happened to me."

"No," Anna Beth was aghast, then she giggled. "Is that true?"

"Absolutely happened," he said, shifting his focus to McKenna. "About six months ago. And I'm still not over it."

"Well, it was fodder for a song that no doubt made you a whole lot of money. If you ever see the girl again, you should thank her."

"I should, should I?" He was licking his lips, eyeing up McKenna.

"Oh my, yes. Of course. Nothing but good came out of that."

"Nothing but good," he repeated.

"Now let me have you sign my copy, so I can move along and give McKenna a chance to talk with you. She's the super fan."

As Jagger signed Anna Beth's cover art, he said, "I'm happy to hear it."

"She's a journalist with our local paper. I'm sure she'd be pleased as punch if you'd allow her to interview you."

"I'm available." Jagger handed Mrs. Wright her cover art. "Single and available," he stated proudly.

Mrs. Wright's countenance lit up like the sun. "McKenna's dating my son."

Jagger's brows rose along with his curiosity. "Your son, wow. Tell me more."

"Well, truthfully I could just bust. McKenna has felt like one of my very own since she dated our other son back when they were in high school." The woman turned her attention to McKenna and simply oozed affection. "Xavier may not have fallen in love with her, but the rest of our family sure did. I don't know what I'd do without her. So you can imagine when she and Xander managed to find love? Well. I'm beside myself. Just bug-eyed with joy."

"I can see that," Jagger acknowledged as he shot a glance toward McKenna's ring finger.

"Perhaps when Xander's back in town, he'll have a chance to meet you as well."

"Back in town?"

"He lives in Charlotte. An investment banker."

Jagger smiled at McKenna. "Interesting."

"Wait until I tell him I've met you. He'll be so jealous."

He eyed McKenna. "I hope to make him extremely jealous." A feeling akin to hope sprouted in his chest when he saw McKenna blush.

"McKenna has turned the entire family into Cavalier fans," Mrs. Wright gushed. "Which is why I was so surprised I'd heard you were in town before she did. Usually, this girl's on top of all things Cavaliers."

"You like to be on top, huh?" He absolutely let his eyes scream the double entendre. "Well, McKenna, maybe the two of us should have dinner." He licked his lips. "You could give me the skinny on Henderson, and I could give you a story for your newspaper."

"That sounds wonderful." Mrs. Wright turned to McKenna. "Wouldn't that be wonderful?"

"Hmm," McKenna hummed.

"I think she's a little starstruck," Mrs. Wright stage-whispered.

"Anna Beth," McKenna scolded with a sigh.

"I'm sorry. I don't mean to embarrass you. I'm gonna go ahead inside. Such a pleasure to meet you, Mr. Yates."

Jagger held out his hand for McKenna's cover art, then sat back down at the table. As he wrote the words he wanted her to see, he asked, "Did that just backfire on you? Bringing your boyfriend's mother to meet me?"

"She insisted," McKenna said wearily.

"She claims you're a big fan."

"That is not news to you."

He stopped writing and looked up at her in earnest. "Did you realize you were my inspiration for 'Babe in a Bar?'"

"Not until you pointed that out."

"And?"

"Annnd." She jiggled her head, her full lips creeping into a cute, little smile. "Maybe it's just moved up from my second favorite song to number one."

He grinned up at her, then stood and leaned over the table with the pretense of giving her back her cover art. "You like me," he whispered.

"Of course, I like you. I'm not above admitting it. And it's not like you didn't know that already."

"Because of the way you stare at our drummer?"

She broke. A real smile coming through all of her you-do-not-affect-me bravado.

He totally affected her.

"Dinner," he said as he held out her signed cover.

"I can't," she said, trying to take it, but he held tight.

"Your boyfriend's mother just suggested it. You don't want to get on her bad side, do you?"

"I'm convinced having dinner with you would land me firmly on her bad side." She snapped the paper out of his grasp and started to move on.

"Good to hear." He smiled at her, at himself, and watched as she headed into the wine shop. And boy, was he ever rewarded for that. Because just as she was about to disappear from view, she turned back to look at him. And that beautiful smile she wore matched his own, megawatt for megawatt.

Damn right, he affected her.

McKenna looked down at the album cover and read what Jagger had written in bold print.

Not.

Going.

Anywhere.

And then there was a scribble that might have resembled his name, maybe. She shook her head wondering why famous people bothered to sign anything if no one was going to be able to read their signature.

Then she read his message again.

Unfortunately, this time it didn't piss her off.

This time, it made her heart beat to the rhythm of "Babe In a Bar."

CHAPTER FIVE

Like any good party, close friends stayed until the end and offered to help clean up. There was no difference with Reds' Grand Opening. After the event officially ended, all the heavy hitters from Team Henderson were there to help Scarlett and Pinks (her very diligent, hardworking boyfriend) clean up and celebrate. After all, opening new businesses in Henderson was the primary goal of Team Henderson, so tonight was a big night for not just Scarlett and her father, Rye Langford, but for the future of the entire town.

After lurking in her shop for the past week and being her number-one customer up until maybe tonight, Jagger felt enough of an affiliation with Scarlett that he didn't feel awkward about sticking around and helping out. He hadn't heard the phrase *Team Henderson* up until now, so when he was introduced to Brooks Bennett (the new mayor of Henderson) and Vance Evans (part owner of Evans & Evans Investments) and Scarlett's man Pinks, (why did they all call him Pinks?), he was eager to ask questions and understand what all the hustle was about.

There were a lot of buzzwords being thrown around. Economic development. Real estate growth. Organic farming. Etc. Etc. But their pride was evident in the details of the Sports Academy for which they'd just broken ground and the projected opening of several new Main Street shops in the upcoming weeks, right in time for holiday shopping.

"We sure wanna thank you for agreeing to Scarlett's little scheme to get the town noticed," Brooks Bennett told him. "The fact that you and your band were willing to come to town for reimbursement of your costs alone … well, I can't tell you what kind of benefit that's gonna bring."

"Because he doesn't actually know," Vance teased, busting into the conversation and introducing himself.

"Cal Johnson is a big name in sports right now," Jagger stated. "And you've got more popular bands than ours on his album. I'd be surprised if you don't see a benefit from sales and publicity."

"We're hoping the music videos will generate interest in our town. Show off the best parts of Henderson. Get people to come play tourist, spend money, consider moving here," Pinks said.

"Well, Henderson got me to stick around, didn't it?"

"I wanted to ask you about that," Vance said. "You're from Nashville, right? So, if you don't mind me sticking my nose in, what the hell are you doing here?"

Brooks jabbed Vance with an elbow to the ribs.

"Ouch," he barked. "Seriously," he said, eyeing the mayor. "Don't you want to know?"

Brooks looked over at Jagger. "I do. I do want to know. I just didn't like the way he addressed it."

"I get it. Nashville is great. It is. It's my home. And it's where I work. So as charming as your Main Street is, I'll eventually be heading back to Nashville."

"Right. So why are you standing here now?" Vance asked.

Brooks took another shot at his ribs.

"I'm here because I felt the vibe."

"The vibe?"

"The vibe. The hustle. The energy of what you're doing. Your rebuilding campaign, if you will. Like so many other small towns formed around a particular industry, once that industry folds, so goes the town. But that's not what's happening here. And I … well, I guess I saw that and was inspired. The Cavaliers aren't touring right now, so I figured I'd stay. See if this vibe, for lack of a better word, can give me some new inspiration for writing songs."

Brooks grinned. "You are absolutely welcome to use the name Henderson in any and all of your songs. In fact, we'd turn one into our town anthem if you would."

Jagger chuckled. "I'll keep that in mind."

"So other than the vibe thing," Vance pressed. "Anything else appeal to you?"

"The rent," Jagger said. "Can't get deals like this in Nashville."

"Maybe that should be our new tagline," Pinks suggested. *Can't get deals like this in Nashville.*"

"Anything else?" Vance urged.

Jagger shrugged. "Anonymity. Before tonight, no one knew who I was, and I wasn't bothered."

"Bullshit," Vance said. "The gossip machine around here is killer. We've got a rock star sticking around after his gig with Cal, that news does not stay quiet. But our citizens, for the most part, are not animals. They're happy to let you do your thing. Happy to have you among us. It's good for Henderson."

McKenna cut in as she hopped off the counter. "Wouldn't hurt to let me put your picture in our paper showing you attended the event tonight. If you do, the article might get picked up by Raleigh or Charlotte and give Henderson a boost. If you want to be that guy."

"That guy?" Jagger asked, stepping back and happily making room for Miss Blakely in their circle.

"The guy who jumps into the Team Henderson spirit. Like the rest of us, doing what he can to promote our fair town."

"While I'm here, I'm happy to be that guy." He threw one arm out and grabbed her around the waist, pulling her toward him as he centered the two of them by an artful display of wine. "Someone snap our picture for the paper."

She tried to pull away, but he wasn't having that. "Settle," he whispered as Brooks and Pinks got out their phones. "You want my picture for your article? This is how you get it."

"I'm the journalist, not the story."

"Smile," he told her as he fell into his publicity stance. The phones started clicking.

"Wait," Scarlett shouted. "Wait. Just let me get this in there." She came running with an absolutely enormous bottle of wine. Not a magnum, but something much larger.

"What the hell is that?" Jagger asked.

"It's called a Nebuchadnezzar. And if you hold it, people might want to come in to see it."

"Or think that I've got a severe wine problem."

"Scarlett, why don't you hold the bottle and stand here next to Jagger," McKenna said, spinning out of his hold and pulling Scarlett into place beside him. "This is the picture. Wait. We need the cover art in there too. Jagger you hold that."

McKenna took her time arranging them and then grabbed the camera she'd left at the register during cleanup. "Smile," she said and started shooting like she knew what she was doing. When she stopped to run through the digital images, making sure she got one she liked, she nodded. "Looks good. This will be good."

"Smooth move," Jagger whispered in her ear while pretending to look over her shoulder at the camera's screen. "You don't like having your picture taken? Or are you afraid of the fallout if out-of-town boyfriend gets a load of us snuggled up together?"

"Stop," she insisted.

"Nope," he told her.

"Let's close up and take a couple bottles back to the Evans's place," Pinks said. "Time to hit the hot tub."

"Hot tub?" Jagger questioned, grinning at McKenna.

"It's kind of a tradition," Pinks told him. "We get food, drinks, music, and a whole lot of primo towels. Then celebrate the latest Team Henderson victory long into the night."

"We're in," Jagger said.

"Great," Brooks agreed. "That will give McKenna and the rest of us a chance to twist your arm to play with Pinks and the Outlaw at Harvest Daze next weekend."

"I'm going to bag out," McKenna said. "Go home and write my article while the details are still fresh in my mind."

"Like hell, you are. Haven't you heard about the weekend rule? Lolly!" Brooks yelled. "Come brief McKenna on the weekend rule."

As Lolly and Piper came out of Reds' storage room loaded down with trays of event leftovers, they were both rolling their eyes. "Come on, McKenna. If *I* don't get to go back to the sweatshop on a Saturday night, you don't get to hunker down and write articles. Brooks is determined to see his work hard/play hard motto carried out."

"Yeah, exactly," Brooks said. "And right now, it's only nine-freaking-o'clock on a Saturday night. We don't continue this party, Henderson's reputation for weekend fun will begin to die a slow death. Y'all do not want to be the cause of that."

"So, *Henderson* has a reputation for weekend fun?" Jagger asked the crowd at large.

"You know it," the mayor insisted. "We may not have your Nashville bachelorette parties or late-night jam sessions, but hot tubbing at the Evans's is an experience you do not want to miss. Vance, you got an extra suit for the Cavaliers' front man?"

"Whatever he needs," Vance said as he took Piper's burden from her arms. "Let's head out."

As Piper passed McKenna, she said, "And I've got whatever you need. Come on. It'll be fun."

"And I am desperate to ease into that hot water. My back is killing me," Scarlett said as she stepped out of her girly heels. "Everybody out. After a very long month, I am finally off the clock. Let's celebrate."

Jagger noticed McKenna didn't say anything as the small crowd was ushered out the door. Everyone else was chatting about the party spread somebody by the name of Genevra had waiting for them.

"So ... we going?" he asked her as the two of them walked slowly down Main Street. His bike was parked in the alley in the back, but he didn't want McKenna to know that. "It seems a bit rude not to show."

McKenna didn't respond, just clicked the locks on an old model SUV that was still in decent condition.

"McKenna?"

After placing her satchel and camera in the back of her car, she turned to Jagger. "Do you really want to go?"

"Why wouldn't I want to go?"

"I don't know. They're not your people."

"I don't have any people. Here, anyway. What? You think I'd be intruding?"

"No. Not at all. I think they'd love to have you."

"Okay, then. We'll go."

"They are going to ask you a lot of questions. Not in an invasive way, but as the newcomer. You okay with that?"

Jagger felt a little burst of joy in his chest. He took a step closer to McKenna. "Are you trying to protect me?" The thought of it almost made him chuckle.

"Maybe."

Aww. She liked him. She really, really liked him.

"Babe. Trust me. I'm tight. I can handle a hot tub party. But I would feel a little more comfortable in my own trunks. That Evans guy, he's stupid fit."

McKenna looked him up and down. "You're fit."

"Not like that Vance. That guy's waist is like a thirty-two. No way am I squeezing into a thirty-two."

McKenna barked out a laugh. "Vance wasn't always a thirty-two. But he runs and started lifting weights to inspire his team. He's our high school's baseball coach."

"Baseball coaches don't look like that. Listen, give me a ride to my place, will you? I'll grab a pair of shorts that'll do the trick." When McKenna just stood there looking at him, he asked, "What?"

"You're human."

"Ah–yeah."

"No. I mean, like, you have hang-ups just like normal people."

"I've got news for you, babe. I am normal people."

"No, you're not," she declared with a rabid grin. She swung her arm out and lightly slapped him on the stomach. "You're … you. You're up on stage most nights, wooing the crowd."

"That's my job. Don't get me wrong, I love it. I'm also freaking good at it. But I am aware of my limits. You don't see me strutting around stage bare chested or in board shorts."

McKenna's eyes squinted. "You totally could."

"Babe."

"I mean it."

"You have not seen me shirtless. And trust me. I take off these jeans, I have twigs for legs."

"I can't believe this."

"What?"

"You are the lead singer of a world-renowned band, and you're worried about how you're gonna measure up to Vance Evans in a hot tub?"

"Pfft. I'm more worried about the mayor. That guy is huge."

McKenna burst into laughter. "You are crazy, you know that?"

"Just give me a ride, will you? And stop laughing at the newcomer."

"All right," she said. "Come on. Get in."

Jagger didn't have to be told twice. He sprinted to the shotgun seat and was strapped in before she could say *boo*. Or, *Wait, I just remembered I have a boyfriend.* Yeah. No moss was growing under his feet. Thank God for the hot tub party.

And the best part? When she cranked up the engine, guess who she had playing through her speakers?

Damn. Straight.

The two of them looked at each other—him grinning, her bursting out in embarrassed laughter. Then he started singing. As she pulled away from the curb, she joined in, glancing in his direction as she matched him word for word.

CHAPTER SIX

No doubt there were plenty of women who could sing the Cavaliers' songs word for word. But·being in the car with this particular one was a little surreal for Jagger. If McKenna Blakely had any idea he'd been fixated on her as he wrote a bunch of them, she might consider slapping him with a restraining order.

Yeah, he was gonna keep all that to himself.

At the moment, things were going too well to throw a lot of *by the way, there was a time I was obsessed with you* into the conversation. For one thing, she hadn't mentioned her fucking boyfriend once in the past hour. Thank you, Jesus. And for another, McKenna was as relaxed and loose now as she'd been during the first part of their telephone conversation the other night. Only this time, he got to see her facial expressions when she spoke. Got to see her crazy-blue eyes roll at him. Got to see her smirk, watch her wince, catch her blush.

And the best part of all? He got to watch her practically fall over and swoon when he walked out of his place with his acoustic guitar in hand.

"Are you bringing that?" She literally started jumping up and down beside her car. Then she squealed, covered her face with her hands, and spun around, as giddy as a woman could get.

"I see McKenna, the fangirl, has made an appearance." They both got back in the car.

"You cannot do this to me," she said, clasping her heart. "You cannot just bring out your guitar like that."

"What are you talking about?" He strapped himself in, and she took off. "The two of us just sang three songs together in this very car."

"Oh my …" Leaving one hand on the wheel, she grabbed her head as if she were in pain. "Don't remind me. That's like. Crazy. I mean, Laidey and Jinx are not going to believe this. I don't believe this."

"McKenna."

"Yes?"

"I really, *really* like you."

"WHAT!" She slammed on the brakes, bringing the car to a screeching halt in the middle of the road.

"Holy shit. What the—?"

"Sorry. Sorry." She apologized. "But you cannot say things like that. Especially while I'm driving. Holy crap! Do you want to get us killed?"

"Nope. Definitely don't want to get us killed."

"Then why would you *say that*?" she shrieked.

"I don't know. It was spontaneous. It just … came out," he shouted. Of course, it did. The girl he'd idolized over seventeen songs was going all gaga on him. Who wouldn't be smitten?

And *fuck* was he ever smitten.

"I'm sorry. I'm sorry," she said. "The last thing I want to do is send my favorite singer through the windshield."

"Good to know."

"But you brought out your guitar," she squealed into her hand.

"I didn't know it would send you spinning into a fangirl cyclone."

"Well, clearly it did," she said, gathering her composure. "Next time, warn a girl, would ya?"

"You got it."

They drove off in silence. Well, the two of them were silent while his band played over the speakers.

"I liked the fangirl cyclone," he muttered.

"What?"

"I'm glad you dig me and my guitar."

She let out a heavy sigh.

"I thought with all the guns those guys are going to be sporting in the hot tub, I ought to bring my weapon of choice."

"They'll love it. But they'll also try to talk you in to playing for free with Pinks at the Daze. And then they'll market the hell out of it because that's what they do."

"What's a Daze?"

"It's a Henderson thing. I'll explain later."

They turned into a circular drive, drove through some fancy-ass gates and pulled up in front of a sprawling brick mansion. "Who are these people?"

"The Evans clan. They're ground zero when it comes to the *hustle* around here. So you know, don't be an asshole."

"When the heck have I ever been an asshole?"

She just shrugged as she exited the vehicle.

"McKenna," he called as he pulled his guitar from the backseat and slammed the door. "WTF?"

"I don't know. I'm sorry. I just …" She came around to his side of the car and ventured into his personal space. "I want people to like you, okay?"

"Ah-huh."

"And they may have preconceived notions."

"Like what?"

"Like you trash hotel rooms or something."

"Why would they think that?"

"You're in a touring band. And you have tattoos."

"We're not a hotel-room-trashing kind of band. And who doesn't like tattoos?"

"I don't know." She laughed. "I'm sorry, I'm talking crazy."

"No." He took a hold of her elbow. "Now, stand here a second and tell me what's going on." He leaned his backside against her car and pulled her to him, dropping his hand to her waist and his voice to a soft whisper. "Babe, is there a reason you don't want me going in there?"

"No. It's not that. And they are going to love you. I'm sure. Absolutely."

"Then I don't get it."

She shook her head, sucked in a breath, and then appeared to gather herself. She held up a finger. "I think it's that ever since I found your music, I've been wanting to turn everyone else into a fan."

"Yeah. Ah-huh. We appreciate that."

"So I'm feeling very invested. I want everyone in there to like you. A lot."

"Oh. Babe."

Suddenly her shoulders dropped, and she shot him an incredulous look. "And stop with the *babe* thing. I'm not your babe."

"Damn."

"Come on," she said, begrudgingly. Like this was the worst thing she'd ever have to do. Walk into this big fucking mansion and introduce him around as her ... what?

He fell into step with her. "Look. I'm tight. I meet people all the time without repelling them. You don't have to worry. If I get the urge to start trashing the place I'll give you the high sign. You can drag me out the back or something."

McKenna stopped abruptly and grinned.

"Seriously," he said.

"I know, I know. I'm being ridiculous. I just ... can't *believe* you're here. That I've been driving you around in my car," she said emphatically. "Granted, this experience has made me a little nuts. But I'll get over it. Or get used to it. Your celebrity status. I promise."

They made their way to the door. "I'm okay with you not getting over it. I kinda like you a little nuts. It's the same way you acted when we first met."

"How did I act?"

The door opened with a spectacular flourish of orange fabric swishing to and fro. "I heard we were receiving a special guest," a Sophia Loren look-a-like cooed in a Spanish accent. "Welcome. Do come in."

"Mrs. Flores, this is Jagger Yates. Lead singer for the Cavaliers. My favorite band," McKenna added.

"Mine too," Mrs. Flores replied.

"Is that so?" Jagger asked, knowing damn well he was being scammed.

"'Babe in a Bar' is my favorite song. Though 'Friday Night Heights' is a close second."

Jagger's eyebrows shot up. "Wow. So you do know our music."

"Doesn't everyone?"

Jagger gave the woman his best smile, already liking ground zero of the Henderson hustle.

"Everyone is in the kitchen preparing libations for the pool."

"I hope you'll be joining us."

"Of course, dear boy. The two of you require a chaperone, and my grandson cannot be trusted." She started moving them all up the stairs.

"A chaperone?"

"Yes. You see, Anna Beth Wright is a dear friend of mine. She has laid claim to this one"—she pointed to McKenna—"in hopes she will become her daughter-in-law. Once I heard you were coming with McKenna well, let's just say I have not forgotten what it's like to party with a famous musician named *Jagger*."

"Ah-ha. And what exactly was that like?"

"*Quite* enthralling."

He grinned when he heard McKenna mutter, "You can say that again."

"So, fear not. While I'm around, everything will be on the up-and-up." She clapped her hands. "Come, you must meet my son, Hale. He has absolutely no musical talent, but he does keep a well-stocked bar."

McKenna watched as the Big Em led Jagger into the Evans kitchen and saw the commotion he made just by entering the room. Everyone immediately stopped, turned, and then dropped what they were doing to welcome him into the fold. Henderson was good like that. You didn't have to be a celebrity to get that kind of greeting. Just a friend of a friend. But considering Jagger was an award-winning musician, he probably was greeted like that no matter where he went.

That truth filtering over her was just as startling as if the Big Em had sprayed her with a garden hose. Which, by bringing up Anna Beth Wright, she figuratively had. McKenna hadn't thought about Anna Beth or Xander for, like, hours. She had lost herself fully in

Jagger. Submerged herself in his presence. And it had been *such* a grand adventure.

But as she took in the room she saw how Jagger was, at once, *everyone's* grand adventure. He walked in with literal rock-star status, yes. But he was so much more than that. He was charisma itself, drawing all the energy in the room in his direction. It was, in fact, his charisma that sold out the Cavaliers concerts on the regular.

He was bigger than this party.

He was bigger even than Henderson.

He was Jagger Yates, and he was bigger than the whole of McKenna's wildest dreams.

She turned around and wandered down a hallway to find a quiet place to change ... and to send off a text to Xander.

As far as chaperones went, the Big Em (as Jagger had discovered everyone called her) was the all-time worst. And thank the good lord for that. Because McKenna Blakely in a bikini was about the biggest turn-on he could recall, and his hands had a mind of their own when she came anywhere within an arm's reach.

He could not stop touching her.

And more than that, once he got a feel of her soft, *soft* skin, he didn't want to.

Fuck sweet Anna Beth Wright and her plans for her future daughter-in-law. There was no ring on McKenna's finger. And if her son had something better to do on a Saturday night than run interference and protect what was supposed to be his? Far be it from Jagger not to take advantage.

And the best part was ... McKenna didn't seem to mind.

It had taken a while getting everybody's cocktails squared away, plus those pitchers of refills, not to mention the coolers stocked with beer and various other liquid offerings. Everybody had something in their hands as they paraded out of the kitchen, going poolside with trays of appetizers and desserts. An Army Ranger named—get this—*Thor,* and his girl Missy were the last of the guests to arrive. Jagger introduced himself since everyone else was busy, and even though, clearly, neither one of them had any clue who he was or what he did for a living, they seemed genuinely happy to meet him anyway.

That felt good. Not bringing anything to the table, so to speak, and being welcomed anyway.

McKenna made sure he was taken care of. Not that he couldn't have gotten his own damn beer eventually, but he was being chatted up pretty good, and she didn't seem to mind playing hostess. In his mind, he was counting up the men and the women, getting a real good sense that this party wasn't just a come-one-come-all. No, this party was for couples. A one-to-one male-to-female ratio, which left him and McKenna paired up. It seemed the stars were definitely aligning.

Waiting for the moment McKenna slipped out of that silky cover-up she was sporting, Jagger kept one eye on McKenna through a whole lot of toasts (once Pinks and his Scarlett emerged from the pool house) to commemorate the start of Reds and the future of Henderson. All the while, Jagger's fingers twitched and grew restless, eager for the unveiling.

Hot tub parties.

Fucking brilliant idea.

As it turned out, she was standing right next to him when everyone started stripping down and getting lost in the steam coming off the water's surface. McKenna was shrugging out of her little silk bathrobe when his hands automatically went to help her. She turned her back toward him, allowing him to ease the fabric from her shoulders and arms as if he were helping her out of a coat. The silky fabric ended up bunched in his hands while his gaze caressed her creamy shoulders and focused in on that tiny bow at the base of her neck where her swimsuit top was tied. She'd piled her hair on top of her head, which appeared no easy feat. As far as he could tell, it took two big clips and a headband to keep the mass up and off her shoulders. He let his eyes travel down her back and was caught gawking when she looked over her shoulder at him. "You can just put that over there. Thanks," she directed.

He nodded mutely, reaching out his arm, and then took a step to lay the delicate fabric on a thickly cushioned chaise lounge. Jagger reached behind his neck with both hands and pulled his T-shirt over his head while toeing off the white athletic shoes to reveal bare feet. He placed his shirt on the same chaise lounge and grabbed two towels off the table beside it. He offered McKenna one as he held out his hand, indicating the hot tub. "Shall we?"

"Let's," she said, taking delicate and deliberate steps on the wet patio surface and then again as she stepped down into the water. All kinds of shifting began to take place in the pool. The thing was big, but this crowd was filling it up pretty good. Glasses and beer bottles were being passed from one to another. Vance reached up to help McKenna down into the pool and Jagger followed her, clasping his towel and beer in one arm and holding on to the handrail as he maneuvered into the hot water. He and McKenna set their towels and drinks on the edge of the pool where others had made room for the two of them to sit.

"Mmmm," he groaned as he sank into the depths of the warm water, realizing there was more to enjoy at a hot tub party than the scantily clad women. "Do y'all do this often?" he asked. "I could get used to this."

"It's become a thing," Pinks said.

"Recently," Vance added. "It's become a thing, recently. There were years this hot tub, and the pool, didn't see a lot of action. But now that we've got so many people living in this damn house, it's a great way to celebrate our smallest victories and continue planning the big ones."

Jagger looked over at Scarlett and held up his beer. "Tonight was no small victory. I know how hard you've worked."

"I appreciate that," Scarlett said. Then she grinned at Pinks who sat next to her. "The dream started out as a website, where I could sell and blog about obscure wines."

"In other words, wineries that had yet to make the connections needed to get their bottles into shops across the country," Pinks chimed in.

"Right. I was headed out to California, but then I met Pinks and he convinced me there was a need for an upscale wine shop in Henderson and I was just the girl to get 'r' done. The rest hopefully— like all good wines—has long legs and will become history."

"Reds is gonna make some good history," Jagger told her. "How about you?" he asked McKenna. "What kind of history are you making here in Henderson?"

"I'm a journalist. I don't make history. I record it."

"Yeah? Is that your passion? Journalism?"

McKenna took a breath, apparently considering her response. "After college, I wanted to live in Henderson and .... well, at that time, jobs were drying up pretty fast. But for some reason, our local newspaper continued to hold its own, even while subscribers moved away. However, the journalists would often leave for bigger cities and larger circulation. I decided to take some courses online and then wrote up a few pieces about things I saw around the area. I took them to the powers that be. They didn't offer me much. Sort of a pay-by-piece deal. But they did give me a desk and access to their databases and technology. Eventually, it became a viable career. Pays the bills."

"How long do you think it will be until *you* move to a bigger, broader paper?"

It was like the scratch of a needle on an album. All the ambient chatter coming to a screeching halt.

"Ah, say there, Rock Star," Vance called from across the pool. "One thing you might want to keep in mind, especially around these folks, is that we are trying to entice people to move *back* to Henderson. Basically doing everything we can short of locking down the perimeter to keep people from escaping."

Jagger laughed.

But he was the only one.

"Hey," he backpedaled. "Sorry. From what I can tell, y'all have things well in hand. I was just, you know, trying to figure things out."

"Things out about McKenna?" Vance asked.

It was not lost on Jagger that Vance's countenance suddenly changed. That his eyes began to shift between him and McKenna. Back and forth. Until he took his arm from around his wife and stood up, making waves as he sauntered through the water, coming at them.

"Move on over, Rock Star. Let me have a seat right here between you two." And without waiting for either him or McKenna to move, Vance began to plop his stupidly fit body down between them.

"What the hell?" Jagger said, dodging the guy so he wouldn't have Vance sitting on his lap.

"Y'all just seem a little too cozy, is all." Vance turned his head to the right toward McKenna and then looked left at Jagger. "See, this is better. Now you and I can get to know each other and my buddy Xander has nothin' to worry about."

"Say what?"

"Yeah." Vance turned his head back and directed his next words to McKenna. "Xander. Shame he couldn't get here tonight."

"He was invited," McKenna said.

"And what's that old saying? Snooze you lose?" Jagger muttered.

"Not on my watch," Vance said under his breath as he took a sip of his beer.

"So ..." Pinks drawled from where he sat in the pool. "Next weekend is the Daze. My buddy's coming to town so we can play a set or two along with various other local musicians. Any chance you'd be interested in jamming with us? For free?"

Jagger smiled. "What the hell is this Daze?"

Brooks filled him in. "The Daze is actually a slang term we've given our hundred-plus-year-old *Harvest Days* celebration. Obviously, it started as a way to celebrate the end of a good harvest. We still have lots of farming in the area, so it's still about that, but it's also about raising money for town projects and getting our citizens of all ages together for some fun."

"So essentially, I'd be fundraising?" Jagger asked.

"That and upping my status," Pinks quipped.

"Sort of," Brooks explained. "We don't charge people to attend the Daze. So the musical entertainment is essentially free and used as a draw. Generally, the high school's marching band performs along with our local barbershop quartet and various other groups who audition for spots. Last year, Pinks and the Outlaw brought down the house as a great cover band and kept everyone dancing late into the night. Pinks plays the drums like twice a year, and the Outlaw plays guitar and sings."

Jagger looked around. "Who's the Outlaw?"

"His name is Jesse James—thus the title. He doesn't actually live in Henderson, *yet*," Pinks explained. "I'm working on that."

"So he just, what, saunters in for a showdown at the Daze?"

"His brother is this town's corporate lawyer. So whenever we need a good party band to play for free, we call Jesse in," Brooks explained.

"And that's the key word there, Rock Star. Free," Vance stressed. "We are a town running on fumes. If you play, you've got to do it for free."

Jagger nodded. "Well, it wasn't long ago I was playing for next to nothing regularly. If I tell my manager it's for a local charity, I don't think I'll get much pushback. Besides, it'd be like playin' for y'all here around the pool. Only on a bigger scale, right?"

"Oh, man," Scarlett said. "If I could get Cal to come to town for the Daze, you two could sing together like you did on the album." Then Scarlett jumped up, splashing Pinks and Piper. "We need to sell the album! And the calendars!" She turned to Pinks and started in on him. "How is it you've let me drop the ball here? We need two separate kiosks at the Daze and staffing for the entire day."

Pinks grabbed Scarlett's hand and pulled her down onto his lap, wrapping his arms around her. "I've got you. You were so busy with Reds I went ahead and started the ball rolling. Happy to hand it off to you tomorrow, if you'd like."

"Oh, thank God," she sighed. "See why I love him?" she asked the crowd at large.

"We do." Lolly smiled at both Pinks and Red.

Brooks growled.

"*Pinks* and *Red*?" Jagger grinned like he'd just caught the best joke.

"It's a long story," Pinks assured him.

"Please. Lay it on me. I've got all kinds of melodies playin' in my head just waiting for the lyrics to this one. And people think 'Jack and Diane' was big."

Everyone chuckled at the thought. Pinks told his story, and then Red told hers, and then the nicknames came out all over the pool. The Lollipop. The Golden Boy. Third Base. The Lawyer Beaumont. King Kong. The list went on, including those who weren't in attendance. Jagger learned real quick that the one thing the nicknames had in common was that Vance had essentially assigned them all.

"Damn right. I call 'em as I see 'em, Rock Star. Except for Davis over there. *Pinks* was all the Golden Boy, back when he was hot under the collar about Lolly's ex coming to town trying to steal her back."

And then *that* story got told.

"Y'all are a wealth of crazy country songs, you know that, right? Maybe that's part of the vibe I felt going on here. Why I stayed."

"I thought it was for the wine," Scarlett quipped.

"And the wine. Definitely the wine," he said grinning.

"What about you?" Jagger pointed his bottle toward the curly-headed blonde with the great rack across the pool. "You're a lawyer?"

Jagger didn't realize that asking that simple question was going to get him exactly what he wanted. Without a word, Vance stood up and walked back through the water, seating himself next to the blonde and copying Pinks by pulling her onto his lap.

Piper laughed as she got herself situated, but never broke eye contact with Jagger. "I am a lawyer, though I don't practice anymore. Right after the Daze, Genevra and I are opening Henderson's Big Pie Plate Shop and Bakery as well as starting an online cooking show. My efforts are now being focused on bringing bakers of all kinds to our town and getting them to invest in Henderson's Big Pie Plate."

"That your place? Down the street from Reds? The one that's got activity going on all day long?"

"It is," Piper cooed. "We'd love you to stop in just as soon as we're open."

Jagger looked to Missy next. "And what about you? What do you do?"

"I'm the CEO of Team Henderson."

Jagger's eyebrows raised.

"She is, and yet she doesn't get paid one dime for it," the Golden Boy/Mayor added.

"I'm a paid consultant for Evans & Evans Investments," Missy explained. "I also have a party planning business where my specialty has become pitting Henderson debutante parties against Oxford debutante parties."

"Debutantes? Is that still a thing?" Jagger asked.

"Around here it is, and thank goodness for it," Lolly piped in. "*My* business depends on it. And weddings. If you're ever in the market for a wedding dress, please remember House of DuVal. One-of-a-kind fashions created not only in the USA, but right here in Henderson."

"Wow. And you?" he asked Thor.

"I inherited a plantation outside of town. My pop and his daddy and my great-granddaddy and so forth grew tobacco. I'm not cool with that, so I'm working on a few new enterprises. All with an eye toward supporting the town."

"Man." Jagger leaned back. "Y'all are pretty much determined to turn the tide here, aren't you? Can't think of much that would be any more heroic than that."

"We're working on it," Brooks said. "Our dream is to eventually have Henderson listed as one of the top places to live in the US. We're coming at it from all angles. The sports academy is our holy grail. Our big push. And knock on wood, that's coming along right on schedule. Still, it's been huge having people like Scarlett and Piper opening shops in town. Giving Main Street a chance to thrive again."

"Y'all could use a music store. You know. One that sells guitars and such."

"Jagger, we'd love for you to consider investing in one," Brooks said. Then he pointed to Pinks. "Talk to that guy right there. He'll research the hell out of it, but with your connections and if you'd put your name on the door, it'd be another destination to draw people to Henderson. Pinks!"

"I'm on it."

"I'm not saying I'm interested," Jagger protested.

"We understand. Just do us a favor and meet with the kid," Brooks suggested.

"Give me a week," Pinks requested.

Jagger shook his head and grinned toward the water. "Y'all are a damn pushy bunch, you know that?"

"See what a hot tub party leads to?" Vance asked. "Lots of great ideas bubbling to the surface."

Jagger did happen to have some big ideas, and he was apparently incapable of stopping himself from acting on them. Because his hand was sliding along the seat underneath the water to graze the side of McKenna's pinkie with his own.

Throughout the conversation, well, after Vance finally gave up his blatant cock-blocking technique in lieu of having his wife sit on his lap—damn that little woman was fine—Jagger had managed to shift and scooch and slide, all hopefully undetected, back to where he'd originally started. Next to McKenna.

If anyone had a problem with it, they weren't voicing it.

If anyone had any idea he was playing pinkies with her right now, they weren't complaining.

If McKenna didn't move her hand away from his, then maybe he didn't exactly have a green light, but he sure as hell had a flashing yellow. And he figured that meant he should go ahead and proceed with caution.

CHAPTER SEVEN

Jagger Yates was secretly trying to hold her hand, and it was the most erotic thing McKenna had ever experienced.

He wasn't even looking at her.

He was acting normal.

Conversing.

Asking questions.

Making inroads with the locals.

For all intents and purposes, he did not look like a man who was making a pass at a woman. Yet all the while, he's dusting her pinkie finger with his. Back and forth. Under the water. Hidden from view.

He seemed completely relaxed and engaged and—*holy shit*—this was making her lungs seize. Jagger Yates was feeling up her pinkie!

Should she … what? Feel his back? Pretend not to notice? And how would that be possible when on the inside, she was *flipping the heck out*. If she acted out what she was feeling, from just the flick of his little finger grazing over hers, she'd be in the center of this Jacuzzi, hands over her head, dancing around like a fool, yelling, "Jagger Yates is *touching* me!"

She was being ridiculous. Completely ridiculous.

Only, NOT.

Because … Jagger Yates was TOUCH-ING her.

Okay. Okay. Deep breath, she commanded herself, while tuning back in to the titillating finger caress happening underneath the water. That's when her natural reflexes kicked in. She turned her head, bit her lip, and gave his sturdy profile a grin.

And maybe he didn't bat an eye or miss a beat as he was involved in an impassioned conversation with somebody across the pool. But *she knew* that *he knew* she was grinning at him, because he busted out a big grin, too, and just kept on talking. In fact, he made the pinkie sizzle go nuclear by wrapping his little finger around hers.

And now they were holding pinkies.

McKenna wanted to squeal. Wanted to kick her feet furiously. But she clamped down on the bounty of internal elation that threatened to wreak havoc by splashing everyone in the pool. She had to stifle her emotions. Try not to call any further attention to Jagger and herself. Because—*Vance* for one thing.

And—*Jagger Yates was holding her pinkie*—for another.

Oh. And now. Now, Jagger's thumb was rubbing the underside of her little finger while he held it captive. He was touching her with two fingers, and instead of giggling or grinning, she didn't move a muscle.

It was such a little thing, hidden from view. But it was sweet and romantic, and on top of that, it was actually quite scandalous. And it was a moment in time she would *never* forget. This whole, *OMG, he's touching me on purpose. In front of my friends. And I'm not sure what this means but oh, would I like to find out.*

It was one of those moments that made you feel happy to be alive. Because sometimes life brings you surprises you'd never begin to imagine.

Jagger Yates walking into your hometown.

Jagger asking you to dinner.

Jagger trying to hold your hand in a hot tub.

Somebody asked a question, she replied with a, "Hmm."

Somebody offered refills. Jagger used his left hand to accept another beer. She used her right.

Somebody got out of the hot tub, Jagger slid closer and put his hand over hers.

Music started playing, and Jagger laughed, took her hand in his, and squeezed it beneath the water as everybody sang the Cavaliers breakout hit.

Together.

In the hot tub.

With the lead singer himself.

There were high-fives all around. He used his left hand. She used her right.

Missy and Thor got out and dried off.

Brooks asked Jagger when he was going back on tour.

Lolly got out of the pool, and Brooks followed.

Jagger's foot ran alongside her own.

Pinks asked about Jagger's guitar. About his bandmates' instruments. About the type of strings they used. What his drummer was like.

Jagger slipped his foot over the top of McKenna's, wrapping up her ankle with his at the base of the pool.

Piper got out to fetch a pie from the oven. Vance gave Jagger a look and followed after his wife.

When it got down to just Pinks, Scarlett, Jagger, and McKenna, the conversation flowed happily, like the bubbling water. Scarlett was direct and inquisitive about Jagger's personal life. And probably because McKenna was presently holding hands and playing footsie with the man, her stomach tensed, worried what his answers might reveal.

Was there a girl waiting for him in Nashville?

But Scarlett didn't go there. Instead she asked about his family.

Mom.

Dad.

Four pain-in-the-ass sisters whom he loved dearly.

All of them not particularly happy he was holing himself up in Henderson and taking time for himself.

"Maybe they'd like to come visit," Scarlett suggested. "Do they like wine?"

Jagger laughed. "They love wine. And if they ever do come to Henderson, they'll definitely want to check out your shop."

"Good. Good." Scarlett smiled and looked between McKenna and Jagger. "You two look good together," she said softly. She gave Jagger a nod. Then she turned to Pinks. "Shall we?"

"Sure. I could use dessert." Pinks motioned toward Jagger. "You okay with me doing a bit of research on that music shop?"

"Depends on how much this research is going to cost me."

"Not a thing. Shouldn't take me long to pull a few things together. I get that you're not here to invest in Henderson. But it's actually not a bad idea. A town can't live on sports and wine alone."

"And pie. Don't forget Piper's pies," Scarlett said, wrapping herself in a towel at the top of the pool steps.

"And pie," Pinks agreed. "With Red producing an album here, who knows where Henderson's music industry could go." He chuckled. "You could be on the ground floor of something big. Think about it."

With that, Pinks sprung out of the pool, not bothering with the steps, leaving behind a small wake.

Jagger shifted around, taking a new grip on McKenna's hand as he turned to face her. "This is quite a group." His thumb brushed over the top of her hand.

McKenna nodded her head, agreeing. Smiling back at him.

"And for some reason, the lyrics to 'I wanna hold your hand' just keep playing over and over in my mind."

They laughed together. Their heads dipping closer.

"Am I getting you in trouble?" he asked quietly.

She laughed softly. "Do you really care?"

"Not about … anybody else. Just about you." He shook his head and pulled her hand closer to him. "I just care about you."

He'd looked her in the eye when he said that. Like he meant what he was saying and wanted to make a point of it.

He could be playing her.

He could be playing her as expertly as he played his guitar.

He could totally be out to simply make her a notch on his bedpost.

But at the moment, she didn't care.

For the moment, she was diving headfirst into Jagger Yates and whatever came along with him.

"So, you've heard me answer everybody's questions. Are you gonna tell me your story?" he asked. "Tell me about the life and times of McKenna Blakely?"

"The life and times, huh?" She licked her lips, letting her gaze travel over his handsome face. Those soulful root-beer-colored eyes. His yummy, thick hair. That trimmed beard that had changed her mind about all beards forever. He had a straight, regal nose. Large, which fit his face perfectly. Below that were lips that conjured impure thoughts. "Well, Jagger Yates," she whispered as she leaned ever closer toward him. "There's a high probability that at this very moment, we are creating one of my life's fondest memories."

"I like the sound of that."

"You are already part of … many of my fondest memories. However, tonight takes My Life and Times with Jagger Yates to an entirely new level."

He let go of her hand. Inched a little closer and laid his right arm on the pool edge behind her. He then reclaimed her hand with his left one. "You want to get out? Wrap up in one of those towels, grab a couple cold beers, and head for that chaise lounge where you can tell me more?"

She grinned. "Sure. I suppose we are getting a little wrinkly."

"I'm okay with wrinkly. And I'm generally okay in the spotlight." He indicated the underwater pool lights. "But I wouldn't mind slipping into a little bit of dark right now."

McKenna checked out the other couples as they were drying off, chatting by the cooler, shifting around the food. No one was paying a bit of attention to them. But they were the last ones in the pool—together—and as Jagger pointed out, the pool was well lit. So yeah, a little bit of dark might be a very good thing.

"Vance is on to me."

"What?" McKenna asked as she stood, dropping Jagger's hand with a keen sense of *damn*. She picked up both their towels.

"Vance. He's not an idiot. Knows it's highly unlikely for a man to sit next to a beautiful woman and not make a move."

"That's because Vance is famous for *his* moves."

"On you?"

"On everybody."

"Seriously? You and Vance?"

"Nooo. Not me and Vance. But Vance and plenty others. And since he was always thinking with his … you know—"

"Dick," Jagger interjected.

"Yeah," McKenna guffawed. "That. He probably thinks every other red-blooded American male does too."

"The guy ain't wrong," Jagger said as he followed her out of the pool.

McKenna sputtered to a stop on the pool deck, turning around to face him. "So he's right? You're thinking with your dick?"

"Like … duh."

"Oh, my God," she muttered. "You aren't even denying it."

"Oh, and like you aren't thinking with your pu—private girly bits."

"Ha! My *girly bits?*" She swung a huge white towel into his chest. Then wrapped one around her body and headed toward the chaise. She was totally thinking with her girly bits.

"We're in public," Jagger explained. "And I don't know how you like … *things.* So, I'm not going to be an ass and … use inappropriate terminology."

She turned and smiled up into his face. Because he was tall, for one. And he was tickling her girly bits for another. This whole comedy routine was more fun than she'd ever imagined possible with Jagger Yates.

"This is so surreal," she said, releasing a breath. "I'm thirty years old, but I look at you, standing here, teasing me, and I feel like a wigged-out teenager who has posters of you plastered all over the walls of her room."

"Do you? Have posters of me in your room?" His eyes glistened with merriment.

"Does my phone's wallpaper count?"

"Totally." He chuckled his delight.

She flew a hand into the air. "And I'm not even embarrassed."

"Why should you be? This is a little surreal for me, too, remember?" He pointed at his chest. "Older than you. Been around the block." He twirled his finger. "And yet, I'm standing here looking at you and thinking—holy shit—the one that got away."

McKenna's breath hitched in dramatic fashion.

"What?" he asked, as if he hadn't just tipped her world upside down.

"Jagger," she half whispered. "Is that—is that true?"

"That I look at you and think, I can't believe I'm standing here with the girl who gave me the wrong number? Yeah. Totally true."

No. No. Am I the One Who Got Away? That was what McKenna wanted to know. Because *that* was how she felt about Xander. *He* was her One That Got Away. And that was the sole reason she'd been granting him so much leeway with this Becca thing. Xander *was* the One That Got Away. She *knew* how that felt. So what she wanted to know from Jagger, was ... *is that how he felt about her?*

She shook her head to clear it.

Of course that wasn't how Jagger felt. She and Jagger didn't have that kind of history. No. The phrase may fit this situation, but it couldn't have true emotion behind it. None of the never-ending longing. Or that grateful, precious relief that had overwhelmed her the moment Xander came back into her life.

"You want a beer?" Jagger's words redirected her thoughts.

"I'd like a water, actually."

"Sounds good. I'll grab two. Meet you back here."

McKenna pulled the towel more fully around her and sank onto the chaise, thinking about Xander. Maybe she should feel a little guilty about holding hands with her favorite celeb and enjoying the night as much as she was, but why?

Xander had been invited to Reds' Grand Opening and for whatever reason decided not to show.

McKenna had been upfront with him. She made no secret of the fact she'd been asked out, forcing Xander to admit they weren't exclusive and therefore he had no right to be upset if she started seeing someone else.

And tonight was a darn good eye-opener for her too.

She now completely understood how a person could be interested in dating two people at the same time.

Like, say ... the One That Got Away and the new one you never imagined—not in your wildest dreams—you could have.

She sighed and flopped back onto the chaise. Apparently, it wasn't just men who thought with their dicks.

CHAPTER EIGHT

Although Jagger's eyes had adjusted to the dark, and the landscape around the pool was generously lit, he began to crave a little more light as he wandered closer to the chaise where he'd left McKenna. Because for whatever reason, she was now sprawled on her back and had thrown off the towel. Her entire bikini-clad body was left exposed to the night air and his regard. *Damn.*

"You okay there?" He cracked a smile, because it wasn't like she was trying to get a tan.

"I'm overheated from the Jacuzzi," she said, propping herself up on her elbows.

Jagger understood. He'd ditched his towel, allowing the cool air to bring down his body temperature. "I hear ya."

"Whatcha got there, handsome?"

Handsome. She called him handsome.

"Vance's wife insisted I grab a piece of her pie. And that little bit of a woman cut me a hefty slice. I brought two forks in case you wanted to help me." He reached out and handed over two water bottles. McKenna took both while sitting up and making room for him at the end of the chaise.

"What kind is it?" she asked.

"Hell if I know."

McKenna opened the bottles while he took up a fork and helped himself to a large bite. "Mmm. Apple," he said around a full mouth. He chewed and then licked his lips. "But it's not just any ol' apple. It's like Nirvana Apple. Or, you know, Decadent Apple. Or—" He took another bite and yummed up more oohs and ahhs. "My God, it's like no apple pie I've ever tasted. This thing is like another level of apple all together." He took a third bite and asked, "What the hell is in this?"

"I don't know, but if you let me have a taste, maybe I can help figure it out."

Jagger smacked his lips and looked at McKenna sincerely. "I would literally give you the shirt off my back. A second case of the wine I sent you. Like, I'd give you anything within my power—except for a bite of this pie. You're gonna need to go get your own."

McKenna laughed uproariously.

Jagger didn't care. He just kept on eating, handing over the fork he brought her but keeping the plate all to himself. "Is this the kind of ambrosia Vance's wife is going to be peddling out of her shop?"

"That's the plan. It's my understanding you are tasting the results of her mother's award-winning piecrust paired with Henderson's Big Pie Plate. Something about the construction of the pie plate making everything taste better.

"They are not wrong. Good God, this is good." Jagger continued to stuff his mouth like he was on the clock. "Seriously. You need to go get a slice before it's all gone."

McKenna snickered, stood, and grabbed up the towel to wrap around her waist.

"And while you're at it, sneak me another piece? You know, on the sly. I don't want everybody to think I'm a pig."

"They won't think you're a pig. Why do you think Piper is opening the shop? Your reaction is everyone's reaction."

He watched her trot off toward the table where most of the others hovered.

As Jagger worked on his last bite, scraping the plate with his fork to get all of the gooey goodness and any bits of that crazy crust into his mouth, he heard a squeal. And just as he was considering putting his tongue directly against the plate, Vance's wife came at him with a big poster-girl smile.

"You liked the pie?" she asked, sweet as sugar.

What he liked was the little baby doll standing before him with that sexy sweatshirt dripping off her shoulder and stopping at the tops of her thighs. His response? "Don't be absurd."

"I'm sorry?" Piper blinked.

"The word *like*. It doesn't do your pie justice. So, no. I didn't *like* your pie. Your pie transported me to a realm of deep appreciation I have never wallowed in before."

Piper breathed in and swung a hand to her throat.

"With every tantalizing, delicious, extraordinary mouthful, all I could think about was my next bite. I kept thinking, *I don't want this experience to end.* I'm guessing it's like people on heroin. The high is so good you just want more and more."

Piper smiled, smug and deeply satisfied. "I like you, Jagger Yates. I hope you stick around."

"Gonna be hard to leave now that I've tasted bliss."

McKenna came back with two pieces and handed him one.

"Bless you."

"It's good," McKenna told Piper. "I mean, I've tasted your Big Pie Plate creations before, so I'm not as overwhelmed as he is," she said pointing at Jagger. "I knew what to expect. Still, when your mouth is ready for apple pie and then it gets hit with this? It's like the brain gets confused. Because it knows it's apple pie, but also that it really isn't."

"No. It really isn't," Jagger agreed. "Do you ship these?"

"Ship?" Piper asked.

"You know, can I order one to send to my parents for Thanksgiving?"

Piper stood there, seemingly stunned. Her pretty face stoic, her eyelashes batting rapidly. Finally, she hollered, "Pinks!" before turning and scampering off.

"What the heck?" Jagger asked McKenna.

She just shrugged, sitting down at the head of the chaise, facing him with her legs crossed. "Maybe she hadn't considered shipping her pies?"

"How could she not have considered shipping her pies?"

"I don't know," McKenna laughed. "But it's a great idea."

"Right?" His face was lit up like who-wouldn't-have-thought-of that?

"It's brilliant. You'll probably get free pies for life if the idea hits."

"Man. Just let me ship a few to my folks, to my crew, the boys in the band, and their folks ... word will spread. Trust me. There ain't nothin' like this in Nashville."

"I'm sure she'd love to sell you a Big Pie Plate. You can take it home to your momma." McKenna savored each bite of her pie, going at it at a slightly slower pace. "So your people aren't happy you haven't come home?"

Jagger shrugged. "They're fine. It's my mother's job to demand to see me. And I appreciate it. But now when I get home, it's become like a damn meet-and-greet. Everybody's friends and neighbors want to meet me. Snap a selfie."

"Ahhh. The price of back-to-back Musical Group of the Year Awards. But isn't there stuff piling up for you back home? Like mail. Bills. A dog?"

"Dog lives with my folks. And I've got a personal assistant who is the most effective human on the planet. Lola takes care of everything so that I don't have to. Frees my brain up to write songs, which is what it does best."

"So this Lola?"

"Pays my bills, checks my condo, waters any plants, returns any calls, books appointments, and takes care of my social media. Lol is so good I do not have to be present to live my life. So I can be here." His hand gestured to their surroundings. "Spending time being amazed by a pie that isn't really pie."

"It's a pie."

"It doesn't taste like pie. Pie is pie. This is absurdly elevated dessert. Or breakfast. I could totally see eating it for breakfast on a Sunday morning. You know. Your day off from eating right and exercising and whatever, whatever, whatever."

"So, you don't have to go home. Lola keeps you informed."

"Correct."

"But you've got friends, right? In Nashville."

He nodded, finishing up his second piece. "I've got my band. My song-writing buddies. My producer, my recording label friends.

I've got contemporaries in my field that I'm friendly with. Lots of people. They all just happen to be in the same industry. So, after several years of nonstop touring, of putting out albums, of making great music, I need downtime. Alone time. If I go back to Nashville, I won't get that. I'll be tempted to jump right back into the hubbub. 'Cause I love it. I do. But, yeah."

"So you aren't here to write songs."

"Yeah. Sure. Writing songs is what I do. So, yeah, I'm gonna write songs. I'm always writing songs. But I'm here for …" he trailed off.

"For?" McKenna prompted.

"A mental health break?"

"Seriously?"

"You know. Time to think. Time to rest. Time to get off the bus and breathe the air and not be on a schedule and not spend time with the same people. Who I love like brothers, by the way. And they needed to get back to their people and get away from me."

McKenna just stared at him, like she was trying to figure him out.

"What?"

"I don't know." Her tongue licked the tines of her fork absently, jump-starting his sex drive. "I think I'd want to get home."

He shifted closer. "To see your momma?"

"Yeah. Definitely to see her. To see Anna Beth and the Wrights. To see this group here and find out what I'd missed since I'd been gone."

"What about your daddy?"

McKenna shook her head, scooping up another bite. "Don't have one."

"Everybody has one."

"Not me," she insisted. Well, it wasn't that she insisted. It was more like she was stating a fact. While she ate pie.

He chuckled. "McKenna. Explain that, please."

She smiled at him while she sucked on her fork, pulling it from her mouth as she savored the last bite. "I think you're right. This isn't pie. It's better than pie."

"Mmm-hmm." He relieved her of her plate and fork, placing them by his feet with his own. "So spill. What's the deal with your nonexistent father?"

She grinned at him. That killer grin he'd loved looking down at from the stage. "Once my single mother decided she wanted a baby, she went to a sperm bank for the assist. Nine months later—voilà." McKenna held her arms wide.

Voilà is right. After a moment of picturing her naked, Jagger got his head back in the game. "So, wow. I mean, I guess you're actually right. Literally, no father."

"Nope."

"And how's that been?"

"Fine."

"Fine?"

She gave him a short laugh. "Yeah. It's been fine. For me. I mean, it might have been a struggle for my mother. She was born and raised in Henderson. To my knowledge, she's the only woman of her generation progressive enough to make the conscious decision to raise a child on her own. Thirty years ago she was a pioneer. For me, by the time I got to school and figured out that the concept of family included a dad, the rest of the town had already accepted my story. I just thought it was normal. It was more of a shock when the concept of conception was introduced to my adolescent brain. Like if that, then how did I happen? When I asked my mom, she spelled it out for me scientifically. Talked to me about the sperm bank, and I went on my merry way."

"Your merry way?"

"Yeah. Basically. I didn't miss having a dad because I've never had a dad. My grandparents were great, my mom's been a role model for independence, and Anna Beth Wright has been a second mother to me for a long time now. Oh, and Mr. Wright." McKenna cocked her head to the side for a moment, silently considering something before she came back online. "You know, I've never thought much about it before," she said, shaking a finger at Jagger. "But Maxwell Wright has been a wonderful presence in my life. He is no-nonsense with his five sons, but with me, that man could not be sweeter. He reads everything I write and is always happy to see me. So, I guess I'm good."

"You're good."

She nodded her confirmation.

Jagger was intrigued. "So your mom? She ever date?"

"Nope."

"Never?"

"Nope."

"She gay?"

McKenna began to form the word *Nope* through her smile, but then she stopped short and just stared at him, her smile fading. She blinked rapidly. "I don't know." She tilted her head, thinking. "I've never thought about it." Her head slanted in the opposite direction for a long, drawn-out moment. Then she abruptly met his eyes. "She has a best friend. LeeAnn Hollis."

McKenna may have been looking at his eyes, but she was staring right through him, thinking. Her head shifted again, as if she were replaying episodes of her life events in her mind.

"LeeAnn Hollis," she whispered.

"McKenna, I just asked the question. Don't think that I've got a clue about anything."

"No. No." She shook her head. "Jagger. I'm a reporter. How have I not considered the possibility before? They're together *all the time.* If my mother is not working, she is at the Hollises'. I mean, when I say they are best friends, I mean, they are *best friends.* And to be honest, I've often felt sorry for Mr. Hollis. It must drive him crazy that my mother is at their house *all the time.*"

"So this LeeAnn is married."

"For *thirty-five years,*" McKenna enunciated. "My mother just threw them an anniversary party," she screeched. "This is so *weird.*"

"McKenna. You may be jumping to conclusions."

"Then why did you ask me, *is your mother gay?*"

"I don't know." He shrugged and held his hands out in a plea. "No man in the picture, I just thought it made sense."

McKenna shot a finger at him. "It does make sense. I mean, it could make sense." She closed her eyes and groaned. "My mother is the proverbial closed book. She tells me nothing. I barely see her."

She opened her eyes and emphatically gestured toward him with both hands. "But I'm a reporter. I do research on everybody I meet. Yet, I've lived with my mother for thirty years, and this is the first I'm considering it?"

Jagger shrugged. "Sometimes what's right under our nose eludes us the most. Besides, it's probably not true."

She closed her eyes. "But it could be."

"Babe."

She opened one eye. "Why do you keep calling me that? Babe?"

He closed in, taking up both her hands, leaning forward so their lips were aligned but there was still enough distance he could see her icy-blue eyes. And then he whispered his truth. "Because I've yet to earn the right to call you *baby*."

CHAPTER NINE

Stick a fork in her. She was *done*.

Her mother and LeeAnn Hollis? Whatever.

Jagger Yates had just whispered the sexiest, the most romantic, the most heart-infiltrating words she'd ever experienced. She equated those roughly whispered syllables to Piper's pie. They rose up to the next level, were created to tantalize, and delivered a shock to your epicenter, leaving you longing for more.

Oh, sweet baby Jesus. She was never gonna be the same. She fell forward, placing her forehead against their clasped hands.

"And what the hell is happening here?"

McKenna lifted her head to find Vance standing next to the chaise dressed in athletic pants and a pullover, beer in hand, sporting a seriously curious demeanor. He threw something at Jagger. "Put this on, grab that guitar of yours, and show us what you're made of." He pointed his thumb over his shoulder. "Over by the fire pit. More pie, more brew, more"—he looked directly at McKenna—"people."

"Well, if there's more pie," Jagger joked, drawing the Henderson Bulldogs hoodie over his head and smoothing it down his body. He stood and motioned toward the house. "I'll just grab my guitar."

"You do that," Vance suggested, holding his ground as Jagger jogged off. Then his gaze landed on McKenna, both of his hands clasped around a beer hanging in front of his hips. His head tilted in an appraising fashion. "How are things with Xander?"

"Complicated."

"I'll bet." He gave her a smirk. Then he rubbed his stomach and bent forward slightly. "Jagger seems like an all-right guy, but he's no Xander Wright."

"And yet, Jagger's here in Henderson, and Xander hasn't bothered to make an appearance for over three weeks."

Vance stood at attention, clearly appraising her irritation. He began slowly nodding his head. "I hear you. I get where you're at."

She highly doubted that.

"I'll be sure to mention it when I relay to Xander how he's left you to your own devices at a hot tub party with the lead singer of your favorite band. Is he even aware that Jagger Yates is in town?"

McKenna shrugged.

"So you didn't tell him?"

"Vance," she sighed. "How could he not know if he's been in touch with anyone from Henderson? When I called Xander and told him someone had asked me out—"

"Jagger asked you out?" Vance was incredulous.

"Why is that so hard to believe?"

"Because he just landed here. It's ... fast."

"Well, this isn't our first rodeo. Jagger and I've met before."

"Before? Like how?"

"After one of his concerts."

"McKenna Blakely," Vance scolded while waving a finger at her. "Do not tell me you're one of his groupies."

"I'm a total groupie. Just not in the way you mean."

"The way I mean is, you allow yourself to be used as an adrenaline release after he gets off stage."

She blew out a deep breath and rolled her eyes. "Of course that's what you meant. And again, no, not like that."

"Then like what?"

"Like we had a conversation, and he asked for my number. I didn't give it to him. I mean, I gave him a number, it just wasn't mine."

"Whose number did you give him?"

"I don't know. I made it up."

"So what? Is he like, stalking you? Tracked you down to Henderson?"

McKenna began to laugh. "I wish," she said, moving off the chaise and pulling on her cover-up. "You know very well why he's here. And I made a point not to cover the Cavaliers' cut on Cal's record in order to avoid this very scenario. We didn't run in to each other until last Monday at Reds."

"Monday, huh?"

"Yeah. Where he immediately asked me out. I told him I had a boyfriend. He said he didn't care. I called Xander, told him he needed to make up his mind, and here we are, Saturday night and Xander's a no-show. Again."

"Wait." Vance squinted. "Make up his mind? Xander needs to make up his mind about what?"

McKenna looked around, making sure no one could overhear. "Vance, please do not repeat this, but Xander is dating another girl. A girl named Becca who lives in Charlotte."

Vance stood alarmingly still. "That's not the word on the street."

"No, it isn't. His parents are unaware. Everyone is unaware except for me and Jinx."

"Jinx knows about this?"

"Yes. I gave her my secret back when I was the only one who knew she was your long-lost sister. I wanted her to be able to trust me."

"You knew about that?"

"I did my research when she came to town. But we're getting off track. You know as well as anybody how much the Wrights mean to me. I don't want to upset them."

"They're gonna be upset. If they catch wind of Xander and another girl, or you and this rock star, they are gonna be upset."

"Exactly. So now you understand. Complicated."

"Hell." Vance rubbed his jaw. "Well, all right then. I mean, you know I'm gonna have to do what I have to do. Make Xander aware he needs to get home and take care of business. But I'll take a step back tonight. Let you have your fun. Only, ya know. Watch yourself. The guy's probably been with hundreds of women."

"Says the pot."

"If I've heard that once ..." Vance's voice trailed off. "You're gonna need something warmer to put on. I'm sure Piper's got something for ya. Come on."

"Any requests?" Jagger asked as he tuned up his guitar around the newly installed fire pit.

"'Babe in a Bar,'" came the response.

He strummed a few bars and smiled, looking up at McKenna, who was sitting next to him. "You got it."

He was not subtle.

Jagger sang the song to McKenna. The rest of her friends be damned. He knew the clock on wooing McKenna was ticking. That Vance was going to get in his way. Or worse, her boyfriend was going to ride back into town on his high horse and bust up what he was working so hard to lay down. He needed to take advantage of this opportunity; once word hit his opponent's ears that there was a new man in town vying for McKenna's affection, everything could unravel. Fast.

So he was winding it tight. Caught up in the ambience of the night, McKenna's beautiful face in the firelight, the mellow group surrounding them, he was weaving his spell as best he could. Not wanting the night to end. Finding it ridiculously poetic that he was singing this song to the girl who inspired it.

It was as if a collective breath was taken at the end of the song. As the last chord dissolved into the night, there was a moment of silence. And then came the smiles. Then the applause.

For the better part of an hour, he played with the group singing along. Songs he'd written and popular hits he hadn't. Pinks started beatboxing the drums on some app, everyone had a request, and Missy and Pinks sang a duet routine they'd apparently performed during a high school talent show.

The banter was contagious. Quick, hilarious, and good spirited. At times, Jagger felt like he was right in there—a part of it all. At others, he felt like he was on the outside of being an outsider. But every time that feeling surfaced, he'd feel McKenna's touch. A hand grazing over his shoulder. A light fingertip on his thigh. He'd lock eyes with her, wanting her to know he appreciated the gesture.

Wanting her to know he was good. So good. Sitting here with her and her friends, playing into the night.

Jagger concluded his concert with a mini riff, the one he and his band used to wrap things up on stage. The tiny crowd applauded and begged for an encore, but Jagger knew to leave them wanting. He also knew it was late, and he didn't want to overstay his welcome.

Because they'd truly welcomed him, and it was his opportunity to say so.

"Scarlett," he said. "I want to thank you for letting me hang out in Reds these past couple of weeks, giving me a place of solace when I had nowhere else to go. And I want to thank the rest of you for including me in this intimate celebration tonight. I have truly enjoyed myself. And if I can be any help at this Daze of yours next weekend, just tell me where to be and when."

"Really?" Pinks asked. "That'd be great. Maybe you and I could meet up sometime this week and discuss the set."

"Sure. Give me your number, and we'll set something up."

The crowd started to pack it in, gathering towels and leftovers and heading toward the kitchen. After exchanging information with Pinks, Jagger caught up to McKenna as she was rinsing dishes and putting them in the dishwasher. He leaned in close. "You okay giving me a ride?"

"Of course." She looked over her shoulder and offered up her infectious smile.

It was all he could do not to squeeze her hip or in some other physical way let her know he couldn't wait to get her alone.

"Hey there, Rock Star," Vance called. "So you're committed to playing with Pinks and the Outlaw at the Daze, right?"

"Like I said, happy to do it."

Vance barked out his first order. "Missy, we need to publicize this."

"Already on it," she said. "First tweet went out ten minutes ago. The Henderson Happenings will send out complete details Monday morning."

"Jagger, you're doing us a real solid," Vance said. "Team Henderson meets at ten a.m. Monday mornings at Evans & Evans located right in the center of Main Street. I expect to see you there.

Pinks can fill us in on the new music store you'll be opening, along with details about your participation in the Daze. Things like riding in the parade, some sort of autograph signing, and selfies to raise money for Henderson Helping Henderson." He clapped his hands together. "This is going to be great."

Jagger had no words. Literally. His mouth was moving, but nothing came out. He turned his disbelief to McKenna, who just cracked up when she saw his face. "It's all right," she told him. "Vance railroads everybody. If it's not him, it's the mayor. You are free to do what you want. Vance is just offering up his preferences. The choices are all yours."

He gazed into her glacier-blue eyes. *Really? Because if that's the case, then I choose you.* He almost said it. Almost voiced those words out loud. And he probably should have, because before he knew it, he was being railroaded again.

"You've rented the old Tolley place, right? Out on Lakeview Road?" Vance asked as he placed a hand on Jagger's shoulder and started walking him away from McKenna.

"That's correct."

"Perfect. Brooks goes right by there on his way home. He can drop you."

"Vance," Piper scolded.

"What?" Vance feigned innocence, pushing Jagger toward the head of the kitchen and out toward the foyer. "It'll save McKenna the trouble. And you don't mind, do you, Brooks? Giving the guy who is going to light up the Daze and its attendance a ride home, right?"

"Be my pleasure," the mayor commented, latching his own mammoth paw onto Jagger's shoulder, the two men propelling him down the stairs toward the front door.

Before he could wrap his head around what was happening, Jagger and his guitar had been railroaded right out the front door and hustled into the backseat of a big, black, well-appointed truck. McKenna was nowhere in sight.

As the doors were slammed and the engine roared to life, Jagger let out a hissing breath and slid himself over to the center of the backseat. He reached forward, grabbing a tight hold on Brooks's shoulder before forcefully patting it a few times. He let his words drip with sarcasm. "Appreciate this man. Real-ly appreciate the ride home."

McKenna stood on the front stoop of the Evans mansion wondering what the hell just happened. She eyeballed Vance before bursting out with hysterical laughter. Which was a whole lot better than going at him with, say, a kitchen knife. "What the hell?"

"It was for your own good," Vance assured her.

"Vance," Piper warned.

"Seriously. We were *all* caught up in his rock-star dazzle. Hell, if I had to drive him home, *I* would have slept with him. I did you a favor, and you know it." Vance turned and stomped back inside.

"How do you figure?" McKenna followed after him.

Vance whirled. "Because you would have regretted it in the morning." He looked to his wife. "Tell her!"

Piper gave McKenna a look that clearly indicated she did not think sleeping with Jagger Yates was going to leave McKenna with any regrets.

Vance sighed loud and long. "Baby doll, that is not helpful."

"He's Jagger Yates," Piper exclaimed.

"Exactly. And she's practically engaged to Xander."

"McKenna is a grown woman who does not have a ring on her finger."

"Yet," Vance yelled.

"Well, until there is one, I suggest you butt out."

"I'll butt out once Xander is made aware some fancy guitar slinger is gunning for his girl."

Piper turned toward McKenna, quieting her voice. "Vance is *very* protective by nature. Sometimes overly so. He likes Jagger. He likes you. But he played baseball with Xander, so that's where his loyalty lies."

Vance harrumphed.

McKenna took a breath and let her gaze graze over Vance's dark features. "Loyalty is a good thing," she conceded. "I know Xander will appreciate it."

"Hey. I heard you earlier. The man doesn't do right by you, I'm hopping the fence and landing on your side. I'm just … trying to slow, you know"—he pointed toward the driveway—"that train down. Give Xander a chance."

McKenna nodded. She understood about giving someone a chance. "It's been over three months," she told Vance, leaving it at that.

Vance nodded. "Time enough. Let's see what happens next weekend at the Daze."

CHAPTER TEN

McKenna ignored the text that pinged while she drove home. It wasn't like Xander would be the one texting her at one thirty on a Saturday night. That thought had her mind drifting to images of what Xander was probably doing at the moment, sleeping in some random bed with the faceless Becca. She grimaced.

Then she sighed, because the text most likely came from Jagger, considering the fact that their enchanted evening had come to an abrupt and disorienting conclusion.

Vance may not have been completely wrong to do what he did. And maybe McKenna would thank him in the morning when the fire Jagger had lit underneath her skin had a chance to cool and higher reasoning prevailed. She was in love with Xander after all, even if her hopes on that front were dwindling.

Still, she talked to herself—out loud—while she drove, convincing herself she needed to avoid checking her texts until tomorrow. Because if it was from Jagger and said anything close to *Can I see you?* or *Stop by on your way home*, after what went down tonight, she didn't trust herself.

Didn't mean she couldn't relive all the night's magic moments with a smile on her face while she fell asleep though.

Which she did.

In great detail.

Sunday mornings had a rhythm. A routine. By eight thirty, she was dressed in comfortable jeans and a pretty top and was out the door. By nine, she was brewing coffee and tying on her apron at the Wrights', helping Xavier and Laidey prepare the family brunch.

Xavier was great in the kitchen, having learned to cook during the dozen years he lived in Phoenix. Most of his specialties had a southwestern flare. Several months ago, he'd moved home to help take care of his mother when they all believed Anna Beth was dying. He'd moved back into his old room and taken charge of the kitchen and everything else, as was his way. Xavier was bossy as hell and proud of it. More often than not, he and McKenna (who could be just like him) butted heads. The one thing the two of them had in common was their love for his mother, Laidey (McKenna's BFF and Xavier's fiancée,) and Xander (Xavier's twin brother.) All of whom possessed gentler personalities able to sway in the gale-force winds that often accompanied McKenna and Xavier.

Like now.

"That's too much bacon in one pan," Xavier bulldozed, looking over her shoulder.

"It's fine. I'm going to scoot the middle slices out to the edges halfway through, and everything will cook evenly."

"Did you bring the coffee cake Ma requested?"

"Yes. Of course. Did you not see me put it on the table?"

"I'm busy making Ma's favorite egg soufflé, and I don't have eyes in the back of my head. So no, I didn't see you put it on the table. Why are you so cranky?"

"I'm not cranky," she yelled. When she turned to yell at him some more, she noticed the youngest Wright brother and Jinx enter the kitchen. "Oh, hey. Morning y'all. Sorry about that. It's just"— she pointed the tongs toward Xavier—"you know, *him.*"

"Yes, we know," Jaxon agreed, dragging his bedhead over to the coffee maker. "Thanks for putting up with *him.* Nobody makes coffee like you do."

"See. You couldn't do it without me." She gave Xavier a cheeky grin.

"It's not like you ever give me the opportunity to find out. You're here all the damn time."

"And that's just how we like it," Mr. Wright asserted as he entered the kitchen wearing casual slacks with a button-down shirt, the Sunday paper tucked under his arm. "McKenna darling, have you an article in today's paper?" He took his seat at the round table across the room.

"I do," McKenna said with a smile. "Under the Style section."

"I thought you didn't like to do puff pieces," Xavier goaded.

"I like having a job. I do what the higher-ups ask of me."

Xavier turned back to his soufflé. "Seems like you should be interviewing with the paper in Charlotte," he said a bit quieter, just enough so McKenna could hear. "My no-good twin doesn't seem to be in any hurry to move back to Henderson."

McKenna shrugged, using tongs to shift the bacon around the pan.

Xavier sidled up to her, lowering his voice even further. "Seriously. I've got things handled here. Ma's still frail, but she's thriving. All her test indicators are good. If Xander is dragging his feet about moving home, there's no reason the two of you can't make a start in Charlotte."

"Your parents would hate that. They want all five of their boys to come home."

"Yes, but *I'm* home now. Jaxon is based out of the damn house for the time being, and Laidey and I are practically moving next door once we're married. You've watched out for my folks for a long time now, and truthfully, as long as you and Xander are together, they'll be happy. And I trust you'll do what needs to be done, which is get him to come visit more often."

The way he said it, McKenna could tell he was as frustrated with his twin as she was.

"He hasn't asked me," McKenna whispered as she followed Xavier back to his soufflé.

"He hasn't asked you what?"

"To come to Charlotte. To put in an application with the paper."

Xavier turned and looked McKenna up and down, his brow furrowed in confusion. "Well then, what's his plan?"

"I don't know." She shrugged. "I do not know."

"And why wasn't he at Reds last night?" Xavier's booming voice grew louder with his frustration. "Why isn't he here?"

"Why isn't who here?" a happy yet gruff voice called.

McKenna's head snapped toward the kitchen's entrance before she let out a squeal of delight. She covered the distance in a flash, throwing her arms around Xander.

Xander, who gave her his adorable grin, kissed her lips, and then asked everyone to give them a second while he picked her up around the middle and backed out of the kitchen with her arms wrapped tightly around his neck.

Mr. Wright chuckled, his attention going back to the paper.

"I can't believe you're here," she told him as he walked backward, carrying her down the hall toward the library. Once he maneuvered the two of them through the French doors and managed to close the things without letting her go, he dipped his mouth to hers and kissed her with a full-on groan. She groaned back, reveling in the feel of his broad chest pressed against her breasts, his strong arms holding her more securely than he ever had. Like he wasn't planning to let her go. He kissed her and kissed her and kissed her, backing her up toward the fireplace. When the backs of her legs hit the leather sofa, she stumbled and fell into it. Xander followed her down, twisting to sit while swinging her body up, around, onto his lap. McKenna eagerly situated herself, her legs straddling him, her fingers going into his hair, her lips drawn to his like a magnet. "You're here," she said in between fervent kisses.

"I've missed you," he said, eventually taking a breath and leaning back to stare into her eyes. He pushed her hair back from her face. "I've truly missed you. I'm sorry I couldn't get back last night. I'm sorry it's been so long since I've been home. I think about you all the time. I do. It's just not easy to leave work and, and my life and make the drive—"

"I know. I know," she said, so happy to have him there. To be touching him. Locking eyes with him. "But you're here now. Your mother will be overjoyed. She misses you, you know. They all do. *We* all do." She let out another little squeal. "This is the best surprise ever."

"Mmm," he said, capturing her mouth with his again and twisting their bodies around to lay her flat against the seat cushions. He crawled between her legs and leveraged his weight over her torso and onto his forearms. "Damn, you feel good," he said as he settled in, stroking her hair back from her eyes.

"You too," she cooed, letting her gaze travel over his beautiful features. His blue-gray eyes, his masculine nose, his cheekbones and jaw. He was big and brawny in the shoulders, but slim in the waist and hips. He had been everything a girl could have wanted back in high school and managed to overshoot the mark as a grown man. She was so lucky not to have lost him completely during the years he'd lived away. Though her relationship with his mother and father and younger brothers had continued, she'd made herself scarce whenever Xander had come home. There was just too much want. Too much longing.

If she'd only known he'd felt the same way. That she was the reason he didn't consider finding work in Henderson. That she was the reason he'd established himself in Charlotte. Because the guilt they shared stood between them.

So foolish, the two of them.

Such wasted time.

But here he was. Just when she thought all was lost, he'd come home. "You came home," she sighed.

"I did," he whispered over her lips.

"To see me?"

"Who else?"

"Your parents, your twin ..."

He brought a hand to her cheek, bringing her focus back to him. "I came home to see you, McKenna. You're my priority. And I've been an ass. And I'm sorry about that. I came home to apologize."

McKenna waited with bated breath, eager for him to say more.

He stroked her hair. "You've been so patient with me, and I can't tell you how much I've appreciated the time and space I've had to work things out. It hasn't been easy on you, and it certainly hasn't been fair." He wet his lips. "I should have been all-in back in June when fate brought us together. I should have confronted my brother. I should have deleted Becca from my contacts. I should have made it clear from the beginning that you have *always* been the one for me."

McKenna wasn't the crying type, but the joy she was feeling welled up from such a deep source, it spilled out onto her cheeks.

"Hey," he said, wiping her tears away. "What's this?"

"I'm just so happy." She pulled a hand out to wipe at her eyes. "Over the last three weeks, I'd convinced myself that you"—she sniffled—"that you"—she breathed—"well, you know, didn't want *me.*"

"I've *always* wanted you," he confessed while leaning down to kiss her slowly. Tenderly. With reverence. But when he finally allowed his body to sink into hers as their tongues touched, things grew hotter. It had been weeks since they'd been together, and their chemistry combusted swiftly.

McKenna was so swept up in the rapture of their physical connection that her brain didn't compute the words being bellowed down the hallway as a warning or alert. So when Xander abruptly derailed the passion building between them, she was left disoriented and aching for more of him. More of this.

Had he really ended things with Becca after all this time? Had he finally chosen her? It felt unreal. And completely unexpected.

"Sorry to interrupt," came the sweet voice of Anna Beth Wright. Her smile didn't waver as Xander dismounted from his prone position on top of McKenna. The Wrights had become, if not immune, then amused by the mix of Laidey, McKenna, and Jinx strolling down the stairs of their home on any given morning. Especially weekend mornings. "Just had to give my favorite son a hug," she said, reaching out to embrace Xander who threw a smug look over his shoulder at McKenna.

"Told ya I'm her favorite."

"Xavier begs to differ," McKenna said, working at the buttons that had sprung loose on her blouse.

"They're *all* my favorites," Anna Beth said, hugging Xander and winking at McKenna. "But this one has made today special, so at the moment, he's my *favorite* favorite."

"Ma," Xavier called from the doorway. "Don't go spouting untruths like that. You know they'll go straight to Xander's head, and he'll think he's too good to do the dishes. Which there are going to be plenty of." He jeered at his brother. "'Bout damn time you made a showing, bro."

"Aww. You missed me," Xander said, letting his mother go as he headed toward Xavier with outstretched arms. When Xavier started to back away, Xander dove for him, wrapping his arms around his twin and slamming him out the door and into the narrow hallway. By the time McKenna and Anna Beth got to the door, the two very large, fully grown men were wrestling on the floor, banging into one wall and then the next. There were muffled groans, a few choice words, and a lot of laughter as they not only tried to one-up the other in physical prowess but also in verbal cheap shots.

Jaxon appeared at the head of the hallway outside the kitchen, chewing on a piece of bacon, delighted to watch his oldest brothers going at it. Especially when his father stepped out behind him and started rubbing his brows. "For God's sake, stop this tomfoolery so we can eat. Your mother's going to perish before the food gets on the table."

"Nope. We've got this," Laidey said as she and Jinx carried platters from the kitchen and headed to the dining room. "They can carry on as long as they want. The rest of us can eat."

Xavier and Xander stopped the wrestling match, both of them panting hard as they untangled themselves and limped to their feet. "Tweets," Xavier shouted after his fiancée. "You missed my full nelson reversal on Xander here."

"Not even close," Xander contested as he forced himself upright. His mother patted his back as she passed him and then took up Xavier's arm to be escorted to the table.

McKenna locked eyes with Xander as he turned to look for her, sweat beading on his forehead. "Damn, you're pretty," he panted, pushing her back into the library, around the door frame, and up against the wall. "I'd wrestle Xavier and ten others like him just to have access to your mouth."

The kiss he laid on her was unrestrained. Demanding. So very hot that when he rolled off her to lean his body against the wall beside her, they were both panting. "Jesus," he breathed. "Thanks for not dumping me." He turned his head to look in her direction, desperate. "Seriously. I don't want to lose you. I'd be a fool to lose you."

McKenna blinked over his words, over the passionate kiss, her mind winding up and starting to spin like a top. Xander had always been passionate. Their chemistry always strong. But he hadn't kissed her like that since last summer when they'd found each other unexpectedly in a bar in Charlotte. "You okay?" she asked. "You're home. You're here. You're not going to lose me."

He slid a strong hand down his face. McKenna noticed the veins that stood out, his long, tapered fingers. "I'm not home, McKenna. Not really. I know I want you. I just don't know how the rest of this is going to play out."

She shrugged, giving him a bright smile. "We'll make a plan. Xavier suggested I apply for positions as a journalist in Charlotte. I'm not real interested in leaving my mom or your parents, but if you need time to extricate yourself out of Charlotte, we can figure something out."

He nodded quickly, over and over. "Okay. All right. Maybe." He stopped and looked at her. "Let's hold off any plan-making until Thanksgiving. Give me a few weeks to talk to my boss, feel him out, review my apartment lease, do some groundwork. Then, over Thanksgiving weekend, we do what you suggest. We make a plan. Get this show on the road."

"Seriously?" McKenna felt unabridged joy. "Is this ... happening?"

"Hell, you've waited for me long enough. But Kens, I need you to hang on a little longer"—he held his thumb and index finger up inches apart—"just a couple more weeks before we make it all official."

Official? Like how official? Her facial expression probably screamed shock, which made Xander smile before he leaned back in to kiss her.

"We better go if we want hot food," he whispered. "Lord knows somebody is bound to come looking for us. Don't want to put you in another compromising position." Xander took her hand, grinned into her eyes, and then led her from the room.

McKenna was dumfounded. She dragged behind him, her legs suddenly sporting the muscle tone of licorice while the blood pumping through her heart became thicker and thicker. She hadn't expected Xander to come home, much less be ready to make things *official*. A part of her was writhing with elation, and another part of her was simply stunned. She took a deep breath and decided to just go with it as Xander, very gentleman-like, pulled out her chair and seated her at the table. Then he took his place beside her and snapped his napkin into his lap.

"Oh, thank heaven," he exclaimed when he saw the hot mug of coffee waiting for him. "Thank you to whoever knew just what I needed. Been up since way before dawn."

"Why didn't you make it in for Reds' Grand Opening last night?" his father asked, the edge in his voice signifying his displeasure.

"Previous engagement." Xander shoveled egg soufflé onto his plate and then jammed a forkful into his mouth.

"What sort of previous engagement?"

McKenna was curious too. Xander had not mentioned any previous engagement to her. He'd just said he'd do his best to make it back for the weekend, leaving things vague like he tended to do. Unfortunately, when you're part of a dating trio, you put up with things like that. But thankfully—thankfully, thankfully, thankfully— no more. Xander had made up his mind, and boy, did that feel good.

"I had to attend a wedding. Work related."

"A wedding," Xavier barked. "When did you stop doing everything you can to get out of going to a wedding?"

Xander shook his head. "Speaking of ... Laidey, how are plans coming along for your Dallas nuptials?"

Laidey dotted her lips with her napkin, reaching for her orange juice. "They'd be going a little smoother if your twin would stop moaning and groaning about every little thing."

"What?" Xavier huffed. "What am I moaning and groaning about?"

"Ah, for one, that it's happening in Dallas."

"Yeah, that doesn't work for me," Xavier said.

"Two, you're refusing to even look at the options for tuxedoes."

"A tuxedo is a tuxedo. Choose one for me and move along."

"Three, you haven't asked any of your brothers to serve as groomsmen."

"Ask? Why would I have to ask? They damn well better know they're wearing penguin suits and escorting old biddies to their seats. I'm not going through this nonsense without dragging them along with me."

"Well, are there other friends you'd like to include?" Laidey asked.

"I've got four damn brothers. How many groomsmen do I need?"

Laidey, exasperated, caught Xander's eye from across the table. "That's how the plans are coming."

"Tweets," Xavier said, dumping his fork and knife and leaning over to pull his petite fiancée right onto his lap at the dining room table. He quieted his voice, looked into her eyes, and spoke as if there were no one else in the room. "Baby, you know I love you to distraction. So anything you want, it's yours. Your wedding, your way. I just have to throw a little badass in so you remember who you're marrying." Then he kissed her.

McKenna, Jinx, and even Anna Beth sighed.

"Well, now you've done it," Jaxon said. "You have set the bar too high. Neither Xander nor myself will be able to look like any sort of hero when our turn arrives."

"Part of my plan to stay on top," Xavier said, returning Laidey to her seat.

McKenna and Laidey shared a smile. It was going to be so much fun to be sisters-in-law with her best friend. If that's where Xander was going with this *make-it-official* thing.

Was that where he was going? She turned her head to spy on his profile. He immediately met her gaze and gave her a happy grin. Touched her thigh under the table a moment before asking Jaxon to pass the coffee cake.

"So Xander, how long are you able to stay?" his father asked.

"Gotta work, Pop. Tomorrow is Monday. Gotta be in early."

"And then you'll be back for the Harvest Days celebration next Saturday." Mr. Wright put it out there as a statement. "Best to drive up after work Friday night. Spend the whole weekend this time."

"That's the plan."

"That good with you, McKenna?" Mr. Wright asked.

McKenna rubbed a hand over Xander's thigh. "It sounds perfect to me." The two of them shared a smile.

Xavier sighed audibly. "Now everything is right with the world, right, Dad?"

"Can't think of a thing I'd change. Can you, Anna Beth?"

"I'm as happy as a woman with five sons can be. I've finally got girls sitting around the breakfast table. Girls I love dearly. We are just blessed. Aren't we, Maxwell? Just blessed."

"We are indeed."

"Oh, Xander," his mother stressed. "Did McKenna tell you who we met at Reds yesterday?"

"No," he responded, appearing much more interested in his food than in what his mother was planning to tell him. "How is the new wine shop, by the way?" He pointedly looked across the table at Xavier.

"It's a beaut," Xavier supplied. "Looks like something you'd find in Napa Valley. Not a bit of Henderson to be found inside the place."

"Oh, stop. That's not true," Laidey protested.

"What? The shop is too over-the-top to be *charming* like you insist for Henderson. It's fancier than anything we've got or anything we've ever had."

"That's not a bad thing," his mother interjected.

"No. But it sure ain't Henderson."

"Again. Not a bad thing," Xander stated.

Everyone at the table stopped eating and turned their heads to stare at him.

"What?"

"What do you have against Henderson?" Xavier asked in a passionate, pissed-off tone. "Laidey and I, and countless others are killing ourselves to pull off something big here. For *your* hometown."

"I didn't mean anything by it," Xander argued, the only one at the table continuing to eat.

"Maybe if you'd bother to show up when you say you're going to. Take the damn time to look around and really see what's happening here instead of rushing in, giving McKenna a quick thrill, and then leaving for Lord only knows how long. What the hell is keeping you in Charlotte, bro? We've got big things happening here, and you're completely missing them."

Xander shook his head, wiping his mouth with his napkin. He held up his hands in surrender. "You're right. I didn't make it to Reds last night, and I'm sorry about that. Really sorry," he added under his breath. "I'm going to do better. I'm going to get involved. I'm just … a bit over scheduled right now. But I'm committed to shaking things loose. Then I'll be around more. Be able to have at least one foot in Henderson."

"Well, we'd all appreciate that," his father said. "Right, McKenna?"

She nodded but, feeling empathy for Xander, was unwilling to pile on. The guy was a raging success in his field. But because his field was located three hours away in Charlotte, lately his family wasn't giving him much credit.

"You know," she started, "I totally get how hard this is for Xander. I appreciate y'all applying pressure to get him home more, but before we started dating this summer, Xander had a life in Charlotte. And y'all were just fine with that. So, as much as I want to encourage him to drive in for the weekends, because I definitely enjoy my social life more when he's around, I don't want to make things harder for him. Especially when he does manage to find his way home. I just wanna be happy he's here."

"Boom," Xander barked his exhilarated response. "Take that. That's my girl giving y'all a one-two punch on my behalf. Appreciate it Be—Babe." He leaned over and kissed her cheek.

Be—Babe? Xander had never called her *babe* before.

Kens.

Kenna.

Micks, even.

Never babe, or baby, or sweetheart, or darling.

Obviously, he was used to spending time with Be-cca, and he had just shown his cards.

The devil in her mind picked up his gaming controller and was pressing all kinds of buttons to upload her fight or flight response. Adrenaline was surging, her heart rate right along with it. She was even starting to sweat. She definitely wasn't hungry anymore.

A few deep breaths, she told herself. Breathe in, breathe out. Breathe in, breathe out. It's not like you didn't know he was seeing another girl.

Breathe in, breathe out.

A girl named *Becca.*

Breathe in, breathe out.

Whom he probably went to a wedding with last night.

Breathe in, breathe out.

He was ending it, McKenna assured herself as she carefully monitored her breath. He'd chosen her. Come Thanksgiving, they were making it official, whatever that meant.

She glanced around the table at the faces she loved. Anna Beth, Mr. Wright. Even Xavier, the ultimate pain in her ass. Jaxon had always felt like a little brother to her, and she adored his Jinx. And Laidey had been such a welcome addition to her life. And now it was all going to be so perfectly wrapped up. They'd all be enjoying brunches like this together for years to come, good Lord willing. Yes. Yes. Because Anna Beth's health was being restored, she assured herself. Jaxon and Xavier were committed to Henderson. If worse came to worst, and she and Xander ended up living in Charlotte, well, she'd find a way to be okay with that. After all, look what blessings she'd have waiting to come home to.

Lost in her thoughts, McKenna's mind drifted from the conversation. But boy, did her radar ping when it picked up on the name Jagger as it slipped from Anna Beth's lips.

"You know, McKenna's favorite singer," she explained to Xander.

"You have a favorite singer?" Xander questioned, giving her a short, inquisitive look.

Was he serious?

He turned back to his mother. "I wasn't aware."

Anna Beth collapsed back in her seat, and from across the table Xavier shouted a hoot. "Then you've been away longer than anybody realized, because we *all* know McKenna's ground zero when it comes to Cavalier fans. She makes us play their albums whenever she's in the kitchen."

"She's definitely made me a fan," Jinx supplied. "And the lead singer is *hot.* Exactly how does Scarlett Langford get every man to do her bidding? I really want to know. I mean, *Jagger Yates,* signing autographs at her Grand Opening. It was arguably the best part."

"Jinx, you can stop drooling now," Jaxon suggested before addressing the rest of the table. "I had to drag her away. She couldn't stop staring at him."

"Well, there's just something about him," she defended.

"Something sexy," Laidey stated.

Once again, everyone stopped eating and turned to stare at quiet, little Laidey. "Say what?" Xavier questioned.

Laidey shrugged, giving him a sheepish grin. "He's got charisma. The kind I'm drawn to," she said as she beamed into her fiancé's face.

"Oh. You mean, like me."

She nodded, and Xavier stood down. Went back to eating. "Maybe I need to form a band."

Titters of laughter and a bunch of ribbing about him fighting his way into black leather pants set everyone at ease. And then Xavier broke into song, which wasn't all that unusual in the Wright household, although Laidey and Jinx had never played witness to it before. Xavier, like his fiancée, was a pianist, and he could carry a tune along with the rest of his brothers. In their youth, the Wright brothers had performed in school talent shows and such, but after they reached a certain age, their enthusiasm for being show ponies waned. Still, they liked to break it out at home once in a while. Especially to show off for their mother.

This spontaneous show of Wright brother talent was usually something McKenna lived for. But she was seriously uncomfortable at the moment. Xander absolutely knew she had a favorite singer, and he absolutely knew it was Jagger Yates. Which was why, when he wanted to know *who* had asked her out, she didn't tell him.

But she was becoming fairly certain somebody else had. Which would explain why he'd unexpectedly shown up this morning, promising her the moon.

"Excuse me," she whispered, rising from the table in search of solace from the chaos inside her mind. She heard another chair scrape against the hardwood floor as she wandered toward the kitchen and then decided to take a detour out into the backyard. She huddled at the end of the patio, folding her arms around herself against the early

November temperatures. Xander came to stand beside her, tucking his hands into the pockets of his jeans. They stood in silence, both of them gazing out at the colorful fall foliage.

Eventually, McKenna cleared her throat and spoke. "Who called you?"

Xander rocked forward, then back. "Vance."

McKenna nodded.

Xander turned his body to address her. "Seriously? Jagger *Yates?* *He's* the guy who asked you out?"

"Yep."

"How the hell did that happen?"

She snapped her head in his direction. "Excuse me?"

"McKenna, stop." He held up his hand. "I get why he asked you out. You're a beautiful, beautiful woman. There's not a guy who passes you on the street who doesn't want to ask you out. That's not what I mean."

"Then what do you mean?"

"Are you the president of his fan club or something?"

"His fan club?"

"Yeah. I mean, how did you two even meet?"

"Oh. I met him after one of his concerts. He asked for my number, I gave him a fake one, and then he recognized me when I ran in to him at Reds."

"Wait. What? When did this happen?"

"Last Monday."

"You went to a concert last Monday?"

"No. I ran in to him at Reds last Monday. The concert was six months ago."

Xander scratched his head. "And why was he at Reds?"

"He likes wine, I guess. And he knows Scarlett from the whole Cal Johnson sing-along thing."

"The Cal Johnson sing—? Oh. Right. The album for Henderson."

"Right. The Cavaliers were here to sing with Cal, and then Jagger just … stayed."

"He just stayed."

"Yep."

"Because he ran in to you."

"No. He decided to stay in town and write songs before he ran in to me. That was just a happy accident." She grinned.

Seeing her face, Xander gave up a brief laugh. "Geez, McKenna, how am I supposed to compete with Jagger Yates? He's like your freaking hall pass."

"I didn't ask you to compete with him. I asked you to make up your mind."

"And so I have."

"Because Vance called you."

"Funny how picturing you holding hands with Jagger Yates in a hot tub put *everything* in perspective."

McKenna's cheeks heated.

"For fuck's sake." He gestured to the house. "Even quiet, reserved *Laidey* thinks he's sexy."

McKenna shrugged. Jagger Yates *was* damn sexy. But she threw Xander a bone. "You're sexy." Which was not a lie.

"But I don't have his"—he flashed his hands around—"*charism*a, and I don't write love songs, or sing in a well-known band."

"No. You don't. But you're Xander Wright. Brilliant investment banker whose career is on the rise. And more importantly, you're the boy I've been crazy about for the last fourteen years."

He pulled her to him, engulfing her in his arms, rocking the two of them gently back and forth. After a moment, he kissed the top of her head. "I'm sorry for putting you through the Becca thing."

"You called me by her name," she grumbled into his chest.

He sucked in a breath but didn't deny it.

"Everything okay out here?" Xavier asked, poking his head out the screen door.

Xander swung their little huddle around to face his twin. "Yeah. We just need a minute."

Xavier's eyes wandered from Xander's face to McKenna's, his eyes searching her for the truth.

"We're good," she agreed.

"All right. Y'all go take a walk or something. Jaxon and the Prom Queen have volunteered to do the dishes so you don't have to."

"I appreciate that," Xander said, letting go of McKenna to look at his watch. "But the fact is, I've got to get back to Charlotte."

"You just got here," Xavier protested.

"I know. And trust me, it's going to be very difficult to get back in the car right now. But I've got a thing tonight and—"

"A thing?" Xavier pressed. "What's a thing?"

"An event. A social thing. Look, man, my calendar is booked in Charlotte. And that's what I came home to explain to McKenna and *Dad,* since he's all up in my ass about it. I have decided to make a conscious effort to extract myself from various obligations in Charlotte so that I'm more able to spend time with y'all in Henderson."

"About damn time." Xavier pulled his head back inside, slamming the door abruptly.

McKenna had lost track of how often Xander had sent her mind reeling this morning, but whatever the total, he'd just added another to it. He had a *thing* tonight? A *social* thing? With *Becca?* She pulled out of his arms, taking a couple steps back. "So, to be clear ..."

"I haven't broken up with Becca yet. That's why I need you to give me until Thanksgiving to get my affairs in order."

"Your affairs?" she choked.

"Just a figure of speech. I wasn't going to break up with her at six o'clock in the morning after reading Vance's text. I figured I'd come settle things with you, and since I'm seeing Becca tonight, I'd break the news to her then."

"So you're ending things with Becca tonight."

"Unless you're planning to run off with Jagger Yates, yes."

"Is that why you drove all this way? To find out if I was running off with Jagger?"

"Maybe."

Well, that certainly explained the overzealous greeting. The desperation in his kiss.

"So, if Vance hadn't called you, or what, texted you, you'd still be on the fence?"

"Like I said, picturing you with Yates in a hot tub put everything in perspective. I don't want to lose you. Not to him. Not to anybody."

She nodded her head, understanding it, but not really liking it. She wondered how long she'd have continued to put up with Xander's double dating if Jagger hadn't arrived, presenting her with a very tempting alternative. "He's a nice guy. I'll introduce you to him at the Daze."

"Sure. Sure. Maybe he'll offer to sing at our wedding."

What? Holy shit, did he just say our wedding? She bubbled with laughter before flinging herself into his arms. For it was the first time Xander had ever talked like that. It was the first time he'd ever mentioned marriage. And it was the very first time she'd ever felt sure about their future.

Oh, it was such a grand relief.

With so many monkeys falling off her back, it was either laugh hysterically or sob into the release. Her One That Got Away was *finally* coming home.

CHAPTER ELEVEN

McKenna, as blissed out as a serious journalist with a Type A personality can get, kissed her beloved goodbye and then spent the rest of the afternoon at the Wright's helping Anna Beth plan Laidey and Xavier's rehearsal dinner. She also gave ear to Jinx, listening to how crazy for Jaxon she was and how much she hated when his business took him out of town for days at a time.

Yeah, tell me about it.

By the time McKenna headed home to catch up with her mother (whose Sunday routine involved brunch with the Hollises—she seriously needed to do some investigating there,) the adrenaline rush created by Xander's surprise visit had finally burned itself out. She was contentedly exhausted.

Strike that.

She was *gleefully* exhausted. For it had been a long, stressful several months waiting for Xander to come around and dedicate himself to her and her alone. Though, there was a tiny place deep in her heart where she felt sorry for Becca's loss. Because Xander was everything a woman could want in a mate. He was handsome, strong, sharp, inventive, had a healthy libido, a commendable work ethic, and then of course, there was his family.

McKenna simply adored the Wrights. Every blessed one of them. And her euphoric optimism resurged as she imagined that perhaps … perhaps at some point during Thanksgiving weekend, she would wind up with a ring on her finger.

Xander's parents will be so pleased, she thought. Heck, the entire town will be pleased. And Laidey and Jinx will be bridesmaids. And how much fun was that? Having best friends who were marrying/dating your groom's brothers made the whole experience even more perfect.

They'd be married in the Wright's church, since she and her mother didn't have any specific affiliation. If she and her mother couldn't afford a reception at the club, the Wright's backyard would make a beautiful setting for a June wedding. Of course, Xander may have his own ideas. Frankly, McKenna couldn't wait to hear them. Maybe he'd want a destination wedding which would suit her fine. She'd never been one to spend time imagining her own wedding.

Until now.

She'd all but given up hope of ever finding love in this town. But through divine intervention, she and her One That Got Away had stumbled into the same bar in Charlotte back in June and *Bam!* Look how her outlook had changed.

As she pulled in to the one-car driveway, she caught sight of a sharp-looking motorcycle parked by the curb next door. For some reason, it made her think of Jagger and the text she never read last night. She pulled out her phone as she walked to the front door, reading the four short words he'd sent at one twenty eight a.m.

Break up with him.

What?

McKenna stopped walking. She stopped breathing. She even stopped thinking. Everything in her awareness ground to a halt as her focus narrowed on those words.

And when things started back up, they did it with a high-speed vengeance. Her walking, her breathing, her thinking.

Break up with Xander? Is he nuts?

Why would I break up with Xander? Xander is like my dream come true while Jagger is just ... just ...

Here.

She'd opened the door to find Jagger on a short ladder in the center of the living room attaching the light fixture her mother had purchased at a deep discount two Christmases ago.

"Hey there," he said, screwdriver in hand, casting his megawatt stage-presence grin in her direction.

"Hi," she said softly, letting the situation establish itself in her brain. "What … what are you doing?"

"Your mom asked if I had any electrical expertise. I don't. But I can google the shit out of anything, so here I am, attaching a new chandelier to your mother's ceiling. Or, your ceiling," he adjusted. He looked up at his handiwork. "Do you like it?"

It was an enormous improvement, as anything would be when you took down the 1970s light fixture and gave the room a 2020s upgrade. She loved it. She wondered why they'd waited so long to find someone to install it. Wondered why she hadn't thought to google it, YouTube it, or hey, hire an electrician herself.

Of course, now the sconces over the fireplace looked dated, and the room screamed for a fresh coat of paint. After all, didn't everything look a little dull and boring compared to the shiny, new thing gleaming so brightly in the center of her universe?

Center of the room, she corrected.

The center of the room.

"I do like it," she said, adrenaline starting to surge once again. "And I appreciate you googling it and getting the job done. I had forgotten it was even there. Sitting in a box in the corner."

"You're home," her mother acknowledged as she came into the room and handed Jagger a glass of wine. "What do you think?"

"I think we should have gotten around to installing it sooner. What a difference."

"I think so too. Of course, now the sconces and all the dang lampshades look woeful."

"And the walls are crying out for a fresh coat of paint. Maybe an updated color."

"This is why we shouldn't start." Her mother sighed. "Update one thing and everything else becomes incredibly mundane."

Hmm. So true, McKenna thought. "So, I see you've met Jagger," she said, recovering from her thoughts and shedding her sweater.

"He'd planned to sit on the front stoop and wait for you, but since we don't have able-bodied men dropping by all that often, I figured I'd put him to work."

McKenna gave Jagger a soft smile. "Thank you."

"No problem. I wasn't doing anything else but looking at my phone every three minutes." His eyes shot her a pointed look. "I needed the distraction."

"I'm repaying Jagger with dinner. Lasagna and salad. Bread too. I splurged at the farmers' market. Jagger you've never tasted anything like Miss Emily's bread. Perfect for an Italian dinner. I hope you're hungry."

"Famished," he said, looking directly at McKenna and salivating like he was the Big Bad Wolf. Without taking his gaze off her, he said, "I'll just put the ladder back in the shed and wash up."

"What is happening here?" McKenna asked. She couldn't help but smile at the storm surge of charisma flowing in her direction.

Jagger folded up the ladder and shrugged. "Just came to see you. Catch up after last night." He stopped and made a point to catch her eye. "Which was awesome," he said softly. "Your mom has been very gracious."

"Once I realized he was *Jagger*, the gifter of delicious wine, I wasn't about to turn him away." Her mom's voice could be heard from the kitchen, proving that they would not be alone in the house. A fact that went a long way to curb McKenna's adrenaline rush. "And I made him sing a couple of his songs for me."

"A cappella," he interjected.

Her mother stuck her head out of the kitchen. "Didn't care for them."

McKenna laughed and threw an I'm-so-sorry look at Jagger.

He shrugged. "Can't please everybody." He picked up the ladder and headed for the back door. McKenna followed.

"You should have heard him last night with his guitar," she told her mother as they passed through the kitchen. "Everyone at the Evans's was blown away."

"Not my cup of tea," her mother insisted. "But I appreciate the get 'r' done spirit he has. Remind me to show you where the ceiling needs patching," she yelled after them.

McKenna shut the slider and followed Jagger across the short span of dormant grass toward the aluminum shed. "I'm sorry about that. About my mom. Making you work like that and then dissing your music." She began to laugh behind her hand. "Who does that?"

"She's testing me," Jagger said as he began to sort out the mess in the shed. "What the hell do y'all have in here?"

"I don't even know," McKenna said, standing outside.

"Bikes? Old bikes. Like for kids."

"Probably mine. Don't bother looking, just come out and shut the door."

"Paint cans. A huge mirror that would not fit anywhere in that house. Boxes of junk, as best I can tell. Tools, all in a pile, not neat. Oh, here's a toolbox." She watched him lean over a pile of boxes, lifting said toolbox and depositing it closer to the door. "I see firewood. Probably best not to use any of that until you've had your chimney cleaned. Could be dangerous."

"How do you know?"

Jagger stuck his head out of the shed and gave her a curious look. "I've got eyes. Soot is piled thick all over the masonry. The flue is bound to be worse. That needs to be taken care of."

He ducked back inside.

"Jagger. What are you doing? Get out of there," she ordered.

"Why?"

"Because … I don't know. It's embarrassing having you see how we keep it."

"This?" His head popped out again. "This is nothing. Haven't you seen that show *Hoarders*? Or *Storage Wars* or *Auction Hunters*? The guys and I love that stuff. So anytime I get to snoop around something like this, I'm on the lookout for hidden treasures."

"Well, trust me. There are no hidden gems in there. Just a bunch of old crap I should probably have carted away.

"I can do that." He came out wiping his hands against each other.

"No, you can't do that."

"Sure, I can. That way, I'll have the opportunity to inspect every inch, make sure there isn't a Rembrandt tucked along the back wall in there."

"There is no Rembrandt, unfortunately. Come on. I'm cold. Let's go back inside."

"Hey." Jagger grabbed her elbow, stopping her from sprinting toward the house. "You good?"

"Yeah," she said, breaking into a smile because his face always made her smile. "I'm good. You?"

"I could be better."

She twisted her lips like she didn't have a clue. "How so?"

"Well, I didn't care much for the change in drivers at the end of last night's festivities. Or that I haven't heard from you since."

"I'm sorry. I literally just opened your text as I pulled in the drive. Imagine my surprise to find *you* here, installing electrical fixtures in my home."

"Well, it was a good way to put a masculine spin on the situation, don't you think? I mean, doesn't the stereotype depict the girl waiting by her phone after a great night out? Waiting for the guy to call? Your mother said it. I was willing to wait for you on the front stoop. She saved my pride by giving me something manly to do while I pined away for my date, who, by the way, left me with blue balls for the second damn time."

She smiled. Smirked even. He was just too cute, complaining like that. She addressed him as a therapist would. "I wasn't your date, and you didn't have blue balls."

"You were my date, and I thought I was going to get laid."

Her brows went up. "Clearly you were counting your chickens before they hatched."

"Clearly this boyfriend of yours has help on the inside. Not fair. Not fair at all."

"That's a small town for you. Everybody's looking out for everyone else, whether you want them to or not."

"So were you happy or sad that I got mugged and thrown into the back of the mayor's vehicle? By the way, it makes total sense, now that I know Bennett and Evans were cops."

"At the time, I was not happy," she assured him. "In fact, I had some choice words for Vance. He explained he was simply trying to slow the Jagger train down. And let's face it, I had hopped that train, it had left the station, and it was gaining speed heading downhill. Probably not a bad idea somebody had the sense to apply the brakes."

"That's a matter of opinion."

"Right. And after a good night's sleep and spending the day with my boyfriend's family, I have come to see Vance's wisdom."

"Or maybe they've just brainwashed you back into submission."

McKenna snickered and started back toward the house. "Just a reality check. Come on. I'm cold. And apparently you are staying for dinner."

"At least your mom likes me," he said doggedly.

"Oh, do not play the sympathy card. You had everyone dazzled last night. Vance said even he'd be tempted to sleep with you."

"Appreciate the sentiment, but I don't swing that way."

"Neither does Vance. But his point was made."

"And what point was that?"

"That the two of us had a lot of energy flowing in a direction that was probably going to feel very, very satisfying but ultimately leave us hungover and miserable later."

"Speak for yourself," he mumbled from behind her.

As they walked into the kitchen, Sandy said, "Wash up. Set the table. Use the good stuff, McKenna. I've already opened the wine. And Jagger, I laid out a silver sharpie for you to autograph the bottles you gave us. If you don't mind."

"You want him to autograph the chandelier he hung too, Mom?" McKenna jested.

Her mother stopped cutting the lasagna for a brief moment and looked toward the ceiling as if she was considering it.

"I'm kidding," McKenna stressed. "Mother. Please."

"Fine. All right." She went back to her cutting. "But Jagger, would you be terribly upset if I sold a bottle or two of your autographed wine on eBay?"

"We are not selling the wine on eBay," McKenna shouted. "Honestly."

With the table set, and the bottles autographed, except for one, which Jagger set aside, telling McKenna he'd get to it later, the three of them sat down to a very gratifying meal. The salad was crisp and delicious, the lasagna full of meat and ricotta, and the sauce loaded with flavor. The wine was as decadent and heady as McKenna had remembered. For a brief moment—the moment she and Jagger clinked glasses—she fell back into fan mode, once again becoming the starstruck groupie, gazing longingly at her idol. Jagger Yates, front man for the Cavaliers, had done something sweet for her mother and had truly been an amazing date last night. In fact, they seemed to be—maybe—becoming friends. It was still freakishly surreal. But as the dinner conversation flowed and she learned more about him, heard more about his life before his band hit it big, and curiously found out more about her own mother, she settled into the new normal.

Calling Jagger Yates a friend.

Only, after dinner was cleaned up and her mother headed back to the Hollises' for the show they watched together on Sunday nights, it became apparent that Jagger wasn't going to be satisfied with the friends thing. He used the dimmer switch to set the mood. The dimmer switch he'd apparently installed. Then, seating himself in the center of the sofa, he reached out, grabbed McKenna's hand, and pulled her onto the cushion beside him. He made a quarter turn of his body, got comfortable with one arm across the back of the sofa and one knee bent on the couch, and then focused all his attention on her.

McKenna was about to blow it off. Blow him off. Inform him that things between her and Xander had moved forward today. Yet, as the words took shape in her mouth, she began to get caught up in the fierce intention of Jagger's gaze.

Because *this* was something new. And something rather intoxicating. Something different than she'd ever been exposed to before.

Jagger was all there. All-in. All present.

His gaze was holding her in rapt attention. Every ounce of his being laser-focused on her.

It created a moment of *Oh wow.*

A moment of *this feels good.* A moment of *man I could get lost in this.* A moment of heartfelt appreciation for finally being *seen.*

It was a moment where more monkeys dropped off her back, and she was able to breathe.

There was nothing to be done but repay his kindness with a smile. And hold him in as much undiluted attention as she could muster.

The two of them sat there. For a long, yet easy moment. Accepting the silence around them. This moment in time. Appreciating the ease with which the two of them were able to share the same space.

"So tell me your story, McKenna Blakely," Jagger whispered as he gently ran a finger over her cheek, tucking hair behind her ear. "About this boyfriend of yours. And make me believe it."

Um, yeah. Okay. At the moment, that was a tall order.

Because sitting here with Jagger was definitely a swoon-worthy fairy tale.

And becoming a member of the Wright family was her real-life dream on the verge of coming true.

Only the one wasn't gelling with the other. Not at all. There was no doubt, with the buzz that was sparking between them, with the sizzle igniting within her breasts, that Jagger Yates was pushing up against her real-life dream. Which made this fairy tale all that more juicy.

She licked her lips and internally grinned at the thought. Finally, she allowed herself a slow smile.

"What?" he asked, touching her hair again, pulling one of her hands into his.

Boy, did that set more body parts a-tingling. And even though the angel on her shoulder gently suggested she shouldn't be holding hands with her—how did Xander put it?—her hall pass, Xander hadn't broken up with Becca yet, so *technically* their relationship status was still *nonexclusive*. Although the angel reminded her that Xander had finally shown his cards, had used the word *wedding* in relation to the two of them, and had dropped plenty of hints about Thanksgiving and making it official.

She squeezed Jagger's hand, forcing herself to come up with words that would help him understand the truth of where things stood. She didn't know how to explain other than just starting at the beginning.

"*Xavier* Wright, Xander's identical twin, asked me out when he was a senior in high school, and I was a sophomore. I thought he was *Xander*. I thought *Xander* was asking me out because Xander and I had shared a few looks, a few smiles the way high schoolers do. I knew he was shy, but I was making it clear that I was interested in the tall, quiet second basemen for the Bulldogs baseball team.

"But in actuality, it was Xavier, dressed in Xander's favorite shirt, who asked me out. I didn't realize my mistake until we were on the date and Xavier honked aggressively at a car that wasn't moving quickly enough for him. Xavier was known for pulling crap like that. *Xander* would have been mortified."

"Wait. These guys are identical twins? Xavier and Xander?"

"Yes. So I found myself dating Xavier because"—she lifted her right shoulder in a short shrug—"well, why not? Xander hadn't asked me out. I figured they were twins, they must have discussed this, right? And Xavier was plenty entertaining. Plus, he took me to his home a lot where I saw Xander and got to know his three younger brothers. *Plus,* I met his mom, Anna Beth, and boy, did I love having a woman like her in my life."

"How so?"

"Well, you've met my mom, right?"

"I have."

"She doesn't have a nurturing bone in her body. And she's the complete opposite of a girly girl."

"A girly girl?"

"She's not much into life's fluff. Dresses. Hairstyles. Nail polish. My mom's never bothered with makeup and has worked two jobs tirelessly for years. I love her for that. She's been a great role model for the value of a strong work ethic. But back in high school, Anna Beth Wright provided a softer side. One I craved.

"And being a mother of five sons, Anna Beth was just as excited about shopping for my prom dress as I was." McKenna smiled at the memory. "She even did my hair and makeup. It was that same night, the night of prom, she confided in me about her miscarriage. A daughter. Miscarried the same year I was born. I suppose I was filling a need in her just like she was filling a need in me. I became the daughter she never had, and I encouraged every bit of it."

"Wow."

"Yeah."

"Makes sense." Jagger nodded. "Okay. Go on."

"When Xavier abruptly left for college in June, months earlier than he needed to, and without bothering to inform me or even say goodbye, I stubbornly refused to give up my place in the Wright's household. Over the summer, I continued to visit and cook with Anna Beth, spending more and more time there since my mother was always working and no one was waiting for me here. I was lonely. And at the Wrights' I was never lonely."

"I get it." Jagger's eyes melted her with their warmth and understanding She took a deep breath before moving on.

"Two months later, right before Xander left for college, he finally admitted that he'd had strong feelings for me even before his brother had asked me out. And that those feelings had continued to grow over the summer. We had a night."

"A night?"

"Yeah. We had a night. One where I admitted I was into him too. One where we *both* ended up feeling a little guilty since his twin had not bothered to officially break up with me on his way out of town. Not that I'd heard one word from him since, I mean the writing was on the wall. But then Xander headed off to the University of Charleston and …" She sighed. "I rarely saw him after that. He didn't come home much, and when he did, he avoided me. I now know it was because of the whole Xavier thing. Which is just fodder for so many regrets. It turns out Xavier hardly ever came home either because *he* felt guilty for asking me out when he knew darn well his brother was into me. So, Xavier, who I'd last been dating, and Xander, who I'd *rather* be dating, both basically left town fourteen years ago and never returned."

"Ouch."

"Yeah. Ouch."

"Then what?"

"Well, as all of Anna Beth's boys grew up, left for college, and then settled elsewhere, the bond she and I had formed just continued to cement itself. I was there for her when she became ill with a rare autoimmune disease that really took its toll. After several years of treatments, she was fading fast. That's what finally brought Xavier home from Phoenix. When all seemed lost he made the plan to move home. He wanted to be with his ma at the end and do his best to take care of her and his dad while the worst was going down."

"Oh. Wow."

"Fortunately, *Xander*"—she smiled—"turned out to be a match for a last-ditch effort bone-marrow transplant and that was what miraculously started turning things around. By the time Xavier actually arrived home, Anna Beth had hope. We all did. And despite a few setbacks, she's been progressing slowly but surely. The doctors are now saying they wouldn't be surprised to see her make a full recovery."

"She looked frail when she introduced us on Saturday, but she didn't look ill."

"Right? She's become accustomed to staying in bed most of the day and letting the rest of us dote on her. Now we are all in cahoots to get her out of bed, urging her to return to participating in life. I couldn't believe she wanted to come meet you."

Jagger reared back as if offended, causing McKenna to laugh. "I just mean, she doesn't like to go out much. So the fact that she was willing to make the effort was surprising. A good surprise."

"Did you tell her I asked you out?"

"Of course not. She's completely besotted with the idea of me and Xander."

"Well, it sounds to me like you are completely besotted with Anna Beth Wright. And for good reason. However, you don't have to go to the length of marrying her son just to stay in her good graces."

"I'm not marrying Xander just to stay in her good graces."

"And you don't have to marry him just because he saved his mother with his miraculous bone marrow. Has he even proposed?"

"No."

"But his mother is acting like he has."

"Well, that's where her preference lies. She'd like Xander to move back to Henderson and settle down with me."

"And that's what you want? To settle down?"

"What's wrong with settling down?"

"Settling. It sounds boring."

"You sound boring," she shot back.

"I do?" A sly grin goaded her. "My life sounds boring?" he teased, pulling on her hand, raising her arm high and over his head so she fell forward, landing on him, chest to chest, lips and eyes aligning. "McKenna, McKenna, McKenna," he whispered. "You are so much more than all that."

Watching his lips move from mere inches away was mesmerizing. She licked her own. "I'm so much more than all what?"

"The Wrights. Those ridiculous twins. This house," he said, his gaze circling their surroundings. "You're thirty years old and live with your mother, who, from what I can tell pays little attention to you while carrying on some kind of crazy ménage à trois with her best friend and her best friend's husband."

"Stop. You don't know that."

"But I know *you*," he promised. "It hasn't taken long for me to realize you're driven and *passionate*, and yet you have set your motor to idle while waiting for *a boyfriend* who lives three hours away. What's up with that?"

McKenna pulled back and off Jagger, situating herself against the other end of the sofa. "It's complicated."

"No. No it's not. He's there. I'm here. There is no ring on your finger, and Anna Beth Wright is going to love you—even if you dump her son—because *you've* been the one constant in her life over the last fourteen years."

Well. What could she say to that?

"Do not *not* give me a chance just because you like this guy's family. Hell, you'll *love* my family. My family is awesome."

McKenna tilted her head and snickered. "Are you saying you want to take me home to meet your family?"

"Yeah, if it'll get me some time with you. Time without good cop and his buddy, bad cop running interference. You like me, you know you do."

"We've already discussed this."

"I know. But I'm making a point. If you weren't involved with this Zoolander—"

"Xander. Oh my gosh."

"Whatever. If you weren't involved with this Xander, and his twin brother which is really just … *eww,* if you think about it—"

"Oh my God, stop."

"—and I asked you out, you would say yes."

"Was that a question?"

"It was a clarification. You like me. In a parallel universe, you'd jump at the chance to date me."

"Jump at the chance to date you?" she repeated in disbelief.

"Yes. You would. So in this universe, the one we are sitting in right here, where there is Frick and Frack and their holy, blessed mother, you still like me, and you're going to give me a chance."

"A chance to do what?"

"Woo you off your feet."

Well ... didn't that sound delicious. So delicious she didn't know how to respond.

"See. So here we are," Jagger went on. "You and me on the couch, Frick somewhere down south doing God knows what, and your mother not coming home until eleven or so."

"We are not watching Netflix and chilling."

"Suit yourself," he said, moving closer and wrapping one arm around her back and his other arm under her legs so he could tuck her into him and throw her legs over his own. "No Netflix."

"And no chill," she ordered, squirming out of his hold, standing up, and backing herself away from the arena of temptation.

For a brief moment, Jagger appeared daunted. Then he held up his hands and said, "Fine. Fine." He stood slowly. "As long as I live to woo another day."

"Jagger," she sighed, because honestly, she loved the idea of being wooed. "Xander came home this morning. He'd heard about last night. About ... you and me holding hands in the hot tub."

Jagger's grin split his face.

"It's not funny." But she let out a little laugh because Jagger Yates was too cute for anyone's good.

"From where I stand, it's a little funny. Was it the good cop or the bad cop who ratted you out?"

"Vance."

"So Frick came running."

"He did indeed."

"He lay down the law? Tell you not to see me, or else?"

"Not exactly."

"Then what exactly?"

"He said he didn't want to lose me."

"Well, of course, he doesn't want to lose you. The guy's dating a ten. No one wants to lose a perfect ten."

McKenna forgot what she was going to say next. "You think I'm a ten?"

"Ah, duh."

"What makes you say that?"

"Have you forgotten how we met?"

"After a concert."

"After a concert where there were hundreds of pretty girls all smiling up at me, singing along. Yet, there was only one who stood out in the crowd. One who—for some crazy reason—I just connected with. I mean, your personality just shines through when you're happy. And I locked in on that because I was happy and letting my personality shine through. You were like the rock-star audience member. You were there. Fully engaged in the moment. I can't get enough of that."

"Wow." She didn't know if she'd ever get enough of *this*.

"And on that note, I'm leaving."

McKenna's heart panicked. "You're leaving? What do you mean you're leaving?"

"Babe, if I've learned one thing about producers, record labels, and women, it's leave them wanting more. Good night."

"Good *night?*"

"Yep." He picked up the wine bottle he'd yet to sign and headed to the door. "Good night. See you tomorrow." He scratched some words on the bottle and set it on the key table beside the door. "And for the love God, have the common courtesy to respond to my texts." He let himself out and slammed the door.

"You have got to be kidding me," McKenna cried, rushing to the door. She whipped it open but didn't know what to yell. She just watched him get on that fancy motorcycle and ride away into the night.

"What the hell just happened?"

She closed the door gently and locked it, figuring she'd just head straight to bed and mull the details of the day over in her mind until she found some solace in sleep. When she turned and saw the bottle he'd just signed and left there, she picked it up and read the same four words again.

Break. Up. With. Him.

CHAPTER TWELVE

There wasn't much that could clear your mind like a good, long ride. So after leaving McKenna "wanting more"—God, what a dumbass thing to say—Jagger rode out to the lake and then cruised some of the main drags. He didn't know the area well enough to venture onto the curvier stuff at night. But it turned out he had plenty of time to explore all the curves he wanted because clearing his mind became a regular pastime.

Monday.

Tuesday.

Wednesday. No McKenna.

She didn't answer his calls, she didn't respond to his texts, and though thoughts of her were lighting off some pretty woeful lyrics for a really sad-sack song loaded with the grief and misery of being in love alone, that was not what Jagger was looking for.

Thursday afternoon, he went riding, *again,* blowing by The Situation, which was the town's lone honky-tonk and noticing a Candy Apple Red bike identical to his own parked outside.

Except his was black.

As every bike should be.

Intrigued, *and since he hadn't a damn thing better to do until he was scheduled to meet with Pinks,* he circled back and stepped into The Situation's darkened interior before it was five o'clock anywhere on the Eastern Seaboard. He glanced around, noted there was only a few in attendance, so he called out, "Who's ride is that?" There was only one bike parked out front, so the question shouldn't prove difficult.

"Who's asking?" The booming voice came from a big guy sitting over at the bar.

Jagger walked himself down the short set of steps and across the open space. He pointed toward the door. "Nice ride. Practically identical to mine."

"Seriously?" The guy's surly face lit up. "A Road King?"

"Same model. Same year, from what I can tell."

"Well, have a seat. How 'bout I buy you a beer and we talk shop?"

"I'd like that. Thanks." Jagger slid a leg over the top of the vinyl barstool one seat down from Candy Apple.

"Where you from?" the guy asked, pointing to his own beer and nodding to the bartender.

"I'm originally from a small town in Virginia. But for the last twenty years, I've called Nashville home."

"Nashville, huh?"

Jagger nodded, accepting his beer from the barkeep and toasting his fellow road warrior.

"Is it all it's cracked up to be? You know, Nash-Vegas?"

"It's definitely got a little Vegas vibe with some serious Southern grits and Texas cowboy thrown in. Plenty of fun to be had in Nashville. Especially if you're a bachelorette."

"That's what I've heard. Hell, you ride all the way from there?"

"Nah. I've never been on a legit road trip. Think about it a lot though."

"I rode over two thousand miles last spring. All the way from Phoenix to Henderson. Took my time and saw the country. Cleared my head."

Jagger leaned over his beer and nodded. "Gotta be the best kind of therapy. Open road, the wind coming at you, all your worries flying away faster than you can remember what they are."

"Pretty much."

The two men sat in companionable silence, drinking their beers. Until McKenna's unexpected arrival.

Both men's heads turned to check out the newcomer and, as Jagger tried to digest her appearance, the man next to him groaned under his breath. "Here comes trouble."

Jagger couldn't have said it better himself. And because she'd been ghosting him for the last three days, he was mildly surprised—and his heart just a little delighted—when her gaze zeroed in and attached to the two of them.

However, after catching the fire in her eyes as she approached, Jagger braced himself for a *This town isn't big enough for the both of us* showdown. So he was dumbfounded when she merely shot him a glance before setting her undeniably irritated sights on the poor dude next to him.

"You summoned?" she drawled.

"I did. Would you like a drink?"

McKenna shot another look at Jagger and then turned back to … to—he hadn't gotten the guy's name. "Am I going to need one?" she snapped.

"Maybe."

She glanced at Jagger again, folded her arms across her chest, and jutted her hip out in an *I don't have time for this* stance. "Just lay it on me."

"He's not coming home for the Daze."

McKenna's arms dropped, and her mouth hung open. Then she caught herself and glanced over at Jagger a fourth time before asking, "Because?"

"Hell if I know, McKenna. The guy could be working for the CIA. I can't whittle any damn information out of him. Not since the two of you hooked up."

"Then why are you the one telling me this?"

"Because he's a freaking coward and afraid to tell you *or* my father that he's blowing off the Daze for one of the *things* he's apparently got jammed into his precious Charlotte calendar."

"I don't understand." McKenna was clearly confused.

"Neither do I. So I want you to tell me just what the hell is going on between you two."

McKenna's mouth opened and stayed that way as she spread her hands in obvious disbelief. "He said he was coming. He said he'd be here."

"Right. And this is a pattern. He says he's coming home for the weekend, and he doesn't. And that sets off Ma being disappointed and Dad being worried about you. So, here I am, *once again,* trying to solve everyone's problems."

Jagger stifled his laugh.

"What?" Candy Apple turned to him expectantly.

"You're the guy who solves everyone's problems?" Jagger asked.

"I am. I don't like it, but apparently, I am. You got a problem you want me to solve?"

"Maybe." He looked pointedly at McKenna. "Although from the little bit that's been said, you might already be helping my case."

"Say what?"

"Jagger," McKenna said. "Could you give us a minute?"

"No."

"No?" Her eyes went scary wide. But not scary enough.

"Yeah. No. Carry on." He motioned for the two of them to continue while he picked up his beer and took a sip.

"Do you know him?" Candy asked McKenna, lifting his chin in Jagger's direction.

This could get interesting.

"Don't you?" McKenna wondered. "I mean, it certainly appears you're sitting here all buddy-buddy, drinking together."

"Because he's got good taste in motorcycles and gets what it means to ride."

"Only I'm not a pussy," Jagger interjected. "My bike's not red."

The *pussy* slowly rose to his feet and started stretching his back and shoulders like he was ready to rumble. "You did not just say that."

"Man, come on. *Candy Apple Red?* Seriously?"

Was it possible that Candy's expression turned sheepish? "I was coming from Phoenix where I'd been doing yoga and meditating. Cut me some slack."

"Fine," Jagger conceded. "I guess there are worse things than red."

"Look. My girl likes the red. So, I live with it, because I love my girl." He stuck his hand out. "By the way, Xavier Wright."

"Oh, ahh," Jagger leaned away from Xavier's hand, bringing his own up to cover his ambivalent grin. "So you're *him*."

"This isn't him," McKenna huffed. "This is Xavier. Not Xander."

Xavier looked between the two, his hand still outstretched. "Yeah. I'm not him. I just look like him. In fact, I look *exactly* like him."

Jagger didn't leave him hanging. He grabbed Xavier's hand hard while running the calculations in his head. If McKenna's boyfriend looked like *this*, Jagger had some serious wooing ahead of him. Not that he hadn't already figured that out by McKenna's *complete lack of response* to his calls and texts. "So, you were saying? To McKenna?"

"Oh. Yeah." Xavier reseated himself, taking up his beer. He directed his next loud outburst toward McKenna. "So what the hell?"

"What the hell, what?" she burst back. Jagger felt like he should rename these two Nitro and Glycerin.

"What the hell is going on with you and Xander? Why is he blowing off the damn Daze? No one blows off the Daze. And when Dad gets wind of this, he's going to flip, and I'm the one who's going to have to hear about how he's letting you down. Again."

"Is he?" Jagger asked. "Is he letting you down? Again?"

Facing Xavier, McKenna did a slow blink, ignoring Jagger. "Why are you the one telling me Xander is not coming home?" She took her phone out of her jeans pocket and shook it at Xavier. "Why isn't he calling me himself?"

"Clearly he doesn't want to hear the disappointment in your voice when you lay yourself out like a doormat and let him walk all over you. *Again.* McKenna, you are a ball-buster. Not a doormat. And for the life of me, I can't figure out why you've turned yourself into one for my brother. I mean, I love the guy dearly, but bullshit is bullshit."

McKenna sighed. She glanced down at the floor and ran the pointed toe of her business-woman shoe along the ground. "He's dating somebody else."

The words came out of nowhere, were clearly unexpected, and sent Jagger's mind reeling.

"Say that again," Xavier dared.

"He's been dating another girl. A girl named Becca. Which is why he hasn't been coming home and why his social life in Charlotte is packed with *things*."

"And the two of you?" Xavier questioned.

"Are dating as well." She lifted her chin, giving Xander's twin a defiant glare.

"So, you're okay with this?"

"I wouldn't say that. But I've known about it since we started dating."

"You have got to be shittin' me."

"And, after word reached Xander that I was holding Jagger's hand in the Evans's hot tub Saturday night, he came crashing home, declared he was breaking things off with Becca and that on Thanksgiving he would be ready to make things official."

"Official?" Xavier questioned.

"Official?" Jagger repeated.

"That's the word he used."

The three of them let that news settle.

"So Xander has another girl, and you have been holding hands with"—he turned his whole body toward Jagger and pointed—"this guy?"

"In my defense, I did call Xander and made him clarify that the two of us were not exclusive, so yeah. Then I held hands with Jagger. Who happens to be my heartthrob."

"Who makes your *what* throb?"

"Oh my goodness, Xavier, don't you ever listen to anything happening at the breakfast table? This is *Jagger Yates*." She stuck her finger in his direction. "Lead singer of the Cavaliers."

"Oh. Dude. I'm sorry. I didn't connect those dots. I get it now. She's a huge fan."

"Well, I'm a fan of hers. Not so much your twin."

"I hear that. But seriously. I mean, you're not actually *interested* in McKenna, right?"

With that, McKenna pushed Xavier as hard as she could and stomped off down a long hallway.

"She'll be back," Xavier assured him. "She's the pain in my ass that never disappears for long."

"If I didn't know better, I'd say there is wild chemistry between you two."

"Nah. Just a couple of hotheads who care about the same circle of people. I'm not going to be able to shake her, so I've stopped trying. But you, sir. What the hell are you doing with all that sass? A guy like you doesn't have to put up with bossy and cranky. Tell the truth: you aren't really into McKenna."

"I'm totally into McKenna. She's not bossy with me."

"Man, that's a damn lie—she's bossy with everybody."

Jagger grinned and shook his head. "I guess I don't see it that way."

"How do you see it?"

He shrugged. "I see it as foreplay. You know, an opportunity to work my way into her good graces and then give her something else to think about."

"She's *dating* my *brother*," Xavier growled.

"Who is *dating* some chick named *Becca*," Jagger growled back.

"True that." Xavier shook his head like a dog before sipping his beer. "It's all making more sense now. But man, my brother is not one to string two women along. And trust me on this. McKenna is not one to let him. This entire episode has blown my mind. I feel like I'm in the dang Twilight Zone. *Plus,*" he exclaimed as he looked Jagger up and down. "What the hell are you doing in Henderson? Total fan by the way. Just don't tell McKenna. I've got to bitch every time she turns on your music. It's what I do."

Jagger nodded as if this made perfect sense. "I won't give you away."

The two men had spun on their stools so, with beers in hand, they now faced the rest of the room. Jagger kept an eye on the hallway McKenna had headed down, wondering if she was calling the boyfriend. Wondering if he should intercede. And underneath all that wondering was a mild form of ecstatic glee. Because he'd heard the big secret right along with Candy Apple here. The *boyfriend* had another *girlfriend* and wasn't coming home for the freaking Daze. Jagger was still uncertain about the weekend's festivities, even though he'd been informed by Pinks that he'd have an official schedule. He was about to bring up this Daze thing to Candy when the tiny one—Laidey—with her bouncy, dark curls and Keds sneakers entered the premises.

"Tweets," Xander called.

"Don't tell me she's yours," Jagger said.

"*All* mine."

Laidey came over, tossing a shy smile in Jagger's direction, but immediately huddled between her fiancé's legs. She wrapped an arm around his waist while he bent his head and kissed the top of hers. "You've finally met Jagger?" she asked.

"He rides a Road King. Like we do."

"I saw it outside. Very handsome, that black."

"Whoa, whoa, whoa. You like the *Candy Apple Red.*"

"I do. Because it's happy. Like the way you make me happy," Laidey said, all the while smiling up into Xavier's eyes. Jagger watched as the dude turned to putty. "But black is sexy. You know, like him." She wiggled short-nailed fingertips in Jagger's direction.

Jagger braced, knowing for damn sure that sentiment was not going to sit well with Candy Apple.

But the big guy just blew it off. "Tweets. Don't be ridiculous. The guy is okay looking, but he's no Xavier Wright."

"Not until you put a guitar in his hand. Then all bets are off."

Jagger held his breath.

Xavier turned Laidey around to face him, encompassing her entire span of vision. "I know what you're doing," he said softly. "And it would totally work if your best girl wasn't in a dire state, in need of your level head and soothing way." He pointed down the hallway. "She's back there. Probably on the phone with Xander, who is not only *not* coming back for the Daze, but is apparently dating another woman."

"What?" Laidey took a step back as she grappled with the news.

"Were you aware?" Xavier asked.

Dark curls bouncing, Laidey shook her head vehemently. "No. No. How would *I* have known?"

"Because McKenna told *me.* Just now. I assumed she'd already confided in you."

"McKenna *knows* Xander's dating someone else?"

"Okay. Clearly, she didn't confide in anyone."

"I don't understand."

"That makes two of us. But it sure explains why Xander isn't driving in every weekend. Go on. I'll be here if you need me."

Without looking anywhere else, Laidey dashed down the hallway.

"Listen, Casanova." Xavier turned a serious face toward Jagger. "When Tweets is around, lay low on the sexy, alright."

Jagger held out his arms, "Hey. It is what it is."

"So, you wanna ride sometime. I can show you Henderson's best twists and turns."

"That'd be great. As long as you're not planning to run me off the road in an effort to get me out of your brother's way."

"Right now, it appears my brother is getting in his own way. Look," Xavier said, leaning closer. "You seem like a good guy, coming to town, playing with Cal Johnson on this crazy record scheme Scarlett's brewed up. And McKenna is thoroughly whacked about your music. And as much as she and I butt heads, she's been a huge help to my family. I owe her a debt I will never be able to repay. She took care of my parents while Ma was sick and the rest of us were scattered across the country. And I will tell you now, I love my brother more than anyone other than Tweets. But McKenna, she doesn't deserve whatever bullshit he's putting her through. So—to be *very* clear—I want Xander to get his head on straight and end up with McKenna. But I will not stand in your way while you give him a run for his money."

"Noted," Jagger said. Feeling right where the guy stood. He held out his hand. "I appreciate that."

"All right then. Now, let's order food. I'm not leaving my girl while she takes care of her girl, and God knows this kind of thing could take a while."

Jagger glanced at this watch. "Sounds good. I'm meeting Davis Williams here any minute. He's giving me an agenda for this Daze of yours."

Xavier's eye lit up. "You totally need to check out *his* ride. But listen"—he shook his head—"you gotta understand something. As well-meaning as they are, they are going to exploit the hell out of you this weekend."

"Who are *they*?"

"Team Henderson. They're on a mission. Well, I'm on the team too, so I guess I should say we're all on a mission. And getting our town's good name into the media is paramount. We are not above exploiting any Major League Baseball players, coaches, or rock stars who wander into town."

"Got it. I'm in. Whatever."

"Because of McKenna?"

"Not necessarily. Although I think she feels a little guilty Team Henderson is throwing all this at me. So, don't tell her that. Because, you know ... sympathy card and all."

"Understood."

"But any publicity Henderson gets by linking my name is also free publicity for my band. So, win-win."

Xavier hit him on the back just a little too forcefully. "Glad to hear it. That's the kind of attitude that will make the Daze go down much smoother."

"How bad does it get?"

"For you? I don't know, but here comes the man with all the answers." Xavier pointed toward the door where Davis stood in the shadows, apparently letting his eyes adjust to the muted light. Once his gaze latched on to Jagger and Xavier, he held up a hand and headed their way.

The dude had a pink shirt on that must have cost a bloody fortune. Right along with the slacks, the belt, and the shoes. His hair was stylish and thick and, even though he wasn't the tallest guy in the room, he was an imposing sight. The guy was either making bank, or came from bank, or enjoyed some sort of combination thereof. He was definitely suited up for a business meeting, standing in front of two clowns wearing jeans and some form of boots. It didn't faze Pinks though. He shook Jagger's hand and seemed genuinely happy to see him.

"How's it going?" Pinks asked. "How are you enjoying Henderson?"

"Going good. Was out riding and saw another Road King. Pulled in and found this guy."

Pinks nodded at Xavier. "How's your mom?"

"Better every day," Xavier said, knocking on wood.

"Happy to hear it." Pinks turned his attention back to Jagger. "I'm starved. You want to get a table in the back, order some food? Xavier, you are more than welcome to join us. I'm going to do my best to sell a few Daze appearances to Jagger. Could always use the backup."

"Don't mind if I do."

The men ordered their food and then meandered toward the hallway where Jagger had seen McKenna disappear. He kept his eyes peeled as the hall opened up into another room with a bar running down the right side, a small clear space over by the jukebox, plenty of tables with chairs, and a couple of billiard tables. He spied McKenna and Laidey perched on barstools all the way down at the end, facing each other, their attention on the crisis at hand and definitely not on the group of men seating themselves at the head of the room.

Jagger purposely took the seat that would put his back toward McKenna. He didn't trust himself not to be overly distracted. It was enough that he had new information and was eager to work out a plan to accommodate it.

Once fresh beers were served, Pinks dug in. "How would you feel about being Grand Marshal of the parade this Saturday? We'd have someone driving you in a 1934 Cadillac, complete with rumble seat, and all you'd have to do is wave to the crowd as you're driven from the high school, down Main Street, and over to the field where the festival is being held."

"I can do that," Jagger offered. "What time do you need me?"

"Parade starts at ten. We like everyone present thirty minutes prior so that we can run it on time."

"Nine thirty at the high school. I know where that is."

"Great. Great. Now, how do you feel about being dunked? It's not going to be freezing out, but it's going to feel like fall."

"Wait. What?"

"Dunked. As in a dunking machine. Let the Bulldogs baseball team or whoever wants to have a chance to dunk you."

"All day?"

Pinks grinned. "No. You'll have a thirty-minute time slot. We've got the mayor lined up and the principal. I'm working on Hale. We've got The Who's Who of Henderson willing to splash down for the cause. All of it raises money for Henderson Helping Henderson."

"All right. Count me in."

"Great. Be sure to bring a change of clothes."

Jagger nodded.

"Now, how about a thirty-minute stint at the kissing booth?"

"Y'all have a kissing booth?"

"It's a thing," Pinks assured him. "We try to man it with athletes and homecoming queens to draw the kids from our neighboring town of Oxford. It's not a full-on kiss. Just a peck. Most of the time, they'll give you a kiss on the cheek and maybe take a selfie."

"Kissing booth? With high schoolers and their phones? Sounds like this could come back to haunt me."

Xavier interjected, "No kissing booth."

"Yeah. No kissing booth," Jagger agreed.

"What about taking selfies with your fans? We can have you stationed somewhere for an hour or so."

"Are they going to have to pay for the privilege?"

"Only a quarter. We don't want people to feel like the Daze is a fundraising activity, even though it is."

"And I get a cut?"

"Ah, no. This is all for charity."

"Henderson Helping Henderson," Jagger stated. "Okay. Fine. No kissing booth, but bring on the selfies."

"Great. Then Red has asked me to see if you'll agree to join her at her booth for a bit. She will be selling the *Hunks of Henderson* calendar, and pre-selling Cal's collaborative album."

"What about Piper's booth? The pie plate booth?"

"You want to sell pie plates?" Pinks asked, surprised.

"I want to be able to nibble on any free samples she's giving out."

Both Xavier and Pinks laughed. "Since Piper's my best friend, why don't I have her bake you a pie for all your trouble. She and I, well, all of us, really appreciate you being so agreeable."

"For her pie, I'll slay dragons."

"Great. All right. So, it's a long day, especially with you showing up for the parade and all the rest because we won't take the stage until seven o'clock at night. I don't know if you'll give us a full hour of your time, but it would be great to have the Daze end on a high note."

"So you're playing from seven to eight? That's it?"

"Well, last year the crowd was up for a good time, so Jesse and I kept going and played for a couple of hours. I don't want you to feel like you have to do that."

"I appreciate it. I'm happy to commit from seven to eight. After that, why don't we just play it by ear? See what the crowd wants. We don't want to play for a handful of people, but if everyone wants more when we pretend to put our guitars down, then we play more." He leaned his upper body over the table toward Pinks. "I haven't performed on stage in weeks. I'm looking forward to a shot in the arm."

"Now, remember. Pinks is not your regular drummer," Xavier pointed out. "This other guy he's got coming in can play the guitar but probably not like your buddies. This is amateur night."

"Hey. We all start out as amateurs." Jagger eyed Pinks. "Your buddy plays and sings. So what's he want me to do?"

"What do you mean?"

"I'm not here to step on any toes."

"Oh, shit," Xavier exclaimed, his gaze locked on something behind Jagger.

Jagger turned in his seat, setting his sights on the two women seated down the length of the bar. "What's going on?"

"They're doing shots. And Laidey, being about four foot thirteen, and weighing all of nothing, does not need to be doing shots in support of McKenna's crash-and-burn."

"You want to intervene?" Jagger asked, watching as the two brunettes in question did, indeed, throw back a shot.

"Maybe. I'll keep an eye on things. If they keep it to one, we'll be good."

Jagger turned back to Pinks. "Where were we?"

"You didn't want to step on my buddy's toes."

"From what I hear, y'all don't really need my help when it comes to bringing the party. I'm happy to take a backseat. Fill in when you want me to."

"Oh, stop with the bullshit," Xavier pleaded. "You get up on stage, McKenna and her ilk will not want to be hearing from anyone else."

"Hey. I've asked around. I hear these guys are good."

"For *amateurs*," Xavier stressed. "Oh, shit."

"What now?"

Xavier elbowed Pinks. "Your Red has arrived, and she ain't here for you."

Pinks watched Scarlett beeline over to Laidey and McKenna. "I can see that. What the hell's happening?"

Xavier rubbed his eyes and groaned. "Word's getting out. And shit's gonna hit the fan if my parents catch wind of this. I need to nip this in the bud."

"What's going on?" Pinks asked, watching his girl gather McKenna into her arms.

"Well, I could tell you, but then I'd have to shoot you," Xavier growled. He rose, chugged a good portion of his beer, and started toward the women.

"What?" Pinks spat.

Jagger pulled his chair in closer and leaned over the nachos, quieting his voice. "Red's going to tell you anyway, right?"

"Probably," Pinks said.

"So you did not hear this from me. Nor will you repeat it to anyone, under penalty of Xavier killing you."

"Go on."

"McKenna's boyfriend? The one that unfortunately looks a lot like him?" Jagger pointed behind him. "He's dating another girl."

"McKenna and he broke up?"

"No. He's dating McKenna *and* another girl. A girl named Becca or something."

"And you know this how?"

"I was sitting next to Xavier when McKenna shared that intel with him."

"*McKenna* told *him*?"

"Yes. Apparently, McKenna has known all along."

"Hmm." Pinks sat back in his chair, and Jagger followed suit.

"What's McKenna's role in this Daze of yours?"

"She's a journalist. She takes picture and conducts interviews throughout the day so she can write a recap of it all for the Monday morning paper. People like to see their picture in the paper."

"Is there any way you could rope her into being my ... I don't know, handler?"

"You need a handler?"

"You could sell it that way. I mean, you want me at the parade, at the dunking booth, at Scarlett's booth, taking selfies, and playing with your band." Jagger ticked the items off his fingers. "Hell, throw in some more if you think we need it to sell the idea."

"She'd make a great handler. Bossy as hell but punctual and always on the job."

"Right?"

"I'm sensing an ulterior motive."

"That's because I'd like to handle her, if you get my drift."

"I do indeed."

"So what do you say, Pinks? You gonna defend and protect the guy who's dating two women and choosing *not* to come home for the Daze? Or you gonna do your newest band member a solid?"

Pinks squinted in disbelief. "Xander's not coming home for the Daze?"

Jagger threw a thumb over his shoulder. "That's what all the hubbub is about."

"Dude. You can't miss the Daze and expect your girlfriend not to be snatched up by a rock star. I'll line up McKenna." He shot out a finger. "As your handler. The rest is up to you."

"That's all I'm asking. Thank you. Now, about our set list."

CHAPTER THIRTEEN

McKenna's call to Xander had been utterly unsatisfying. He, indeed, was not going to make it home for the Daze. Which put her into a daze of her own.

Until Laidey showed up, McKenna had stood in the corner at the back of the room, facing the damn wall like she was a kindergartner in a time-out. Her mind reviewing the words Xander had uttered on Sunday combining with the disappointment they created now. Had the hope she'd cultivated about where their relationship was heading been misplaced? Had she read him wrong?

Fuck no. Her mind yelled. You heard him loud and clear. He was breaking up with Becca. He was coming home for the Daze. And by Thanksgiving, he'd be ready to make plans and make things official.

She'd *definitely* heard those words. All those words.

She wasn't crazy. Xander had come home and said all those things. But in keeping with his SOP over the last couple of months, he was once again making excuses about missing one of Henderson's events.

As if the Daze was just some random event. The Daze was *the* event. If you were raised in Henderson and didn't get home for anything else, you made it home for the Daze. Because that's when you saw everyone who had ever meant anything to you. That's where you caught up on the good, the bad, and the ugly. That's where you drank a little more than you should, and it usually turned into a hard-to-remember night that you never forgot.

No one missed the Daze.

And Xander's explanation was as flimsy as it always was. Needed to play catch-up. Was coming back for Thanksgiving, so he couldn't lose the time.

WTF?

She flat out asked him if he'd broken up with Becca, and he said he was working on it.

Working on it? Her mind screamed. Her mouth could form no words. Then he's all like, "I know you're upset, and I'm sorry. I promise I'll make it up to you."

"How?" she spat. Because Xavier was right. She was done being a doormat.

"I'll plan something special. As soon as I'm out of Charlotte, I'll plan something special to celebrate."

"Out of Charlotte? You mean …?"

"I meant what I said Sunday. I'm talking to my boss. I'm looking at my lease. I'm striving to shake myself loose."

"Xander," she sighed.

"Kens, it's what you want. I know. I'm finding out what needs to be done. Taking the steps. For you. For us."

"Thank you. Thank you. Thank you. I don't like not seeing you until Thanksgiving, but I do get that you've got a lot on your plate. You've got to know how much this means to me."

"I do, Kens. I do. Now I've got to go. Do me a favor, and please get my father to chill about this weekend, will you?"

"Yes. I will. I'll get him to chill."

"No one can handle him like you. I gotta go, babe. Bye."

The babe thing again. It grated. He'd *never* called her babe.

And could he have been any more desperate to get off the phone?

And did she just go from a girl with a backbone to a doormat in the span of that short conversation?

All those questions had her mind going numb until Laidey approached, and McKenna realized she'd been staring at the wall.

Now, one shot in, she was releasing all kinds of tension. Tension from her shoulders, tension from her questionable backbone. Tension from not having shared her saga with her closest friend, who was now grilling her in her Laidey-like way—where Laidey's brain went down a very intelligent list of questions for which there were absolutely no intelligent answers. Because intelligence had absolutely nothing to do with the situation in which she and Xander found themselves.

Passion.

Lust.

History. That is the stuff that created this kind of melodrama.

"He's coming home," she told Laidey. "He's working on coming home for good. Which is more than I'd hoped for at this point." She should be smiling, she realized as she said those words. But she wasn't. Nor did she feel like smiling.

"So he's not coming home for the Daze. Big deal," McKenna went on. "I don't know why that just—ugh—gets me right in the gut." She looked into Laidey's eyes and dug for understanding.

"The Daze is a big tradition. You anticipated him sharing it with you."

"Yes," McKenna jumped on that. "Yes. That's it." Only it really wasn't it. It might be part of it, she thought, but shouldn't she be focusing on the end game? Xander was working to move back home. He was going to make things official. What really was the big deal if he didn't make it home for this one Daze?

And then the jukebox began to play "Babe in a Bar," and McKenna knew exactly why it was such a big deal that Xander make it home for the Daze.

She'd been avoiding Jagger Yates like he was the tax collector. And after one shot and half a beer, she didn't even try to avoid the beautifully muscled, guitar-playing arm reaching into the crowd that now surrounded her. That voice—the one she heard every time she turned on her music—now asking her to dance.

I tried, Xander, I tried. The words swam in her head as Jagger Yates, lead singer of the Cavaliers, pulled her into his embrace and danced them both in a slow, sultry circle while the rest of the room looked on.

"You okay?" he whispered in her ear.

"Hmm," she sighed, thinking that yep, she was now very okay. Thinking about how much she was enjoying this slow dance with Jagger. How good his arms felt wrapped around her. How nice it was to lay her head up against his shoulder. How romantic it was the way their hands were clasped together, resting against his chest. She closed her eyes and just took in the moment. One she was going to be able to take with her and relive forever. "This is very nice."

He didn't respond. His body just sort of sank into the moment with hers. She felt that when his shoulders relaxed a bit. When his hand re-gripped hers. When he dipped his chin and brushed his lips over her hair.

The part of her that never let go of harsh reality was very aware that they had an audience watching this show. She couldn't guess how Pinks and Red were feeling about it, but she definitely knew Xavier and Laidey were probably uncomfortable.

Whatever.

Take a video, she thought. Text it to Xander.

Annnd that's when she heard the record needle screech inside her head.

Her body stopped moving, halting their dance. In fact, she stepped back out of his arms. "We need to talk," she told him.

"Okay," he nodded agreeably, like he'd give her anything in his power right about now.

"Okay," she nodded back. "Ah"—she looked around—"maybe not here." Her gaze came back to his. "Meet me at my place? In a half hour?"

"Sure. Sure," he said. "Sounds good. I'll, ah, just settle up at the bar. Are you okay to drive?"

"Ah?" She thought about it. "I think so. It's not far. I'll be careful."

"Because I'm sure any of your friends would be willing to drive you and your car home. Hell. I'll do it. I'll just leave my bike and, here. Give me your keys. I'll drive you home."

"You think that's okay?" she asked.

"Why wouldn't it be okay?"

She shook her head. "I don't want … I don't want people to get the wrong idea." She held out her hand indicating the double duo watching them from the bar.

"Hey!" Jagger called out. "McKenna needs one of you to drive her and her car home."

Xavier was off his barstool and on the move.

"I'll see you in a half hour," Jagger told her and then left her waiting for Xavier as he headed back to the others.

She heard Xavier ask, "You wanna get home?" while her gaze was latched onto Jagger's back. When she finally pulled it off him, she simply nodded. "I probably shouldn't drive."

"Not a problem."

They drove in silence for a bit. Finally, McKenna turned to Xavier and said, "Please don't use Jagger to bait your brother."

"What do you mean?"

"That dance with Jagger back there. It doesn't change the way I feel about Xander. I don't want it used against me or against him. I don't want him to feel pressured to drive home at daybreak because he thinks he's going to lose me. He knows Jagger is here. He knows Jagger is interested in me. He also knows that I am committed to him. And I am." She turned her head to look at Xavier. "I'm committed to Xander."

"No one's doubting that, McKenna." Xavier turned in to her drive and put her car in park.

She gave a half smile with a short laugh. "Good. So don't bait him. Okay?"

"I don't like how all this is playing out. I'm not happy to have been kept in the dark about the nonexclusivity of your relationship. And I hate the idea of Ma and Dad finding out that things are not as they seem."

"I totally get it. This is what I've been struggling with for weeks. And like you said—rather ineloquently—I have turned myself into a doormat. I don't enjoy feeling pathetic."

Xavier looked confused. "In what way are you pathetic? Am I wrong, or did you not enter into this third-party arrangement with your eyes wide open? It's the rest of us who are looking pathetic for believing in something that didn't exist."

"But it does," she explained. "He's coming home. All is well."

"It better be. Look, you know I'm happy to pay the guy a visit and see what's what. Now that I've got all the intel, I'm happy to drive down there and set my bro straight."

"No. I mean, that's sweet of you, but no. He's doing the best he can, Xavier. I believe that. I'm going to give him the benefit of the doubt. And I want you to do that as well."

"Done."

"And don't goad him into action by telling him I danced with Jagger. He doesn't need that. I don't want him committing himself to me simply because Jagger Yates happens to be in town."

"Well, why the hell not? Something needs to light a fire under the two of you. You can't be his side piece forever."

McKenna flinched.

"Aww. I'm sorry. I didn't mean …"

"I know what you meant," she grumbled, reaching for the door handle. "Now get the hell out of my car and find a way home."

"Attagirl. There's that backbone."

Jagger showed up twenty-nine minutes later, giving McKenna a chance to change into comfy jeans and a very soft, yet very hot-girl, fleecy-feeling pullover. Since it was only a Thursday and the Daze was looming, she poured herself a sparkling water but iced down a couple beers for Jagger.

She hadn't worried her mother would be around since her mother was never around. Thursday nights, she played mahjong with LeeAnn and other neighborhood gals. So when Jagger came inside, there was soft music playing, and the light from the new chandelier had been turned down a few notches.

"Hi," he said, shooting up her heart with his cute front man grin.

"Beer?"

"Sure." He followed her to the couch where they'd last sat together. The night he declared he was going to woo her. They each took an end, turning toward the other. She hiked a knee up onto the cushions and reached over to clink her glass with his bottle as a sort of green flag for their conversation.

"Thank you for … the dance," McKenna started, reseating herself, getting comfortable but still focused. "I was really enjoying it." She shot her eyes to his, giving him the truth. "I mean, really enjoying it. Until the thought occurred to me that if Laidey or anyone decided to video us and send that to Xander …"

"Hm-hmm. It would put you in hot water with the boyfriend."

"No. It might serve to spur the boyfriend into action. Action he might be unwilling to take on his own."

"And that would be a bad thing?"

She shrugged. "He came home Sunday and promised me the world because *you* were a threat to our relationship."

"Ah-uh."

"Not because he wanted to see me. Not because he'd finally made up his mind. Not because he *wanted* to promise me the world. All that was incentivized by you holding my hand."

Jagger took a sip of his beer. "You're welcome."

She huffed and rolled her eyes. "He knew someone had asked me out. He didn't like it, but he didn't change his plans and come home last weekend. Not until he heard it was you."

"Right. So, I'm helping your cause."

"Well, I'm not sure you are, and that's why we need to talk."

"O-kay. Talk."

"I want Xander to choose me. I want him to break it off with Becca and dedicate himself to me. That is what I want. What I don't want is for him to be forced to make a decision and then later regret it."

"Break up with him."

"What? No."

"McKenna, your relationship is bullshit. You know that, right? He's got a girl where he works and lives and plays, and he's got you doting on his mother and his father and waiting to welcome him home with open arms whenever he *has* to make the drive. What part of this is not computing?"

"He's my first." The words popped out. McKenna hadn't meant to provide that kind of intimate information but there it was, pouring out. "He's my first. I willingly gave my virginity to Xander, and for one night and a few days, he treasured it. And then he left for college. We both felt guilty since what we'd done could be construed to be cheating on his brother, and Xander never pursued me again. I pined for years over the loss."

"He was your first." Jagger's hands massaged the leg he'd crossed ankle to knee.

"Yep."

"That can create a mighty strong attachment."

"One I've never been able to shake."

"I hear you. And you were how old?"

"Sixteen."

"Hmm. So …"

"So, when he came back into my life this past summer, it felt extremely satisfying. Deep down to my soul satisfying."

"Mmm."

"And I was willing to do anything to cultivate that feeling."

"So you cut him some slack when it came to Becca."

"They'd already started dating, so yeah."

"And how did that feel?"

"Pretty spectacular when he was coming home every weekend to see me. But as the summer wore down, so did his road trips to Henderson."

"And now it has all boiled down to this."

"Yeah. It has."

"Break up with him."

McKenna sprung off the couch. "You aren't hearing me."

He stood up with her. "I'm totally hearing you. You're holding on to a relationship that you fell in love with back when you were *sixteen years old.*"

"I am not," she shouted.

"You so are," he shouted back.

"This is not the same relationship we had when I was sixteen."

"Agreed. Because back then, the two of you were cheating on *his brother.* Now, the two of you are cheating on Becca."

"Oh!" McKenna stepped back, crossing her arms over her chest as tears sprung to her eyes. She was so *angry.* Angry at Xander for not being man enough to stand up to his brother all those years ago. And angry at him again for not making the hard choice between her and Becca immediately.

But most of all, she was furious with herself.

She'd let the hope of Xander Wright and all he brought to the table blind her to how compromised her sensibilities had become.

As the uncomfortable silence dragged on, McKenna struggled not to dissolve into all out bawling. She'd never felt more embarrassed than she did in this moment. And the more she felt the depth of her embarrassment, the more she struggled to catch her breath, to keep the tears at bay.

"I'm sorry," she heard Jagger say. "That was completely insensitive. But you gotta understand, from my perspective, a guy like that does not deserve a woman who is as kind and generous as you are to his mother. He does not deserve your loyalty, your dedication, or your unending patience just because his last name is Wright. Nor because you gave him your virginity back when you were sixteen. He's the one who owes you his love, his affection, and his undying gratitude for all that you have been to him and his family. And yeah, I've got a vested interest in the outcome here. But that doesn't make me wrong."

"Jagger. I'm so embarrassed." A small sob broke loose, but she suppressed the ones that wanted to follow.

"Embarrassed? *He's* the one who should be embarrassed. Allowing you to misrepresent your relationship to everyone you know, including his own family? It's unconscionable."

"*I* allowed it. That's why I'm embarrassed. We should never have misled his folks back at the very beginning. We should have made it clear that we were not exclusive. But Anna Beth and Maxwell were so delighted, and I was so happy, misguidedly assuming Xander's relationship with Becca would be short lived. I mean, how could he not choose me?" And that's when the floodgates burst.

"I don't know," Jagger said as she fell into his arms and sobbed against his chest. "I honestly do not know."

CHAPTER FOURTEEN

"So, that happened." McKenna came out of her bedroom after washing her face following a crying jag unlike any other. All it took was one look at Jagger sitting on the couch and her life became surreal again. She had just sobbed all over the Cavaliers's lead singer. Like, *what* was her problem?

"Can I take you to dinner? Tomorrow night?"

McKenna chuckled under her breath. The man was nothing if not persistent.

"It occurs to me that had I simply accepted a date when we first met, your infatuation with me would have ended by now."

"Not likely." He shifted his head, looking at her speculatively. "Your infatuation with me gone?"

She gifted him a smile. "I'm afraid I'm going to be a fan forever. How much longer are you planning to be in town?"

Jagger was visibly taken back. "What do you mean?"

"I mean," she said as she put a tentative knee on the couch vacillating between sitting back down or ... something else to put distance between them. Eventually, she sat. "Are you heading home for Thanksgiving?"

"Nope."

"Why?"

He blinked. "Because Thanksgiving is your deadline."

"My deadline?"

"On Xander. And my intentions toward you haven't changed. In the least," he assured her. "So, yeah. I'll be sticking around. Seeing what sort of doubt I can wheedle into that head of yours."

"Stop. I can't believe you just let me sob all over you, and yet you're still at it."

"I want what I want, McKenna. And if I see a foothold, I'm going to use it."

She jumped off the couch. "You need to go."

"Bullshit. There's nobody here videotaping us and sending it off to dumbass Xander. Sit your ass back down and get back in the game."

"The game? This is not a game, Jagger. This is my life."

"Life is a game, McKenna. And just because you've been playing it with the wrong partner and coming up a loser doesn't mean your luck can't change."

"Oh my god. If that's a veiled insinuation that I should *get lucky* with you, you have lost your ever-loving mind."

He grabbed hold of her hand and pulled her down onto his lap, wrapping his arms around her and holding tight. "Kiss me."

"What?"

"You heard me. Kiss me. You know you want to. And we owe each other *at least* that much after what happened last Saturday night."

"Owe each other?"

"McKenna, you cannot deny that after our hot tub date, you and I were headed for a long—*very long*—make-out session in your car."

She took his head between her two hands, added pressure, and shook it as she spoke. "Jagger. I'm dating somebody else. I'm not going to kiss you—"

Well. That ended that.

McKenna's tongue was tangling with Jagger's before she had any idea what hit her. And her body was sooo into the kiss that it overwrote any thoughts she had to … to … yeah, whatever. Her hands were still on his face, but the rest of her body was sl-o-w-ly wallowing, sinking into the experience of Jagger Yates playing her mouth as well as he played his guitar.

The.

Guy.

Could.

Kiss.

Oh dear heavens, she was never going to be the same. Her lips wanted more. And more. And more as every muscle that had been fraught with tension eased into the bliss that was Jagger Yates's kiss.

How could one man know how to do so much so well? It defied the imagination.

"Jagger," she whispered over his lips as she briefly changed the direction of their kiss.

"McKenna," he responded, using his lips to explore hers.

"This is …"

"Yeah, it so is."

Her mind tugged on the word amazing. Other words floated into her awareness. Sensual. Intimate. Gratifying. "Decadent," was the one she voiced with a small moan, her brain equating him to a dark chocolate truffle.

"Mmmm." He pulled her further across him so she was better situated in his lap. The back of her hips hit the arm of the sofa, and both her legs dangled across his. She let her hands drift into his hair, luxuriating in the feel of the longer strands at the top. She could hardly focus. So enveloped in his kiss it was as if gravity had released its hold on the two of them and off they floated in a bubble all their own.

Kissing Jagger Yates was everything she'd imagined it could possibly be.

Eventually, he slowly pulled his mouth from hers, gifting her with a mini grin that was lit up by the sparkle in his eyes. His hand came over her hair, caressing it from the top of her head to the tips of the strands. He picked up her hand and brought it to his lips, kissing it reverently. "If you're gonna keep exceeding my high expectations, I cannot be held responsible for the trouble we're gonna get into."

She sighed, placing her forehead against his. "Is there anything you can't do well?"

"Plenty." His hand grazed over her back, as his other slid along her thigh. "Where's this headed McKenna?" he whispered, tucking his head in to kiss her neck. "Are you sending me down the block, or are we headed down that hallway?"

That had all her faculties coming back online. She sat up straight. "I'm going to get you some dessert. How does ice cream sound?"

He nodded, eyeing her, whispering, "I'm happy to take what I can get."

Friday mid-day, McKenna sent a text to Xander.

Team Henderson has asked me to be Jagger Yates's handler for the parade and other events tomorrow. Give me a good reason to turn them down.

It took two hours and seventeen minutes for him to reply.

I'm working on it.

"Not good enough." McKenna said, turning her phone all the way off because she was so angry. And then, after walking very quickly toward Reds, stopping, and then shifting directions and walking very quickly toward the library, her anger burned into irritation and then simmered into frustration. Finally it just sat in her chest as resolve. She decided the best thing to do was walk home, get in her car, and head toward real solace. Anna Beth Wright.

"What a surprise," Anna Beth said, checking her watch. "It's not cocktail hour yet, although I'm happy to join you with one of my mock-tails whenever you're ready."

"I'm good. Just finished up early and wanted to come see how you were doing."

Anna Beth spun slowly in the center of the foyer, showing off how she'd dressed herself in a new pair of slacks and pretty pale-blue sweater. "Well, check me out. I had my hair done over at the salon today. I actually drove myself over to Biddies for the first time in ages. Why, you would have thought I'd risen from the dead the way everyone stared at me when I walked in."

"No. Seriously?"

"Then they applauded. All of them. And I let them. Wasn't even embarrassed about it," she said as she waved McKenna into the living room and past the grand piano. "I felt rather proud, getting myself up and out of the house today all on my own."

"I'm rather proud of you too," McKenna said, her eyes shining with a few joy-filled tears. "My, we have come a long way."

"We have indeed." Anna Beth took hold of McKenna's hands and shook them both. "And I thank you for sticking by my side."

"No thanks necessary."

The two of them sank into the couch while Anna Beth went on. "I believe I shall actually live to see my firstborn wed." She beamed from ear to ear.

"I believe you will." McKenna beamed back. "How's your energy after the trip to the salon?"

"Pretty good. I mean, once I got there everyone hovered over me, and they did all the work. I just relaxed and read a magazine while I was shampooed, colored, and cut. But it felt good to be out and on my own. I had forgotten what independence felt like. I enjoyed it."

"That is so good," McKenna said.

"It is indeed. So tell me your news. What's up with you and Xander?"

And there was her opening. Her opportunity to explain exactly what was up with her and Xander. She didn't take it, but the long, drawn-out silence that ensued was a telltale sign that not everything was as it may seem.

"He'll come around," Anna Beth said softly.

McKenna looked up from the piece of fuzz she'd been digging at. Of course, the woman who she was so close to had concerns of her own. "You think?"

"I do. Xander's not spoken to me directly, but he called his father a few days back. Although I wasn't privy to the conversation, I will tell you that Maxwell has been in a much better mood since they spoke."

"Is that so?" McKenna's spirits lifted immediately. Mr. Wright made no secret about where he wanted McKenna and Xander's relationship to head.

"It is. So, if you just hang in there, I believe everything between the two of you will sort itself out."

"I've been asked to be Jagger Yates's handler for the parade and festivities tomorrow."

Mrs. Wright's eyes lit up. "Well, that's exciting. Oh, I'm thrilled for you. I've been feeling badly that Xander isn't going to make it. But now, well, you'll have your hands full with your idol."

"I will indeed." McKenna tried not to laugh at the irony.

"He's really quite charming. I can definitely see the appeal."

"So …" she dragged out. "Jagger has also asked me to dinner."

"Oh. For the interview? That's wonderful. What an opportunity for you to get into the head of a man you so admire."

Admire wasn't exactly the way McKenna would describe her feelings for Jagger. A couple weeks ago, she would have classified herself as a maniac fan. Now, she was somewhere between cloud nine and a reality check. Jagger was becoming a slippery, slippery, slope.

"Anna Beth. Jagger asked me out. On a date."

"Oh." Her brows rose. "Oh. I see."

"Ha-hum." The two women nodded at each other. "I tell you this because, well, because I'm human, and Xander isn't coming home for the Daze."

"I understand." Anna Beth nodded her head slowly. "You'd like to go out with Jagger."

"I'd like to feel on firmer footing where Xander is concerned. And, although last Sunday he promised me, ah, well, I'm not sure what he promised me exactly, but you must realize …" she trailed off.

"Realize what?"

"That there's a reason Xander isn't coming home as often as any of us would like." She literally couldn't spell it out any clearer. Not that she didn't own the words, but she didn't have the heart to upset Anna Beth on a day that had been going so well.

Anna Beth patted her hand reassuringly. "I believe when Xander arrives home on Thanksgiving, you'll find your peace. And I want you to trust that."

"You do?"

"I do. Jagger is a lot of excitement, especially for a fan such as yourself. But he's not solid like Xander. He's in town for today and will be gone tomorrow."

"That's true." McKenna smiled a sly smile at Anna Beth. "But you even thought his beard was sexy."

Anna Beth hooted. "Oh dear Lord, I dare say I did. Trust me, his appeal is not lost on my generation."

"No. And he's a really nice guy," McKenna said, sinking back into the cushions and making herself comfortable. "Did I tell you he installed a chandelier for my mother?"

"No—"

And the conversation went on, with McKenna singing Jagger's praises and Anna Beth eagerly hanging on to her every word, just like they'd always done. Just like they were sisters or best friends. She'd left out all the *good stuff* of course. But in truth, when all the Xander drama was said and done, Jagger was going to end up being a friend. At least that's what it felt like. Of course, there would be a few fine memories too. And, for the most part, he wasn't something McKenna wanted to hide from Anna Beth.

"Ma!" The bellow came crashing through the front door, announcing Xavier's arrival. He stomped his big motorcycle boots into the living room wearing a leather jacket and jeans, carrying his helmet in his hands. His hair was messed up good. "Oh, hey."

Xavier stopped dead. Which meant that the leather jacket-and helmet-clad biker behind him ran smack into his back. "Ouch."

"Yeah. Okay. So, McKenna," Xavier stumbled.

Jagger looked around Xavier, loosening his chinstrap. He pulled off his helmet and ran a hand through his hair, breathing quickly. His happy, famous, onstage grin practically busted her heart. "Hey." Then he addressed Anna Beth. "Mrs. Wright. It's good to see you again."

"Ma, you got your hair done," Xavier noticed.

"I did." She touched it with obvious pride.

"Looks good. What's she doing here?"

Anna Beth harrumphed. "Xavier, really. I thought you were getting used to McKenna being around."

"I mean that in more specific terms." He eyed McKenna directly. "Like, literally, *what* are you doing here?"

"I'm catching up with your mother."

"Catching up with her about *what?*" The threat was implied. Xavier, ever protective of his mother, wasn't interested in her being brought into the Xander drama.

"Xavier, please don't be rude. Mr. Yates, would you care to sit down? I'll fetch some sweet tea."

"No, ma'am. I appreciate that, but Candy Apple and I are heading out on a ride."

"Candy Apple?"

"Don't mind him. Ma, if Tweets gets here before I do, put her to work in the kitchen, will ya? And Jagger's gonna stay for dinner. Poor guy's got no one looking out for him, so we're gonna do it. Not like we aren't used to taking in strays," he said, eyeing McKenna pointedly.

"That's a grand idea. Jagger, did you know Xavier plays the piano?"

"None of that, Ma. Just tell Tweets I'll be back."

"You play?" Jagger asked as Xavier herded him back out the door.

"Don't start," Xavier huffed. And then the door slammed shut behind them.

CHAPTER FIFTEEN

It was eight thirty Saturday morning, and the sun shone brightly over the Daze. Jagger had a toothbrush in his mouth and a towel wrapped around his waist when a knock came on the door. Not thinking much about anything, he answered.

"Holy shit." McKenna's expression was priceless.

He grinned, left the door open as he turned around, and headed back into the bathroom to finish brushing. He rinsed his mouth and shouted, "To what do I owe the pleasure?" God, she looks good, he thought. That face of hers does it for me every time. And then he thought about her lips, and then he replayed their kiss, and that just wound him up tighter. And he was already tight enough and sooo glad to be getting a chance to get on stage and play tonight. Tiny crowd, amateur band members, whatever. He needed to burn off energy.

He stuck his head out the bathroom door when he didn't hear a response. The front door was still wide open, and McKenna was nowhere to be seen.

"McKenna?" He went to find her. He didn't have to go far. She was right on the stoop where he left her. "You okay? Come in."

She clapped her open mouth shut and ordered, "Put on some pants."

"Sure. Yeah," he agreed. "Come on in. I'll just be a second." He held himself back from actually doing the fist pump that he was envisioning. Until he got into his room and closed the door. Then he indulged.

McKenna.

First thing in the morning.

This was going to be a great day.

He chose a shirt he'd wear on stage. Slipped on jeans with holes in them because he had a reputation to uphold and he didn't want to let Henderson down by pulling out a pair of khakis. Not that he owned any, but hey—he was going to give Team Henderson the performance they asked for all day long. Then he stuffed what was practically the identical outfit into a duffle bag. He grabbed his phone, his watch, his wallet, and his leather jacket and headed out his bedroom door. He found McKenna in the kitchen making coffee.

"Hey," he said. When she glanced up at him, he noted, "You look pretty." He hadn't planned on those words falling out of his mouth, they just did. And when she did a bashful drop of the chin and blushed, his heart beeped a little.

Although he had to admit, after last night, his feelings upon seeing McKenna were a little conflicted. The Wrights were good people. The best kind of people. Mr. Wright was gruff as hell, but he doted on his wife and he'd molded five hell-raising boys into some form of respectability, so gruff was probably expected.

Anna Beth had fawned over Jagger, mothering him like his own mother would have if he'd unexpectedly slipped home for a night or two.

Xavier and Jaxon gave him shit on top of shit, so basically they treated him like one of the guys. Sadly, after three weeks of being off the tour bus, Jagger missed that kind of camaraderie.

So yeah. He could certainly understand from where McKenna's loyalty to the Wright family came. The house was big and everyone in it—except Mrs. Wright—was loud. There was constant motion, all of them busting on each other. And with Tweets and Jinx joining in for cocktails and dinner, the place was alive. Alive-alive. Like, completely opposite from what McKenna found at home.

"Apparently," McKenna said, "I drew the short straw." But then she grinned and ruined her opening line.

"Did you now?" Jagger leaned a hip against the counter and folded his arms over his chest. He crossed one ankle over the other as he watched the leggy brunette with all those lush curves work his kitchen.

"Yep. It was between tending the Jones's prize-winning pig during their lunch break or babysitting a pampered rock star all day long. Thor won. He got the pig."

"So I'm stuck with a bossy, snarling, she-wolf all day, and Thor gets it easy with a fat, sassy hog?"

"Something like that. How do you like your coffee?"

"Black's good."

She handed him a cup. He watched as she fixed herself one all doctored up with stuff she'd found in his refrigerator and cabinets. "Did I have cream?"

"You had milk. It will do."

"Did I have sugar?"

"You had honey. Again. It'll do."

"How about I buy you a cup of what you'll really like on the way to the parade?"

She jerked her head to the side. "I'm okay. Not used to fancy coffee like you are, no doubt."

He lifted his cup. "Black, remember?"

They both took a sip, eyeing each other. "How was dinner at the Wrights?" McKenna asked.

"Good."

"Good?"

"Yes. Good."

"That's all I get. A good?"

"How about this? You tell me why you *weren't* at dinner at the Wrights' and I'll give you all the details you want to hear."

"You know why I wasn't there."

"I have no clue. All I kept hearing was how often you have dinner at their place. And Mr. Wright couldn't comprehend that you would miss dinner, especially since your *favorite* singer—*his words*— was gracing them with his presence."

"Jagger, I couldn't be there if you were there."

"Why not?"

"Because. We kissed. And I like you. And I would have felt guilty the entire time, which would have led me to act guilty, like probably not even able to make eye contact with you and then … it would have just been obvious."

"You like me?"

She huffed, throwing him a look while setting her stance. The one with her hip jutted out. It was a damn fine stance, especially while wearing those particular jeans.

"Show me your shoes."

"What?"

This totally unnerved her.

"Your shoes. You always wear fancy business-girl shoes."

She lifted the hem of her jeans and displayed a pair of low but sharply heeled shoes. The toes just as pointy as the ones he'd noticed before. But these were fresher, more fun. Blue-and-white pinstriped fabric.

"Are those practical for a parade?"

"I'm riding with you, so I figured I'd be okay. Not sure about tromping around in the old Myers field though, so I brought some flats with me. They're in the car."

He didn't mean to unnerve her by letting his eyes roam from her shoes, up her legs in those mighty-fine jeans, to the heavy leather belt at her hips. She wore an ice-blue long-sleeved T-shirt, tucked into the belt, the color enhancing her eyes. And over that she wore a long, fitted navy cardigan left open. Each piece of her ensemble was understated—except for the shoes—and yet each was fresh and in like-mint condition.

The woman had a style. One that worked for her.

One that worked for him too.

"McKenna, you appear to be a woman who knows who she is and what she wants."

She sipped her coffee. "And?"

He gave her a chin lift. "I want you to want me."

Her immediate grin dissolved into embarrassed laughter, hanging her head so her hair covered her face for a moment. When she looked up at him, her eyes glistened with mirth. "We cannot be obvious," she warned him. "You've met Xander's family. This entire town thinks I'm going to be engaged to Xander. I don't want to embarrass myself or the Wrights today. And I especially don't want Xander rushing in tomorrow because he thinks I can't give him until Thanksgiving to sort things out. I don't want him thinking you're a threat."

"But I am a threat."

"Jagger, you're not. Not really. I mean, if there were no Xander, then yeah, I'd totally be jumping your bones right now. But that would only be temporary."

"Why do you say that?"

"Because you don't *live* here." She said it as if it was the most obvious thing in the world. "You're just holing up here to write songs or get away from Nashville or whatever. But you and I both know you aren't buying this place or planning to set down permanent roots."

"What does that have to do with anything? McKenna, you're a journalist. You can journal shit from anywhere."

"But I *live* here."

"Right. But you don't *have* to live here."

"This is a ridiculous conversation."

"I don't think so."

"Trust me, it is. As fond of you as I usually am, I am committed to Xander and am giving him what he's asked for. Trusting him to come through by Thanksgiving."

"As fond of me as you usually are?"

"Well, you're sort of pissing me off right now, so I clarified."

"Got it. Let's go." Jagger knew when he was spinning his wheels, and this conversation was the epitome of that. "You want a to-go cup?"

"They'll probably have coffee and donuts at the gathering site." She washed out her cup in the sink, then took his from him and did the same.

"I like having you here," he whispered as he moved in close, standing at her back, his chin hovering just above her shoulder.

He could tell she was smiling.

"Maybe after the concert tonight, you and your friends would like to come over. There's a good old-fashioned hole-in-the-ground fire pit in the backyard. I bought marshmallows and graham crackers and chocolate bars and a case of beer at the Gas and Go, just in case. Might be fun."

She nodded her head. "That would be nice of you. Invite some people back after the concert."

"I wanna do my part. Try to fit in."

She turned around to face him and didn't seem to worry about how close he stood. "Jagger. This is really gracious of you. What you're doing today for the Daze. What you've done for Scarlett and the town by recording a song with Cal. There were plenty of bands that said no. Even with Cal Johnson being such a big deal in sports right now. But you and your guys came in and … well, you proved that what I see on stage when you perform is exactly who you are in real life."

"And you like it." He grinned.

"I have liked it since my first Cavaliers concert, and I like it even more today."

"In the spirit of being genuine, I really want to kiss you right now."

She laughed softly, gently pushing at his chest.

He didn't budge.

He slid one hand up into her hair, cupping the side of her head, and pulled her lips to his as easily and deliberately as he knew how. He was giving her a chance to balk or escape or whatever, but she didn't take him up on any of that. She let him lead her to his lips, and she allowed him to coax her into a kiss, and then she participated like Xander Wright didn't exist.

And in that moment, hope was renewed.

"Okay," he said as their lips parted and he looked her over. "That was a good way to start the day. Let's get this show on the road." He turned her toward the door and pushed her gently in front of him, giving her ass a soft pat.

"Okay, so no more of that," McKenna bossed as they stepped outside the door, and he turned to lock up.

"No more of that when the Wrights are around," he clarified.

"No more of that when anyone is around," she ordered as they crossed the lawn to her car. "What the hell?" She stopped and stared at the rusted-out bucket of bolts that may have been a light blue pickup in its former life.

"That was a must-have purchase. The kid next door was selling it."

"And you took one look at the piece of crap and thought, 'I must have that?'"

"Not exactly. The urge to own it was born out of necessity. See, I had ridden my bike to Scarlett's Grand Opening and left it in her back alley because I wanted to get a ride with you."

"Okay–"

"And then, as you know, Brooks dropped me off on his way home. The next morning, I'm stuck out here without my bike. And since y'all are like the only place in the free world that does not have Uber, I had to buy the damn truck so I could pick up my bike."

McKenna burst into laughter. "That only proves one thing."

"What's that?"

"You have more money than sense."

"I don't know. The truck comes in handy."

"How so?"

"Much easier to haul groceries and firewood."

"Well, that's true. How did your bike get to Henderson anyway?"

"I attach it to the back of the tour bus. Sometimes I just need to ride a bit. Get off somewhere by myself."

"I am so the opposite. I go home at the end of the day, and most days I'm alone. I mean, Mom comes in and goes out. Sometimes we enjoy dinner together, most times not. I love her, but she's got a full plate, and I just have my one job. Speaking of, I'll be working today."

"Pinks said you'd be taking pictures and doing interviews for the Monday morning recap."

"People love seeing themselves in the paper," they both said at the same time, ending up eye to eye in a grin fest.

"Do you enjoy the publicity?" she wondered as they both moved to get in her car.

"I don't mind it. We worked so hard for so long to get noticed, it's hard to cry about being recognized now. We are smack dab in the middle of living our dream. We had fun getting here, we are having fun being here, and what comes next is going to be good too. I can't complain."

"So, you'd give me an interview?" She pulled away from the curb and headed toward the high school.

"McKenna. Of course, I'll give you an interview. In fact, I am willing to give you a very in-depth interview. A hard-hitting, deeply *penetrating* interview."

She blinked a few times. Took her gaze off the road a moment to assess him while she was driving. "Are you ... are you like hitting on me?"

"Yep."

She shook her head, smiling. "Jagger. I like kissing you. But kissing you is as far as it's *ever* gonna go. I feel guilty enough already."

"Need I remind you, your boyfriend has another girlfriend."

"Whom he is breaking up with."

"So he says. And until you have confirmation about that, *you* need to consider *me* as *your* other boyfriend. I told you you needed two."

She pulled into a parking spot behind the high school gym. "I have not forgotten those words."

"Good. So, you and the asshole—dating. You and your favorite singer—also dating." Jagger exited the car. Quickly.

"We are not dating," she said as she slammed her door shut and clicked the fob to lock up.

"You just kissed me not ten minutes ago. We're totally dating."

"Oh my God, Jagger."

"And"—he held up a finger—"it is completely guilt-free dating because that asshole—"

"I know, I know. Has another girlfriend. Come on. And enough about all this. From here on out, I'm your handler."

"And I plan to give you something to handle."

She broke into a smile, which grew to a grin. "Stop being so ..."

"So what?" he asked as they began to walk toward a field crowded with marching band members and a number of homemade parade floats.

"So *you*," she sighed as she walked in step with him.

That's when he knew he had her.

CHAPTER SIXTEEN

The Daze lived up to its billing. By the time Jagger hit the stage, everyone between the ages of sixteen and sixty was feeling no pain and eager for a show. Pinks and his buddy the Outlaw did not lag behind. They brought some real talent to the stage and were overly solicitous, allowing Jagger to take the lead and show off.

Which suited him fine. He wanted to show off for McKenna. She'd been happy, generous ... not exactly carefree because—yeah, not her. But she was kind and patient with him and with everyone who approached him all day long. She was an excellent handler.

She made sure he was in that damn dunking machine for thirty minutes and thirty minutes only. Then she took him into the back of Piper's Big Pie Plate tent and let him warm up and change. Even brought him a cup of coffee and a piece of his favorite apple pie. Since they were pretty well hidden from view, he pulled her onto his lap and force-fed her a few bites of pie just because he wanted to.

And she'd allowed him.

The best part of the day had been the selfie booth. McKenna stood with him for close to three hours, taking pictures of him with everyone who asked. She was good about helping with the small talk, giving him a little tidbit on everybody in town. How she knew everyone, he couldn't imagine. Henderson was small, but it wasn't that small. She was a journalist, so he figured part of it was that. But he wondered if her upbringing—being an only child and brought up in a quiet house of two—might have been the catalyst that formed her curiosity about other people's lives.

When he was doing time at Scarlett's booth, explaining that he was not one of the hunks pictured in the calendar, but he'd be happy to sign their copy anyway, McKenna brought him sample after sample of all the treats available at the Daze. Things like corn dogs, fried Oreos, homemade ice cream, pig ears, and a damn good local brew that had yet to be put on the market.

He could see the appeal of the Daze. A chance for the community to come together and play. The old crowd brought lawn chairs and set up in groups around the perimeter. The families with young children laid out picnic blankets where they'd congregate between trips to the makeshift petting zoo, the bouncy house, face painting, or other various attractions.

But it was the twenty to forty-somethings that were having the most fun. If he'd witnessed a happy reunion of old friends once, he witnessed it fifty times. What he'd been told seemed to be true. Everyone came back for the Daze.

Which had Jagger's thoughts turning to McKenna's boyfriend. Xavier's brother. This *Xander* everyone was sweating about. *Why wasn't* he here? He could see why Xander's family was taking it so hard. He now understood McKenna's reaction when she'd heard the news. It was funny, because now Jagger felt like he had a stake in this Xander thing. And not just because he wanted McKenna. He absolutely did want McKenna. But because he was suddenly more aware of the complexities that surrounded all the drama.

And it sort of put the kibosh on his behind-the-scenes seduction of Miss McKenna Blakely. Not that he was stepping back from his pursuit, necessarily. It's just that as he continued to gather more information, he was able to see the entire picture at play.

He kept replaying Xavier's words in his mind. "I will not object to you giving him a run for his money." At the time, he'd taken that for a green light. Presently, he was reevaluating.

Jagger sat at Scarlett's booth, sipping a glass of wine she'd offered him as the sun started to descend. It was that time of day where the light was magical, everything cast in a golden glow. And since the crowds had run themselves out at the various and sundry booths and were looking for food, or bathrooms, or partners in crime, he had a quiet moment to observe McKenna as she tirelessly conducted interviews.

She was a beautiful woman. There was no doubt about that. People were attracted to her, but he realized it wasn't because of her looks. Hell, the locals were probably used to how pretty she was. Not Jagger. She was his kind of pretty in a deep, visceral way, and those glacier-blue eyes of hers hooked him every damn time. But he was coming to understand the beauty beneath those eyes and that face. The bossy woman Xavier carried on about had a softer, gentler side. And he'd seen the evidence of it today and over the last couple of weeks.

McKenna was kind. And she was loyal.

And all of a sudden, Jagger didn't want to mess with that. He didn't want to be the cause of McKenna being less than she was. If she wanted to be loyal to Xander—give him until Thanksgiving to break up with this Becca and show up for real—Jagger wasn't going to interfere.

Well, he was. But less conspicuously.

He leaned back in his chair, sipping his wine, watching McKenna interview a woman whom he assumed was a mom. Because McKenna was stroking a little girl's hair, calming her down while she asked the mother her questions. Then she took her time setting up a picture of mother and daughter, perching them on a grouping of hay bales decorated with pumpkins and gold-and rust-colored mums.

A mother and daughter. Was there more to that family? Was McKenna choosing them because it was just the two of them, kind of like her and her mother Sandy?

It was interesting being the outsider. Interesting to observe interactions between people with a level of detachment because he didn't know them intimately. He hadn't had the opportunity to study *the boyfriend*, but he had spent time with his brother, with his family, with his girl.

And had witnessed the Daze that the boyfriend had missed. He had watched as life in Henderson moved along—including McKenna and the Wrights—without him.

And with all he knew and all he saw, he made a prediction.

One he decided to bet on.

CHAPTER SEVENTEEN

I am so sleeping with Jagger.

That's the thought that went through McKenna's mind while watching the hipster perform on stage. He was so in his element. So much larger than life. So freaking sexy that she could hardly contain the joyous desire bubbling underneath her skin. She shouted and sang and whistled and applauded along with the crowd as she always had whenever she'd seen the Cavaliers play.

This concert was pretty much the highlight of her Cavaliers' concert run. Yeah, the rest of the band wasn't backing him up tonight, the sound quality was just okay, and the stage lighting was nonexistent. Yet their front man did his thing, regardless. Jagger engaged the crowd with his voice, his songs, and his gratitude for their enthusiasm. He was as he had always been when she'd seen him on stage. Simply Jagger. At his best.

Only this time, it was personal. This time, she was screaming for the man, not the rock star. This time, she was more in tune with the hidden talents of the gorgeous hunk who was rocking her world. Because she had come to know the man, Jagger, over the last few weeks. So even though she'd fantasized about sleeping with mythical rock star Jagger Yates while she stood within the embrace of a shouting, dancing, eager crowd, this was the first time that fantasy was an actual possibility.

She was definitely sleeping with Jagger.

Tonight.

While he sang cover songs and his own songs, and did an off-the-charts duet with the Outlaw to a song she'd never even heard before, she came to a decision. If there was no text or voice message from Xander by the end of the concert, she was going to assume their nonexclusive status ruled the day. And she planned to make one fine memory of the man, the myth, and the legend to encapsulate this Cavaliers-crazy time in her life.

She was sooo sleeping with him tonight.

After having made that momentous decision, her nerves, her adrenaline, and her excitement were vibrating just like the strings of his guitar, creating a rhythm and music McKenna could feel down to her soul.

She was amped up good. Eager to touch him. Eager to harness that smile and have it focused solely on her. Once the concert ended at nine thirty, it took forever to get him off the stage and then out from the mob scene that was his new fan club. She prayed for patience as she watched him graciously sign autographs on T-shirts and hats and calendars and Cal's album's artwork. He even signed arms, but thank God, no breasts. Yeesh.

Standing a short distance away from the crowd, McKenna felt the zing of anticipation surge through her veins whenever he shot a smile or a wink in her direction. She passed the time happy, humming the encore tune while contemplating how big a hit Jagger had become with the locals and thinking how much she couldn't wait to surprise him the next time he hit on her.

As the good citizens of Henderson finally dispersed, McKenna and Jagger planned to hitch a ride with Pinks and the Outlaw, the two who now appeared to be Jagger's best buddies. While the men loaded their concert gear into a black Range Rover, McKenna slid into the backseat, moving to the center, so either way he entered, she'd be close to Jagger.

He got in but didn't seem to notice.

Immediately, he sat forward, speaking over the front seats. "How 'bout you two come on over to my place? Make a fire out back and see who can eat the most s'mores. I've got an acoustic guitar. We can keep jamming."

"Can I bring Scarlett?" Pinks asked.

McKenna slid a hand onto Jagger's thigh as he sat back.

"Sure," he said. "Absolutely. Bring whoever you want. In fact, bring Piper," he said, sitting up again causing her hand to fall from his thigh. "Because she'll bring pie. The hell with s'mores, I want pie."

McKenna rolled her eyes.

"Piper's headed home to her baby, VJ. Probably can't get her to come out," Pinks told him. "But I can call Lolly and Brooks, get them to grab any leftover pie."

"There aren't any leftovers," McKenna interjected. "She and Genevra barely made it through the afternoon."

"Damn," Jagger said, sitting back once again, hip to hip with McKenna and throwing his arm over the top of the seat behind her. "Not surprised, but I've still got a craving. That stuff is like a drug. One bite and you're hooked. You getting her hooked up with shipping?" he asked Pinks.

McKenna leaned her weight against Jagger, hoping he'd take the hint and drop his arm down around her shoulders.

"I'm on it."

"Good. Good. I'm gonna need a way to get my fix when I'm back on the road. But for tonight"—he pulled his arm back down and clasped his hands in his lap—"I guess s'mores will have to do." Then he started using his hands as he spoke, causing his elbow to poke McKenna. "Jesse, you got a girl you want to bring?"

"I have a girl. But she's not here," the Outlaw grumbled.

"Jesse's madly in love with his girl," Pinks provided. "But he doesn't let her come to Henderson. She doesn't even know *he's* here."

"What? Why?" Jagger inquired.

"Because she worries, and I don't want her to worry," Jesse proclaimed.

"She worries about what?"

"About women throwing their panties up on stage." Jesse James turned around, looked over the backseat, and flailed a finger. "That happened one time. One time, and now she flips out every time I play."

"So where does she think you are?"

"Lacrosse tournament." Jesse plopped himself back around facing front.

Jagger looked at McKenna, who shrugged.

"But yeah, let's keep this buzz going," Jesse continued. "Pinks and I've had good crowds before, but nothing like the energy we saw tonight. I've never given much thought to making a career out of music but, I can tell you, tonight has opened my eyes."

"It's like Piper's pie," Jagger acknowledged, rocking a little. "Addictive."

When they reached the high school, Pinks asked if it was okay to invite some of the others to Jagger's place. Jagger said, "Whoever," then jumped out to retrieve his guitar and amplifier from the back of the SUV, leaving McKenna to exit the vehicle on her own.

As McKenna drove them back to Jagger's place, they had no idea who might drop by. But it didn't matter. They were both riding the high, reliving individual moments from the concert. When they arrived, McKenna shut off the car and turned to Jagger. His chocolate eyes met hers over the dashboard light, and she licked her lips, dipping her gaze for a moment to collect her thoughts. "You were … breathtaking," she told him, finally settling on the word. "On stage. Your showmanship. Your energy. There was no difference between what you gave Henderson tonight and what you give a full arena when you're actually being paid."

He gave her his sexy half smile while his gaze wandered her face. "A stage is a stage, McKenna," he said softly. "I do what I do whenever I have the opportunity to get on one."

"So you enjoy the limelight. Being front and center."

"I love it. The Outlaw is not wrong. Enthusiastic crowds are addictive. And trust me. I've spent a lot of time playing in front of unenthusiastic crowds. So I don't take one person who stuck around tonight for granted. If someone shows up, I'm going to give them my best. I don't have a second speed when it comes to showmanship. Except back when I busted my knee. Then I was forced to slow down."

"You got such crap on social media when you rescheduled that concert in Iowa."

"Hated to let the fans down, but for the show to go on, I needed surgery."

She glanced down at his knee. The one that stuck out of the stellar rip in his jeans. "Seems it's healed up pretty good."

"Good as new."

The air around them became quiet then, their vibrational energy simmering down from a boil. She wanted him to lean in and kiss her. She wanted him to pull her into his lap so they could make out until they had to stop. When the quiet stretched out, becoming just a smidge uncomfortable, she asked, "You got everything we need? Want me to run home and get more beer or anything?"

"Nah." He pulled back and went for the door handle, popping it open and moving out. "We'll be good. I'm guessing Pinks isn't going tell the general population where the after party is."

"No," she agreed, taking her time to exit while he pulled his equipment from the back. "I'll meet you around back. See what it's going to take for the two of us to get a fire started."

It took some work, some newspaper, and some kindling, but the come-sit-by-me fire beckoned when Pinks, Scarlett, and the Outlaw arrived with Scarlett's sister Tansy and her husband Crain Carraway in tow. Jagger hadn't had the pleasure of meeting the C.C. of C.C. Henderson, but he seemed to be taken with the guy immediately.

When Xavier and Laidey showed up, the entire group regaled Jagger with the story about how Laidey had come to town with the C.C. Henderson group from Dallas. A half hour after that, when Jaxon and Jinx came around the house to find them all in lawn chairs, the story of Jinx's ultra-secret ties to Henderson were once again revealed. And by the first strum of Jagger's guitar, Missy and Thor arrived, after having put the Daze's cleanup crew through their paces.

"Had to get the whip out on some of those football players," Thor said. "Lazy bunch of pip-squeaks. Not a damn one of them would have made it through thirty minutes of Ranger training."

"I don't know a soul who could," Jagger told him.

McKenna was at Jagger's side when he greeted his guests, whispering their names and reminding him who was who. She brought out the s'mores fixings they'd arranged on a tray they'd found after stumbling over each other and opening every one of the kitchen cabinets. Somehow, he was never more than an arm's length away. And while he made a point to continually catch her eye, she counterpointed by brushing the exposed part of his arm lightly with her fingertips whenever she needed his attention. Likewise, she made a point to touch him whenever she had to move past or when she offered him a beer or when she decided to head inside for a trash can and paper towels. Jagger was so busy being chatted up by everyone, she was happy to play hostess.

It wasn't like she darted for the lawn chair next to Jagger's when the music started to play, but inside her mind she was daring Scarlett or Tansy or even her BFF Laidey to take that seat. She wasn't sure how she would have handled it, but the way she was feeling right now—possessive and turned-on—there was no doubt it would have been handled.

"All right," Jagger said, stopping the hum of his strings with a slap of a hand to his guitar. "Who, besides my man Jesse over here, can sing?"

"Sing like we're on stage or sing around a campfire?" Scarlett clarified. "Because I can sing with a group, but no one wants to hear me do karaoke or anything of the like."

"How 'bout you?" he asked McKenna, giving her his half stage grin that felt so intimate she had trouble finding her voice.

"No." She shook her head vehemently. "I cannot carry a tune. I mean, I love to sing, but I'm with Scarlett, not on my own."

"All right. Campfire tunes it is. Any requests?"

Pinks suggested an old Fleetwood Mac song that had withstood the test of time. Maybe not so much their group's pitiful rendition of it, but the song was a pretty one, fun to sing and somehow, they all knew the words.

And then the night spiraled on from there. Lots of singing. Lots of jokes. A few good ol' Henderson stories tossed in to delight Jagger and Crain and Jinx and Laidey alike.

"So all y'all weren't born around here," Jagger surmised, scanning the circle.

"No," Pinks said, looking around the group. "In fact, we're about half and half. Missy and I are from Baltimore. Laidey and Crain are from Dallas. Jinx is from Richmond. Ahh, just Scarlett, Tansy, Lolly, Brooks, Xavier, and Jaxon are from Henderson."

"So basically, I fit right in," Jagger said, making McKenna smile.

He didn't fit in. He stood out. Just as Crain and Pinks had when they'd first arrived. And it would have been a mistake to think Jagger was going to be seduced by Team Henderson or even lend his name and a monetary investment to a music shop in town. McKenna knew this, and still she was allowing him to seduce her with his guitar and his voice and his cute grin and his happy manner.

He was the outsider, but he ran this show just as he had the one he'd put on onstage. He couldn't help it. Put a guitar in his hand, and that's who he was.

A star.

A beautiful, masculine, high-energy, take-no-prisoners rock star. And didn't McKenna feel like she was falling just a little in love with her heartthrob.

The night wore on even as it turned chilly. She and Laidey headed inside in search of blankets to keep the fireside party going.

"He's amazing," Laidey whispered as they gathered several throw blankets from a linen closet. "What are you going to do?"

"What do you mean?" were the words she spoke. Inside her head, McKenna thought, *I am going to sleep with him, and I'm determined not to regret it.*

"He's completely into you. He hasn't made a secret of it since that first day at Reds. What are you going to do?"

McKenna blinked at Laidey, not sure how to answer. "I'm … going to enjoy being his friend."

Laidey nodded.

"That okay with you?" McKenna snapped.

"Yes. Absolutely. I just, I mean, if I were standing in your shoes, knowing what I know now about Xander's life in Charlotte, I might … want to … *experience* more of Jagger Yates."

McKenna laughed. "You are reading me like a book. Am I that obvious?"

"*He's* that obvious. He *sings* to you."

He did. He definitely did. "I know," McKenna whispered as they herded the blankets outdoors. "And I can't help but eat it up with a spoon."

"Xander doesn't sing to you," Laidey said.

"Nope. Xander does not sing to me." With that, they separated, dispersing blankets to those around the fire.

An hour went by, then two. The last beer was gone. The s'mores fixings tray was close to empty, and the Daze had finally taken its toll on everyone, made clear by the yawns that were being performed. When the party broke up, it broke up all at once. Lots of bro hugs and back slaps, all the girls hugging Jagger, and plenty of help getting the trash and blankets back inside.

And then … it was just the two of them.

McKenna stood beside Jagger inside the door they'd just closed on his departing guests. "That was fun," she said. "Everyone appreciated you doing that. I think they liked having the chance to get to know you better."

"Likewise," he said quietly, his gaze zeroing in on her lips.

This is it, she thought. This is when he's going to pull out his *Moves Like Jagger* and seduce me into staying the night. And won't he be surprised when I let him.

"I know we're becoming … friends," McKenna said. "But when it comes to you, there is always going to be a fangirl side of me. And that side wants to make sure you know that you made all her dreams come true tonight."

"All?" Yep. There it was, that part happy, part super sexy stage grin.

"Well, just about all," she whispered, purposefully eyeing his lips.

With one hand on the wall next to her, Jagger Yates, lead singer of the Cavaliers and personal heartthrob of McKenna Blakely, leaned in and gave her a good night kiss.

She knew it was a good night kiss because even though it was delicious and heartfelt, it lacked the emotional intimacy his kisses normally conveyed. There was no yearning, no hunger. And if that wasn't enough to clue her in, when their lips parted and his head moved back from hers, he said, "Good night, McKenna."

Ahh—yes, yes, but nooo.

"Good night?" she questioned.

He nodded, lifting himself from his sexy lean-in and straightening. "Come on. I'll walk you out."

"Walk me out?" Like she was a discarded contestant on The Bachelor?

Jagger opened the door and took hold of her elbow.

"You're walking me to my car?"

"Yes. Of course. I'm not a Neanderthal."

"No. I mean. You're walking me to my car, now?"

He blinked like he wasn't tracking. "You want to stay?" he asked. "You want a nightcap? Or want to watch something on TV? It's late, but if you want to stay, I'm up for whatever."

A nightcap? TV? Where the hell was the Holy Grail of Seduction when she needed him? McKenna was so doused in a fog of wonder that she turned and headed out the door. She noted that Jagger followed along with his hands in his pockets, leaving the front door cracked. *WTF?*

"Thanks for everything today. I couldn't have done it without you," he said.

"Sure, you could have." It came out snippy. Very snippy. It came out like a woman who thought she had a sure thing locked up and yet was coming out empty-handed.

"No. You're amazing. The way you knew everybody by name. The way you managed things when crowds began to congregate." He took hold of her arm and pulled her to a stop. "Look at me."

She gave him her eyes.

"You know I was a fan of yours already. A big fan. But after today—hell after these past few weeks—I want to put a poster of *you* on *my* bedroom wall."

That had her smiling, sighing, but still feeling defeated. After all they'd been through together, she decided to simply put it out there.

"Jagger, if you'd asked me to spend the night, I would have said yes."

He stood up a little straighter, stepped in a little closer, his hand still on her arm. "Nothing I'd rather do," he said solemnly. "My feelings haven't changed. I just … well, I see the big picture."

"The big picture?"

"Yes. Your big picture."

"*My* big picture."

"Right. And I understand it has to play out."

"What? What has to play out?"

"You and the boyfriend. It has to play out."

"Jagger." His name came out sounding like she was exhausted. "Xander will be home in a week and a half. If there is going to be a you and a me, this ... *tonight* is our moment."

"I don't think so."

"I'm telling you, it is."

She felt herself deflate. Jagger Yates was turning her down. After all the pursuing he'd done, she'd finally come around, only to be reduced to throwing herself at him—literally becoming the groupie she'd never wanted to be.

She spun and stomped off toward her car.

"McKenna," he called.

She kept stomping.

"McKenna," he said as he caught up to her and gripped her upper arm, halting her abruptly and spinning her around. "I want you," he said, panting. "You know I want you. Fuck," he swore before pulling her against his chest and wrapping her up in his arms. His lips gave her everything she asked for this time. His kiss was full of want and desire. He groaned when their tongues met, and his hands came up into her hair, turning her head the way he preferred. "I want you," he repeated. "Right here." His lips melded over hers. "In my bed." His tongue demonstrated what he had planned. "On the trunk of your car." One arm reached down and cupped her ass, pulling her tightly against his firm—very firm—rock-star package. "I want you, and I don't want you to doubt it. I said I'm not going anywhere, and I meant it. I've stated my desires plainly and more than once." He pulled back, a hand still clasping her head, the other firmly gripping her hip. "Break up with him."

"Jagger," she whispered because her brain was still lollygagging on the trunk-of-your-car part.

"Break up with him. There's no doubt in my mind that you and I would burn up the damn sheets, and God knows that's where I want tonight to head. But I can't stop the sun from rising tomorrow, and if I've learned anything about you, I'm guessing sleeping with me will not make you feel better about the boyfriend. Because I realize I was wrong. You don't need two boyfriends. You're a one-man woman. I want to be that man. So either dial him up right now and settle all that or get in your car and go home."

When she stood there, startled and paralyzed, he moved back in and clasped her face between both his hands. After he kissed her soundly, he said, "I'll see you tomorrow." He turned and left her thoroughly …

Dazed.

CHAPTER EIGHTEEN

McKenna was infuriated. With Jagger. With herself. With Xander most of all.

She spent most of the week writing and posting snippets and pictures from the Daze on the newspaper's website while writing more in-depth articles for the physical paper. She wrote a couple of book reviews, headed to Raleigh to cover the opening of a fancy new design center, interviewed Lolly DuVal and Annabelle Devine *James* (James since she'd recently been married) about the upcoming debutante season and the dresses they were selling. As a follow-up to that interview, she tracked down Missy McReady in an effort to wheedle out some newsy tidbits concerning the upcoming debutante parties Missy had been hired to plan. That woman was as tight as a tick. However, Missy did give McKenna some fabulous teasers for the society section, which she greatly appreciated.

McKenna always held off publishing anything about Laidey and Xavier's wedding plans because that just hit too close to home. She never wanted her nearest and dearest to feel like she was using them for a story. However, when it came to Henderson's hard news columns, she treated them as she would any other citizen of the county. So when Laidey had a sound bite about the coming sports academy, or Xavier was hired for a new construction project, their names landed in the paper.

But this week, the more she worked on her news stories, the more she considered doing a true interview with Jagger. She sporadically jotted down the questions she'd like to ask him. As an overzealous fan, she'd already heard most of the interviews he'd done (thank you, YouTube) and most of the questions put to him were redundant.

How are things different now that you've hit it big?

What was the moment you knew you'd finally arrived?

Blah, blah, blah.

But now she found herself caught between journalist and friend. She'd obviously learned much more about him in the past few weeks than she had through all those interviews. If she wrote about him, it would feel the same as if she were squealing on Laidey and Xavier.

Maybe her focus needed to be on the band, not the front man. And that thought had her grimacing.

Easier said than done.

What she really should be focusing on was Xander Wright and the fact that Thanksgiving was now mere days away. *Finally.* Although … like, wow. What to think about all that? What to think about his two a.m. phone call that went to voicemail the night of the Daze.

Xander had been a little drunk. Like, cute-boy tipsy. He'd sounded a little homesick, a little nostalgic now that he'd missed the Daze. He wanted to know how it went. Who she saw. What she did. And if Jagger Yates had swept her off her feet and the two of them had run off together before he had a chance to get home and make things right.

"Almost, Xander. Almost," she had said aloud after hearing his message the next morning.

And then the regret set in. And the guilt.

The tricky thing was she just couldn't figure out exactly what she regretted and what she felt guilty about it. Jagger was stirring things up in her that felt important to pay attention to. Something completely different than the desperation she'd been experiencing throughout her relationship with Xander.

With Jagger, *man,* things were so easy.

With Xander, everything felt so ill at ease. They were still lying to his parents. There was still no concrete evidence he'd dumped Becca. And with the words *make it official* running through her head every time she thought about Xander and Thanksgiving, she felt confused and disjointed and frankly like she was running in circles.

So she called him. Xander. And within minutes slid right into the understanding, nonthreatening, easy-going girlfriend she'd always been but never really felt on the inside.

Although, Xander—surprisingly out of character—followed their call up with a sexy text, a sweet phone call the next day, and then a string of texts indicating his desire to move forward—to come home and be with her and his family without the cloud of secrecy surrounding them. He indicated that he was eager to be free from the situation, and he—more than once—offered his gratitude for McKenna's patience and perseverance and affection, allowing him to sort things out within his own time frame.

His texts were extremely encouraging. Heartfelt. Humble and funny, even. The old Xander shining through. Not the stressed out, double dating, workaholic Xander of the past few months, but the true Xander. The one she'd fallen in love with.

When his beautiful floral centerpiece was delivered addressed to *The Blakely Ladies*, McKenna was all-in. As she admired the beautiful and unique fall-colored roses, she let out a long, grateful sigh of happiness.

Xander Wright was finally coming home to her.

That didn't mean that Jagger Yates wasn't still part of her life. Her fangirl side was alive and well, responding to his texts immediately. Meeting him for a quick cup of coffee during her lunch break where the two of them stuck their noses up against Henderson's Big Pie Plate Shop and Bakery, watching as the finishing touches were applied to the interior.

"Are they really going to do an internet cooking show?" Jagger asked as they peered around the workmen, trying to imagine pies being created on the massive, marble countertop.

"From the looks of all those cameras, I guess they are." McKenna pointed out the cameras hooked up all over the place.

"Makes me think about writing a song about pie, just so we can have a video done in there. You think Piper would want to be in it? We could make sure to promote the Henderson Pie Plate throughout."

"You want to write a song … about pie?"

He shrugged. "Damn good pie. Totally songworthy."

"Hmm. Well, you're not wrong about that. I just … can't see it."

"That's because we aren't indulging in her pie right now. If we were, the lyrics and melody would spring forth around the excitement of your taste buds."

McKenna laughed at him.

"What? There are a zillion country songs written about beer. Why not pie? It would probably go something like … you can have my girl, you can have my truck, but keep your damn hands off my slice of Piper's pie."

Laughing, McKenna said, "If you can write a song—a good song—about pie and make your video right here? There is nothing this town would not do for you. Or, shall I say, nothing the Evanses wouldn't do for you."

"What about you?" he asked, moving in and lowering his sexy voice. His hands landed gently on her waist. "What would you do for me if I wrote a good song about pie and that big-ass pie plate?"

"I'd buy it, stream it, play it over and over again," she said lightly, as if he hadn't just propositioned her. "I'd even write about it. In the paper."

"Hmm. I was thinking of a little more … personal appreciation for my efforts."

"Well … all right." McKenna pretended to think. "I know. I'd bring you one of Piper's apple pies. That's the one you practically had an orgasm over, isn't it?"

He stepped even closer, running a slow fingertip down her arm. "I was thinking about an entirely different type of orgasm."

"Sorry," she said blithely. "You had your chance."

"But I'm going to write a song about pie," he reiterated in a deeper, even sexier voice.

"And Xander is coming home next week." She took a step back.

"And how is the boyfriend and, ah, what's her name—oh, Becca. How are those two?" He leaned in from his hips as if he were seriously curious.

"Xander is just fine," she said pointedly. "*Xander* is very sorry he missed the Daze and is looking forward to coming home and putting the whole secrecy thing behind him."

"Is that so?"

"Practically verbatim."

"Huh."

"Huh, what?"

"Nothing. Just huh."

"Jagger."

"Look," he said, holding up his hands. "I'm not trying to cause trouble. Well, I absolutely am, but the situation is what it is. Considering that I actually *like* the Wrights—except for this *Xander*—I'm just curious how this is all going to play out."

"I am too," she told him plainly as they resumed their stroll. "I mean, he's been far more attentive since the Daze. Phone calls, texts, all about coming home, looking forward to Thanksgiving, etc., etc." She stopped and turned to Jagger. "Are you okay with me talking about this?"

Jagger stuck his hands in his jeans pockets and looked to the sky as he sucked in a deep breath. "Am I okay with you sporting a goofy grin while going on and on about the boyfriend with whom I told you to break up?" He lowered his gaze to hers. "I told you. It is what it is. I'm resigned to watch it play out."

"What does that mean?"

"It means, *no,* I don't want to hear about him. And *yes,* maybe you haven't asked, but yes, I'm kicking my own ass about not pulling you into my bed the other night instead of playing the goddamn hero. Hero? Check that—nice guy. You know what? Check that as well. *Sucker.* That's what I was. Nice guys finish last, so that makes me a sucker. I don't know what the hell I was thinking."

McKenna burst into giggles because in that moment, Jagger was everything any girl could ask for. She wanted to jump all over him. Cover his face in kisses and run her fingers through that beard. He was so deliciously good for her ego she wanted to jump with the joy of it. "Ahhh," she sighed coming down from her high, feeling the wide smile that split her face, knowing the smile he'd mentioned as she talked about Xander was no match for this gleeful Jagger-smile she sported now. "I wish I were single." Because the Jagger Yates carnival ride might be a short, fast twirl, but there was no doubt it would be a fun one.

"I wish you were too," he said, reflecting her smile back at her.

"Jagger Yates, you're a good sport."

"Ugh. Stop. That's just another synonym for sucker."

They began strolling back to McKenna's office.

"It's better this way," she tried to convince him. "You and I as friends. It'll last longer. Along with the whole rock star/crazed fangirl thing we've got going."

He was silent for a bit.

"You okay?" she asked.

"Not really, no," he admitted. "Got more than a little regret hanging over me at the moment. I like your company, McKenna. A lot. We've got more going on than friends here. Much more than the fangirl thing."

She didn't disagree. Couldn't disagree. But couldn't let herself think too deeply on it.

"May I take you out to dinner?" Jagger halted their forward progress. "We can head to, I don't know, somewhere out of town. Tonight?"

She stared into the face that always made her feel happy—even before she'd come to know the man behind it. Friends had dinner together. It wasn't an odd request. They'd shared meals and more since he'd been in town. But Xander's homecoming was only days away, and somehow she felt as if this … dinner would open the door to more intimacy than sleeping with Jagger after the Daze would have.

She needed to turn him down, although she experienced an intense internal struggle to actually do it. "It would be too dangerous," she whispered.

"For whom?"

"Xander."

"So that's where your loyalty lies? With the guy who's been two-timing you."

She flinched at that.

"I'm sorry," Jagger said, stepping back and giving her space as he kept moving away from her. "Still." He pointed to himself. "Not going anywhere."

McKenna watched as he shot her his patent stage grin and then turned and strolled away with every bit of swagger he had. And he had it in spades.

"Damn," she whispered, regretting so very much about all of this. If he'd told her once, he'd told her a thousand times he wasn't going anywhere.

It was just a shame she didn't believe him.

CHAPTER NINETEEN

Turns out, Jagger could write a hell of a song about pie. A little country, a little hip-hop, a kickass chorus that everybody was gonna wanna sing to. Don't tell him he couldn't write about pie. He was totally nailing a song about pie.

And don't tell him he and McKenna were just friends. He was so damn deep in that woman he saw no way out. He wasn't sure how he was going to pry her away from dickhead Xander, but he was sure as hell going to do it. How could he not? For him, there was only McKenna. As was indicated by the three other songs he presently had in the works. One about unrequited love. One about a broken heart. One about singing around a damn campfire like he was a fucking Girl Scout. McKenna was hot and sassy and loyal to her goddamn boyfriend, who was cheating right in front of her.

Yeah, he got the whole Wright family thing. She didn't come from much. Much money, much family, much action. And Xander sure brought all that to the table. And not once had Jagger spent time at the Wright's with Xavier where he hadn't heard the words *the daughter we never had* when the Mr. or Mrs. referred to McKenna.

Yeah. He got it.

He just couldn't live with it.

He couldn't get her to go out with him either, try and try as he might.

So now he had a new plan. One he just hatched up as he waltzed out his front door and headed to his godawful truck. Since McKenna was the daughter the Wrights never had, he was going to become the son that Sandy Blakely needed.

By the time McKenna came home from work, he was halfway through that old shed, dragging out everything from old mattresses to boxes on top of boxes of new light fixtures, faucets, knobs for cabinets and drawers, and an endless array of stockpiled household accoutrement that had yet to be installed. If he wanted to find a way to make himself useful to the women inside that house, he'd just uncovered a gold mine.

"What are you doing?" McKenna called from the kitchen slider.

"What are y'all doing?" he called back. "From the looks of things, you've got a brand new house hanging out in bits and pieces out here."

"What are you talking about?" McKenna came out from the slider and closed it, wrapping her arms around herself against the cool autumn air. She strolled toward him, dragging her hair out of her eyes and from between her lips as it swirled around her. It was beautiful stuff, her hair. A deep, dark chestnut color, cut long in the back, tapered in the front, curling just a bit at all the ends, giving it a bouncy quality. He'd had many a fantasy involving that hair. Most of them had his hands locked up in it, gripping tight. Like really tight, because apparently he was a dirty bastard who hadn't been aware of what the hell kind of depravity he was capable of.

That or he was simply horny as all get out.

Because ... yeah, McKenna.

"Jagger?"

"Yeah, right," he said coming back online. "You look good. What's up?"

"I look good?"

"Yeah. You look good."

McKenna glanced down at her standard working-girl trousers and shoes.

"I mean, you look pretty," he stumbled. "Your hair. Your eyes. The color of your eyes always gets me."

She grinned. "The color of your eyes gets me too."

Jagger's brows came together as he screwed up his lips. "My eyes are brown. Like, just dark brown. They aren't ice-flow blue."

"Ice-flow blue?"

"Yeah. You know. That crazy blue color of the ice up in the Arctic."

"You've seen ice in the Arctic."

"Damn straight. I've even had a drink made with Arctic ice."

"That's pretty cool."

"Definitely was. You ever been to Alaska? Seen an iceberg?"

"I have not."

"Well, they are mesmerizing. Just like your eyes."

"Jagger," she breathed with a half laugh, half sputter. "I'm sooo going to miss you when you're gone," she sighed.

"Baby," he whispered, stepping in closer. "I keep telling you, I'm not going anywhere."

"But you will," she whispered back, her face lifted toward his.

"Not today. Not tomorrow. How am I gonna go anywhere when it feels so good right here, looking at you?"

He watched her throat as she swallowed. "You just called me, baby."

He nodded. "Felt right."

She nodded, then dipped her head and took a step back.

He could have kissed her. He could have taken advantage of that moment. Lord knew he wanted to kiss the memory of the boyfriend out of her head once and for all. But he'd started on another path, and it felt right, too, at least for the moment, even if his filthy-dirty mind was begging for something entirely different.

"How was work?" he asked. He was honestly interested. He'd been reading her articles, as diverse as they were. Which brought up another fantasy of his. Reading a review of a Cavaliers' concert from her perspective.

"Work was a stretch."

"In what way?"

"Not much going on in town since everyone is focused on next week's Thanksgiving preparations."

"What about the pie shop opening?"

"It's been pushed back."

Jagger's lungs seized. "Oh my God, why?"

McKenna threw him an incredulous smile. "You are seriously addicted, aren't you?"

"Who isn't? Please tell me it won't be long before I can get a daily dose of pie."

"Minor glitches with the operation of some of the cameras. A couple of setbacks with cookware and ingredients arriving. Piper and Genevra want everything just-so when they open their doors. You'll hear about it. I know they'd like to be up and running for the Christmas season." She leaned to the right and made a grand show of glancing around him. "And you're here looking for ... treasure?"

"And I've found plenty." He stepped back to show off his wares. "I'm getting the feeling your mom finds a deal and drags it home. Not so big on the follow-through though."

"Hmm." McKenna glanced over the boxes. "No truer words," she sighed. "Once those boxes started taking over the living room, I was the one who dragged them all out here and shoved them in the shed. I guess we both forgot about them after that."

"Seems like decent stuff. You want me to install some of this?"

"Oh, no. Jagger, please no." She rubbed her head as she looked around at all he'd pulled out and then walked over to duck her head inside the half-empty shed. "Lord, what a mess."

"My mess. Not your mess." He took her by the shoulders and turned her around to face him. "Let's leave this and go out to dinner. I heard from Xavier that the Tavern has a great burger. I'm in the mood for a great burger."

What he was in the mood for was a great lay. And putting his hands on McKenna was just jacking that shit up.

"Well, you're in luck."

Good. He wanted to get lucky.

"I'm making burgers for dinner tonight, and you are welcome to join us." Then she glanced around him. "As long as you clean up this mess so the neighbors don't rant."

"I'm going to toss all the crap that's going to the dump into the back of my piece-of-shit pickup. Then I'm going to bring in all those unopened boxes and pile them up inside the kitchen so while I eat your burgers, your mother can tell me what she wants to go where. And then after dinner, I'll make a plan to get started."

"Jagger."

"McKenna."

She sighed and looked away briefly, bringing her gaze back to him as she spoke. "It feels like you might be trying to ingratiate yourself into my mother's affections."

"Hmm."

"Hmm?"

"Well, yeah. Sure. Maybe. But I've got nothing to do but write songs, and cleaning out this pitiful shed has conjured up a song idea." He started twirling a finger beside his forehead. "'This Old Shed.' About the stirred-up memories each unearthed item evokes."

McKenna thought for a moment, her head tilted in speculation as she stared at the shed. "It could work."

"Right?"

"And I'm thrilled to have had a hand in the inspiration, but it certainly doesn't mean you have to actually clean the thing out."

"McKenna. Out of the last twenty songs I've written, the song you've had the least influence over is 'This Old Shed.'"

She blinked a couple times.

"Yeah," he grumbled, stepping by her to get back to work. "The song whose working title is 'I Hate Her Boyfriend' is number one in that category." She laughed like he was trying to be funny. Whatever. "What time is dinner? I do want to make one trip to the dump."

"Fine," she said, all disgruntled like. "I'll go change my clothes and help."

"Did I ask for help? This is *my* job. You offered to make dinner, so that's your job. And, speaking of jobs," he stated firmly as he turned to confront her, "you did not write one word about the Outlaw, Pinks, or me in the entirety of your Daze reflections. What's up with that?"

"I … I …"

"You, you, what?" He stomped back toward her.

"I have no rational perspective," she argued. "I have no journalistic focus when it comes to you. I can't write about Jagger Yates or the Cavaliers without gushing all over the place."

"And what's wrong with that? You afraid the boyfriend might see it? Get upset?"

"I hadn't even thought about that. I mean, I tried Jagger. I really tried. But I'm so personally tied up in your Henderson story I can't be objective. So tied up in my own Jagger Yates story. Please, don't take offense. You know how highly I think of your music. How highly I think of you."

He softened his tone, coming up close and gifting himself with permission to touch her cheek. "Yes, but I was looking forward to seeing it in print. Something I could cut out of the paper and stick in my wallet. Carry with me."

"Oh." She seemed genuinely taken aback.

He dropped his hand. "What time should I be back for dinner?"

"I'll hold off tossing the salad and putting the burgers on the grill until you get back. Take your time. I'll make sure Mom's here at dinner so she can talk to you about those boxes."

"That'd be great. Thanks." He turned and pulled his work gloves on.

"I still think you're gonna need a hand getting all that stuff to the dump."

"Got one coming."

"Who?"

"Who else?" the boisterous greeting came. The two of them turned their heads as Xavier marched toward them from the side of the house. "Who else is gonna bail either one of you out of a tough spot? Me, that's who."

"You?" McKenna scoffed.

McKenna and Xavier's relationship was more like oil and water than any other Jagger had observed. And yet, they tolerated each other far better than most.

"Yes, me. Of course, me. Your problem is always my problem. Isn't that the way we work?"

"I think you mean you are the cause of all my problems."

"Don't get me started," Xavier shot back.

"Don't get *me* started," McKenna snipped. "Whatever. You two, don't throw out anything that looks important. But get all this in the truck quick before Mom gets home. Lord knows she'll want to go through every inch of it."

"We're on it," Jagger soothed. "She's not going to miss anything that's tossed. Believe me."

"All right. And thank you. Thank you both." She twirled and left the two of them to it.

"So," Xavier said as they lifted the first of two full-sized mattresses and carried it to Jagger's truck. "You get in McKenna's pants?"

Jagger snorted, holding the mattress in one arm while he opened the tailgate of his truck with the other. "Do I look like I'm a happy man?"

"Hard to tell with you." They shoved the thing in so it stood up on its side against the side of the bed. "Can't figure why you'd be playin' *1-800-Got-Junk* for her ma if you ain't getting any."

"Because what the hell else am I gonna do?" Jagger asked as they headed back for the second mattress. "I can only sit around strumming my damn guitar so many hours a day. And I guess I could clean out *your* ma's shed, but since she's got five strapping boys and McKenna and Sandy have nobody I figured this was a good plan."

"A good plan if you want in McKenna's pants," Xavier huffed.

After they shoved the second mattress against the first, Jagger turned toward Xavier. "I have been completely upfront with you about my intentions toward McKenna. Don't go getting on your brother's high horse and taking aim at me now."

"Yeah well, McKenna and my relationship is complicated. I mean, we dated in high school, which was total bullshit because the only reason I asked her out was to get back at my twin. And now that she's dating said twin, I'm feeling guilty because I loused it up for the two of them up way back when. Only he's clearly not rising to the occasion." He paused, his already pained expression becoming even more intense. "On top of that, somehow I have befriended his rival—you—and, get this. Ma, who has no idea the extent to which you have designs on McKenna, wants me to ask you to join us—and when I say us, I mean Xander, McKenna, and the rest of our family—for Thanksgiving dinner."

Jagger just chuckled and headed back to the shed. "You tell your ma I appreciate the invite."

"Nope. No. She's like a dog with a bone when she gets something in her head. And it would make her happy if you'd be there. I get you may not enjoy the romantic reunion between McKenna and my brother, but what else are you going to do?"

"I'm going to enjoy a very good bottle of wine and the fully-cooked turkey my mom's promised to send."

"I think you should come." Xavier gathered more junk into his arms than Jagger would think to try to haul at one time. Jagger grabbed three ancient paint cans in both hands just to keep up with him.

"I think you're crazy."

"No, I'm not," Xavier stated. "Seriously. Listen to my rationale."

After they dumped their wares into the truck, Jagger turned to Xavier stabilizing himself with a hand on the tailgate. Not because he wasn't interested in hearing what Xavier had to say, but because he suddenly found himself emotionally weary.

"I think you *should* be at our house on Thanksgiving. You're from out of town and without family this year. You and I are friends. My parents find you amusing and like having a celebrity in the house. One who's not a complete asshole. My fiancée thinks you're sexy, which sticks in my craw, but whatever. Because the most important thing is that you and McKenna are friends. And even though it's not exactly the relationship *you* desire, the two of you are friends, and I think she'd like to cement that."

"I'm not following."

"She's not going to want to lose being your friend just because Xander's back in town."

For the first time since this situation had developed, Jagger felt like his back was up against the wall. In his mind, he and McKenna were friends, but on the way to something else entirely. He had no plans to stop at *friends*. He didn't want to just be her friend. And he sure as hell hoped that whatever was in all those boxes her momma had stockpiled gave him enough work to be around McKenna for a long while after the prodigal boyfriend's return.

"Xavier, that's a very generous offer, and I appreciate it. Especially under the circumstances. But McKenna would have a fit if I showed up during her big reunion with … your brother."

"Which—I'll just go ahead and say—is exactly what delights me about the whole idea."

"Delights you?"

"Absolutely delights me. Just the thought of watching that girl squirm, trying to negotiate between her boyfriend and her heartthrob? Frankly, it gets me giddy. Look man, Xander deserves a hard time for what he's put McKenna through. Having you in the house is sheer payback. And selfishly, I think it will cement his focus where it needs to be."

"So, you are encouraging me to accept your mother's invitation just so you can watch the three of us squirm?"

"Well, not you particularly. But sure. Watching McKenna squirm will be highly entertaining."

"She's not going to squirm. She knows who she wants, and he's guaranteed to be at your Thanksgiving table."

"She'll squirm. I'm not blind. I see the way she looks at you. McKenna needs to step up as well. Needs to get her head on straight."

"About what?"

"About you being nothing more to her than a friend. Her big-deal, rock-star friend. That is all."

Jagger shrugged.

"What's that?" Xavier pointed to his shoulder. "What the hell was that?"

"Nothin'."

"Bullshit that was nothing. You've got a plan. You've got designs on McKenna, even though you are fully aware my brother is coming home to propose marriage."

That bit of news hit Jagger hard. "Is he?"

"Yeah, man."

"Are you sure? I mean, like he told you himself?" Because that was not the vibe—not the intuitive feeling—Jagger had been betting on.

"I've refused to talk to the asshole. But I have it under good authority—meaning my pa—that Xander is indeed ready to make McKenna his wife."

"Well, damn," Jagger said. "Not gonna lie. That smarts."

"Dude."

Jagger looked around at the rest of the mess sitting outside the shed wondering for the first time what the hell he was doing here.

Damn. "Okay, help me get this handled, will you? And stop talking. I had this killer tune in my head, and you've just annihilated it."

"Oh. Sorry. What's the tune about?"

"A shed. What else?" With that, the two of them got to work in complete and utter silence.

When the truck was loaded and the tailgate was closed tight, Xander offered to ride his motorcycle to the dump and help Jagger unload. Jagger turned him down, eager to work alone.

"Okay," Xavier relented. "Call if you need me. I'm going to stop by Tweets's and make her feed me if she's there."

"Where else would she be?"

"Work. She loves work. Almost as much as she loves me." He grinned, and then he stood there for a moment. "I think you ought to come for Thanksgiving dinner. Just saying."

"I'll think about it," Jagger mumbled.

"I'm gonna tell Ma yes."

Jagger didn't have the energy to argue.

CHAPTER TWENTY

Jagger's presence at the Blakely's dinner table that night became the household's standard operating procedure. Every evening thereafter, when McKenna arrived home, Jagger would greet her from the top of a ladder while installing sconces or with his head shoved beneath cabinetry while he tightened up new plumbing fixtures. He'd never felt so handy or useful and he sure enjoyed the way the Blakely ladies smiled at him after completing another job that updated their surroundings.

He'd never painted before, but after walking into the local hardware store and asking a few questions, he realized it wasn't rocket science. If he purchased the proper tools, he could offer to paint the interior walls, something both women kept insisting they needed to have done. And it would give him an excuse to hang around once Thanksgiving had come and gone and the dreaded boyfriend was back.

Ugh.

The boyfriend—the nagging gnat that was ever-buzzing around his ear. It never failed. Every time Jagger found himself luxuriating in McKenna's enthusiasm as he demonstrated, say, the new faucet in the bathroom, her phone would ring with a call from He-Whom-Jagger-Refused-To-Name, and suddenly the smile that had been all his morphed into an I'm-so-sorry, twisted grimace before she whirled away, slipping into her bedroom and closing the door to take the cheater's call.

At least Sandy was on his side, he thought, encouraged by the roll of her eyes and the commiserative frown she showed him every time Dick Head called, or texted, or in some other fashion sent McKenna into a twirl.

Each night Jagger willingly submitted himself to this suffering. He showed up to work and then stayed for dinner. Afterward, he'd linger to watch television or play a board game or cards. He remained to remind McKenna he wasn't going anywhere, even if the current scenario continued to shatter the edges of his heart bit by tiny bit. Because once McKenna's adrenaline over the boyfriend's call dissipated—and it always did—Jagger was there to share her evening. Not Dick Head.

He had to believe that was something.

He had to believe that the laughter they shared over her mother's table meant something.

He had to believe that the quiet evening hours they passed on the couch together were bringing them closer.

He had to believe that when she laid her head on his lap so she could stretch out as they watched TV, it brought her the same sense of ease as it gave him.

She was his person. She just didn't know it yet.

He contemplated telling her the night before Thanksgiving. *Thanksgiving*—the taboo subject that neither of them had brought up once in the past three days. It was this crazy deadline looming over their intimate time together. As much as he couldn't kid himself—it was obvious McKenna was eager for the boyfriend's return and all that might mean for her—he couldn't give up hope either.

His plan was to stay the course. He assumed the boyfriend would be home for the long weekend and then make his way back to Whereversville, North Carolina by Monday. And then Jagger would swoop in with paint chips and reinsert himself into McKenna's life.

Boldly.

"I'm going to miss you," she said quietly as their third episode of the latest Netflix sensation concluded. Her head was resting on his lap, and he was stroking her hair slowly, mesmerized like he tended to get when enthralled with her hair.

"I'm not going anywhere," he replied.

She started to shift, moving to a sitting position beside him, all sleepy and sweet as she brushed her hair back from her face. "If things go the way I think they will tomorrow …" Her voice wavered as she shrugged.

"Then I'll be happy for you," he lied. He wasn't giving up. How could he give up? "And we'll still hang out. Just like we do now."

She sat back, lounging into the back cushion. "Maybe. We'll see."

"What are you trying to say, McKenna?" *Because whatever you say next is probably bullshit, and I am prepared to discredit it.*

"I like you more than I should."

Okay. Maybe not bullshit.

She went on. "If, say, Xander does *make things official* tomorrow, it would probably be best not to … hang out as regularly as we do now."

"So you don't think he'd be down with me coming over every night?"

She smiled at him. "No."

"So if he *makes things official,* then he becomes the boss of you, and you don't get to choose who you hang out with anymore?"

"Jagger," she huffed. "Stop being an ass."

He slapped a hand on his knee. "Well, I would, except it's hard when I'm competing against the king of all asses and you think he's going to be a better choice."

"You don't even know him," she defended.

"I know you, McKenna. I don't need to know him."

"What's that mean?"

"It means that I'm crazy about you. And I'm a damn fine choice. It means you don't have to settle for a two-timing jackass just because his last name is Wright."

"That is not why I'm settling for him."

"But you admit that you're settling."

"That's not what I meant."

"Kiss me. Shut up and just … kiss me."

"Fat chance," she said, tossing off the throw blanket and preparing to stand.

Jagger lunged forward, all but tackling her down to the couch. "Kiss me," he demanded. "I don't want you walking into Thanksgiving dinner at the Wrights' thinking you don't have a choice. Because you do have a choice, McKenna."

Her facial expression softened. Her hand came up to his beard, and she gently scratched her fingertips through it. "Jagger," she breathed. "You aren't real life. You're a fantasy. Albeit a really *good* fantasy."

Cue sexy background music.

In his mind, Jagger threw on his favorite make-love-to-this album. Damn right, he was a really good fantasy, and it was about time McKenna got a taste of what she'd be missing by playing life safe. By not giving herself what or whom she really wanted. Tucking his arms underneath her body, he rolled them so that she was in the dominant position, even though he planned to maintain complete control. His pelvis lifted, his prize-worthy boner performing a slow glide against her most intimate juncture.

As predicted, *that* caught her attention. "Jagger," she breathed. "Stop."

"Stop what?" he asked. "Stop this?" He did it again, only slower, and more drawn out.

And when her mouth hung open but no words came out, he did it again while nudging her lips closer to his, capturing her mouth with his own.

She didn't protest his kiss. No, she did not. She met him lip for lip, tongue for tongue, with a couple of teeth and a lot of sexy little peeps and moans nestled in. He knew he had her right where he wanted her, so he kissed his way over to her ear. "We'd be good together, McKenna. So good," he whispered as he kept up the slow and steady grind. "You have options. No matter what happens tomorrow, you have me as an option."

When she tried to protest, he kissed her again, ran his fingers through her dark hair, felt her luscious breasts mold themselves against his chest. He wanted to flip her back over. He wanted to be on top. To show her how good things could be. But he'd done enough for now. If he'd managed to get McKenna half as hot for him as he was for her, his mission would be accomplished.

"We are good together," he proclaimed quietly as he brought the petting session to a close.

"You're a tease," she said, dropping her head to his chest.

"Don't you threaten me with sex. I'd take you to bed right now if I didn't think you'd hate yourself in the morning."

She looked up at him as if she were actually thinking that over. As if she were contemplating giving him the gift of her body on the eve of the boyfriend's return.

"Stop looking at me like that," he warned.

"Like what?" she denied.

"You know like what. Come on, off me." He nudged and prodded and untangled himself from the disgruntled, snarling she-wolf. "I'm just as turned-on as you," he told her, standing and straightening out his clothes. "But until *I'm* the boyfriend, you get no more of this."

"I was wrong," she grumbled from her sprawl on the couch. "You're not a fantasy. You are quite literally my worst nightmare."

CHAPTER TWENTY-ONE

Thank God, it's Thanksgiving.

That was McKenna's first thought as she woke to a chilly but sunny Thursday morning. It was such a relief to know that she was finally going to be able to put her hands on Xander, because the truth was, she didn't know how much longer she could go without jumping Jagger's bones. Seriously, Xander was showing up at the eleventh hour, and her nerves had been rubbed severely raw trying to maintain a romance with him and a friendship with Jagger. It had felt far more the opposite over the last several weeks, and man, thank goodness it was all coming to an end.

During their latest conversation, Xander had assured McKenna he'd be at his parents' by noon. So, not wanting to miss a minute with him, McKenna jumped in the shower and then labored over her blowout and makeup application, rolling her eyes at the shit she was going to take from Xavier. Because on past Thanksgivings, she'd join the Wrights in their kitchen early to help with the cooking and setting the table before returning home to dress up for dinner. But she didn't want to take the time to come all the way home and shower and change. She wanted to be ready for whatever Xander was bringing with him. Hopefully, their future. Perhaps even a ring.

She glanced down at her hands and grimaced. She'd made the effort to have a professional manicure—just in case—and didn't that send the entire beauty shop into a spin. She'd tried to pass it off as getting ready for the holidays, but those old biddies knew she wasn't one to spend hard-earned money on her nails unless she had a very good reason. She shook off the nerves that invoked. It wasn't like the entire town didn't expect the same. She wouldn't be the only one disappointed at the end of the day if Xander didn't propose.

Regardless, she told herself as she chose a fancy blue sweater to go over her priciest pair of slacks, Xander was showing up, and they were making a plan. Either way, it was going to be a very good day.

The relief she began to feel as she drove to the Wrights' was noteworthy. No more misrepresenting. No more worrying. No more wondering. Xander had sounded so confident over the last few days that she allowed herself to experience that same confidence now that the day of his homecoming had finally arrived. She opened the Wright's front door feeling refreshed and invigorated and was immediately met with the happy sight of Anna Beth fully dressed in beautiful new clothes that actually fit her tiny frame. The two women embraced, sharing in the enthusiastic knowledge that this was going to be a very special day.

"Xavier has one bird in the oven already," Anna Beth said. "And he's pulling the second out of the marinade, preparing it for the fryer."

"Right on schedule. Maybe the two of us will be able to watch the first hour of the parade before we have to start on the potatoes and the rest of the sides."

"Stuffing is all done," Anna Beth said, the two of them walking side by side with arms linked toward the family room. "The dough for the dinner rolls is rising. I've had Jaxon prepare each of us a very light Mimosa to enjoy while we watch."

McKenna laid her head briefly on Anna Beth's shoulder. "Thank you for always including me," she told her second mom. "I love Thanksgiving at your house."

"Oh, darlin'. What would we do if we didn't have you? Now, what time is your mother planning to arrive?"

"I told her cocktails start at three o'clock."

"Wonderful. And Xander is arriving at noon?"

"That's what he told me." McKenna gripped Anna Beth's hand before they separated and took their seats in the family room.

"Well, I have a feeling it's going to be a very good day," Anna Beth said.

"Me too." They clinked their flutes.

It wasn't long before Jinx showed up in a dress that was straight off the latest designer runway but curiously resembled a traditional pilgrim ensemble. "It's too much, isn't it?" she asked turning this way and that to show off the creation. "I mean, it's a hoot, right? The only place you could possibly wear it is to Thanksgiving."

"Yes, but …" McKenna stuttered, mesmerized by the dress and wondering if she was falling in love with the oddity. "It is sort of perfect for Thanksgiving."

"I think you look darling," Anna Beth said. "Don't you think Jinx looks darling, Maxwell?"

Poor Mr. Wright was just trying to walk through the room without notice, but at his wife's insistence, he stopped and gave his attention to Jinx and her pilgrim dress. "Good morning, Jinx. Why, yes. I agree. You look darling." Then he glanced in McKenna's direction. "McKenna, you look as you always do. Perfect." His smile was as bright as always. This gruff man, who was known for swatting at the heads of his offspring more often than not, always treated her with kid gloves. The gratitude she felt over his smile, his words, ran right into the joy she was experiencing watching the parade with her favorite women. The feeling was overwhelming. The emotion that welled up inside her chest was nothing short of euphoria. She was so very happy, today of all days, to be part of the Wright family.

At ten o'clock, the ladies went to work in the kitchen, tuning in to the rest of the parade on the tiny television that flipped down from under the upper cabinetry. But there was enough chatter between them that it soon became background noise as Jinx learned how to roll out dough and McKenna prepared the oysters for their casserole.

Xavier, in his notoriously bossy way, had left a list taped to the refrigerator with explicit instructions on who was to do what, including who was to teach Jinx as they went. (Jinx had arrived in Henderson with no serviceable background in cooking, having been raised in a household with *help*. Xavier seemed to be on a mission to ensure Jinx would be able to feed herself, and his brother Jaxon, when and if it came down to that. Not that Jaxon didn't have his own talents in the kitchen. But he wasn't one to jump at the chance to do any cooking if someone else was willing.)

Anna Beth seemed surprisingly full of energy and checked her watch almost as often as McKenna did. Every time they caught each other doing so, one would say to the other, "He'll be here soon."

It was close to noon when Anna Beth led McKenna and Jinx into the dining room located off the foyer and directed them where to find the long linen tablecloth she wanted to use as they stretched the dining room table to its maximum length by adding two leaves. Butterflies rose in McKenna's belly as she draped the table and folded the napkins, knowing any minute Xander would be walking through that door.

And the moment the front door opened, all three women stopped to stare. McKenna's heart beat rapidly in anticipation, every bit of her ready to fling herself into Xander's arms. But it was Xavier who came through the door, escorting Laidey who had her arms full of what looked like a beautifully packed picnic basket.

"Oh, it's only you," his mother sighed, clearly disappointed.

"Ma," Xavier exclaimed. "Is that any way to greet your future daughter-in-law and the only son you got right now who is giving you any hope for legitimate grandchildren?"

"Stop," Anna Beth said, coming up to hug Laidey. "I adore the two of you and can't wait for those grandchildren."

"Darn right," Xavier said, taking the basket from Laidey and handing it to McKenna. "I'm not sure what all's in here," he said quietly. "But it's junk from Dallas, where they probably eat squab for Thanksgiving because … *Texas* and they just don't know any better. If you'd do me a favor and hide this, I'd appreciate it. Don't want to hurt my fiancée's feelings, but she ain't messing up our traditional, tasty, Wright family Thanksgiving dinner."

"Squab," McKenna laughed. "You're insane."

"Whatever, just deal with this, please. And thank you." Xavier returned to help Laidey off with her coat while lavishing his mother with praise along with a good ribbing.

McKenna took the basket into the kitchen and set it on the table. But with her anticipation of Xander's arrival now at a fevered pitch, she retrieved her phone and texted him before another moment could go by.

Are you close? What's your ETA?

The response came back after a few moments.

No. Sorry. Got a late start. Don't expect me until closer to three. Please soothe Dad's ruffled feathers.

McKenna's spirits plunged. How could he be late today of all days? Her mind was in a spin as she looked down into Laidey's basket of treats. Maybe Xander was packing up a truck and moving home. That would be a wonderful surprise, she thought. He hadn't given her much detail about his talk with his boss, and she'd assumed he'd take more time, easing out of one job before starting another. But hey, if he was bringing all his stuff back with him today, all the better. She grew ecstatic at the thought.

Now feeling particularly giddy, she began to investigate the assortment of beautifully wrapped pantry items. "Happy Thanksgiving," Laidey said, coming into the kitchen and giving McKenna a full hug. "Is your mom here yet?"

"No," she answered as she dug through the basket, setting jars and bags on the kitchen table. "She'll be here at three. What is all this? Everything looks wonderful."

"My parents sent it. Some of our family's favorite holiday treats. Xavier did not want me bringing it, worried I'd try to mess with his exalted menu."

"Did he even look at it? He's a closet chef. He's going to flip when he gets a load of this assortment."

"I tried to tell him it wasn't for Thanksgiving dinner, but you know him. Mr. Jump To Conclusions. Whatever. He'll figure it out."

"I'm going to put all this back just as I found it so you can present it to Anna Beth and Maxwell when the time is right. Maybe when Xavier is out frying the bird."

"Smart," Laidey said, watching McKenna carefully repack the items. "And …" McKenna could actually hear Laidey's smile, "Has Xander arrived?"

"He hasn't," McKenna said, abruptly spinning to face her friend. "He's going to be late." She grinned like it was the best news ever. "Do you think that means he's packed a U-Haul and has moved out of his apartment?"

Laidey's eyes went wide. "Wow. I don't know, but that would be wonderful."

"Right?" McKenna's level of giddiness reached frenzied proportions. She took a deep breath. "I need to chill. I might be reading too much into this. But why would he be late if he didn't have a good reason?"

"Exactly," Laidey agreed.

"Come on. Help Anna Beth and me set the table. Then we'll get something to drink before I mash the potatoes. Oh, and since this is your first Wright family Thanksgiving, you need to prepare the hot pepper jelly appetizer," she bossed. "It's Mr. Wright's favorite, and it'll gain you his undying love. Not that you don't have that already." She whirled around, facing Laidey directly to make her point. "I mean you are taking his most obnoxious son off his hands, so pepper jelly or not, he's always gonna be crazy about you."

Laidey laughed and then did what she always did. Followed McKenna wherever she led.

The four women worked together to create the sprawling but low-lying centerpiece for the long dining room table. Hollowed-out mini pumpkins and gourds served as candleholders and vases for colorful mums and berry sprigs all found in the Wright's backyard. McKenna and Anna Beth stood back from the table, ordering Jinx and Laidey to move such-and-such over a smidge there and replace that droopy flower here. Finally, votives were set within the garden they'd created. Then came the fine crystal water glasses, the Wright's best wine glasses, the silver they'd received as wedding gifts, and their good china. The table came together beautifully just as Anna Beth appeared with a stack of place cards.

"I wrote these out in calligraphy last night," she told the girls. "We have a surprise guest joining us."

"A surprise other than Xander?" McKenna laughed.

"Maybe a surprise for Xander," Anna Beth said. "And you, my dear." She dramatically handed over a singular place card to McKenna.

McKenna blinked. Then swallowed. Then her breath halted completely. *Jagger?* Her brain couldn't quite compute. "Jagger?" she managed to eek out between the swallowing and the blinking and the nonbreathing.

"Isn't that exciting?" Anna Beth beamed. "When I found out he'd still be in town, I asked Xavier to invite him. He's such a darling man, and no one should be alone on Thanksgiving. Plus, I knew you'd be tickled sharing Thanksgiving with him. And since Xander hasn't had the chance to meet him yet, well"—she clapped her hands together, pleased as punch—"it will be such a surprise."

It was definitely a surprise, McKenna thought, working her brain in the direction of no, no, no, and *please, no*. She needed to figure out some way to derail this without admitting to Anna Beth that Xander would not be pleased since he hadn't thought much of the idea of her holding Jagger's hand in the hot tub a few weeks ago.

And Jagger. *Poor* Jagger. McKenna couldn't imagine why he would accept Anna Beth's invitation, knowing that Xander was coming home to *make things official*. He didn't need to witness that.

And the last thing she needed was to have Jagger's eyes on her when Xander finally walked through that door. It would be so uncomfortable for everyone, except maybe Xavier, who would no doubt find excruciating delight in her discomfort. He probably set the whole thing up. She checked her watch, breathing a sigh of relief that there was still time. Time to fix this debacle before it came to a head.

"So, I think, as the guest of honor, Mr. Yates should sit to my right. Unless you want him on the other side of you, McKenna."

"No. No, I think you're right. Jagger will enjoy sitting next to you. If he's able to make it."

"Oh, he'll be here," Anna Beth assured her. "He told Xavier he's bringing pie."

The damn pie.

"Maxwell will be at the far end, I'll be at this end. We'll put Jagger right here." Anna Beth indicated the spot to McKenna. Begrudgingly, McKenna set the place card down. "Laidey, we'll seat you next to Jagger."

"Ah, that's not happening," Xavier interjected. He stood at the head of the dining room, sipping some deliciously dark liquid over one big ice cube. McKenna wanted to kill him but only after he fixed her a drink exactly like that. "Put Tweets at the other end of the table with Dad. I don't want her anywhere near the guy with the beard."

"*You* have a beard," Laidey protested.

"I have scruff. Perfectly manicured, very sexy scruff. Jagger's got a full beard." The contortion of his face conveyed his distaste. "I mean, I get he wants it to show up on stage and all, but really, it's not a good look."

McKenna, Laidey, and Jinx burst out laughing. "If that's not a good look, I don't know what is," Jinx said as she exited the room.

"Tweets," Xavier ordered. "You're down with Dad, and I'm next to you. McKenna, you're also down there with Dad, and let's not forget *my twin* will be sitting by your side."

"Fine with me," McKenna agreed. In fact, once the place cards had been set, she snuck back into the dining room to swap sides of the table with Laidey and Xavier. She wanted to be on the same side of the table as Jagger so none of them had to face each other.

If he showed.

Her intention was to text Jagger and ask him to politely decline the Wright's invitation, but every time she thought to do it, something else would call for her attention. She was busily making the gravy with the entire kitchen in a last-minute flutter as the three o'clock hour approached. The hors d'oeuvres had been placed in the sunroom, where Maxwell and Jax had created a full bar. The socializing part of Thanksgiving was about to commence.

And, more importantly, Xander would be arriving within minutes.

CHAPTER TWENTY-TWO

Jagger stood outside the Wright's front door beside McKenna's mother.

The woman had called him this morning and requested a ride—on his *Harley*—to the Wright's Thanksgiving party. She said that McKenna had already driven her car over, and it didn't make sense to muck up the Wright's driveway with more than one of their cars.

"How did you know I'd been invited?" he asked.

"Anna Beth told me Sunday when I ran into her at the farmers' market."

"So McKenna is aware?"

"Not to my knowledge. She was out of here before I woke up this morning, and Anna Beth had wanted it to be a surprise, so I didn't say anything."

"I'll bet you didn't," Jagger mumbled.

"So, I've borrowed a helmet from the kid next door. You okay with taking me for a spin beforehand? I've never been on a motorcycle and figure this is my chance."

"McKenna hasn't even been on my bike. I get the feeling she prefers the beat-up pickup."

"She's a little cautious, that one."

"But not you?"

"I'm cautious, but I'm also old. I've been thinking about my bucket list lately."

"So riding a motorcycle will check something off your list?"

"Only if I add it on there first."

He laughed. "I'm happy to give you a ride. Truck or motorcycle, your choice."

"So you were planning to go?"

"Actually, no."

"What's changed your mind?"

"You. Calling for a ride." There was a quiet break in the conversation before Jagger added, "Something you want to tell me?"

"No. I just ... the Wrights are good people. They love my McKenna and have taken her under their wing, giving her the kind of lavish attention I don't have in me to give."

"Is that true?" Jagger didn't think that was true.

"It might be. My daughter and I see eye to eye on plenty, but in some ways, we are completely different creatures. There's a side of McKenna I just don't get. Her less practical side. I can't nurture that side like Anna Beth can. I don't even understand it."

"Give me an example."

"I don't have a dress in my closet."

"Ah-huh."

"I know that McKenna owns several dresses, but I've never actually seen her wear one."

"That seems ... odd." Jagger had never seen McKenna in a dress either. She was always in slacks or jeans or yoga pants or a bikini. Man, he really liked McKenna in a bikini. Her work uniform was just that, a uniform. She wore the same type of thing every day. A white or soft-colored blouse, a pinstriped or blue jacket with matching slacks. Her shoes changed. Her work shoes and her weekend shoes were completely different things. "Maybe she saves them for special occasions?"

"Exactly. So apparently, we have no special occasions."

"She's probably wearing a dress today," Jagger grumbled, knowing McKenna was likely getting engaged—unless the boyfriend threw up on himself. One could hope.

"I don't think so. I mean, maybe, but ... see, what I'm trying to tell you is, the Wrights are good people. They understand McKenna. Anna Beth and Maxwell practically adopted her years ago, and I'd be lying if I didn't acknowledge that I'm grateful she's had people— extended family, if you will—who could be there for her. And although I'm not happy about this runaround Xander's been giving her, he too is a good man. As good as the rest of them."

Jagger didn't have any words to contribute.

"So rest assured, whatever happens today, my daughter is going to be fine."

"I don't doubt that," he grumbled.

"And you'll be just fine too."

"Hmm." He doubted that immensely.

"I know you're attracted to her, and quite frankly, I thought you were going to give her more of a run for her money."

"Since the Daze, I've been playing a hunch. One, as it turns out, looks like it's going to cost me."

"Day ain't over yet," Sandy told him with a chuckle. "I think it's important you show up. Xander will take one look at you and wish he'd come home weeks ago."

"McKenna's pretty set on him."

"McKenna's never had much of a choice before either. The Wrights are her favorite thing about this town. Xander was her first love. Rock star or no, that's a lot of history to push against. She cares for you, this I know. I think you know it too."

"Apparently not enough."

"Oh, quit your damn moping. Won't be long until you're back on stage and women are flinging hotel keys and what-not at you. Put on a clean shirt and pick me up at two forty five on that Harley. Make that two thirty. We'll take the long way to the Wrights'."

Short, stubby Sandy Blakely had been a natural on the Road King. She was all about leaning into the curve and moving out on the straightaways. As far as moms went, she was cool.

"You think McKenna's gonna kill me for showing up?" he asked as Sandy rang the bell.

"We're about to find out."

Anna Beth opened the door, greeting the two of them warmly. Jagger didn't have to wait long to get a feel for McKenna's mood. As soon as he stood in the foyer and looked down the hallway toward the back of the house, he saw her standing in the sunroom—not wearing a dress—watching him enter, a grim expression on her face.

Xavier came forward with a boisterous greeting. "Damn better than eating alone," he told him with a hand grab, a bro hug, and a back slap.

"Xavier, I rode over on Jagger's Road King," Sandy said. "I can see why you enjoy that thing."

"Now that's a fine way to start Thanksgiving. Feeling the wind in your face."

"And I had a leather jacket just for the occasion."

"Let me help you with that."

"Oh, and here." Jagger stepped outside the door once again and leaned down to pick up a huge box. Like an extra-large pizza box. "I dropped this off earlier because I wouldn't have been able to carry it on my bike. It's that crazy-good apple pie that Piper Evans makes. Figured in this town, no Thanksgiving would be complete without it. The pie plate is my gift to you for inviting me."

"I'll take that," Laidey said as she greeted the new guests. "Xavier, see that your momma gets off her feet for a bit."

"Will do," he said, helping Sandy off with her jacket. "Ma, take our guests out to the sunroom and grab a seat. I'll be right there to fix drinks."

Jagger followed dutifully behind the three women, noticing that McKenna had disappeared from view. He'd be lying if he said he wasn't feeling remarkably uncomfortable. Any minute, he expected a Xavier look-alike to stroll around the corner with his arm tucked around McKenna. Good Lord, why did he decide to submit himself to this? He should have stayed the course. Follow his post-weekend, paint-chip infiltration plan.

"Jagger, the bar is open, Help yourself," Xavier said as he mowed his way back into the party, taking over the care and seating of his mother. Jagger shook hands with Mr. Wright, shared a greeting with Jaxon, and kept an eye out for McKenna and the boyfriend while he made his way over to the bar and poured himself a double shot of tequila on ice. One shot of tequila was his band's traditional pre-stage ritual. He figured he was going to be *on* tonight one way or the other. And then he sensed her standing close, smelling like apricots and ginger, her voice seducing him as she whispered in his ear.

"Fancy meeting you here." He couldn't tell if her tone was combatant or faux-friendly.

"Happy Thanksgiving, McKenna," he said, offering her his drink. She took it and sipped. He quirked an eyebrow and then proceeded to fix himself another.

"When I saw your name on a place card, I had half a mind to text you and tell you not to come."

He took his time adding ice to a fresh glass. Took great pains to use a shot glass to precisely measure two pours. He squeezed the lime wedge until there was no juice left and then used a plastic stirrer topped with a turkey to combine the contents. He turned to face her, taking a sip before delivering his truth. "I said I'd let the boyfriend thing play out. I never said I'd make it easy on you."

"Hmm," she grunted, looking away, her gaze circling the room. Probably looking for the boyfriend. "And here I was worried this wouldn't be easy on *you*."

Jagger's gaze took a stroll around the room. "Where is he?" The two of them moved away from the bar as Xavier moved in to fix his mother and Sandy drinks.

"I don't know," she huffed, becoming more like herself. More open. More honest. Jagger wanted to shake her, because it was so obvious they had something between them. Something good and easy. Yeah, they were at odds on the boyfriend thing, but even so, he was standing here for her and she was leaning on him. "He was supposed to be here at noon. Said he got a late start, and now he's still not here. Frankly, I'm worried that he and his U-Haul have run into trouble."

"U-Haul?"

"I'm sort of guessing he's packed up his apartment and is surprising me with a move home."

"Oh." That sucks, Jagger thought.

"Which would be great, but the freaking anticipation of his arrival is grinding my insides to dust."

Okay. There was only so much leaning he was willing to tolerate. "Good luck with that. I'm gonna go talk to Jaxon about NASCAR."

"Sure. Fine. Whatever," she said, storming off in a snit to the kitchen or wherever she landed.

But before heading down the hall in search of Jaxon, Jagger slid quietly into the dining room and rounded the table at a leisurely pace, taking note of the place cards McKenna had mentioned. When he was sure no one was looking, he very casually switched his name with the boyfriend's, moving Xander down between Mrs. Wright and Sandy, placing himself next to McKenna. The act of defiance caused him to grin.

The party went on, and it was a fine one. The middle two Wright brothers, Huxley and Rex, arrived and found Jaxon and Jagger watching football in the library. They were not nearly as big as the oldest, Xavier, nor quite as tall as the youngest, Jaxon. But they made up for it in sharp, cutting one-liners that cracked Jagger up, making him feel a little more relaxed. That and the tequila. It was darn good tequila.

It did not escape Jagger's notice that whenever he spied McKenna, she was glancing at her phone. Then he overheard Mr. Wright ask her about Xander's arrival time while Jagger was passing the sunroom in search of a bathroom.

"I haven't heard from him since he said he'd be here by three," she told Mr. Wright. "I tried to call, but his phone is in *Do Not Disturb* mode, so I assume he's driving. He shouldn't be too much longer."

"Everything is being kept warm, and we won't cut the turkey until he gets here," Anna Beth said.

"Hmm," Mr. Wright grunted. "The boy should have driven in last night."

"You always say that," his wife soothed with a hand to his thigh.

On his way back to the library, Jagger took a quick detour, finding the place cards had been rearranged back to the original seating. He figured McKenna was the culprit and smiled as he once again traded places with the boyfriend.

With a break before the next kickoff, all the men gathered in the sunroom to refresh their drinks and eat a few more hors d'oeuvres. That's where Jagger was when he spied McKenna with a confused look on her face, reading her phone. He couldn't help himself and wandered over in her direction.

"Everything cool?" he asked as casually as he could muster.

"I don't know," she blurted in a half laugh/half disbelieving snort. She held up her phone for Jagger to read.

Forgive me. I promise I'll make this up to you.

"Make what up to you?"

She shook her head. "I don't know."

But as the front door opened at the end of the long hallway, everything—and Jagger meant *everything*—was revealed.

He took one long look at the petite, strawberry blond cutie walking in with a guy who looked exactly like Xavier and immediately turned to find a back way out.

"McKenna's not going to want me witnessing this," he whispered to a stunned Xavier. "I'm gone."

CHAPTER TWENTY-THREE

Forgive me. I promise I'll make this up to you.

McKenna had read the text, her heart sinking over the fact that once again Xander wasn't making it home. But before she could even address the absurdity of that hypothesis, the front door opened and in walked Xander.

With Becca.

At least, McKenna assumed it was Becca.

The sweet, little peach dressed in cocktail attire certainly looked like a Becca. Certainly looked like she'd been dating Xander for a good while with the way she touched him, gently laying a hand on his arm, gifting him with a shy smile when he looked at her solicitously.

McKenna felt people gather around her as she stared—disbelieving and certainly not breathing—down the hallway at the handsome couple. It wasn't until she felt the keen presence of the only two Wrights she loved more than Xander that she remembered to take a breath. Anna Beth stood solidly on McKenna's left side while Mr. Wright flanked her right, as her mind frantically worked to sort out what she was witnessing.

There was nothing but silence—a shockwave quieting the crowd—while McKenna took in the chagrin on Xander's face, along with the curious, sparkling eyes of the woman he obviously loved.

She didn't know where she summoned the grace, or the strength, or the will to move toward them. She only knew that it was born from a keen desire to protect Xander's parents. Their son showing up with another woman? At Thanksgiving? While she and her mother were present? She could imagine their shock.

So McKenna did the only thing she could do to salvage the moment. She made the first move. She forced her legs to carry her in the direction of the pair and willed herself to greet Becca as graciously as she was able.

Because this was not her fault.

And her beloved Anna Beth did not need a scene.

"You must be Becca," McKenna said calmly, plastering on some semblance of a smile. "I've heard wonderful things about you," she said, taking Becca's hands in both of hers.

"Xander," Mr. Wright barked from behind McKenna. "What's going on here?"

"Mom, Dad, … McKenna. This is Becca McNamara."

"Hello," Becca said, her eyes moving to glance at everyone standing in front of her.

"And?" Mr. Wright snapped.

"And," Xavier said, "since her flight to Boston was canceled and she wasn't going to be able to make it home for Thanksgiving, I knew *my family* would be eager for the chance to share their bounty."

"Absolutely," McKenna said.

"I'm not sure I fully understand," Mr. Wright pressed.

"Xavier." McKenna signaled him from the growing crowd in the foyer. "Becca, this is Xander's twin, Xavier." She introduced him as he approached. "Xavier, would you mind fixing Becca a drink. Xander will join you in just a minute," she finished, ushering Becca toward Xavier and his parents toward the kitchen, assuming Xander would follow.

"What's the meaning of this?" Mr. Wright asked in a hushed and irritated tone. McKenna had motioned them all to the very back of the kitchen so their discussion would not be overheard. Fortunately, the kitchen was old and still had doors that were able to be shut between it and the dining room and the hallway. McKenna quietly went to shut both as Mr. Wright started his interrogation.

"Dad," Xander said.

"Who is she? This Becca."

Lord knows, Xander didn't deserve her support, because being thrust into this situation was untenable for both her and his parents. But at least she had prior knowledge of *this Becca*. McKenna knew that for the sake of the Wrights, she needed to bail him out or the day would never recover. She went to stand next to Xander and faced his parents. Even put a hand on his back to show support and solidarity.

"It's all right," she told everyone. "I've known about Becca since Xander and I started dating."

"What's to know?" Mr. Wright argued.

"Xander started dating Becca prior to the two of us meeting up in Charlotte last summer. He was upfront with me about it. I've known all along."

"I don't understand," Anna Beth whispered.

"I know. We didn't mention Becca to you because you both were so happy that we were together."

"Yes. We are very happy the two of you are together," Mr. Wright insisted. He looked directly at Xander. "What's the purpose of bringing her here?"

"I told you. Her flight was canceled. You must have heard about the Nor' easter dumping snow on New England."

"I don't give a devil about the snow in New England. What is that girl doing here? Today of all days?"

Xander spread his hands in apology. "I just … couldn't leave her."

And weren't those the truest words McKenna had ever heard Xander utter.

He just couldn't leave her.

Well, she could see it. The girl was young and pretty and probably sweet, just like Xander. It would be hard for any man to leave sweet behind when faced with a ball-busting, domineering, stuck-in-Henderson woman as your alternative. She couldn't compete with sweet or little or docile or creamy. Becca's skin was definitely creamy. And, as all those thoughts took aim and hit the bullseye of her heart, she realized she needed to leave. Quickly.

She turned to Anna Beth and looked her right in the eye. "I love you. I'm going to quickly grab up the place cards from around the table, and my mother and I will leave without incident. Xander is your son, Becca is his choice, and you need to open up your heart just a little more and give her a chance. You and I will catch up tomorrow. I promise."

She couldn't risk looking at either Mr. Wright or Xander. She had about ninety seconds of control left before things got ugly. She didn't want ugly. Not for the Wrights, not for her and her mother, not even for Becca.

Becca.

McKenna squeezed Anna Beth's hands one time as her eyes started to mist. "I've got to go," she whisper-choked.

Her mother was standing in the dining room, holding her jacket and McKenna's coat at the ready. McKenna brushed tears from her cheeks after donning the coat and then picked up every place card and tucked them in her coat's pocket on the way out the door.

Sandy put her palm out, silently asking for the keys. McKenna fished them out and handed them to her, her momentum gaining as she sought the security of her car. She couldn't get in the passenger seat or close the door fast enough. She buckled up and looked straight ahead, desperate to be out of the Wrights' driveway.

The two of them drove home in complete silence.

Well, McKenna thought, what was there to say? Becca had missed her flight, Xander chose to bring her home. As he so eloquently declared, he couldn't leave her. Not back when McKenna and he had first started dating, not throughout the months he'd kept her on pins and needles, not even after he'd raced home weeks ago to declare his intentions. He couldn't let Becca go.

McKenna finally had her answer.

It entered her awareness that her mother was driving slowly. Which, ya know, was fine. It wasn't like the two of them had anywhere to be. There was no turkey dinner waiting in their kitchen, she thought as her brainwaves slowed to a crawl. She still felt the deep pain of Xander's rejection. Or maybe she didn't. Maybe this catatonic state she was slipping into was her brain's way of protecting itself from the anguish that was screaming within every other part of her body.

Should she have seen this coming? She wondered. She tried to replay the conversations she and Xander had had over the last few weeks and struggled to read things differently. *But does it really matter?* The thought came from some form of internal wisdom.

"No," she whispered. "I guess it doesn't."

"Doesn't what?" her mother asked."

"Matter," McKenna answered.

"You matter, McKenna," her mother offered, pulling the car into their driveway.

She nodded in her dazed state. "I know I do. To you." She pulled at the lever to open her door but sat for a minute before summoning the strength to get out and walk to the house. She stood on the front stoop, allowing her mother to unlock the door. She entered, walked through to the kitchen, and sat at the table in her coat.

Her mother came in quietly behind her. Opened a cabinet, then a drawer. McKenna could hear the sounds in the periphery of her sorrow, the periphery of her shock, the periphery of her grief, but she didn't pay any attention. Eventually, she noticed a glass of red wine had been placed before her, and her mother was seated opposite, sipping a glass of her own.

They sat in silence for a long time.

Eventually, McKenna took the pains to unbutton her coat. Then she took a sip of the wine. Then she laid her forehead on the table and sobbed.

CHAPTER TWENTY-FOUR

Not long after McKenna's catatonic state broke and the tears and the anguish and the outrage and the misery played out in front of her mother, who was—it was fair to say—*ill equipped* to handle emotional meltdowns, McKenna hit the shower, where more of the same poured forth. At least now she was alone, and her poor mother was spared … whatever. She let her mind drift to how Anna Beth would have handled her. If this had happened back when Anna Beth was bedridden, McKenna would have simply crawled in with her. Anna Beth would have wrapped her up in her arms and held her until she was all cried out.

Sandy was not the warm and fuzzy type.

And those thoughts drifted to the Wrights' Thanksgiving table. McKenna wondered how Anna Beth and Maxwell, not to mention Xavier and Laidey and the rest, were handling the new addition at their table.

And then she cried some more, thinking of all she'd now have to give up since foolishly falling back in love with Xander. No more Thanksgivings at the Wrights'. No more Christmases. No more anything when Xander and Becca came to town. She'd have to steer clear. She'd have to give stupid Xander his family back, and wouldn't that just make Xavier the happiest he's ever been, getting her out of his hair for good.

"And, oh, the wedding," she sobbed. Xavier and Laidey's wedding in Dallas was going to be sooo uncomfortable with both she and

Xander in the wedding party and Becca sitting in the Wright family pew, looking all peachy and perfect.

Those miserable, horrible, no-good thoughts just kept coming. Because if Jaxon and Jinx ended up together, she'd probably have to be in their wedding too. On and on and on those thoughts came until she was all cried out and the shower had run cold.

And then there came a knock on the bathroom door.

"What!" Seriously, her mother couldn't give her a little bit of space?

"Get your ass out here," came a low, luscious voice.

Jagger? She wrapped a towel around her body. "Jagger? What are you doing here?" she asked through the door.

"Feeding you and your ma."

Yeah. No. That wasn't going to work for her. "Thanks, but no thanks."

"McKenna," he coaxed. "You gotta eat."

"Actually, I don't have to eat. I don't want to eat," she snapped. "And I really don't want your pity. What I want right now is to have the house to myself."

"Yeah. That's not happening."

"Seriously, Jagger. I don't want to deal with you or anybody right now. Tell Mom she can head to LeeAnn's. I'll be fine."

"I hear ya."

There was quiet. She didn't hear him move away or anything. "And?"

"And tough shit. Get your ass out here and eat dinner."

"Oh, my gosh."

"And put on a dress," he ordered before she heard him backing away and stomping off toward the kitchen.

A dress? I don't wear dresses. And then she heard her stomach grumble and realized she was in the process of accruing a splitting headache. She was spent, heartbroken, hadn't eaten much all day in her excitement over Xander, and truly just wanted to collapse into bed. So she stood there, staring in the mirror at her drowned-rat-looking self and contemplated her choices in the moment.

She could crawl into bed and pull the covers over her head. Certainly Jagger and her mother would understand and most likely leave her be. Annnd then she'd have to face them tomorrow.

Or she could throw on some clothes and join them for a bite to eat, letting them throw platitudes around for a night.

Or … she thought, as Jinx's words from back when Jagger first arrived in town rang through her mind … Jagger Yates would be a great way to get over Xander Wright.

"Ah, yes he would," she told the mirror, picking up her blow dryer. The devil on her shoulder also mentioned Jagger would be a great way to get *back* at Xander. Not that Xander cared because … clearly.

And even though neither the mini adrenaline rush nor her enthusiasm about using Jagger as a healing balm lasted very long, she did manage to dry her hair *and* her body *and* find a pair of special-occasion jeans she'd been saving for some special occasion that was never going to come. She slipped those on, picking out the top she wore to the last Cavaliers concert she attended. The one where Jagger had asked for her number.

Now, that thought made her smile. Internally. Apparently, her face was still catatonic.

Slipping her feet inside fuzzy slippers, she moped her way into the kitchen where a huge box with the words Williams Sonoma sat discarded by the back door. The lights were bright, the oven was on, three burners had pots stewing, and the microwave seemed to be working overtime. The kitchen table had been set for three using placemats, and another opened bottle of wine served as their centerpiece. Her mother had on an apron. Jagger had on an apron. And when her appearance was noticed, he ushered her into her seat at the table and poured her a short glass.

"I drank the rest of the one you left," he told her. "This wine is even better."

"Where did all this come from?"

"My mom. She said she was sending a turkey, but it arrived with stuffing and gravy and potatoes and green beans and cranberry sauce. The turkey looked pretty good. I sliced it at home and brought the meat over. We're reheating it in the microwave."

"Smells good," she commented. "And I am hungry. Thanks."

"Glad I had it to fall back on."

"Hmm," she said through her sip of wine. "Me too."

And that's all that was said. Jagger turned away to continue preparing their dinner and left her alone to breathe. And drink his wine. Which, like Jagger, was layered with such delicious complexities.

The dinner hour started quietly since by the time Jagger and Sandy sat down, they were all ravenous. Both McKenna and Jagger had seconds. McKenna didn't know if she was eating her feelings or was simply famished by the ordeal she'd endured. Whatever it was, food had rarely tasted better, and she was truly grateful Jagger had thought to share his bounty with the Blakely girls.

"Mom, are you headed to LeeAnn's for dessert?" McKenna checked the clock. It was already eight.

"They won't miss me," her mother said.

McKenna narrowed her eyes. "They won't miss you? You're there almost every night. How are they not going to miss you?"

"It's fine. I *am* there almost every night, so if I miss one, no big deal."

McKenna stared at her mother, her eyes making an impassioned request. "I'd like you to go and not say anything to the Hollises about what happened today. If you stay home with me, they will wonder why you're a no-show. The news about Xander and me, or rather Xander and Becca, will be out soon enough."

Her mother calmly placed both her hands on the table. "Maybe you should accept the situation with Xander at face value. Maybe the only reason Becca was with him was because her flight was canceled. I'm guessing he drove her to the airport, found out her flight was canceled, and couldn't leave her stranded."

"Maybe," McKenna said. And maybe she could go on lying to herself and the Wrights for the rest of her life. "Go on," she urged her mother. "Jagger will help me with the cleanup, right?" she asked him.

"Absolutely. And I'll be over tomorrow night to help with the leftovers."

Sandy looked back and forth between the two of them, as if assessing the situation. "Go on," McKenna told her. "Thank you for backing me up today. Thank you for getting me home."

"I love you."

"I know you do."

"And I'm sorry."

"I know you are."

"And—"

"Ma," she abruptly interrupted. "Go. You're about to make it worse."

"All right." Her mother nodded contritely and then, after a moment, quietly got up, cleared her place, picked up her coveted pecan pie and left the house.

McKenna eyed Jagger. "I apologize. That probably sounded harsh."

Jagger grabbed his chest with one hand. "No need to apologize to me. I'm not the one you were swearing at."

"I didn't swear at her."

"Sounded like you were about to."

She huffed and gazed at him, dropping one ear to her shoulder. "She can't make this better for me. It irritates me that she would try."

Jagger turned his chair in her direction, scooting it up closer so he could touch her knees with his fingertips. His dark head hung low so that she could see the top of his hair. The top of *Jagger Yates's head*. Even after all that had passed between them, it still felt surreal.

"Is it going to irritate you if I try?" He looked up, their faces now close. His dark, chocolate eyes empathetic.

"It will irritate me to no end if you say one word."

"What if I just do this?" Jagger brought both his hands to her face and tugged her closer, placing his lips over hers in a tender, easy, soft, damn good kiss. Then he slowly backed away.

When she opened her eyes, she said, "Surprisingly, that doesn't seem to irritate me at all."

"Good," he said, moving his chair back and standing. "You put on some music while we clean up this kitchen. Then we can Netflix our way into a chill, or take a walk, or I can put you on the back of my bike and we can just ride."

"Music sounds like a good start."

He nodded. Then licked his lips. Then grinned.

She should have stopped him right there.

"Or," he said in that charmingly magical voice of his. "We can head to my place, where it's guaranteed to remain just the two of us," he said slowly, reaching out a hand to grab hold of hers, pulling her to her feet.

"Hmm." She practically melted against him. "Just the two of us does sound good." More wine, more Jagger, and getting away from her present reality sounded very good. Right now, Jagger's arms linked around her back felt better than good. Too good, if she was listening to the angel on her shoulder. Because the devil in her head was all-in for wherever *just the two of us* might lead.

"Did you happen to bring your guitar?" she asked his chest.

"No. Why?"

"I just had this Jagger Yates fantasy. Where you're sitting at my kitchen table playing the guitar while I cleaned up." She pulled back and gave him a genuine smile. Then she actually laughed. "That is such a good fantasy that I am going to stop being miserable. Because maybe you aren't playing a one-man show for me right now, but if we put on your albums and you sing while we clean up ..." She shook her head in amazement. "A girl couldn't ask for more than that."

"Your wish is my command. You get the music going, and I'll put on some rubber gloves and handle the dishes. Your job is to wrap up the leftovers for tomorrow."

"Dinner was good." She pulled back and went to do his bidding. "So good."

"I'll let my momma know you approved."

"Please do."

The two of them got down to work with a Cavaliers playlist piped in over an Echo. Jagger sang his lead, McKenna sang the background vocals, and her mood continued to shift and change until McKenna's soul was soothed by the man and his music, just as it had been for years before he'd come to Henderson.

Only now, she was crazy about him on a personal level.

Still just a fantasy, this Jagger Yates. McKenna wasn't going to kid herself about that. But one that was now free for the taking if she chose. Jagger had not minced words. He planned to offer everything she needed to get over Xander. And basically, him being so sweet to her and her mother, him singing in her ear right here in her kitchen, his touch, his eyes, his delectable mouth …

Yeah. *Xander who?*

At least for the moment.

She was only human, after all.

CHAPTER TWENTY-FIVE

Jagger may have seemed loose and easy while doing dishes, and why not? He was singing the songs he wrote, recorded, and sang on stage to thousands and, at present, he was on a stage of sorts, singing to his number-one fan. And generally, when he was on stage—*man*—nothing could touch him.

He equated it to going underwater. That sensation of no noise, just this moment of peace and calm while you held your breath and hung. That's what he felt when he walked on stage. Like here he was, doing what came naturally, and for the next ninety minutes, nothing could touch him.

Only that wasn't really what was happening now, was it?

He wasn't on stage, although he was acting pretty nonchalant for McKenna as they headed to his place. However, internally, he was yinning and yanging with all sorts of emotional dilemmas. In his mind, what happened at the Wrights'? Fucking brilliant. He could not have orchestrated a better scenario if he tried. The dreaded boyfriend—first in line for McKenna's affection—walking in and shocking the livin' shit out of everybody with that sweet, little Georgia peach hanging on his arm. What the ever-loving hell?

The man must have a death wish. Because knowing McKenna as he did, she was likely to castrate the bastard tomorrow and hang his testicles from the flagpole at the top of Main Street.

And, also knowing McKenna as he did, she was going to give Jagger this night that he'd been wanting for far longer than she knew, only to screw it all up in the morning.

Of that he was sure.

She was going to be all *rebound* this and *using you* that. So Jagger decided to go ahead and get that bullshit out on the table now. He held the front door of his rented home open with one hand, allowing McKenna to enter, holding up a re-corked half bottle of wine in his other. He raised it up. "More?"

"I'm good for now, thanks." McKenna took off her coat and hung it on the brass coatrack.

The woman looked good. Damn good. He recognized the blouse. Had definitely seen that blouse before, though he couldn't remember exactly when. It might be the one she wore when he first asked her out after that concert, but he remembered it being tighter with more buttons undone. He studied the curve of her ass in those killer jeans, watched as she lingered for a moment, dragging her fingers across the top of the couch in his family room. She seemed to not want to take a seat, as if she was ready—not unlike him—to move things along.

He cleared his throat and rubbed his hands together. "McKenna, *I*"—he stressed, holding a hand to his heart—"happen to be convinced that the two of us have staying power. So I'm gonna go ahead and ask you a question, but trust me, there's no correct answer." He took off his leather jacket and hung it with hers. "I just don't want to get stuck in my own head wondering what's in yours. So, either way, I'm good."

"And your question?" she asked coyly.

"Are you here with me because you're mad at Xander or because you want to be with me?"

She gazed at him, her lips quirked up in a half amused, half considering gesture. "Both?"

He nodded figuring that was honest.

She held up a finger. "However, I'd like to further clarify by saying that had I not been dating Xander when you first arrived in Henderson and asked me to dinner, I would have accepted your invitation immediately, and we likely would have arrived here weeks ago."

"Well, I'm not gonna lie"—he approached her slowly—"tonight's turning into a really good night." He slid a hand into her luscious, dark mane, cupping the side of her head. His eyes fell to her dazzling arctic-blue irises, feeling like he was finally cashing in his winning ticket. "You are far more than I imagined you'd be. Full-on feisty and giving me one long run for my money."

"And finally, I'm yours."

He grinned, licking his lips. "Those words." He bit his lip, essentially stomping down on the grin she'd prompted. He didn't want to show his damn hand because … yeah … she was totally on the rebound. In his head, the words, *Rebound this,* sprouted as he leaned down and kissed her the way she liked to be kissed. Easy, sweet, and then just a little deeper.

"Xander's a fool," he said as he applied and released pressure to her lips. "I'm no fool. I've known what I wanted for a long time now." He eased back, looking into her eyes. "And if you'd given me your number way back when, he'd have never had his shot."

"Mmm."

Her *mmm* was noncommittal, but her eyes smiled. He released his hold, his palm sliding over her shoulder, down her arm so he could take her by the hand. "You are about to find out what you've been missing by chickening out."

"Did I chicken out?" she wondered aloud. "Or was I just not interested in hearing from you?"

"Obviously, you chickened out, because what woman in their right mind wouldn't want to hear from me?" He was backing his way down the hall, pulling her along. "And I get it," he continued to jest. "I'm intimidating. You and your ladylike upbringing were afraid of the fierceness of your attraction."

McKenna grinned, her eyes shining.

"What?" He prompted, grinning back.

"You're not wrong," she admitted. "You think you're teasing me, but you are not wrong. I was—I *am* afraid of the fierceness of my attraction. Back then, it was based on your stage presence, your charisma, and your voice. I was terribly attracted to you. Just like every other Cavaliers fan."

"It was more than that, even back then." He pulled her into his bedroom. (Which he'd cleaned from top to bottom before heading to her place with dinner.) "There's chemistry between us. I felt it from the stage."

"There's definitely chemistry between us."

"And it's only grown." He pulled her to him, the two of them standing at the foot of his bed. Jagger gripped her jean-clad hips and slipped his hands into her back pockets, shortening the distance between them to next to nothing. "But from the stage, I couldn't fall in love with the lilt of your voice. I couldn't know that you had gumption in spades. I wasn't able to feel the softness of your skin, predict the extraordinary color of your eyes, and I could only imagine what it would be like for you to kiss me." His voice trailed off. "Kiss me," he whispered.

She looked toward the ground. With her head bent forward, her freshly washed hair—begging to be touched—fell over her shoulders, hiding her face. As she brought her head up, she settled her hands on his chest. It didn't take much for her to lean in, lift to her toes, and place her lips against his.

"Kiss me," he whispered against her perfect mouth. His eyes were open, noting that hers were closed. He saw the movement of her head, the tilt. Felt her hands move to his jaw, smooth over his beard, clasp his cheeks in her hands, tug his head forward and down just a tad before she opened her mouth and really laid one on him.

He didn't leave it one-sided. How could he? She was everything he'd wanted for the last eighteen months. If he told her that now, like he really, really wanted to, it wouldn't sink in. She'd just been dumped by the guy the whole town thought was her fiancé. He wasn't going to waste his first vocal confession of love tonight. But he could demonstrate his intention. He could show McKenna how much she meant to him. Show her that in his mind, she'd never come in second. She had always been ... the one.

But apparently, his stupid mouth wasn't on board with all that. Because after kissing his way from her mouth to her ear, he revealed, "I'm crazy about you." Not that she couldn't have deduced that over the last several weeks of him dogging her. And crazy was an apt description for the culmination of feelings he was sorting through at the moment.

Euphoric ... about how this was all working out for him.

Desperate ... for it to work out for her as well.

And let's not forget *horny* as all fuck.

His capacity for breath shortened considerably at the same time his heart rate was kicking in, like he was sprinting at the end of a marathon. He pulled back, double-checking her features. Then he pushed the hair from her face so he could stare into the arctic abyss of her eyes. "We doing this?" he asked. "Tell me we're really doing this."

"We are so doing this," came her reply, which threw him out of his head enough to see that she seemed to be right there with him in the hyperventilating department. And from the wild look in her eyes, probably the horny department as well.

"I changed the sheets," he told her as he toed off his boots. It didn't take long for her to slip out of her fuzzy slippers.

"So you were expecting company?" Her eyes sparkled as she started unbuttoning her blouse.

"Not expecting. Just hoping." He pulled his shirt over his head, threw it to a chair.

With the buttons of her blouse completely undone, her shirt hung open and loose, giving him a beautiful glimpse of her pretty bra and smoking-hot cleavage. She reached out and touched his chest with both hands, her fingers splayed. Her eyes were definitely not on his face.

Wanting to indulge in much the same, he fit his fingers into the collar of her blouse and backed it off her shoulders, pushing it down her arms, causing her to release her touch for a moment while she extracted herself. Her fingers came back to caress him as he tossed her shirt over to land with his. His breath halted as he looked his fill, not wanting anything to take away from this moment. She was a mighty-fine babe in her bikini. But having her standing in his bedroom with a lacy bra on was far more intimate and awe inspiring. "You're a beautiful woman, McKenna. You literally take my breath away."

"Right back at you, Jagger Yates."

He smiled at the use of his full name. "Call me Jags."

She looked up curious. "Jags?"

"My parents, my siblings, they all call me Jags. To you, I want to be Jags. Not *Jagger Yates*."

She stood there—half naked—actually thinking about it. "I'm not sure that's possible." Finally, she shook her head. "Sorry. To me, you'll always be heartthrob, rock-star, man-of-my-dreams Jagger Yates."

"Man of your dreams? Well, hell. I can live with that." He bent down and pulled off his socks before easing her up against him, chest to chest. The fingers of his right hand sought the back waistband of her jeans and lingered just a moment before sliding inside, feeling his way into her panties, enough to cup her bare ass. "I can't tell you how right this feels."

He meant to say good. How *good* this feels. Her bare skin against his. His hand on her bare ass. Not that it didn't feel right. It felt damn right. He just didn't want to continue to show all his cards.

Well, why the hell not? his inner rock star wondered. *You told her last night she had a choice. Show the fuck up and make it a good one.*

Right then.

His left hand felt for the hair falling down her back, tugging on the ends so she'd lift her face to his. Then he made his move. His—wait for it—*rock star* move. He captured her mouth in a searing kiss. A blow-the-lid-off-what's-happening kiss. A take-it-to-the-next-level-and-keep-right-on-going kiss. And during that kiss, he slid his hands to the front of her jeans, unfastening the button, sliding open her fly. His fingers lingered, treading over tender flesh, luxuriating in the soft feel of her body where he'd yet been allowed to touch. His fingers drifted to the skin over her hips, teasing all the sensual spots her jeans covered. Caressing, molding his fingers to her body, all the while using his kisses to continue to stimulate both of their desire.

There was no holding back on McKenna's part, and he appreciated that. Was desperate to *explore* that. He longed to play her body as confidently as he did his favorite guitar. Get her vibrating against him, learn how to string her along. So he took his sweet time, tuning into her sensitive spots. God, she felt good in his hands. Beyond the newness. Beyond the excitement.

Eventually he couldn't stop his hands from sliding farther into her jeans, down her hips, on to her thighs, dragging the denim down over them. He kept on going, finally having to break from her lips as he pushed her clothes toward the floor, feeling her hands hold on to his shoulders as she stepped out.

The lingerie she had on was not your everyday fare. It was nude in color, skimpy in design, appealing without screaming *Fuck me*. It was definitely saying something more along the lines of *I have shown up for you, so make love to me and don't let me down.* At least that was Jagger's interpretation. He intended to embody that sentiment even if his heart was beating too fast again. He wasn't going to rush this, no matter how much his dick was yelling that it needed to get off.

Simmer down, old friend. We've got some serious business to attend to.

All this conversation with his dick and McKenna's lingerie happened in a split second. Because McKenna's hands had decided to reciprocate and were now unbuttoning, unzipping, and pushing down his own jeans.

"I love your hands on me," he said, leaning into the feel of her. His legs shimmied his jeans loose.

"Mmm," came her response.

The two of them stood there, taking in each other's bodies.

"You are really quite remarkable," McKenna commented.

"Me?" He looked down at himself, a little distracted by the tent in his boxer briefs. His dick was average at best for a guy his height, but in front of McKenna, it was doing its best to look mammoth. Kinda like if he were standing on his tiptoes while bench-pressing his maximum weight.

"Do you think all the women in the audience undress you with their eyes while you're on stage? Or is that just me?"

"Just you."

"Pfft," she blurted, smiling.

"Those little goodies you have on." He wagged a finger at her lingerie. "You put those on for me?"

"I did."

"So when you got out of the shower tonight, you thought …?"

"When I got out of my shower, I thought I was going to crawl into bed and stay there. But after you knocked on the door and told me to put on a dress, I remembered that there was a very attractive man in my life I was now free to pursue." She waved her hands down the length of her body. "I was saving this ensemble for a special occasion." She looked him in the eye when she admitted, "I didn't realize just how special it would be."

God, she made him happy. So happy he'd like to weep. Instead, he ducked, threw her over his shoulder, and grinned as she let out an "Eep." Then he walked to the side of the bed and dumped her on it. He stood back, hands on hips, basking in the glory of finally having the woman he'd lusted after for so many months right where he'd envisioned her.

"You were my muse for 'Babe in a Bar.'"

She grinned, curling onto her side, letting her sexy hair fall all over the place as she propped an elbow on the bed and then supported her head with her hand. "When you alluded to that at the signing, it made my head fill up with joy bubbles."

Joy bubbles. Yeah. He was experiencing a few of those joy bubbles himself. He stood his ground, his erection a minor distraction as they talked. "You were my muse for 'My Kinda Woman.' For 'Missed Again.' For a song called 'Wrong Number,' which will never see the light of day because of its overzealous use of profanity."

"Jagger," she whispered in awe.

"For so many of the songs I've written during the past eighteen months, McKenna, *you* were my muse."

"Oh my gosh," she said sitting up, looking serious. "What if us getting together squashes that?"

"Squashes what?" he said, putting one knee on the bed.

"Your creative genius? What if this chemistry between us combusts, burns out, and ... and then so do your lyrics?"

"Something tells me our chemistry is going to have a long run, and I'll never run out of lyrics. Regardless, I'm willing to risk it."

"I'm not sure I am," she said as she backed away from him. 'Babe in a Bar' is a damn good song."

"It is," he said, grabbing up her hand so she couldn't get that far away. "Imagine how well I'm going to be able to write once all this pent-up, angry lust is no longer angry."

"You have angry lust?"

"Not at the moment. At the moment, I have raging lust. Irrepressible lust. Hardcore lust."

"Hmm. Hardcore lust," she whispered. Then grinned.

He grinned back. Right before he pounced on her, curling her body underneath his, and arranging her legs so he could press himself right at her heat. "This feels good," he said. Then he manned up and said, "This feels exactly right."

"Jagger," she whispered, looking at him like he was all she'd ever need. And he so wanted to cash in on that.

He rocked himself against her slowly. The pain so good he shuddered. Nothing but exquisite torture. His eyes locked onto hers, their bodies finally having a go at what they'd been working toward since he'd first noticed her from the stage. He didn't want to stop the very slow, very potent body engagement, so he kept it up.

McKenna began contributing to it with more than a bit of enthusiasm. "This feels good," she agreed in a breathy bit of vocals. "You feel good. Against me. Like that."

"Imagine how good it's going to feel when we get these damn clothes out of our way."

"I don't know. This feels pretty good." Her eyes were closed. She was biting her lip. He leaned in to kiss her.

"Take off your bra for me," he whispered.

She grinned before opening her eyes. Releasing her hold on his forearms, she drew the straps down off her shoulders, pulled her arms out of the straps, and then sashayed the fabric around her torso so the clasps were in front. She twisted and tugged and eventually freed herself. "There." She laid her head back on the pillow, looked down at her breasts, and then back up at him. "All yours."

It didn't take him long to make them his. His mouth came down and sucked in not only a nipple, but a large portion of flesh as well. The feel of her soft, supple skin in his mouth was soul satisfying and served to rev his engines even higher. Her breasts were more than a mouthful, full and cushiony. He sucked and suckled himself into distraction, hardly aware he'd moved down, his hips no longer working against the juncture of her thighs. His body still eager, but his senses enjoying one bliss-filled moment at a time.

McKenna's fingers were in his hair, stroking his scalp. His hand came up to replace his mouth as he moved to lick her other nipple. He squeezed and kneaded, tugged and twisted. God, he loved tits. And as tits went, McKenna's were spectacular. Just as he'd imagined.

And then his imagination flashed to McKenna riding him. Imagining how he'd have his mouth on her breasts, his hands on her ass.

His mouth was on a roll, sliding, sucking, nipping kisses down her stomach. When he reached her bellybutton, he swirled his tongue and then caught the edge of her panties with his teeth. She giggled as his teeth went to work, pulling her panties down, using his hands only when he had to, uncovering the pinnacle of what made her female.

The scent of her sex sent his senses soaring. His dick pulsing thickly at the sight of her well-groomed curls. His tongue craved a taste of her, while his fingers longed to stroke her from top to bottom and drive her wild. His cock, yeah his cock had a couple ideas of its own, causing him to move quicker, relieving McKenna of her clothing once and for all. He even took time to drag the remnants of her bra from underneath her and, while on his knees, he slowed things down to a crawl as he sprung his cock free of his boxers.

McKenna's greedy gaze latched on to his erection. Glancing between it and his eyes.

"Okay. Wow."

He stroked himself proudly, never feeling more like a rock star than when her eyes were on him.

"That's hot," she said.

"You're hot."

She moved to sit up. Then came to her knees. She placed a hand on his shoulder and with the other one she took him to heaven.

"Jesus," he hissed as her hand cupped his balls. She immediately drew her hand away.

"Did I hurt you?"

"God, no. No. Please." He guided her hand back to where she'd touched him. "No hurt. Extreme pleasure," he said, continuing to stroke himself while she used her fingers to fondle him gently.

The two of them were kneeling in the center of the bed, both of them focused on his junk. Jagger hadn't realized he had closed his eyes until he felt her licking and then sucking on the skin at the side of his neck. She abruptly pulled back.

"Sorry. Sorry," she whispered, kissing the area tenderly. "I don't want to leave a mark."

"Hell. Mark me. Wherever. Put your mouth on me. Please."

He felt her grin against his shoulder. Her talented fingers still playing with his balls. She opened her mouth and bit down gently on a tendon there, the one that was moving because … yeah, he was still jacking himself. *Fucking best fantasy ever.*

Her hand eventually moved from his balls up his shaft, taking over the hand job with her soft palm. Her mouth lavished his pectorals with kisses and little bites. She spent time on his nipples, and damn if he didn't think that was a good idea. Who knew? Nipples!

His hands were on a mission to touch her body every place she'd normally be covered in clothes. So while the exquisite sexual sensations shot up and down his shaft and throughout his chest, his fingers teased her breasts, her underarms, her waist, her hips, her ass. He was able to get a fingertip in between their bodies without messing up her rhythm … because yeah, not gonna fuck that up. Sweet baby Jesus, was she ever hot and wet and ready for him.

She'd probably be okay if he tossed her on her back, spread her legs, and plowed inside. Just go for broke until she came and then he came. But first times were first times, and man, he'd never wanted anything more than to make this first time last—make this experience more than memorable for both of them. It was the first time he had her naked. He wasn't going to rush a damn thing.

But he did want more. He wanted to give more, and he wanted to receive more. And he didn't really know how he managed the move, because damn, it was smooth. Like, he could write a how-to book smooth. It involved hugging her close, laying her down, shifting his own position as they went. It involved parting her legs and putting his face between her thighs. It involved his mouth and tongue and the art of pleasing a woman.

And it involved a heavy dose of hope. Hope that she might go ahead and follow his lead.

As he taunted and teased with nothing but his fingertips and his mouth, he felt McKenna's hand return to his cock. Another hand on his balls caused his hips to jack involuntarily against the sublime friction she created.

Yesss, his mind hissed, causing him to go after her sweet pussy with zeal.

And then he cried out as he felt the warmth of her mouth on the tip of him. Even though it was what he craved—really craved—it landed as a shock to his system. That first touch of her tongue. That first suck on his tip. That first feel of her mouth claiming him, going down his shaft, sliding back up—damn that was good. So good. So crazy good.

He had to pull his mind out of the sensations and refocus on her pleasure; he was not going to last long if he didn't spend most of his consciousness focused elsewhere.

Although …. *fuck that feels so damn good I could come in the next fifteen seconds.*

Nope. Nope. Back to the game plan, he told himself. She gets hers, then, maybe, you get yours.

Inspired, he rolled, pulling her legs on either side of his head, bringing her body on top of his. He felt her hands and mouth adjust. McKenna was now stroking his balls as she made sweet, sweet love to his cock with her mouth.

The rock star in him refused to be outdone.

He used his fingers to spread her open and prolonged the strokes of his tongue, making a point to use his beard to add sensation. McKenna's hips responded, pressing in and releasing. He held her steady, wanting to make this as diabolically exquisite for her as she was making it for him. Because he was getting off so good right now that if this were the last sex he was ever going to have, he would not be able to complain.

Best. Sensations. Ever.

Of course, it was. Because McKenna was the One.

He was so overwhelmed by the physical sensations they were sharing that he wanted to consume her. Somehow inhale her into his body. He had the sensation of struggling to get close enough. The sensation of wanting more, more, more.

So, relishing the lust-laden haze his mind had entered, he gave *her* more. Following his instincts, he sucked on that beautiful, sensitive nub and felt her strain against him. Then shudder against him. Then spasm, her thighs gripping the sides of his head, her pussy pressing into his face.

His dick felt her hum her reaction. And he couldn't help lifting his hips, pushing deeper for his own release. Her hand at the base of his cock tightened, and that was all she wrote. His body let loose into the most rewarding, most hard-won, most orgasmic orgasms of all time.

And, as his mind drifted back down from heaven, all he could think about was his next song entitled "Sixty-nine."

CHAPTER TWENTY-SIX

McKenna was so out of her league she didn't know whether to laugh or cry.

Sixty-nine? WTF.

And that was WTF as in Why The Fuck have I waited so long to try that?

"Jagger." She sighed his name, not like he was a rock god, but like he was an actual god. Like the offspring of Venus and Zeus or something. The god that would naturally have all the right moves because he came from the right stock.

She didn't know how to dislodge herself from this crazy tangle he'd manipulated them into, and what the hell did it matter, she thought. She wasn't sure she even survived what had just happened. But of course, the god of sex managed to untwist them slowly and delicately, flipping himself around so that both their heads were now at the top of the bed. They were both on their backs, both a complete mess. She'd never felt so satiated and yet so rattled at the same time.

"Stop thinking," he demanded, pulling her against him. One arm under her back, the other arm bent under his own head. He glanced down at her.

"I can't ... think," she uttered. "I'm stunned."

His brows drew together. "Good stunned or bad stunned?"

"Amazingly stunned. Sweaty stunned. Messy stunned. But mostly that-felt-so-good-I-want-to-cry stunned."

He snuggled down, wrapping his arm around her middle and pulling her to him. He kissed her hair. "I'll be right back."

She grabbed on to his arm. "Where are you going?"

"To wash my face. I want to kiss you."

"So kiss me."

He stared down at her. "You sure?"

She smiled. "Very."

"Hmm, okay McKenna Blakely," he said moving to hold her against him again. "You asked for it."

They kissed. Well, they didn't just kiss. They made out. They made out like they were feasting on each other. Open mouths and lots of tongue. And it was sexy as hell tasting the salt of their sweat, the other flavors of their lovemaking mingling within the kiss. It served to add to the intimacy between them. She relished their dirty passion. The grit of being so physical. They didn't use their mouths to talk about what they'd just shared. Their kisses, their hands, their bodies were having the conversation. And the conversation was going very, very well.

Get the rest of the world out of their way and man, could they communicate.

Eventually, she had to use the bathroom, where she did wash up. And he took his turn, which included a quick dash into the shower. He returned to her minty fresh.

Their mouths couldn't get enough of each other.

His hands were having a hard time too. He propped himself up against the headboard then pulled her over his lap. His half-hard dick brushed against the juncture of her thighs. She thought round two was about to begin, but Jagger surprised her. He looked his fill of her face, her hair, her breasts and then angled his head.

"The first time I noticed you from the stage, it was your grin that grabbed my attention." He leaned in, plucked her bottom lip with his thumb and forefinger, and gave her a kiss. "Of course, your physical beauty caught my eye. How could it not?" He started playing with her hair, something he was beginning to make a habit of. "But there was something else that intrigued me. That first time. And I'd forgotten about it. But after your mom filled me in on how you handled the scene with the Wrights tonight after I'd left, it reminded me."

"What was that?"

"Sometime early in our show, you turned completely around and faced the crowd behind you. I'm not sure what was happening, but from my vantage point, it appeared as if you reached into the crowd and extracted an older woman who was quite short. I watched as you swung her in front of you, pushing against the people around you, pointing her out to those who were standing too close. I saw them nod at whatever you told them and give the two of you space. Then you turned back around. Immediately, this huge group started looking for something. I'm not sure what, but it must have been important. Whatever it was was found fairly quickly. It was passed to you, and you gave it to the woman. You couldn't see and probably weren't aware of what happened next. But the woman burst into tears, hugging whatever it was you gave her to her chest."

McKenna didn't recall any of the incident until he said that. "Oh." She pouted. "It was sad, actually. That lady had dropped her son's dog tags. He was supposed to have been at your concert. He was this huge fan and had been killed in a car accident just the weekend before. She came in his place, hoping to feel close to him."

"How did you know all that?"

"I didn't. She told me later because I walked her out to her car."

"How did you even know what was happening behind you?"

"I was pushed. And then I heard some frantic commotion. She'd been buffeted by the crowd as everyone swarmed forward when y'all came on. She was trying to tell people. Get them to help her find the dog tags. Only she wasn't as mouthy as I was."

He laughed. Grinned. Slid his hand through her hair. "You got everyone's attention—*while I was singing*, I might add—and found the dog tags."

"It had to be done. I wasn't going to enjoy the concert until that lady was settled."

"That was kind of you."

She shrugged.

"Nah. Don't do that. You're kind." He held up a hand to stop her from disagreeing. "You have an attitude. One I love. But underneath that bravado, you are kind. You are thoughtful. As evidenced tonight by your lack of exploding all over Xander."

She shook her head. "I honestly don't know how I managed that."

"Me either." He laughed. "I mean, come on."

"I know, right?" She laughed with him. Actually laughed at the absurdity of Xander showing up with her archenemy on the day she thought he was going to propose. "I probably would have exploded—in magnificent fashion—if I hadn't felt Anna Beth and Maxwell flanking my sides. Anna Beth is doing well, but she is not out of the woods with this autoimmune thing. Stress is not helpful, and I have sat by her bedside too long to risk going back to the days where she was hanging on by a thread. I, at least, had knowledge of Becca. His parents were completely taken by surprise."

"And so you handled the situation. Like the pro you are."

"Like the pro what I am?"

"Maybe not pro. Maybe just like your Southern roots and your momma brought you up to be?"

"Humph."

He leaned in and kissed her. "You did good," he whispered. "You're kind. You think of others. I could use someone like you in my life."

She glanced at him curiously, wondering what he meant by that.

"That's a song for another time," he assured her while using his growing appendage to distract her.

And oh what a distraction it was. With her legs sprawled on either side of his pelvis, her body was spread perfectly to feel the sensations of his long …slow … glide. And it was *sublime*. And powerful. All her focus narrowed, zeroing in on the really, damn good, over-the-top feelings below her waist. Jagger was good with his hands, he was good with his mouth, and now she was finding out he was good with his—

The pounding on the front door brought them both to a quick halt. The two of them held their breath, not moving, unsure of what they heard or what the hell was happening.

It came again, the pounding on the door. Then they heard her name.

"McKenna!"

McKenna's eyes flew to Jagger's only to see his close as he cursed under his breath.

"It's Xander," she said, even though it was obvious Jagger knew exactly who'd just stolen their moment.

Jagger started to shuffle from underneath her. "What are you doing?" she asked.

"I'm going to answer my door."

"Why?"

"Why?" He fought his way loose, although she noted he was careful as he deposited her from his lap onto the bed. "Because he's pounding on it and it's"—he checked the clock—"eleven thirty."

"But why is he even here?"

"Well, since he called your name, I'm guessing he wants to talk to you. Which, you know, gets a no-fucking-way from me."

McKenna scrambled out of bed and over to the rug to find her clothes. She began tugging on her jeans over her bare body. "Stay here," Jagger insisted, pulling on his own jeans.

"I'm not staying here."

"I'll tell him to go away. It'll take me thirty seconds, and we can get back to what we were getting to."

McKenna stopped buttoning her blouse and stared at him. "My ex pounds on the door as we are about to have sex and you don't think that has blown the mood? You stay here. I'll deal with this."

"Not in thirty seconds, you won't."

"Watch me," she assured him as she managed to hang on to her adrenaline surge long enough to button three buttons on her blouse before bolting out of the bedroom.

"McKenna," Jagger called, dogging her, reaching out and spinning her around.

"Look, let me deal with him. You don't need to deal with this. Not tonight."

"Where's Becca?" She flung hair out of her eyes. "Why is he here?"

"McKenna!" The pounding on the door commenced again. Clearly, Xander could hear them.

"Jagger, just let me deal with him."

"Yeah, no. My house. My door he's banging on. And frankly, it's my girl he's harassing. Not gonna back down from all that."

McKenna turned back toward the door, wondering if the pampered rock star was equipped to tussle with an oversized banker. With the mood she was in at the moment, she wouldn't mind watching the two of them have a go at each other.

Of course, with the mood she was in, she could probably take both of them down. Simultaneously.

She swung open the front door and folded her arms over her chest. "What?" she snapped.

Xander stood there looking stunned, like he hadn't really expected anyone to open the door.

"Xander?"

"I'm sorry. About tonight. Can we, ah, talk?"

"No. She's on a date. With me," Jagger said, coming up beside McKenna and wrapping his arm possessively around her middle.

McKenna looked toward the ground a moment, debating on whether to permit Jagger's he-man routine. Quickly, she decided Xander deserved that and more. She looked up and threw a thumb at Jagger. "Yeah, what he said."

Xander's eyes darted between the two of them. Then his gorgeous gray ones settled on her. "McKenna. I'd like to explain to you how I didn't have a choice. I'd like for you to understand how that happened. How I was stuck between a rock and a hard place. Did you get the text I sent? I told you I'd make it up to you."

Was he serious with this? McKenna's inner voice shouted inside her head. She literally had to close her eyes and take a breath in order not to reach out and strangle him.

From somewhere deep inside her came an extraordinarily calm voice. "Xander, you've actually had a choice for a lot of months now. And boy, did you finally make it. In rather spectacular fashion. I may have preferred not to have it revealed to me with the equivalent of fireworks and balloons, but hey, I have clearly received the message, and the nicest thing I can say right now is that I hope you will be very happy living in Charlotte with your sweet Becca for the rest of your goddamn life. Now, if you'll excuse me, I'm going to go have sex with another man." She leaned forward. "You were good, but you are no rock star."

Then she slammed the door in Xander's face.

CHAPTER TWENTY-SEVEN

So, that happened.

Jagger's head was reeling as both he and McKenna stood side by side unmoving, their gaze on the back of the door McKenna had just shut in the boyfriend's face.

"You okay?" he whispered.

"I'm not sure," she whispered back.

"You were brilliant. Like, a heroine in a movie, brilliant."

He felt her nod as they both continued to stare at the door.

Then an abrupt sound made them jump. Xander had either kicked or punched the door. They continued to stand together until they heard feet move off the stoop, a car door slam, and a motor start up. They stood there even after they'd heard him drive away.

Finally, Jagger placed a kiss on her head. "How about some wine?"

She nodded.

He wasn't an insensitive idiot. He knew their lust-laden evening had just taken a turn for the worse. His semi was certainly hoping he could get things back on track fast, but his years of being a human adult tuned him in to the fact that McKenna was probably going to struggle with this.

Even though she'd nailed the asshole good.

That scene right there was something Jagger was *never* going to forget. Nor was he grown up enough not to repeat—verbatim—that last little ditty she threw at the boyfriend. His band was going to eat that *rock star* shit up.

But for the moment, he had McKenna's heart in his hands, and he needed to show up for her and let her deal however she needed to.

He left her standing, staring at the front door and headed over to the galley kitchen to pour a couple glasses of wine. He then pulled out some cheese and crackers because even though he'd eaten his fill of Thanksgiving dinner earlier, he'd worked up another appetite. Maybe McKenna had too.

He kept glancing in her direction as he worked. Wondering, as she continued to stand right where he'd left her, what was going through her mind. When she finally turned to look at him, he wasn't prepared for what came out of her mouth.

"I've got to go home," she said, buttoning the remaining buttons on her blouse. She turned to head down the hallway into the bedroom.

"Whoa, whoa, whoa." Jagger leapt around the counter to go after her. "What just happened? I mean, I get that we aren't going to jump right back to the action," he said, pointing at his bed. "But we can certainly sit on the couch, enjoy some wine, and rehash all that."

McKenna was stepping into shoes and picking up her lingerie.

"Baby, please."

"I'm not your baby," she said as she strode past him and into the hallway.

"So we're back to that again," he muttered before turning to chase her down. "McKenna. Stop. Please." She was putting on her coat, pulling her hair out from the back of it. "Give me five minutes so I can understand what is going through your head right now."

She raised her hands over her head. "I don't know." Then she dropped her arms, defeated. "I don't know what's going through my head." She stepped forward. "I mean, why did he come here? Why did he search me out? Where the hell has he stashed the peach?"

"The peach?"

"You know. The peach. Becca, the darling peach."

Jagger's brows raised briefly. "The same word floated through my mind." And then a horrible thought occurred to him. "Are you … are you going to run after him?"

"What?"

"Are you leaving me to run after Xander? After everything he's put you through?"

"No. Of course not."

He shook his head. "I don't believe you." And his heart sank. Like, truly sank. Because he realized there was no way he could win the battle for McKenna's love if she could go through what the asshole boyfriend put her through today, not to mention the last few weeks, and *still want* him.

As if she'd heard his inner fears, McKenna raced into his arms, throwing her own around his middle and holding on tight. "I'm not running after him. I promise. I just don't understand why he bothered to come over. And it has me worrying about Anna Beth. Not to mention the glaring spotlight his arrival on your front stoop put on the fact that I'm here, with you, after I just was dumped, by him."

"Well, you said it yourself. If you hadn't been dating Xander, you would have ended up here prior to tonight."

"Yes, but people don't know that."

"What people?"

"All the people."

"I'm not following."

"Look." She began to pull away. "You and I have a thing. A thing that's been brewing."

"Yeah."

"But the people out there"—she pointed to the front door—"and most importantly, Mr. and Mrs. Wright, have no idea that we have a thing. That's been brewing."

"McKenna," he growled.

"Just hear me out."

"I will if you take off your jacket and sit on the couch and drink wine with me."

She actually struggled with the idea.

"Jesus, McKenna. It's almost midnight. Where else do you have to be?"

"Right. Sorry. Okay. I just feel, guilty, I guess. For being here."

He wasn't going to touch that one. At least not until she took off her coat and had a drink in her hand.

CHAPTER TWENTY-EIGHT

After ninety minutes and a full bottle of wine on top of the half bottle already opened, the mostly consumed cheese platter embodied the battle that had ensued between Jagger and McKenna.

McKenna beseeched Jagger as he stood next to the couch, hands on hips, leering down at her. "Why can't we just lie low for a few weeks as I've requested? Let me ease Anna Beth into the idea of you and me dating so it doesn't appear that I've abandoned her overnight."

"McKenna. How are you abandoning Anna Beth by dating me?"

"Up until today, she thought I was marrying her son."

"Not. Your. Fault."

"True. I get there has been something brewing between us since you've been in town—"

"Exactly"—he poked a finger at her—"something very naughty, something very risqué, something even downright lewd has been brewing between us, and I've had to simmer it the fuck down because *I* wasn't the boyfriend. But guess what?" He clapped his hands and rubbed them together. "I *am* the boyfriend now. So nothing has to simmer. Nothing is going to simmer. And if you'd like me to escort you to see Anna Beth so that I can explain to her how much things are boiling over now that her son has gotten his ass out of my way …"

"Like that's going to help."

"She likes me," he claimed. "And she loves you. Ultimately, I know that she's gonna want you to be happy. And McKenna," he said, sitting back on the couch, taking up her hand. "Are you happy? With me?"

Was she happy with Jagger? What McKenna knew was that she was *crazy* about Jagger. That she was physically *drawn* to Jagger. That she was revved up whenever Jagger was around. But happy? Happy wasn't even in the realm of how she was feeling about Jagger.

Clearly, he didn't like her hesitation. "McKenna," he barked. "The proper response to that question is yes. Yes, Jagger, I'm very happy with you."

"I'm sorry," she pleaded. "I was thinking about the question. About whether I'm happy. I have to say that there are a lot of really strong emotions swirling around you, and they are all good, and exciting, and crazy even. I'm mad for you. You have to know that. But just simply happy? Like content? Or at peace? I'm not anywhere near any of that. I'm in the *holy shit, is this really happening* stage."

"Well. Hmm." Jagger regarded her thoughtfully. "See, I'm happy. I'm extremely content. I'm definitely at peace for the first time in almost two years."

"Because I'm the girl you've been writing about. The one you've finally caught up with. But for me, for the past many months I've been worried about losing my first love for the second time. Then suddenly I'm in bed with a rock star, the embodiment of my maddest obsession, the one-and-only *Jagger Yates.* I am on cloud nine and having to pinch myself that this is even real."

"I'm pretty sure the feeling of happiness is included in there somewhere."

She nodded, giving him that. "Yes. I'm sure it is. It's just more exciting and unworldly. That's why I need a little time to digest what's taken place. And on the broader scale, if I have to digest it, I'm pretty sure everyone else who hasn't been living this dream is going to have to digest it too."

"That is bullshit."

"But it's my bullshit."

"Oh, fuck. Now I've got a song in my head," he said staring at the ceiling right before he returned his glare to her face. "You want to wallow in your small-town bullshit while I write an award-winning song about it, be my guest." He got off the couch and started stomping around. "The hits are just gonna keep on coming, aren't they?" he shouted.

"I'm glad I can be an inspiration."

"Oh, you're an inspiration." He definitely didn't sound as enamored with her as he had earlier.

"I'm sorry I'm dragging you through this."

"Whatever," he said, heading down the hallway. "I've gotta write this down."

CHAPTER TWENTY-NINE

While Jagger worked, wrote, whatever he was doing back there in the second bedroom, McKenna got herself off the couch and cleaned up the wine bottles, the glasses, and the mess they'd made of the cheese board, adding on whatever cleanup she could in the kitchen. Then she straightened the pillows on the couch and made his living area look tidy. She'd never been around Jagger while he was working, so she quietly wandered down the hall and leaned against the doorjamb as he picked a melody out on his guitar.

It was two o'clock in the morning.

Part of McKenna wanted to find her phone and film him at work. Another part of her wanted to curl up in the armchair across the room and close her eyes, letting herself fall asleep while listening to him create. She thought about leaving him be. About going home and sleeping in her own bed with her own thoughts. But then she remembered Jagger wasn't going to be in Henderson forever, and however much time she had with him here, like this, she didn't want to squander.

So she curled up on the armchair for a few minutes before Jagger set his guitar down and approached.

"What?" she asked sleepily.

"You're distracting me." He leaned down and wrapped his arms around her, gathering her together enough to pick her up.

"I thought I was your muse."

"Ah-ha. Therefore, I can't create while imagining how uncomfortable you are. I'll be better able to write if I know you are tucked in bed across the hall." He carried her from one room to the other.

"Leave the doors open," she said. "If you wouldn't mind."

"Don't mind a bit." He laid her down, kissed her on the forehead and covered her up. "Sleep," he said. "I'll get you home before too long in the morning."

"Night, Jagger."

"Night, baby."

CHAPTER THIRTY

Jagger didn't sleep.

He wrote, he composed, he continually reframed the story within the song. He hummed the harmony. He liked what he'd come up with as the sun started to rise. He knew it could grow into something special by tweaking a word or two, finding the precise turn of phrase that presently eluded him. But the chorus was there. The chorus was prime stuff, and he was eager to share it with McKenna just because it was really going to piss her off.

He smiled at that. Not that he wanted to make his girl mad, but come on. She was putting him through the wringer, and she was getting off scot-free.

Well, maybe not scot-free. I mean, she did get dumped in front of the entire Wright family yesterday. And maybe he could see her point a little. She didn't want her infamy to be about a big breakup at the Wrights' on Thanksgiving and hopping into the roving rock star's bed the same night.

Even though it was totally true.

Yeah. He didn't necessarily want to admit it, but he understood it. He'd grown up in a small town. He knew that the worst things you'd done were the first things people remembered when they heard your name.

So instead of jumping into bed with her right now and finishing what they'd been so grossly cheated out of last night, he was going to earn some points. Some new-boyfriend points. He was going to get her home before all the talk started.

He had a song going.

He had a couple weeks before he needed to be anywhere.

The cheating boyfriend was now well out of the picture.

He could be magnanimous, even if his dick was not exactly onboard. It wasn't like he and McKenna were going to stop hanging around each other. They could be sneaky while the gap between the big breakup and her new relationship with him widened.

He could be supportive with all that. In fact, it would give him a chance to publicly woo her. A little bit at a time. Here and there. Let all of Henderson watch them fall in love. Again.

So off he went to brew some coffee. To find a suitable easy-fix breakfast to offer McKenna in bed.

Then he'd hit the shower, because after kissing her awake, he'd definitely need a cold one before driving her home.

They'd make a plan.

All would be well.

They were finally moving on.

CHAPTER THIRTY-ONE

"Oh, fuck no," Jagger said aloud as he saw what was happening in his rearview mirror. He immediately decided to turn left and circle back to McKenna's place. Because if his eyes weren't deceiving him, the boyfriend—*the ex-boyfriend*—just got out of a car where he'd apparently been hunkered down, lying in wait for McKenna. And, as Jagger turned the corner, he could see that the ex-boyfriend was now heading straight for her front door.

"You've got to be kidding me, dude," he shouted as he stepped on the gas and made his way back around the block. "She told you goodbye last night. In rather triumphant fashion, I might add. Remember? You're good but you're no rock star. That's right," he yelled. "I'm the rock star, and it is time for you to back the fuck off."

Once back at McKenna's, Jagger saw no one standing on the front stoop even though the jackass's car was still parked up the road. "Did she let him in?" His head hurt at the thought. He pictured himself parking, getting out, slamming the door, and rocketing himself up those front steps and into the house to put an end to whatever the hell shouldn't be happening inside.

And then he remembered to breathe, because with the tendons in his neck bulging, there was a lack of oxygen getting to his brain, making him lightheaded and ready to pass out. So he parked, breathed, breathed some more, and then decided to play things a little cooler.

Like, not that much cooler. Just, ya know, not stampede the place. No, he was going to wait it out. McKenna would probably appreciate that, he thought as he extracted himself from the pickup. He closed the door and then leaned back against it, one booted foot crossed over the other, his arms crossed over his chest, his ball cap covering most of his face as he waited to have a word with the lying, cheating, thorn in his side.

CHAPTER THIRTY-TWO

"Xander?" McKenna couldn't believe he was here. In her house. "Where's Becca?" *Why was she so worried about Becca?* she wondered as her internal dialogue played out an entirely different line of questioning than the one she was vocally engaged in.

"Becca's on a plane. I think you and I should talk."

"So talk."

"Can we sit?"

"No."

"All right. My parents are furious with me. And they aren't happy with you either."

"Me?" McKenna was horrified.

"We weren't honest with them, and they feel like they've been blindsided."

"Oh," she half laughed, half sobbed. "*They* feel like they've been blindsided. Well, I guess they do. I know I sure felt *blindsided*."

"And I'm sorry about that, but Becca's arrival at Thanksgiving didn't mean what you thought it did. I didn't choose Becca over you."

"Ahh, yeah. You actually did."

"No. I was taking her to the airport, shipping her back to her family for the holiday, and I was going to break up with her during the drive. It's a long drive. I figured I'd have time to explain about how I wanted to move back to Henderson and date you exclusively. And just as I was about to get into the whole thing, she got a text that her flight had been canceled."

"Wait a minute. You waited until *yesterday* to break it off with Becca. And not only that, your big plan was to do it before you dropped her off at the airport?"

"Yes. Because I've been busy gearing up for a move, making my boss understand my desire to work from Henderson, and figuring out the details of how that was going to go. I haven't seen Becca in two weeks, and although we have communicated, I didn't have it in me to break up with her over the phone. And yeah, I could have asked her to dinner, or met her somewhere, or just stopped by her place, but like I said. I have been *very busy*, working *very hard*, making this happen for *us*."

"That *us* sounds very angry."

"I am *beyond* angry."

"You're beyond angry? How do you think I felt when you walked into Thanksgiving with the peach?"

"The what?"

"Xander, I was under the impression that you were going to *propose*," she shouted. "I thought you were late because you had packed up a U-Haul and were moving back. And then, in walks Becca." She was enraged.

"I just explained that. I might be callous enough to break up with her before putting her on a plane to her family where she could mourn with those she loved, but no way am I asshole enough to literally dump her at the airport and then leave her on her own on Thanksgiving. And, oh by the way …"

He got down on one knee and pulled out a box, opening it to reveal a diamond engagement ring. "Would you marry me?"

"You can't be serious."

"I'm completely serious."

She smacked the box out of his hand. "Don't you dare do this to me."

He stood up and leaned into her face. "Do what to you? Go through with my intention? The intention I set, the intention I told you about weeks ago. The intention I followed up on just like I said I would. The intention I shared with every phone call home to you?"

Xander was furious. His beautiful gray eyes were as stormy as McKenna had ever seen them. His hands were on his hips if they weren't flailing around when he spoke. Check that—when he *shouted.*

"You didn't give me a chance to explain. I mean, I knew it was going to suck for you watching us walk in together. There was only so much texting I could do in front of Becca. I had planned to grab you away as soon as possible to explain all this. Yeah, it wasn't going to be the Thanksgiving we thought it was, but all I needed was another eighteen hours of your patience. Instead, you drag my parents into it, *tell them I've been dating Becca for months* and then leave in a blaze of glory. Wasn't all that exactly what we'd been trying to shield my mother from? Wasn't that what we were doing? Together."

And then he grabbed his head and spun away from her. "And don't get me started on how fast you did exactly what I asked you not to do."

"We're friends. Jagger and I are friends."

"Trust me. I got that impression loud and clear last night." He turned around. "I've been sleeping with Becca for months. I get that you probably suffered with that. I also get that paybacks are a bitch, and I deserve exactly what I'm getting." He stopped himself before saying more. McKenna watched him bite his lip to hold the words back.

"Xander," she whispered.

He just shook his head and then took a step back. "I did what I said I was going to do. I got out of my lease. I changed my job so I could move back here. I bought a ring." His eyes were so full of hurt McKenna felt his pain. "I did what I told you I was going to do."

She sucked in a breath, digesting his words. Then, just too curious not to ask, "Tell me, when was the last time you slept with Becca?"

He hesitated only a moment before he admitted, "Last night."

Under the circumstances the truth hurt way more than it should have. It took a full minute before she was able to ask her next question. "And this morning, when you put her on the plane?"

"We broke up. Only you should know, she was the one who did the breaking."

McKenna cocked her head in question.

He shrugged. "She found your ring. Thought it was intended for her. Told me she wasn't ready, and that I was probably too old for her."

The thought went through McKenna's mind, *How could anyone break up with you,* and then she realized that's exactly what she needed to do. Right now.

Only.

"Look," Xander said. "This is a colossal cluster-fu—mess. I needed to come over and have my say. I know I'm not as good as a rock star, *believe me,* but you need all the facts before you throw me and my family away. And let me reiterate. They are *not* happy about this."

"You didn't tell them you found me at Jagger's, did you?" Anna Beth certainly didn't need to know that.

"No. I told them he was here. With you and your mother. I might have mentioned that the two of you seemed cozy as I threw a glass against the wall of the back porch."

"Did you explain all this—all this Becca stuff—to them?"

He was immediately weary. "Nah. I mean, yes and no. The whole day went to shit as soon as you walked out. No one was happy. The tension was so thick you could cut it with a knife. Becca didn't get it because Beavis and Butthead kept her entertained, finding the entire thing amusing. They loved the fact that Dad and Xavier were arguing over who was going to kick my ass the farthest."

"That's Hux and Rex for you. I guess Xavier too."

"And Dad. You know Dad."

They slid into a silence that could have easily gone on forever.

"Any other questions?" Xander asked.

"Questions?"

"Yeah. I figure I'll give you a chance to digest everything I just said. Hopefully, sooner rather than later, because no one back home is going to stop dogging me about it, you'll contact me so we can sort through all of this."

"Sort through all this?"

"McKenna. I just asked you to marry me." He pointed at the ring box on the floor. "My intention has not changed."

"Xander," she whispered. "We have deviated so far off course."

"You and I have done that before. And yet years later, the flame still burned. Pretty sure if we can withstand this trial, we'll be able to stand together against anything." He turned and showed himself to the door muttering, "Even Jagger Yates."

CHAPTER THIRTY-THREE

Jagger's head popped up when he heard McKenna's front door open and close. He watched Xander, who had his head down and his hands in his front pockets, descend the steps and move toward the street. When Xander looked up and spotted Jagger, he froze.

That's right you, son of a bitch. Stop. Right. There.

Pushing himself off his truck, he took a few steps forward. "You done here?"

Xander stared him right in the eye. "Not by a long shot."

"She's my girl now," Jagger claimed.

"Maybe. Until you leave town and get back to rodeo clowning or whatever it is you do."

Asshole.

"Y'all head on home," came the voice of Sandy Blakely. McKenna's momma had stuck her head out the door and was shooing the two of them off with a dishtowel. "This town's gonna have enough to talk about without you two brawling on the sidewalk. Now get."

"Sure thing, Ms. Blakely," Xander said like the well-bred, Southern ass kisser he was. Of course, to his credit, he flipped Jagger the bird before he strode to his car.

Jagger stood his ground and watched the guy leave. Then he looked directly at Sandy wanting desperately to get inside to McKenna.

She simply shook her head.

Damn.

He got back in his truck and drove home, the song he'd been working on blown completely out of his mind.

CHAPTER THIRTY-FOUR

"You done with him?" Jagger asked McKenna over the phone. "With Xander?"

She was *so* done with Xander.

The insanity of the last twenty-four hours prompted McKenna to barricade herself inside her room with zero distractions. It was time to take a long, hard look at how she'd arrived here. And she realized that introspection needed to include a giant step back to examine her history with Xander—with the entire Wright family—from a more neutral position. One that wasn't so fraught with emotion.

She'd fallen in love with Xander when she was a kid. *In tenth grade.* And he'd been handsome and a senior and a whole lot nicer to her than his brother had been. And she had really appreciated his mother that whole summer when her own mom was working two jobs and probably struggling to make ends meet. So, yeah, it made sense for her to carry a huge soft spot for Xander.

But not today's Xander.

Not thirty-two-year-old-Xander. Not the double-dating, workaholic Xander who'd strung her along for months making her doubt her own self-worth. It was the *memory* of twelfth-grade Xander and their one romantic summer together that had a stranglehold on her heart. Of course it did. He was her first love. But if she were honest with herself, and right now she couldn't afford *not* to be, she didn't particularly like or respect this grown-up Xander. And as much as she dreaded hurting Anna Beth and Maxwell by not accepting their son's proposal, she simply couldn't do that to herself, or to Xander.

"Tell me you're done with him," Jagger repeated.

"Jagger, Xander proposed."

"Hold on. What?"

"It was crazy. He came here this morning, got down on one knee, whipped out a ring, and proposed."

"Holy fuck. What did you do?"

"I knocked the damn thing out of his hand and sent it flying across the room."

"That's my girl."

"I'm not really your girl."

"You are. You are definitely my girl. Now pull your momma away from the front door so I can come over and prove it to you. Better yet. Why don't you just come over here? We can get back to what we were doing last night before we were interrupted."

"Oh my goodness. I can't just … come over."

"Of course, you can."

"No. No. I've gotta, like, deal."

"With what? You and Xander are history. You have moved on."

"Yes. Yes, I have. But …"

"The ball is now firmly in your court. You are the one with options. And, let me remind you, I am a big option."

She chuckled at that. "Yes, you are. You are one big option."

"Right? Lest you forget, you were sort of digging on me when you didn't even know me. And now that you *know me,* well … seriously, I'm not sure why Xander has ever been in the conversation."

She took a breath. Blew it out.

"Come on. Trust your instincts. We are good together. And there is so much more to come."

"Jagger."

"I'm here. Not going anywhere."

"Jagger," she whispered.

"Baby, I'm crazy about you. Like, really wild about you. I haven't felt like this in … well, ever. And for me, like you, I was already digging on you long before I had the chance to get to know you. You and I … maybe it really was love at first sight, and we just had to find our way to each other. Okay, *you* might have had preconceived notions about me, but now that you've gotten to know the man behind the myth, you know that what you see is what you get. I've got a voice, I can write songs, and that's pretty much … it. I've got a talent that is helping me make a living just like everyone else has talents that help them make a living. But when I'm not on the road making my living on tour, I've got a home, I've got parents, I've got siblings, I've got friends. I'm just like everyone else. And yeah, we'll need to figure some stuff out, but that's just where we've landed. At the holy-shit, this-is-awesome, so-let's-figure-stuff-out stage."

"Right. Yes. I agree with that." McKenna took her time, drew in a deep breath, and sighed it out because … because … she still had to face the Wrights.

"Mmm-hmm. So what's that big sigh about?"

"I've been rehashing all of the history between me and Xander. Between me and the Wrights. It's a big chunk of my life and it's not incidental."

Jagger was quiet for a moment. "You absolutely have history with the ex-boyfriend and his family. You do. And I can't change that. But I've got a momma and daddy who are gonna love you. I've got sisters coming out of the woodwork dying to meet you. I've written more songs about you than I've written about sunsets, and I've written way too many songs about the damn sunset. I'm honest. I'm true. I'm head-over-heels mad for you. I deserve a shot. A real shot. And if we somehow crash and burn, well, it's not like your ex isn't going to be waiting in the wings, is it?"

"Jagger," she sighed, "it's just … *hard.*"

"It's not that hard, McKenna. You don't have to give up Anna Beth. You don't have to give up Mr. Wright and Xavier and the rest of them. But you're too much for Xander. Too much for most men. Hell, any man would take one look at you and want you, but few have the balls to step up and give their best effort to handle you. Xander's not man enough for you. Just look at Becca. She's half the woman you are. In stature, in beauty, in personality, in presence. You need somebody who can step up to the plate and not let you down. Ever. Baby, I am that man."

There was a good amount of silence as his words buzzed around her head and flowed into her heart. If that wasn't a love song, she didn't know what was. And what woman wouldn't succumb to Jagger Yates spouting all that? Not her. That was for sure.

"I'm going to have to go find Xander's ring, pick it up off the floor, and return it to him."

"Happy to come with you."

That made her shout with laughter. "Ah, no thank you."

"Seriously. I'm happy to back you up."

"I understand that, but I've got to do this myself. And I'll probably speak to Anna Beth and Maxwell while I'm there. See if I can let the two of them down gently."

She thought she heard Jagger breathe a sigh of relief.

"You okay?" she asked.

"You really going through with this? You're giving me a chance?"

"Didn't you just sit here and spin a web of seductive words to talk me into exactly that?"

"I did. I just didn't know they'd work so fast."

"Jagger. I'm not immune to anything about you. Especially the way you weave words together. I've got all the feels, too, believe me. I'm not lying when I say I would have jumped at the chance to go to dinner with you if I hadn't been dating Xan—the ex."

"Sweet, sweet music to my ears. So how about that date?"

"Yes."

"Yes?"

"Yes."

"Tonight?"

"Yes. But out of town. In fact, let's just plan to get out of town for the rest of the weekend."

"I'm in."

"All right. So. Give me some time. Don't be blowing up my phone. Just … pick me up at six tonight, and I'll pack a bag and we can go … somewhere. Anywhere. Give ourselves a chance to get all sorted out."

"Sorted out?"

"Right. Like, come up with a game plan."

"A game plan?"

"Yeah. You know, like I was talking about earlier? You and I come up with a game plan to lie low while the whole McKenna-and-

Xander-are-not-getting-married gossip train steamrolls itself through Henderson."

"Hmm."

"Jagger."

"I hear you. I will consider a game plan while I make reservations for a weekend getaway. I will pick you up at six o'clock and if—McKenna, hear me on this—if you are a no-show, I will come looking for you."

"You afraid the Wrights are going to hogtie me and force me to marry Xander?"

"I wouldn't put it past them."

"Me either," she grumbled. "Oh God, how am I going to do this?" She braced her head in her palm.

"Same way you'd eat an elephant. One bite at a time."

CHAPTER THIRTY-FIVE

Jagger didn't waste time pacing around his rental home. He did stand still for thirty seconds debating whether he could trust the outcome of McKenna heading to the Wrights' alone.

Without him as back up.

Or muscle.

Or whatever.

But McKenna would probably bite his head off if he drove over and parked himself at the edge of their driveway. And … she was either going to go through with it or not. He'd said his piece. She'd heard him. She seemed to be in agreement and so … he called his assistant.

"Lol. I need you to hook me up with a romantic getaway. Someplace within driving distance of Henderson."

From the other end of the phone he heard … nothing.

"Lol?"

"Ah–here. I'm here. I'm … not exactly sure …"

"What the word romantic means?"

"Ah. Maybe?" she squeaked out. "I mean, when it comes to you?"

"What the hell?"

"Well, what is this *for*?"

"What do you mean what is this for? I need a romantic getaway so I can seal the deal with the woman of my dreams. What do you think it's for?"

"There's a woman? Of your dreams?"

Jagger placed a hand on his hip and harrumphed. "Very funny. You know, you don't need any details to do your job. I don't pay you to need details."

"Since when? I totally need details. Is this why I haven't heard from you? Is this why *no one's* heard from you?"

"No. But, yes. Sort of. I don't know. Just, can you handle this for me please?"

"I suppose, if you tell me where Henderson is located. And why you're still there? And why you aren't here? Oooh. I know. Bring her to Nashville so I can meet her."

"How about you plan to come here in a couple weeks and meet her?"

"I come there?"

"Right. You come here. Bunk with me. I've got an extra bedroom."

"In Henderson?"

"Did I stutter?"

"Nashville is Nashville."

"And McKenna lives here. Like, she's got roots here. The kind of roots that won't let her leave. *Yet.* I've got to gently dig around those roots and loosen the soil so that she feels comfortable moving around a bit."

"Loosen the soil? Is this one of your song metaphors?"

"Maybe?" He thought about it. He could totally write a song about this.

"What are you going to want me to do in Henderson?"

"Same stuff you do for me there."

"Right, so why do I have to leave here?"

"Because I'll pay you to come, to meet McKenna, to work with me to roll out the news that I have a woman in my life and now the band is going to have to deal with it."

"Ooooh."

"Yes. Ooooh."

"Right. Okay. I'm on it. When do you want me?"

"In two weeks. We'll work out those details between now and then. But this is what I need from you now. Remember that real pretty bracelet? The one the rest of the band bought their significant others?"

CHAPTER THIRTY-SIX

After falling into a nap due to her emotional turmoil, McKenna took a long shower, hoping the water would wash away any lack of clarity. She changed from her regular jeans, into a dress, and then back into nicer jeans. As she walked out of her bedroom, she called out to her mother.

"Did you find Xander's—"

Her mother stood in the center of the kitchen holding the ring box in the palm of her hand.

"Did you open it?"

Her mother nodded.

"Is it pretty?"

Her mother nodded again.

McKenna slumped down into her kitchen chair with a sigh, staring at the box in her mother's hand. "If Jagger had never come to Henderson, I would be completely content to marry Xander."

"Well then, you've dodged a bullet. Life isn't about what's gonna make you content."

McKenna picked up her head and gave a short chuckle. "Maybe you ought to take your own advice."

"What's that supposed to mean?"

McKenna sat up. Leaned her elbows on the table and let the question she'd be holding on to for weeks, fly. "Mom. Are you … gay?"

Sandy Blakely blinked, raised one eyebrow and then sat herself in the chair across from her daughter. She plopped the ring box on the table between. "Now what in the world ever gave you that idea?"

"After I told Jagger about the sperm bank, he was curious. Thought maybe you were gay. And, you know I'd be okay with that, right?"

Sandy chuckled. "I'm not gay."

"Well then, are you and the Hollises a throuple?"

"What in the world is a *throuple*?"

"It's a polyamorous relationship."

"Like, a ménage à trois?"

"Yes."

"Darlin' girl, are you asking me if LeeAnn and Ray and myself are … involved? Sexually?" Cassandra hooted a laugh and then just kept rolling with it as she fell back into her seat. "Oh, goodness me, no. The two of them are as uptight as a preacher. But they get my warped sense of humor and put up with my bad taste in television. They are my dearest friends and have been since I can remember. But no. You can tell Jagger I'm just plain ol' boring. No erotic stories to share."

"Then why the sperm bank?"

"I was thirty. And I'd just turned down a third marriage proposal."

McKenna's eyes bugged out. "A *third* marriage proposal? From the same guy?"

"No. No. Three different men."

"What?" McKenna shouted and then roared with laughter. "You've had three marriage proposals? That is far from boring. How have you never told me about this?"

"Four. I've had four marriage proposals and I never told you about any of them because well, one, you never asked. And two, I didn't want to make you feel bad."

"Feel bad?"

"McKenna, you're thirty, and right now you have two men fighting over you, but up until now? Baby, you've been in a helluva drought."

"Oh my God. Mother!"

"Sweetheart. The truth is the truth."

"Well, what about you?" McKenna scoffed. "It's not like you have a parade of men knocking on our door."

"Darlin', you don't actually believe I'm over at the Hollises every night, do you?"

"Why, yes. Of course, that's what I believe. Why wouldn't I believe that?"

Sandy shrugged her shoulders. "I don't know. I just figured at some point you'd be old enough to figure it out."

"Figure what out?"

"That I have a lover."

"You have a *lover*?" McKenna shrieked. "Why have you kept that from me?"

"Uhh, it's not really any of your business. Or anyone else's. I mean, if it ever gets serious, I'll bring him around. But I like to keep my private life private. Always have. I've never been a big sharer of my thoughts and feelings. I mean, you know that. That's why you love your Anna Beth so much. She's like you. Needy."

McKenna's mouth hung open. "I'm needy?"

"Well, no, I suppose. But in a lot of ways you're the opposite of me, and I'm … well I'm decidedly *not* needy. I don't need other people interfering in my life. You're naturally more social than I am. You like getting out in the community and finding out what's going on."

"Because that's my job. Although clearly I'm not the investigative reporter I thought I was."

"You're exceptional. Interviewing, hobnobbing, writing it all up for others to read? Lord knows, if I get stuck making chitchat around the water cooler, it about drives me insane. But being around people is one of your talents, your strengths. And you've used it well, especially to mold your career. I'm not saying I don't need people in my life, but where I'm content with one or two close friends, you need more."

"So you're content."

"I am."

"And yet you just told me life isn't about being content."

"Well, it sure shouldn't be. Not when you're thirty and dating a freaking rock star."

McKenna eyed the box sitting between them. "I could be marrying Xander Wright."

"And you'd be miserable doing it."

McKenna drew back and blinked. "I wouldn't be."

"Imagine how you'd feel every time you heard a Cavaliers song on the radio."

McKenna's chest tightened. Her mouth hung open.

"You can't do that to yourself. You need to live. Really live. You need to reach for happy. Not just settle on being content. And then … if your great love affair with Jagger Yates explodes, well, you can always come find your way back to content. Trust me, it'll be here, waiting for you."

CHAPTER THIRTY-SEVEN

Breaking up with the Wrights.

That's what McKenna was here to do.

Sure, she was shaking all over as she approached their front door, but there wasn't a whole lot of indecision going on. She needed to end things with Xander and do what she could to ease Anna Beth.

Xavier greeted her by opening the front door as she approached. It didn't escape her that his eyes shot first to her ring finger. Her empty ring finger.

"Gol-damnit," he uttered, holding open the door and allowing her to step into the foyer. "He fucked it up, didn't he?"

She shrugged.

"Took him too long to make up his mind."

She nodded.

"And then there's Jagger Yates," Xavier scoffed with a grimace. "Pretty sure that didn't help."

McKenna met his eyes, rubbing her hands together. "You gonna hold this against me?"

"Yep." Then he pulled her into a tight hug. "I gotta live here with Ma and Dad. So until I'm a married man and move out, you're on my shit list."

"After that?"

"We'll see about after that."

She nodded. Gave him a squeeze and pulled back, teary-eyed. It was the nicest exchange she'd ever had with Xavier. "Where is he?"

"Getting drunk out back."

She nodded, heading in that direction.

"You gonna need back up?" he asked.

"Maybe with your mother."

"Oh, hell no. You're on your own with Ma."

Ugh. McKenna couldn't think about Anna Beth right now. She first had to deal with Xander. She found him out on the back porch, sitting in a rocking chair, staring into the backyard, beer in hand. He didn't move or look in her direction when she stepped out. Nor did he move when she came over and took a seat in the rocker next to him.

She decided to join him in looking toward the horizon.

Eventually, she took out the ring box and placed it on the arm of Xander's chair. "I'm sorry we aren't going to work. I truly thought it was the perfect situation, the two of us. That's why I pushed so hard. Waited for so long."

She watched him nod. Take a sip of his beer. When he didn't comment, her gaze wandered to the backyard again.

"He's not going to marry you," Xander finally said.

She nodded. "I know."

"Then what are you trying to prove?"

Without a lot of thought, she turned her face toward him and blurted, "That life holds more for me than the Wright family?" The words were a shock. A truth she hadn't seen coming. "I will always love you, and I will always love this family. But you left me a lot of years ago and didn't look back. And when we got together last summer, you still weren't all-in. I was. I was all-in."

"Until you weren't," he grumbled.

"Up until I had another option."

Xander turned his face in her direction. The anger seething from him was palpable.

"I never allowed myself other options. I pined for you while finishing high school. I pined for you in college. I found a job here in Henderson so I could be close to my mom and your family. To see you when you bothered to come home ... which, you know, would reel me in for more. And then this summer happened, and I thought, man, it has all been worth it. We were finally getting our shot. And wasn't it just the best kind of icing on the cake that I loved your mother more than just about anybody else on the planet and your brother was marrying my best friend? I just knew we were gonna work. And we did. For about three weeks."

"So this is my fault," he groused.

She looked him in the eye. "You didn't choose me. Not until you had to." She looked back toward the horizon. "Kinda says it all, doesn't it?"

"Don't put words in my mouth. I love you. So, I didn't jump at the chance to move back to Henderson right away. Doesn't mean I don't love you. That we wouldn't be good together."

"We'd be good together," she agreed. "You'd make us a ton of money, and I'd take care of your family and everything else. We'd be very content."

"Then what the fuck?"

She sighed. Was quiet for a spell. "With every word that comes out of Jagger Yates's mouth, he's writing me a love song."

Xander flinched, took a sip of his beer.

"That man has pursued me for longer than you know with a single mindedness that is not only soul satisfying, it has lightened my spirit."

Xander's chair started to rock.

"And I have no idea if he and I can make a relationship work, considering his crazy lifestyle. But shame on me if I'm willing to use you to ensure I'm content, when there's a big world out there and, at least for the moment, Jagger Yates is mine for the taking."

"I can't compete with that."

"No. But when you find the girl who makes every word coming out of your mouth sound like a love song …"

He eyed her before taking another sip of beer. "I hope you two crash and burn."

"If we do, you'll be there to see it. Because I'm not giving up your parents, or your brothers, or my future sisters-in-law."

"You can have them," he said, finishing off his beer before standing. "I'm going back to Charlotte. Beg my boss to forget everything I said about working in Henderson and assure him that I am done with women."

"Well, that would just be cruel and unusual punishment for all womankind. You're a good guy, Xander. Except for the simultaneously dating two women thing, you check all the boxes. So go live where you want and work on forgiving me and Becca for screwing you up. And forgive yourself, while you're at it. Then ... jump back into the game."

He whirled on her. "This isn't a game, Be...McKenna. This is my life."

She nodded her head, not missing his mistake. "Except over the past many months you've been treating me like a pawn on your personal chessboard, keeping Becca as your queen. So, you lost. *This round.* Refine the rules and next time you'll come out ahead."

He grunted, shook his head, and then opened the back door, leaving her alone on the porch.

"Whew," she whispered aloud, her hands gripping the arms of the chair. "I did not think I had that much to say," she muttered, rocking herself back and forth, wondering what kind of words she had left for Anna Beth.

Turns out she didn't need words.

Anna Beth had taken to her bed, as if she'd had a relapse. When McKenna saw her there, she simply slipped off her shoes and crawled in the bed, holding Anna Beth in her arms until both of them were all cried out.

CHAPTER THIRTY-EIGHT

It was five forty five. Jagger was due to pick McKenna up in fifteen minutes and, per her request, he hadn't blown up her phone with texts or calls.

And he hadn't received any either.

Given the intensity of the silence, he considered calling his buddy Xavier for an update. But his *buddy* might not be in such a friendly mood since it was his twin getting dumped and Jagger was all set to reap the rewards.

So he stewed, he planned, he packed, and thank the freaking Lord, it was finally time to go get his girl.

He hoped. He hoped McKenna was now his girl.

"Dude," he said aloud. "You seriously need to man up." He grabbed his duffle, the cooler loaded with four bottles of wine, and the address he was going to need to sneak off to once he got McKenna settled at the Umstead Hotel and Spa, located an hour's drive away from Henderson.

Getting a glimpse of the rusted bucket of bolts sitting in the driveway he reconsidered. Was this truck really the kind of thing he wanted to drive to a romantic getaway? Would it even make it? He had serious doubts, and he did not need any other serious doubts at this point. Not when he was engaged in mission countdown. He didn't know why, he didn't know how, but he had Pinks's number listed in his phone, so he dialed the kid up and simply asked, "Where can I get a better car for the weekend?"

He assumed Pinks would direct him to the nearest rental dealership, but Pinks told him to swing by the Evans estate and he'd see what he could do. Curious, he hit McKenna up with a text saying he was trying to improve their ride and he'd be just a few minutes late.

When he finally arrived at the Blakely girls' humble abode, he was driving a vintage Corvette the shade of a pumpkin. The thing had a stick shift—one you really had to operate. The experience got his blood pumping, his heart beating, and that's before he realized he hadn't received a text back from McKenna.

Which made his heart beat and his blood pump even more.

He locked the 'Vette and was making a plan to storm the Wrights' home in order to extract his girl when the prettiest sight he'd ever seen stepped out onto the front stoop.

McKenna Blakely, with her raven hair all dolled up in curls flowing down past her shoulders, had come out to greet him in a *dress*. A very sophisticated, very clingy, very plunging neckline, long-sleeved navy dress. The word *voluptuous* sounded like an alarm in his brain. And right behind that word came other words like *sex, fuck me,* and *Holy Jesus.* The word *lips* snuck itself in there every once in a while. *Incredible tits* flashed like a neon sign. *Fantastic ass* practically shouted as she did a slow twirl while he tried to lasso his tongue and pull it back into his mouth.

The woman had legs for days, and they did not disappoint. She was born to wear dresses, yet she had spent every moment he knew her in a fucking pair of pants.

From somewhere deep, he dragged up his rock-star swagger and screwed it on good and tight, because no mere mortal was going to be able to handle all that. McKenna Blakely, muse to so many of his hit songs, goddess of his future dreams, was grinning down at him like she knew all his secrets.

"I …" he stumbled, hands spreading out before him. "I have no words." A complete lie. His brain was still coming up with all sorts of words. Just none that were at all appropriate.

"Well, that's disappointing," she quipped. "I'm usually pretty fond of your words."

"First of you all, you're here," he said in awe.

She glanced down at the slim little watch on her beautiful wrist. "You said six o'clock. I think you're going to find that I'm generally punctual."

He nodded, grinning. Folding his hands in front of him, just taking in the scene she made. Then he shook his head, chuckling. "I don't know," he admitted. "This may be one of the single greatest moments of my life, right here."

"Aww," she sighed. "See, you do have words. And I am very fond of those."

"So, I ah, borrowed a car." He threw a thumb over his shoulder. "Flashy. Fun to drive. Gives us a better chance to get where we're getting to."

"I'm a fan of the Corvette."

"There's not a lot of room for luggage."

"I've got a small bag."

He started forward slowly, coming up to meet her at the top of the stoop. His hand went to her hip and then slid up to the back of her waist. "So you're coming with me?" he whispered just a breath away from her lips.

"I am." She grinned.

He grinned.

Then she lifted to her toes and planted a lingering kiss on his lips.

The moment was absolutely perfect until she pulled away, quickly looking right and left. "Come on inside while I gather my stuff."

She was trying to hide him. From her neighbors.

Yep, Jagger thought as he followed her indoors, he was definitely going to need the secret weapon.

CHAPTER THIRTY-NINE

"The Umstead Hotel and Spa?" McKenna wondered. "Isn't that pricey?"

"Ah … to tell you the truth, I don't know."

"What do you mean you don't know?"

"I didn't make the reservation. My assistant made the reservation."

"And why did your assistant make the reservation?"

Jagger turned his head to look at her while doing ten miles an hour over the speed limit. "That's what assistants do?"

"Oh. I wouldn't know. I've never had one."

"You can share mine."

McKenna chuckled. "I think I'm managing well enough on my own. But thank you."

When the silence dragged out, Jagger had to ask, "Are you going to tell me what happened at the Wrights'?"

From his peripheral vision, he watched McKenna nod. Only she didn't speak right away. When he finally looked in her direction, she shrugged. "It went as well as could be expected."

When she didn't elaborate, he doubted that was the truth. He reached over and took her hand. "Thank you," he said quietly. "I know that wasn't easy."

"No," she sighed long and hard. "But I bet once we get to the spa I'm going to feel a whole lot better."

"You know what made me feel better?"

"What?"

"You. In that dress."

CHAPTER FORTY

"Don't change, we have to be downstairs for our dinner reservation in five minutes." Jagger tipped the bellman who'd brought their bags up to the room. As suites went, this one wasn't terribly large, but the bed was big and inviting, and the place was tricked out. The bathroom was a stunner and made Jagger think about shower sex and Jacuzzi sex. It also made him think about bathroom counter sex, and when he walked out into the bedroom again, he thought of good, ol'-fashioned comfy, bed sex.

He noticed McKenna was staring at the bed and hoped she was thinking about comfy bed sex too.

She turned to him abruptly. "How many hotel rooms do you think you've stayed in?"

His eyes widened. "I don't know. Plenty. Too many." Then he smiled. "But this one is my favorite."

She gave him a soft chuckle, her gaze drifting toward the floor.

"I've been waiting on this dinner date for a long time, McKenna Blakely. So how about we get to it?"

She eyed him, grinning. "Our first date."

He nodded briefly, staring at her, grinning back. "Our *official* first date."

The restaurant's menu was high-priced and exotic, its food poetry promising deliciousness. McKenna looked high-priced, exotic, and delicious too. So much so Jagger couldn't keep his hands off her. By flashing a twenty-dollar tip, he'd managed to talk the maître d' into seating them at the cozy-looking booth he'd spied in a quiet, dark corner of the restaurant. The booth was curved, one bench seat around a cloth-topped table for two. All of this suited Jagger perfectly. McKenna slid into her side, he slid into his, and then he moved toward the center. While they enjoyed their cocktails, he slid his hands underneath her fanny and pulled her body closer to his.

He could tell she kinda liked that.

They'd opted for champagne, and he didn't know if it was the bubbles making him dizzy or whether it was McKenna's perfume. Hell, it could easily be her smile, because the one she kept flashing him was soft and sweet and relaxed. Yeah, this tipsy feeling probably had a lot to do with that … and the fact that her right breast kept threatening to spill out of her deep V-neckline. So between the soft and the sweet and the tipsy and her breast, Jagger was plenty distracted. Wanting to lean in and kiss her right there. On the soft, plump bulge of her breast. He gave the idea serious consideration. Thoughts of dropping his napkin—in her lap—and then going to retrieve it—with his teeth—and accidentally on purpose landing his lips on the sweet spot.

And that whole line of thinking got him nothing but caught when McKenna snapped her fingers in front of his face. "Jagger."

"Sorry. Sorry." He laughed. "Your dress is very distracting. In fact, *you* are very distracting."

"I think it's knowing our room is a hop, skip, and jump away."

"Please tell me that you're finding it distracting too."

She grinned before sipping her champagne.

He leaned closer, completely forgetting about his half-finished foie gras. "I am seriously contemplating how to go about putting my mouth right there"—he indicated her breast with his eyes—"without anybody noticing."

Her hair fell, hiding her adorable blush when she lowered her head. "Jagger," she whispered.

"What? I'm, like, starving, but food is the last thing I've got on my mind." When she didn't say anything, he asked, "Aren't you, ah … starving? Just a little?"

Her beautiful grin returned, and she met his eyes, those icy blues of hers dazzling their way into his heart, and quite frankly, down into his pants. "I'm … famished," she said, biting her lip, her fork toying with the scallop on her plate.

Setting his fork down, Jagger gave up all pretense of eating. Instead, he reached into the ice bucket and retrieved their champagne, refilling both their glasses. "So, once we take that hop, skip, and jump—I'm totally writing a song with those lyrics, by the way—what's the first thing you think we should do?"

"Hmm," she wondered, picking up her champagne glass. "What? Are we like brainstorming here?"

"Brainstorming, yes. Or fantasizing. Fantasizing is good. I've been doing a lot of that lately."

"You have, have you? Anything worth sharing?"

"Well, let's see." He sat back, holding his champagne, one arm laid out behind her along the top of the booth. "Once I get a good look at you hopping, skipping, and jumping to our room in that dress—because I'm definitely going to be walking behind you for that—I plan to lock the door to our suite right after I hang the Do Not Disturb sign outside."

"Mmm. Yes." She took another sip. "Good plan."

"Then, I'm gonna use my hands to find out if your beautiful dress has a zipper, or if I just simply have to untie that knot at your waist for it to fall off."

"An excellent use of your hands."

He lowered his voice from every-man-Jagger-Yates-interview mode to I'm-doing-my-best-to-reel-you-in-darlin' mode. "I think it might add a little something if I closed my eyes, just so I'm tempted not to cheat."

"And maybe I'd return the favor, running my hands over that dress shirt you're wearing, which is the equivalent to an aphrodisiac, by the way. You, in a suit, is killing me."

He leaned in and kissed her lips. "I want your hands on me, McKenna. Anywhere. Everywhere."

"Likewise. By the way, are you a lingerie guy?" she whispered even as the waiter came to refresh their water glasses.

"If it's on you, I am."

"Then please be sure to open your eyes after you figure out how to get me out of this dress."

"Is that right?" He grinned.

She nodded.

"Any hints?"

Without hesitation, she pulled his arm down from behind her and drew his hand onto her thigh. When she brought her own hands together, elbows on the table, she simply said, "See what you think?"

Well, isn't this one unexpected gift. "Yeah?"

She nodded.

He rubbed her knee first. Running his hand over it gently, letting his fingertips dip down and graze the soft spot behind it. He did all this to lull her into a state of ease right before he firmly gripped her lower thigh and pulled her leg tight against his own. He heard her breath catch, as if she realized he was no longer fooling around. He leaned his mouth close to her ear. "You may be in for more than you bargained for, Miss Blakely."

Her response was a sharp intake of breath.

Yeah, he was totally going to deliver a little rock-star treatment.

CHAPTER FORTY-ONE

Firm and sure, Jagger's palm smoothed over and down the inside of her knee causing delicious side effects to dance all over her body. Then he abruptly pulled her leg against his, causing McKenna to sit up sharply.

Jagger said some words, words that swam into one ear, caused her brain to swirl, and then swam out the other ear. She had no idea what he'd said, but the low, sexy rumble of his voice made her very aware of his intent.

She drew her thighs together, trapping his hand in between. "I just wanted to … ah, stimulate your imagination. Give you a brief … preview of what's in store for you after dinner."

"Mmm," he soothed with that devastating voice of his against her ear and the long, slow caress of his hand. "Nicely done. Now … *relax.*"

McKenna had no choice, really. She could have slapped his hand away, but between his gorgeous suit, the champagne, the freaking Umstead Hotel and Spa, not to mention his glorious beard tickling the side of her face—ah, no. There wasn't much else he needed to do to seduce her.

Jagger's hand slid down and brazenly dragged her left knee up and over his right thigh, causing her upper body to snuggle tightly against his. She could smell his delicious aftershave which was just another item on the long list of aphrodisiacs. She didn't see it happen, because her eyes closed as she inhaled his scent, but she felt his left hand sneak under the table and place a secure hold on the leg he'd just draped over his own. The fingers of his right hand began a massaging motion on her lower thigh that soothed as much as it excited. She was enjoying this sensuous attention. Especially enjoying the secluded table and the heat of his body tight against her. Mmm, and the tantalizing way he kissed her behind her earlobe. His hand motions were controlled and rhythmical, lulling her into hardly noticing and frankly, not really caring that his fingers, and thus the hem of her dress, crept higher with every pass.

McKenna's vision seemed a little blurred as she set her champagne glass down. Every bit of her awareness tuned in to Jagger's fingers and the ricochet of delight his fingertips were creating throughout her body. The phrase turned-on was inept. Having her legs splayed like this under the tablecloth where anyone who dropped a napkin might happen to see? A shockingly hardcore aphrodisiac.

She tried to be subtle, slowly easing a long-held breath from her lungs, releasing some of the tension building within her. She became aware of the heavy weight of her breasts and the ache in her nipples. Jagger hadn't touched more than her inner thigh, yet she was wet in anticipation. Finally his fingers brushed softly—erotically—over the silky face of her thong while his left hand gently massaged the crest of her inner thigh.

The man did not hesitate to demonstrate his sex-god status by pretending to be shy. He leaned in close against her ear again and whispered, "This is so hot for me. Kiss me if it's hot for you." She turned her head and pressed a hard kiss to his lips. It wasn't a long kiss, because … restaurant, but yeah this was hot for her. *Was he even joking about that?* The devil in her was curious to see just how far he would go.

His fingers went on a discovery, feeling their way around her panties, slipping inside the tiny strap that circled her hip, dipping slightly into the top of her lingerie. Then he brushed the backs of his fingers down over the silk that was now clinging to her most sensitive area. "Don't move." Jagger squeezed her thigh lightly before drawing his hand slowly from underneath the table to take up his champagne. "For some reason, my throat is getting terribly dry." He smiled at her, his playful-fun-happy smile, before he took a sip. Then he leaned in and kissed her with wet lips, letting his tongue drift over hers before backing away.

He shifted in his seat while his long, talented, and hidden-from-view fingers drew the silk barrier of her panties out of his way. She sucked in a breath, feeling the air swarm over her nakedness just before Jagger used his fingertips infuriatingly, lightly—and way too cautiously—to explore the tender skin that longed for his attention.

Swollen, wet, and craving more direct touch, McKenna shifted her hips reflexively, working to achieve more pressure. Working to force his fingers through the downy barrier he seemed content to toy with. When the results produced less than she was after, a deep hum—maybe even a groan—vibrated involuntarily from her chest. Her eyes sprang open, her gaze darting around, fearful she'd been overheard. Her brain responded by instructing her body to sit up straight and draw her leg from Jagger's thigh, thus ending this madness. But Jagger chuckled and slipped his hand back under the table to hold her firm. At the same time, he jacked the craziness up a notch by slipping one long finger into her dampness, stroking her from bottom to top.

Holy shi—

It felt good.

It felt so decadently good she prayed to the god of waiters everywhere, begging that she and Jagger be left alone for the time being.

In a far-off, distant part of her brain, she realized Jagger was literally playing her. And, yeah, there was a good chance he was getting off on this, but she couldn't shake the idea that he was also feeling a little smug. So, doing her best to assume a calm, outward demeanor, she slid her left hand from the table and placed it ever so deliberately over Jagger's crotch. She lifted her gaze to his face and detected a subtle change in countenance. Then he grinned, and while his eyes were focused on her face, his finger found her epicenter.

Stop the presses.

Of course, Jagger didn't just find her clitoris. No. Being the rock-star sex god he was, Jagger's finger tantalizingly circled it. Then he added a little pressure and a rub. Then her heartthrob-in-the-flesh performed a figure eight over and around it. His finger circled again, and then he did the meanest thing. A slow, luxurious, up-and-down stroke featuring less pressure, then more pressure, and then all of the same over again. For a long, patient, exquisite minute he … Worked. Her. Over.

While McKenna's aching need tightened, her desire to be filled deepened, and when the breath she'd been holding finally gave way, Jagger slid his finger down to the junction where her bottom met the cushion and used his elbow to gently push her torso back against the booth, enabling McKenna to cock her hips forward. He slowly began to press, and her eyes fluttered shut as he slid the tip of his finger inside. Her head rolled back.

Thoroughly beyond caring they were in public, McKenna planted her free hand on the seat to steady herself as she began to gyrate her hips as slowly and inconspicuously as possible. Jagger matched her rhythm pushing in, pulling out, creating excruciating orgasmic tension right there at the table. His palm fastened over her sensitized clit, massaging it back and forth with the movement of his wrist as his finger copulated at an increasing pace. She needed to get there, she thought, biting down on her lip, determined to keep silent but get her fill right here. Right now.

And she got there.

Boy, did she get there.

When she came, her thighs clamped together, crushing his hand to a stop. Her body shuddered and shuddered, and she dared not take a breath for fear of drawing attention. She so wished they were upstairs with their hotel door between them and everyone else. What she wouldn't do to thank him.

"That's enough. That's enough," she whispered when Jagger tried to loosen the bear trap her thighs had turned into.

"Just trying to get my hand back, baby," he whispered against her ear.

"Oh." She immediately released his hand. "Sorry," she said. "Sorry," she breathed, reaching for water and scraping hair back from her face.

Jagger leaned toward her. "Nothing to be sorry about." He kissed her lips. "I'll be right back."

He left her panting and delirious while he traipsed off to God only knew where. Oh, maybe to wash his hands. Yeah, that was probably a good idea, since they were *supposed to be eating.* Holy crap, had he just rocked her world.

Who does that kind of thing in public? her mind screamed.

Apparently, rock stars.

And they were good at it.

She didn't want to know how he learned to be so good and yet so damn subtle. It was way too much and yet not nearly enough all at the same time.

She drank more water. Downed the rest of her champagne. Suddenly she was famished for their entrees, which arrived at that exact moment.

"Yes," she said when asked if her scallop appetizer was to her liking. *It was only that I was distracted by the sex god I'm dating. Otherwise, I'm sure I would have cleaned my plate. And, oh, by the way, do you think anyone will notice when I slip under this table and give the lead singer of the Cavaliers a blow job? I can't tell you how much he deserves it.*

Maybe she kept that part to herself as she dug into her five-star lamb dish with gusto. She was halfway through her meal when Jagger returned.

"What took you so long?" she asked with a full mouth. "I'm sorry, I couldn't wait. Apparently, I've worked up an appetite."

Jagger sat down and replaced his napkin on his lap, using the salt and pepper before even tasting his meal. "I had a little business to take care of."

"What kind of business?"

He turned his head and stared at her pointedly.

She burst out laughing. "You did not."

"Of course, I did."

"In the bathroom?"

"Where else?"

"You couldn't wait?"

"Could you?"

She stifled her laugh with her fingers to her mouth, chewing and then swallowing. "No, I guess not. Sorry." She gave him a sheepish grin. Then a wag of her head. "I'm starving after that." She pointed a fork in his direction. "And you will be richly rewarded for your undercover efforts. Trust me."

"Yeah?" He took the first bite of his meal, drew his eyes closed and moaned.

"Yes, and if you don't moan at least that loud for me, I'll be disappointed."

He pointed his fork at his plate. "This is some good food."

"It is. I'm glad I didn't make us leave. I almost made us leave."

Jagger kept shoveling food into his mouth. "You were so hot. Damn hot. I've never been into public sex, but I can see how it's a thing."

"Don't tell me you've never done that before."

He looked at her like she was crazy. "With whom? Where?" He set down his fork and knife and took the time to wipe his lips with his napkin before leering at her. "Is that something *you've* done before?"

"No," she stammered. "No. But you were so good at it, I just assumed …"

"I was good at it because I was highly motivated to get you off. Fast. Before the waiter came back. Before you came to your senses and told me to stop fooling around." Then his happy, life-is-awesome grin came back. "I like fooling around. With you."

She matched his grin as best she could. "I like fooling around with you too."

"Good. Then let's say after we take our time and enjoy this very-expensive-but-worth-every-penny meal, we go upstairs and fool around some more."

McKenna was game. Oh boy, was she game.

CHAPTER FORTY-TWO

The way the two of them waltzed slowly toward their room, hands clasped and swinging between them, McKenna assumed Jagger was going to take his sweet, sweet time making love to her. There was no sense of urgency. Just a sense of *finally*. Finally, it was just the two of them. Finally, they were free to be together. Finally, they could explore the possibilities of a … *relationship?*

Did Jagger Yates even do relationships?

And if he didn't, what the hell was she doing here?

She wanted a relationship, right? With Jagger.

She was fairly certain that Jagger was interested in a relationship. With her. But she had been fairly certain Xander was going to dump the peach last week so …

"Ah, Jagger." She pulled him to a halt in the hallway just before they reached their door.

"Yep?"

"What are we doing here?"

Jagger eyed their door a few feet away. Then he stepped into her, wrapping her up in his arms. "Whatever you want." His voice was low, sweet yet erotic. He leaned in and kissed her softly, with a little tongue and a lot of feeling. Seducing her all over again. The man was one big, drinkable love potion.

"I mean, are we here to start something?" she asked breathlessly. "Or are we simply finishing what we started?"

"Start something." He gently held her face between his palms, leaning down a bit so they were eye to eye. "Something big. Something long term. How's that sound?"

She nodded. It sounded good. Really good. Only …

"Yeah, I know," he said before she bit through her own lip. "Lots of details to work out. I've been putting together a plan. One you're gonna like. Trust me."

She nodded again. Jagger had never given her reason not to trust him. It was all her preconceived notions about rock stars in general that kept getting in her way.

"Good? Now," he tipped his head toward their door. "Are you running the show, or am I?"

She blinked and then blurted a laugh. "Does somebody need to run the show when it comes to … sex?"

"Ahh, when it comes to us? Probably, yeah."

"Why do you say that? Don't tell me you've been listening to Xavier preach about how bossy I am. He's the king of bosses."

"Which is why he doesn't like you giving him all that competition. Come on." He moved her toward their door, taking out his keycard.

"So what are you saying? That … *you're* bossy?"

He slipped the card in the slot and gave her his onstage, killer grin. "I'm not the front man for nothin', babe."

"You're the front man because you can sing better than most."

He shook his head as they entered the room. "I'm a darn good singer, but I'm *not* great. What I know how to do is emote a song. I reveal the meaning of the words with inflection. That's my gift. Oh, and I'm fearless on stage—absolutely no nerves whatsoever. So, you can understand how I like to run the show."

She grinned at him, understanding. "And you'd like to run this show?"

"I'd like not to butt heads on how this is going to go."

"So if, for instance, I decide to reach for your belt buckle, unscripted. You're gonna what? Swat my hand away?"

His cute lead-singer smile was gone, a smirk in its place. "Why don't you try it and find out."

McKenna reached out slowly, her gaze linked with his, her lips forming a sly smile as she wondered what he might have in mind. But he didn't slap her hand when she gripped him by the belt and tugged him a little closer. And he didn't protest at all when she started to loosen the strap from the buckle. Instead, he whispered to her while looking down at the top of her head, "A man would have to be crazy to swat your hand away. Please feel free to touch any of my clothes or any part of my body at *any time*," he stressed as she pulled his belt from the loops and tossed it on the floor.

"Where did this suit come from?" she asked quietly as she reached her hands underneath the lapels of his jacket and pushed it from his shoulders.

"I had it on me when we hit Henderson. I rarely have to wear it, but there are times when wearing it is a necessity. Or a privilege."

"A privilege?"

"A privilege." He kissed her. "Like when escorting a beautiful woman out to dinner."

She smiled at that, allowing her gaze to drift over his puppy-dog eyes and his well-trimmed beard. "How long have you had the beard?"

"Before beards were cool."

"Really?"

"I also had long hair years ago. I looked ridiculous."

She began unbuttoning his shirt, wondering if that could be true.

"I was totally into the grunge band thing growing up."

"How about the tattoos on your arms?" She helped him pull his arms from his shirtsleeves. He pulled the tails from his pants and took the shirt off, checking out his own tattoos. "Badges of honor, maybe. Commemorating the major events in my life, definitely." He pointed to a guitar. "My move to Nashville." He pointed to a bunch of carrots. "When we got our first number-one song."

"Why carrots?"

"From a children's book, The Carrot Seed. Little boy plants a carrot seed and everyone's telling him it won't grow. But he has faith. He *knows* it will happen. So he waters it, he pulls weeds, and eventually …" Jagger pointed to his carrots.

"So you had faith. That your music career was going to grow."

"And I didn't listen to the naysayers. At least, not for long."

"And this one?" She pointed to a scary-looking mask or face.

"Stupid teenage angst. Poor decision, that."

McKenna let her fingers run over his arms where the tattoos were engraved. Her focus left the artwork and fell to the muscles in his forearms, the definition there. "Is playing guitar hard?"

"Learning to play guitar well may be considered hard, but if you love doing it, practicing is fun—so, playing guitar was never hard for me. Playing guitar is just what I do."

"Like journalism has become for me."

He nodded solemnly. "That's something we have in common, isn't it? We both write stories. Lucky for the both of us, we're able to make a living doing it."

"Well, you are. I'm guessing you make a very good living."

"Now. Now that the money has started to flow. Whether our band has the staying power to draw crowds years from now? That remains to be seen."

McKenna pulled away, blinking rapidly. "I can't imagine the Cavaliers not putting out another album."

"Neither can I," he said, stepping forward and clasping both her elbows. "Especially when I've got such luscious inspiration."

"Luscious?"

"*Extremely* luscious."

He shoved his hands into her hair, gripping her head firmly as his mouth dropped to her lips and began to plunder. Her fingertips restarted the job they'd begun earlier, feeling their way to the button on his pants and then the zipper, making slow work of both while Jagger continued to work his magic at her mouth. She definitely didn't want to break the kiss, but she did want to show Jagger how eager she was to reciprocate for that no-holds-barred, hella-sexy interlude at dinner.

She stroked her hands over his shoulders while they kissed, then used them to explore the musculature of his arms. Slowly, she extracted herself from the kiss to slide down his torso, taking his pants to the floor as she lowered herself to her knees.

His erection was magnificent as the tip popped free of his boxer briefs. She watched the rest unleash itself in a bounce as she pulled down his briefs by grabbing at the hems. Reaching between his thighs, McKenna cuddled his balls while putting her mouth on the top of his cock. Jagger groaned and jutted his hips forward, probably dropping his head back as he told her how good that felt. How much he enjoyed her mouth on him. And then how he was going to let her make him crazy just a few more moments before he tossed her on the bed and fucked her senseless.

She grinned. And hummed. And when that triggered a tight response from his body, she groaned around him, longing to drive him wild now that she had the chance.

Jagger's hands rooted themselves in her hair, his fingers latching on and tugging. His hips jacked forward and back, giving her as much of him as she could handle. It was a euphoric feeling, knowing she was capable of giving him this kind of pleasure. Realizing the power she held. Exulting in how he wasn't able to talk like he'd been doing, now making only visceral noises that conveyed his rapture.

And he wasn't kidding when he said he was good at emoting his vocals, because she felt every ounce of his profound praise when he said her name. *"McKenna."*

She didn't know how he did it. She certainly wouldn't have pulled away had she been the one in the throes of that kind of ecstasy, but somehow Jagger released himself from her mouth, backing off just a bit to reach down and help her to her feet. Then he turned her around and rubbed his hands over the back of her dress, searching for a zipper that just wasn't there.

"Damn. So it's just the tie?" He spun her back to face him and pulled the sash, loosening the dress, finding the hidden second layer of strings that held the dress in place. He pulled at those as well. McKenna shrugged out of the sleeves, allowing the clingy material to slide to the floor.

His mouth was on the swell of her right breast before she could look up. She reached behind her back and unhooked her bra, carefully extracting it from her arms while Jagger's tongue and teeth created dark, screaming sensations emanating from her nipples all the way to her groin.

Things were hot and getting hotter.

Jagger lifted her from the floor, his arms around her hips, raising her high enough so her breasts were level with his mouth. He lavished attention on one and then the other as he walked them to the end of the bed, allowing her to fall back onto to it while he followed. He was on his knees, feasting on her breasts, driving her crazy with his licks and nips and appreciative moans. The man was *vocal*—which you know, made sense—but for McKenna, his sounds heightened her awareness of what was happening and who exactly it was happening with. And how right—*how amazingly right*—and easy, and oh-dear-God, just how good the two of them were together.

"Jagger," she panted. "Jagger. Jagger." It was all too much for her mind to hold on to. She'd blissed out into a zone of bodily awareness and complete non-thinking. Her hands fell to the bed beside her head. Jagger's body was up over hers while he worked her torso with his hands, with his mouth. She pulled one knee up and Jagger's body landed in between her thighs. His mouth moved up to capture hers as he snaked a hand between them, his thigh nudging hers farther apart, the tip of his shaft rubbing seductively inside her crease, pressing against her nub, circling, and drawing moans of rapture from her soul.

He took his time. Found her center and slowly pushed in, releasing himself and moving his hand to her head as he started moving, finding a rhythm. Finding their rhythm.

"Baby," he pleaded. "Open your eyes."

McKenna opened her eyes as their bodies united. There was Jagger, his beautiful brown eyes focused and searching. "You good?" he asked.

She nodded, mesmerized by the reality of Jagger and her together. Reveling in how amazing it felt.

"You're more than I imagined," he told her. "Better than my wildest dreams." He was perfecting the moment. Their moment. Because McKenna saw the honest, raw emotion in his eyes even within the sensations of their wound-tight lust. "You're it for me," he grunted as he went deeper. Going at her harder.

"For me too." She lifted her head to press her lips against his, and he fell into it—into her—engaging in the kiss that sealed their future while their bodies sealed the deal.

And it was a big deal.

A long, intense, two-orgasm deal, before Jagger reached for his own, moaned through his release, and came inside McKenna.

Without benefit of a condom.

CHAPTER FORTY-THREE

"What do you mean, you didn't use a condom?" McKenna was still thoroughly satiated, so this revelation didn't penetrate her brain as dramatically as maybe it should have. The fact that Jagger Yates was snuggling her, kissing her neck, and clearly not in a panic about this latest plot twist served to keep her body and her mind calm. Along with her immediate thought, *I'm on the pill.*

Of course, Jagger didn't know that.

"Please tell me you're on the pill," he said, continuing to nuzzle her neck, which felt so glorious. "Not that I shouldn't have used one anyway, because my momma doesn't want a whole lot of mini-Jaggers running around out there, as she's mentioned to me at least once every time I see her since moving to Nashville."

"Jagger. Are you clean?" McKenna asked, continuing to lazily scratch his back.

"Yes. And, don't ask me to elaborate or I might have to admit that this is the first time I've had sex in a while."

She turned her head to look at him.

"Don't ask."

Okay. She wouldn't. But damn, she was curious.

"And you?"

"The last time I had sex was six weeks ago. With Xander. He was covered."

"But you're on the pill?"

"I am, but you were crazy to assume that."

"I assumed nothing. I just totally forgot."

"You're forty years old. How could you forget?"

"Well, I don't remember you suggesting we stop the action to find one."

"Well … no … I."

"Ah-ha. It was so good that both of us lost our minds. Admit it."

"It was that good," she admitted. "But boy, that was stupid, right?"

"I don't know." He propped himself up on his elbow and started playing with her hair. "We've gotten to know each other pretty well. If there was going to be an issue, it would have come up."

"You're being way too trusting for a celebrity."

"Like I'm a celebrity."

"You're worse."

"I'm not. I'm just … a guy. In love with this freaking-hot babe I finally get to put it to, and poof." His hand created an exploding motion next to his head. "No brain cells."

"I would be all over you right now about the *get to put it to* part, except my brain would like to track back to the *in love* part. Jagger?" She held her breath for a moment. "Are you in love with me?"

His mouth cracked into that happy, delirious grin. "Well, yeah. Of course. Like that's news to you."

"You've never said it."

"Well, neither have you."

"I just broke up with my boyfriend. How could I have said it?"

"I mean, you *have* said it. Just not with words."

"How? How have I said it?"

"We've both said it," he assured her.

"Really? Like when?"

"Like every time you look me in the eye and smile that pretty smile of yours. The one you never, and I mean never, give anyone else. Not even your mother or Anna Beth."

McKenna blinked. "Is that true?"

"Oh yeah, it's true. You are one serious chick when you're dealing with everyone else. Especially Xavier. But with me? *Butter.*"

"Butter?"

"Yeah. Sweet and smooth. Delicious. Like butter."

She laughed, for some reason completely delighted he found her equivalent to butter."

"Well, I suppose you said I love you when you cleaned out the shed and updated my mother's home."

"I'm not sure that was an act of love. It felt a little bit more like desperation. And I probably shouldn't admit this, but y'all were about to get the interior of your house painted. I wanted an excuse to hang around after this weekend. You'll probably do better if I just pay a real painter to come in and do it. Now that we're …"

"We're what?"

"Together."

She smiled, realizing immediately she was grinning Jagger's *love* smile. "So are we? Together?"

"Absolutely."

"Okay. I like that. I *love* that," she emphasized. "But if you wouldn't mind keeping this quiet while people ease off me being engaged to Xander before they start yakking about me hitting the sheets with the visiting rock star, I'd appreciate it."

Jagger didn't say anything. Though he did give her a nod.

"Jagger?"

"McKenna?"

"We good?"

"Oh … we are very good," he said, rolling her over and starting to kiss his way down to her ass. "I really love the sight of you naked."

"I like you naked too," she said through her face plant on the pillow.

"So are we good to go? No condoms?"

"As long as you aren't worried about things getting messy."

Jagger chuckled. "Woman, with you I ain't worried about a thing." Then he smacked her ass and told her to get on her knees.

CHAPTER FORTY-FOUR

For two nights and a full day, they hardly left the bed.

At one point, Jagger said he had to run an errand, so that gave McKenna a chance to finally hit the spa and indulge in a hot-stone massage.

A freaking hot-stone massage.

It was as ridiculous and as wonderful as she'd imagined. Being rubbed by rocks sounded unspeakably painful, but the experience was anything but. The rocks were touted to be from some sacred river, and they were smooth, and large, and *hot*. And since Jagger had worked her over pretty good, they felt amazing everywhere. The massage left her feeling like an overcooked noodle, so when she arrived back in their freshly cleaned suite wrapped in a fluffy white bathrobe, she was in no mood to dress for lunch. Jagger brought lunch to her from a delicious deli that had good reviews on Yelp.

Of course, when he arrived to find McKenna with a clean face, her hair piled up on her head, all cozy in a robe, their lunch sat for a spell while he came over and untied the robe just to see what she was wearing underneath. That led to bare hands scoping over well-oiled skin, which led to a slow exploration of bodies in the bright sunlight, which led to some afternoon delight, which led to a very late lunch. Which is how their Saturday turned into a Saturday night and how dinner turned into a midnight snack before McKenna became Jagger's nightcap.

They could not get enough of each other.

"What's this?" McKenna pulled her hand from under the pillow as she awoke Sunday morning to find a bracelet dangling from her wrist. Her first thought was *how lovely.* She blinked and rubbed the sleep from her eyes with her free hand to better inspect the costliest piece of jewelry she'd ever worn. The bangle bracelet was obviously real gold and it sparkled. As she spun it around, she realized it wasn't just any bracelet. It was ... *holy shit* ... were those diamonds?

"Jagger," she whispered in awe. "Oh, Jagger."

"You like?" he asked, bracing himself on his elbow, his big, brown, puppy-dog eyes looking hopeful.

"I *love.*"

"Oh, thank goodness." He exhaled his relief as he fell to his back. His hand going to his forehead. I just wasn't sure of what color gold you prefer. You wear zero jewelry."

"Because I own zero jewelry. Well, zero *good* jewelry." She was still in awe of the gift. Still watching the beautiful piece dangle from her left wrist. "Are these real?" she asked as she spun the bracelet. Four, five, six, seven, eight tiny diamonds.

"It's from Cartier, so yeah, they're real."

"*Cartier?* Like Cartier, Cartier? You've got to be kidding?"

"Dead serious," he smirked. "It's called the Love Bracelet. I only know about it because the rest of the guys in the band bought them for their significant others to celebrate when we won our first award. I didn't have anyone to buy one for at the time. But I do now," he whispered, moving in to smooch her on her nose.

"So what's this?" she asked, pointing to a little screw while still marveling at the bracelet overall.

"It screws on. It's Cartier, so you don't want to lose it. But also so you'll wear it every day. Not just for special occasions. My love for you doesn't just happen on special occasions. My love is an every day thing, McKenna. And I want you to know that."

"Jagger, this is beautiful. Thank you." Then she thrust her wrist at him. "Now show me how to take it off."

"Ah. I think I just mentioned that you're supposed to wear it *every day.* Like my love."

"Yes, and I get that. Only no. I can't do that."

"Can't do what?"

"Wear it every day. In fact, right now I can't wear it at all."

"Hmm."

Jagger's *hmm* seemed more of a noncommittal placeholder for words than a question or a consideration.

"Jagger. You know I can't wear this in public right now."

He shrugged. "I think it looks beautiful on you."

"It is beautiful on me. That's the problem. I head into the paper tomorrow, or visit with Anna Beth, or go to cover Henderson's Big Pie Plate Shop opening and everyone's going to notice it." She tried to pull it off over her hand with no luck.

Leaning forward to kiss her on the nose again, Jagger said, "That's the point. I *want* everyone to notice it."

She blinked. "I don't understand."

"Yes, you do." He rolled over to the other side of the bed and got out, pulling on his boxer shorts before heading to the bathroom.

"Jagger," she called after him. Then she lounged back against her pillow, her left arm hung in the air so she could admire the beauty on her lonely wrist. She was giddy. So crazy about the man she was sleeping with. So happy he wanted to gift her with something so extravagant. And then their conversation replayed itself and his *that's the point. I want everyone to notice* suddenly landed. She bolted upright. "What the hell," she cried.

The handsome fiend came out of the bathroom and leaned against the door jamb, brushing his teeth.

"You want to out us, don't you?"

He shrugged, brushing away.

"You know everyone is going to take one look at this bracelet, know that I could never afford it, and then ask the pertinent question. Where did you get it?"

He grinned before ducking back into the bathroom.

"And I'm going to have to tell them you gave it to me. Then, in about five and a half seconds, it will be all over Henderson that I'm throwing myself at the rock star because Xander won't have me."

"And, really, who could blame you?" he said with a doubly fiendish grin.

"Jagger. We talked about this. I can't jump from Xander to you and hold my head up in Henderson."

"That makes zero sense."

"No one knows that we've been falling for each other for the past few weeks."

"Years. I've been falling for you for years," he insisted.

"You haven't been falling for years. It's only been months, and … and falling for me is not exactly the case."

"It is exactly the case. I have written seventeen songs about the woman who gave me the wrong number. If that's not pining away, if that's not falling for a woman, I don't know what is."

"Then you wear the damn bracelet."

"Nope. You're wearing the bracelet. And you're going to admit to everyone who asks that I am now *the boyfriend*."

"And what happens when their heads spin off their shoulders because they all think I'm supposed to be engaged to Xander?"

"You'll pick it up, help them reattach it, and explain that as much as you love all the members of the Wright family, you were meant to be mine."

"Aww." McKenna felt herself soften immediately. She went from being up on her knees to settling back onto her haunches, her right hand gripping the object of their argument. "Meant to be yours," she repeated. "I really love that line."

"Well, it's the truth. You were never meant to be Xander Wright's. You were meant to be mine." He came onto the bed and wrapped his arms around her, kissing her lips. "I love you. I want you. I don't want to hide what we finally have. Especially from *my* family and friends. So … I've lined up a photographer, and we are going to have some pictures taken. My publicist needs something to post on my social media accounts."

"Holy crap."

"What?"

"I don't think that's wise. Being single is part of your mystique. Your fans don't want to know a thing about me. In fact, it's better for you if they don't. Better for me too. I can't imagine the haters that will come out of the woodwork."

"Fuck 'em. I've got a life. *Now*. I want people to know about it. The love story that wrote an entire album of songs. People will eat this stuff up."

"Not in Henderson."

"Bullshit. Henderson wants to see you happy."

"Not this fast."

"Look. I get this is going to be news to your nearest and dearest and every-fucking-body else wandering the streets of your hometown. But so what?"

"They won't understand. They're just going to think I'm on the rebound."

"Who cares? Let them all think I'm a lucky son of a bitch to be in the right place at the right time. Let them all gossip about us until they're bored to death, and then they'll be eager for something new and finally able to hear the true story."

"The true story?"

"Yes. That we fell in love at first sight. A long time ago. It's just taken a while for the universe to lead us back to each other."

She sat there. Staring at her beautiful bracelet. "Jagger. I need you to take this off," she said quietly.

"Absolutely not." He backed off the bed and stood. "I've sat on the sidelines for weeks waiting for you to figure your shit out, and I'm done with that. You can make up a story about the bracelet, but I'll be kissing you on the lips every time we meet, so rest assured, we won't be a secret for long."

"Jagger, please listen to reason."

"McKenna, please get your head in the game."

He looked so irritated she had to laugh.

"Are you really not going to take off this bracelet?"

"Yes, I'm really not. I love you. Use it as an excuse to inform people we're dating. Or not. I won't hassle you in public. I'm going to give you your space. But in less than two weeks, my assistant is coming to town. We will be lining up a photographer and outing the two of us on social media." He sat back on the bed. "Can you handle that? Because from what I've witnessed, you're perfectly suited to handle the public side of my life. You're a journalist. You get the media. You understand what they want. What makes a good interview. I think you can help me—well, the whole band—in a professional capacity when we go on the road."

"On the road? You want me to go on the road? When you tour?"

Jagger gave her a well-duh blink. "Now that we're together, I want us to be *together*. We'll hit up Henderson as often as we can, but I think you're gonna fall for Nashville. At least, I really hope you do. And the tour thing is negotiable. You get a say in all this, obviously. But baby, I'd really like it if you'd be willing to change things up a bit. Maybe a new job in a new place to go along with your new man."

McKenna didn't mean to hold up both hands in front of her, but in her mind, she needed a hard stop. Because in her mind, it was only a couple of days ago that she had planned to marry into the Wright family and live in Henderson forever. And now, now she was in love with Jagger Yates, and he was spreading out a whole new life plan in front of her.

"I've lost you," Jagger noted.

His words had her gaze shifting from the bed to him.

"You got lost in your head."

"Yeah. I did. I hadn't … Jagger, I've never thought about what it would mean to … to be with you."

"Not just be with me. McKenna. I want to *marry* you. So let's work from that premise."

"We just started dating."

"We can date. I get we're kinda new, even if our story started a while back. But I'm just stating a fact. I want to marry you someday. And I'm not getting any younger. So take me at my word, because I'm definitely *in* this. And I want you to be *in* this too."

"I'm in," she said, shaking her head in disbelief. "I'm totally in. I just can't really believe I'm this in." She laughed as he tackled her back to the bed, wrapping his arms around her, positioning them both on their sides so they could look at each other.

"Yeah? You're in?"

"I'm in," she promised.

"Good. Because I had an entire speech planned about how you've outgrown your hometown and how I've got this big, exciting life that I've been hoarding all to myself. But now, I've found the right girl who can not only handle the big dream but expand on it as well. McKenna, I have no doubts, you are it for me."

She leaned over and kissed him with a megawatt smile plastered on her face.

"And my band is going to love you."

"You think?"

"Oh. Once they get a load of the bossy side of you, they'll go crazy."

"Why is that?"

"Because they'll know I've met my match." He reengaged their lips, slipped her a little tongue.

"I don't boss you."

"Get on your knees."

"No. I wanna be on top," she said as she pushed him to his back and climbed on.

Jagger spread his arms wide. "I rest my case."

CHAPTER FORTY-FIVE

"You want me to do what now?" Jagger scratched his head, sure he hadn't heard McKenna right.

"I know it sounds crazy, but things are so strained between me and Anna Beth right now, and Mr. Wright's face is as stern as I've ever seen it. He can hardly look at me. Thankfully, Jax and Xavier sort of get it. Although Xavier always gives me shit, so it's hard to tell whether he's actually angry I've dumped his brother and am dating you or if he's just being his regular, irritating self."

"And you want to what?"

"Show up at breakfast like I usually do. Only with you in tow, and in a more dramatic fashion. To make a point."

"And breaking and entering is a part of this plan? This plan you believe is going to get you back into the Wrights' good graces?"

McKenna frowned. "Well, now that you've added the words breaking and entering, it just sounds crazy."

"Because it *is* crazy. I'm not crawling up a ladder, climbing into a dark bedroom, and spending the night in the Wrights' house without their knowledge just so you can surprise them in the morning by making their coffee."

"But I'm the one who makes the coffee. They all love my coffee. That's probably the biggest reason they are all so grumpy."

"And you don't think the fact that you're not marrying into the family—the family who would like to shackle you to their coffee maker—is not the leading cause of their grumpiness? McKenna, this is crazy. I mean, the Wrights have been as cordial to me as I can expect, but finding me lurking around their home in the middle of the night is not a good idea. I am not interested in jail time."

McKenna sputtered. "Like they'd throw you in jail."

"Why not? It sure would get me out of their hair and away from you for a spell. Xander would be back in town so fast your head would spin. No way. No, thank you. The Wrights will come around when the Wrights come around. You're just going to have to be okay with that."

Annnd that was the last word on the subject until McKenna refused to sleep with him. Which is how the following Saturday night, Jagger found himself dressed in black from head to toe creeping through the Wrights' neighbors' yards like a damn cat burglar—scared to death of getting caught—as the woman he was jumping through hoops for led the way.

"Why are you not more nervous?" he whispered.

"Because I know who lives in these houses, and they aren't going to call the cops if they know it's me who's trespassing."

"But they don't know it's you."

"They will if we get stopped. And we aren't going to get stopped. Come on."

It was close to midnight, and Jagger thought he truly might need to have his head examined. This was the craziest scheme he'd ever heard of, and frankly, he still didn't fully understand it. Yet, him having agreed to this scheme vividly clarified a few things for him.

One, he truly loved McKenna and was willing to do anything to get her to leave her hometown.

Two, his sex drive was alive and well and completely insatiable. It was like he was twenty again. And McKenna was, well, McKenna was gluttonous. She'd even agreed to have sex with him during this crazy escapade. Which is why he found himself lurking around one of the nicer neighborhoods of Henderson at one in the morning, wearing all black.

Not that black was unusual for him. It wasn't like he had to dig through his wardrobe to find the perfect cat-burglar attire. But at the moment, he sure felt like he was dressed for a movie role. Black knit cap, black sweatshirt, black jeans, black sneaks. Black gloves because it was cold in the middle of the damn night, and he had allowed

McKenna to talk him into leaving his leather jacket in the truck a few houses down.

And if *he* was dressed for a movie role, McKenna was a damn shadow. She'd pulled her sexy hair back in a ponytail and also donned a knit cap. Only hers had a cute pom-pom attached to the top. He couldn't see that or anything else as they traveled through backyards, scooting through the gates of a picket fence. She did have on a puffy winter coat—black—a dark pair of jeans, and some kind of reasonable footwear for this activity. The activity of lurking through neighbors' yards.

She had also strapped on a small backpack. When he'd asked her about its contents, she simply said, "You'll see."

"Here we are," she whispered as they found a break in a tall hedge that separated the Wrights' backyard from their neighbors. She slipped through first. Then he slipped through before letting out a "Crap" and backing himself up against the hedge.

The place was lit up like a runway. "Jesus, are they trying to land planes back here?"

McKenna chuckled softly. "Xavier knows we're coming. He's making it easier on us."

"What?"

McKenna pointed to the back of the house where a long ladder was stretched tall, leading up to a second story window.

"Last summer, when Xavier was dating Laidey, he forced her to climb up to his bedroom this way. To hear Laidey tell it, Xavier had this high school fantasy he wanted to play out. So they did. And it sort of became a thing. Jaxon ended up using the same ladder to kidnap Jinx from the Evans's estate and then used it to get her up to his bedroom.

"Of course, then Vance climbed up the same ladder to rescue Jinx early the next morning. We all ended up downstairs in the kitchen cooking breakfast and making a party out of it."

"You were there too?"

"Yeah." He might have seen her shoulders shrug. "I never got to climb the ladder, but that was the last weekend Xander came home before you arrived so, I was here, just like Laidey and Jinx. But me being here for breakfast wasn't unusual. Much to Xavier's chagrin, it's a regular thing. I eat breakfast with the Wrights three or more times a week. Which is my point."

"I'm still not sure the two of us coming down their stairs and arriving for breakfast is going to endear either one of us to them. Especially me. Shouldn't we just show up at their front door like normal people?"

"But that's exactly the problem. I'm not normal people. Yet Anna Beth and Maxwell are treating me as if I am. They are treating me just like they would anybody else. Definitely not like the daughter they never had. Not like I'm me. It's just … so awkward. For all of us." She huffed. "I want them to see that I'm still me. Even though I'm in love with you. And they aren't losing me. They're just gaining … you."

"Like they need more testosterone around here."

"Well, Xander's threatened never to return, so until he does, you can fill in."

"Fill in?"

"Yeah. Fill in. Come on." McKenna moved across the well-lit backyard.

"So Xavier set this up? Left the ladder like this? For us?"

"I got nervous, so I decided to give him a heads-up. In case he heard anything. Because he's the wild card."

"Wild card?"

"You know. He's a lot of bluster most of the time. But if he thought something was threatening Laidey, I wouldn't want to be the one standing in the middle of that."

"Yeah, those two are interesting. She's all …"

"Quiet," McKenna supplied.

"Yeah, and he's all …"

"Obnoxious."

"Loud was the word I was going to use."

"Oh, he is that. So there again. Didn't want him waking up the entire house if he found us back here. I want this to be a sneak attack."

"A sneak attack?"

"Well, maybe not a sneak attack. I actually just want it to be *normal*." McKenna grabbed the ladder with both hands, setting her foot on the lowest rim.

"This is anything but normal," Jagger assured her. "I'll hold the ladder steady while you climb up."

"Thanks."

"Is the window going to be unlocked?" he whisper-shouted.

"I hope so," she whisper-shouted back as she climbed.

Jagger watched her climb, muttering, "I swear to God this better end up making a great story for the band."

"One way or another, I'm sure it will," came McKenna's reply.

He had to smile at that. She was absolutely correct.

One way or another, this was going to make an epic story.

McKenna gave a shout of alarm when the window flew open just as she arrived at the top of the ladder. "Xavier" she whisper-scolded. "You scared me to death."

"Oh, like I'm the one creeping in somebody's window in the middle of the night." He extended a hand, which McKenna took, letting him help/drag her through the window and onto a desk placed directly underneath it. She crab-walked two steps and hopped down to the floor.

Xavier stuck his head out the window. "So you brought him, huh?"

"That was the plan."

"Humph." He turned back toward McKenna, leaning his big body back against the desk.

"You like him," she insisted.

"I like Xander better."

"Well, that's fine. Now you and your twin can enjoy time together without me interfering. I'm surprised you haven't figured out the upside of all this."

"You, taking off with this guy?" Xavier pointed over his shoulder as Jagger stuck his head through the window. "That's actually a big upside … *for me.* Not so much for my ma."

"I know." McKenna started wringing her hands. "I'm trying to fix things. Before I have to leave. I know this seems like a crazy scheme, but I don't know what else to do."

Xavier shrugged as he made no move to get his huge body out of the way, forcing Jagger to become a contortionist, getting himself through the window and off the desk without bumping into Xavier. With the level of meticulous care he was using, it was clear Jagger didn't want to rock the boat any more than he already had.

"I've got a menu planned." Xavier went on talking as if Jagger hadn't just entered the room. Through the window. "A few of Ma's favorites. Laidey should be here soon. And I've sort of let Jax and Jinx in on the plan. They're sleeping next door"—he nodded his head in the direction of Jaxon's room—"instead of at her place, so they'll be here in the morning too. And all of us," he stressed to Jagger, "will act as if nothing is amiss. We'll act like you two belong here instead of the fact that you stomped my twin's heart into the ground and then danced on it."

"Xavier."

He waved his hand. "I'm just busting your chops. Still. Him?" Xavier pointed to Jagger.

"Yes. Him," McKenna declared. "I choose him. I'm in love with him."

Xavier folded his arms over his chest while turning his head, taking a long, hard look at Jagger. Finally, he moved to his feet, held out his hand, and said, "Welcome to the family."

Laidey was halfway through the window before anyone knew she was there.

"Tweets," Xavier nearly shouted. "Aren't you a sneaky little thing. Look at you, practically leaping tall buildings in a single bound." He had his hands on her, lifting her from the window and over the desk like they'd done this before. Many times.

"Hello," Laidey said, looking from McKenna to Jagger. She was grinning from ear to ear. "I heard we might have company. I did not realize it would be you."

McKenna went over and embraced Laidey. "Can you believe it's come to this?"

"You climbing the into the Wrights' second-story window with a man who is not their son? No." She grinned. "I do not believe it has come to this."

There was a knock on the door. Everybody stopped moving and held their breath.

"It's just me," came Jaxon's voice.

"Come in," Xavier called.

Jaxon turned the knob and entered with Jinx on his heels. They were dressed in cozy pajama bottoms and long-sleeved T-shirts. Jinx also had on what looked like a cashmere, zip-up hoodie to keep the chill of the night at bay. "Somebody shut that window," she said as she scampered onto one of two queen-sized beds, tucking her bare feet beneath her. Laidey and McKenna immediately joined her, bouncing and squealing as girls were wont to do when greeting their best friends.

Jagger had to smile. And he also felt a great sense of relief knowing that for him, McKenna was willing to leave all that happiness she was knee-deep in over there. He knew she'd want to come visit as often as possible, but he also knew she was ready for a change. A big change. He was planning to make it a big, exciting, but not overwhelming (as best he could manage) change.

"So what's the plan?" Jaxon asked the two men left standing there, staring after their women.

Xavier clapped his hands and rubbed them together. "Sunday morning breakfast as usual. Ma and Dad will walk in when they walk in, and we'll all be cooking like we used to do before this guy busted things up."

"Stop. Jagger didn't bust things up," McKenna insisted. And then in a very sweet tone none of the men (other than Jagger) had ever heard her use before, she said, "He's made them complete."

Xavier looked around the room. "Three girls. Three guys." He nodded. "Maybe she's right."

"Even though she'll never officially be a Wright," Jaxon said as he took a hop and landed in the middle of the bed, scattering the girls with muffled shrieks.

"McKenna Blakely Yates," Jagger insisted.

Xavier's eyes went wide. "I'm going to hold you to that, bro. You make an honest woman out of her within a year, or you answer to me."

"I knew you liked her," Jagger bragged.

"Pfft," Xavier sneered. "I like that you're taking her away. Tweets," he called. "You hungry? How about a midnight snack?"

"I could go for some hot chocolate and one of your famous grilled cheese sandwiches."

"The woman works herself to death," Xavier muttered. "So this is what my Saturday nights have turned into. Saving McKenna's ass while waiting on my fiancée to show up for hot chocolate." Xavier moved to grab Laidey's hand, extracting her from the gang on the bed. "Y'all take this room. That bed." He pointed specifically. "We'll grab the room down the hall. I'll get y'all up in the morning. Not too early," he said, saliva practically dripping from his mouth as he leered at Laidey.

"Sounds good," Jagger said, sitting down on the other bed, feeling as if this crazy plan of McKenna's just might work now that two of the brothers were on board. It made him realize just how important McKenna was to all of them.

And then his heart hurt a little thinking of how important she'd become to him.

He felt their pain at losing her.

Well, not losing her. Just doing without her for a few months at a time. He wouldn't want to do without her for one day.

It was then he decided he was all-in. He was going to make this crazy plan of McKenna's work. He was going to play his part tomorrow morning. Do his best to soothe Anna Beth's heart over giving up the daughter she never had.

CHAPTER FORTY-SIX

"McKenna?" It was Maxwell Wright with the Sunday paper tucked under his arm, entering the kitchen, sounding surprised to find her in her pajamas at the coffee maker. Then his astounded expression swept the room, taking in Xavier and Jinx at the stove, Laidey preparing an egg mixture at the counter, and Jaxon at the table with his feet propped on a chair enjoying a cup of coffee, before landing sharply on Jagger, who had his arms full of the fruit he was retrieving from the refrigerator. Maxwell stood quietly, assessing Jagger and the situation, noting Jagger's bed head, bare feet, pajama bottoms, and Old Dominion sweatshirt.

Finally, he pointed his paper at Jagger. "I thought your band's name is The Cavaliers."

"It is, sir."

"So what's with the sweatshirt?"

"I'm a fan," he said, stretching the material from his body.

Maxwell nodded. Then said, "Me too." And with that, Maxwell took his seat at the kitchen table across from his son before accepting a hot mug of coffee from McKenna. "How's my girl?"

McKenna beamed. Just lit up and then fell over to hug the poor man like he'd probably never been hugged before. Jagger could tell she was emotional. Like teary-eyed, probably trying-to-swallow-it-down emotional. And from what he could tell, she wasn't going to unleash the poor man's neck until she got a hold of herself.

"There, there." Maxwell patted McKenna's arms. "You're always going to be my girl. And I'm very much looking forward to the first decent cup of coffee I've had since Thanksgiving."

McKenna laughed, and choked, and coughed, and laughed some more before kissing Mr. Wright on the top of his head and moving back to the coffee maker.

"Do you have an article in today's paper?" he asked.

"Style section," she told him, grinning.

"All right then. Jagger, you a newspaper man?"

"I've found reason to read the Henderson Daily from cover to cover since I've been in town."

Mr. Wright nodded, like that was the right answer. "What's for breakfast?"

"All Ma's favorites," Xavier replied.

"Why?" Mr. Wright asked as he snapped open the paper. "You think she needs buttering up?"

"Maybe," Xavier replied. "She definitely needs fattening up."

"And how are Laidey and Jinx this morning?"

"Good, thanks," Laidey replied, smiling her shy smile at her future father-in-law.

Jinx brought Maxwell a small chunk of cheese. "I bought this at the farmers' market a week ago and have been hoarding it. Tell me what you think?"

He took the sample and popped the whole thing into his mouth, chewing thoughtfully. He began to nod in earnest. "Yes," he said, smacking his lips. "I would hoard it too."

"I'm donating it to the baked egg casserole." She smiled before she whirled around as Xavier barked for her attention.

"So are we going to be able to expect this on the weekends you're in town?" Maxwell hadn't addressed anyone specifically, but they all knew it was directed at McKenna. She shot Jagger a quick glance.

"You've been telling me I'm part of the family for years now. Where else would Jagger and I show up for Sunday brunch?"

The man's head was stuck in the paper, but he nodded. Everyone watched him nod.

Jagger finally turned from where he'd been frozen in place. *One down and one to go*, he thought, moving to the sink and dumping his wares on the counter. He began the process of washing blueberries and decapitating strawberries as he'd been instructed by Xavier. He wasn't sure what was going to happen when Mrs. Wright arrived for breakfast, but he felt a little more confident in the situation now that Mr. Wright had not thrown him out.

And then the music started to play from the Echo on the counter. McKenna must have started it from her phone. It was "Babe in a Bar." He sidled over to McKenna and whispered, "Really? Don't you think that might be a little much? You're already jamming me down their throat. Isn't this akin to throwing salt on the wound?"

"It's what she makes us listen to while we cook," Jinx said from the makin'-bacon center. "It wouldn't be Sunday without a few Jagger Yates ballads."

"Perhaps you can make yourself useful for more than washing strawberries and go ahead and chime in," Xavier ordered. "Let us hear if you sound as good in person."

"It's morning, and I'm a rock star. I don't do mornings." He was grinning the whole time he said it. Still, Xavier shot him a scowl—until he realized Jagger was joking.

"Asshole." He poked tongs toward him. "You want Ma to jump on your bandwagon, you'd better sing. Use that voice of yours to make her forget whose place you're takin'."

"I am not takin' Xander's place. I'm simply hoping to become an honorary member of the Wright family someday."

"Honorary member, huh?" Xavier grunted. "Maybe. Someday." He glanced at McKenna. "He gives you one moment of trouble, you call me. Immediately."

McKenna smiled. "Since when do you care one iota for my welfare?"

"Since you're dating somebody other than my twin. And hell, try as I have, I finally realize there's no getting rid of you. So, to be clear—he gives you trouble, call me," he emphasized.

"I will. And thanks."

"Do we all hate Xander now?" Jax asked from his seat at the table. "Because with Xavier not trying to bully McKenna out the door, and Dad being okay with Jagger here in pajamas, I'm thinking the world has come to an end."

"We don't hate Xander," his father insisted. "We are disappointed he let McKenna slip through his fingers. And, since Jagger probably makes more money than Xander, your mother and I will now be moving in with him and McKenna in our old age."

Jagger spouted a laugh.

Mr. Wright mumbled, "He thinks I'm kidding," from behind his paper.

"Well, that's good," Xavier said. "Because you sure as hell aren't moving in with me and Tweets."

"Rather hear the boy sing than you shouting directives," Maxwell supplied.

"Pot calling the kettle black, Dad. Who do you suppose I learned that from?"

"Well, it certainly isn't your mother."

"Got that right," Xavier muttered.

"Speak of the devil," Jaxon said, standing as his mother shuffled into the kitchen like she would have rather stayed in bed.

The entire kitchen ensemble stopped what they were doing and turned to stare at Anna Beth, who was sporting black yoga pants, a long lilac sweater and some fuzzy lilac slippers. She blinked a few times, taking in Jagger at the sink, and then her gaze quickly darted toward the coffee maker to find McKenna. Her breath caught in a "Wha–?"

Mr. Wright, who hadn't bothered to take his head out of the paper, said, "Look, honey. Son number six."

"Son number six?" she repeated.

"Once our money runs out, we'll be moving in with him and McKenna."

Anna Beth didn't laugh or snicker. She stood dumbfounded, apparently adding the situation up in her mind. Jagger didn't think it through, he just moved in her direction with the berry bowl he'd been filling.

"Strawberry?" he offered.

"Well." She looked around at the rest of her growing family. "Yes. Thank you, Jagger." She took one and held on to it. "When did you two arrive?" She was looking at McKenna, so Jagger let her answer.

"Last night," she said, as if this was not going to raise eyebrows.

"Last night? Where did you sleep?"

"In Xander's bed. You don't think he'd mind, do you?"

With that, Jaxon began to howl with laughter. Xavier piped in, "Not unless he wanted to come home. Which we all know he never does, so ... Ma? You okay with that? You okay with the daughter of your heart wanting to be here first thing in the morning? Wanting to indoctrinate Jagger over there into the weekend rituals of the Wrights?"

"I suppose," Anna Beth said softly.

"How about we get you a chair and a cup of McKenna's coffee, let you think on it a while."

An unexpected lesson was playing out in front of Jagger. And the shock of it was, he hadn't realized a guy like Xavier had it in him. This guy, this big, brash, loud, bossy SOB was paving the way for him and McKenna to find a place within his mother's broken heart.

And this big, brash guy did it softly. With love.

Jagger turned around and gave him a grateful smile. Xavier winked. McKenna got Anna Beth seated and brought her a doctored coffee the likes of which Jagger had never seen a barista take on. He watched as Anna Beth sipped it, eyeing McKenna over her cup with an emotion Jagger could not name.

And he was a songsmith.

"I love her." He hadn't meant to say those words. Break into their moment. In fact, he'd not only startled his audience, the words escaping his mouth had startled him. But he followed through, speaking directly to Anna Beth. "I just thought you should know. And she's not leaving town with me unless she can come back here whenever she wants, spend the night, and make you coffee."

Anna Beth nodded, setting down her cup. She turned her head toward Maxwell. "Darling?"

"Hmm?" Mr. Wright replied from behind the paper.

"I bet we're going to enjoy living in Nashville."

Jagger grinned. "You are welcome at any time." Then he looked over at McKenna. "Remind me to call a real estate agent. We're gonna need a bigger house."

McKenna—bossy, sometimes surly, McKenna—had become a giddy woman. The day she found Jagger Yates in Henderson, she turned giddy. And right now, sitting at the Wrights' dining room table with her two best friends, and the rest of her favorite people, she was as jubilant, blissed out, over the moon—basically as giddy as a serious journalist could ever hope to be.

There was interesting conversation.

There was unadulterated laughter.

There was the typical fighting.

There was the merciless teasing.

There was love.

And best of all, there was Jagger, holding his own.

And Anna Beth, looking healthier than ever.

How this scenario had come to pass was almost too hard to account. And with the knowledge that she would always be welcome at the Wrights' came tremendous relief.

She now had it all.

The man of her dreams, who just happened to be her one-and-only heartthrob.

A grand adventure awaiting her journalistic curiosity.

And the crazy Wright family she could look forward to coming home to.

Giddy.

And in love.

All of my Heroes of Henderson novels and novellas are complete romances in and of themselves and do not need to be read in any particular order. However, it's a little more fun that way.

Heroes of Henderson full-length Novels

Good Cop
Bad Cop
Top Dog
Tempting Vivi
UnderDog
Mr. Wrong
Mr. Wright
Mr. Wright Now
Rock Star

Heroes of Henderson Novellas

Playin' Cop
Taming Molly
Kissing Cooper ~ A Christmas Quickie

Listed in order

Countdown to a Kiss
A New Year's Eve Anthology

Playin' Cop
Heroes of Henderson ~ Prequel
Previously published as
The Keeper of the Debutantes in
Countdown to A Kiss

Good Cop
Heroes of Henderson ~ Book 1

Bad Cop
Heroes of Henderson ~ Book 2

Taming Molly
Heroes of Henderson ~ Book 2.5
A DuVal Cousins Quickie

Top Dog
Heroes of Henderson ~ Book 3

Tempting Vivi
Heroes of Henderson ~ Book 3.5
A DuVal Cousins Novel

Kissing Cooper
Heroes of Henderson ~ A Christmas Quickie

UnderDog
Heroes of Henderson ~ Book 4

Mr. Wrong
Heroes of Henderson ~ Book 5

Mr. Wright
Heroes of Henderson ~ Book 6

Mr. Wright Now
Heroes of Henderson ~ Book 7

Rock Star
Heroes of Henderson ~ Book 8

All Star
Heroes of Henderson ~ Book 9
Coming in 2021

Sign up at *www.LizKellyBooks.com*
to be alerted when new books are released.

About the Author

Growing up every summer in a place where *dancing and romancing* are literally part of its theme song, Liz Kelly can't help but be a romantic at heart. And since her favorite author, Kathleen E. Woodiwiss wrote some of the world's greatest romances, she's just trying to give the world a little more of that. (Okay, maybe a little sexier *that*, we are now in a new millennium after all.)

A graduate of Wake Forest University, where she met her handsome golf-addicted husband (who is now sporting dark glasses everywhere he goes), Liz is a mother of two grown sons (also sporting dark glasses) and a miniature Labradoodle named Annabelle. They've recently become residents of the great state of North Carolina spending summers in the mountains there, and winters in luscious Naples, Florida.

Rock Star celebrates Liz's twelfth published work.

Made in the USA
Monee, IL
12 February 2021